THE BUSINESS OF LOVING

This edition, issued in 1962, is for members of The Companion Book Club, 8 Long Acre, London, W.C.99, from which address particulars of membership may be obtained. The book is issued by arrangement with the original publishers, Victor Gollancz Ltd.

Also by
GODFREY SMITH

★

THE FLAW IN THE CRYSTAL
THE FRIENDS

"A blessed companion is a book"—JERROLD

THE BUSINESS
OF LOVING

*

GODFREY SMITH

THE COMPANION BOOK CLUB
LONDON

© Godfrey Smith 1961

Made and printed in Great Britain
for The Companion Book Club (Odhams Press Ltd.)
by Odhams (Watford) Limited
Watford, Herts
S.862.V.R.

FOR
MISS CHARLIE SMITH

What will happen will happen
The whore and buffoon will come off best;
No dreamers, they cannot lose their dream.

Louis Macneice

"FELIX! It is you, isn't it?"

"Of course it is, Benny. But what a surprise. How are you?"

"I'm fine. But how extraordinary. What an odd place to meet. Are you a member here?"

"Yes. Well, I thought it would be an amusing place to bring people, though I doubt if I'll ever be called. Don't tell me you're reading for the Bar too?"

"Good heavens no. I came in with Jeremy Grumman. Do you know him?"

"Not yet I'm afraid. I hardly know anyone. Which is he, the old boy with glasses sitting on your left?"

"Yes, that's him. He's not so old. But what a coincidence. I can't get over it. How many years is it since we met? Twelve years?"

"Twelve or thirteen. You haven't changed much. A bit plumper perhaps."

"I recognized you at once. You look thinner."

"Even thinner?"

"Well, you always were a bit scraggy, Felix. But tell me about yourself. What are you doing beside reading law? Are you married? Where are you living?"

"I'm in the export business. I expect you remember."

"Yes of course I do. What's it like?"

"So so."

"And your father?"

"Oh fine. Taking it a bit more easily now. Writing fewer pamphlets than he used to. He's had a spot of blood pressure you know. Nothing to worry about, but he snoozes in a big chair every day for an hour after lunch."

"That's good. But what are you doing Benny? You look disgustingly prosperous."

"I've got my own business. I make gramophone records."

"You don't say! Gramophone records! I remember you always used to be a keen collector. That confounded club of yours . . . but how did you ever come to be in the business?"

7

"It's a long story. I'd like to tell you. Couldn't we meet for lunch or something?"

"Love to. One day next week?"

"Yes. Let me look at my diary. Tuesday?"

"Yes, I can make Tuesday. Have lunch with me. Come down to Pimm's in Threadneedle Street. Do you know it?"

"Yes I do; but I'd like you to have lunch with me."

"Oh but let me——"

"No really. To tell you the truth, I have to follow a strict régime."

"A diet? Surely not ulcers already, Benny?"

"Good Lord no. I mean—I have a sort of routine I keep to. I have lunch in my office. Don't worry, it's quite nice. I have a good chef."

"A *chef*? Benny you're not serious?"

"I'm afraid it must sound a bit extravagant. But after a lot of trial and error, I decided it was much cheaper than taking people to the Mirab—to restaurants. You know how it is."

"I wish I did! Well, you intrigue me. O.K., I'll come to you. Now what's the address?"

"It's Diskon House in Curzon Street."

"Diskon? Surely that's not your company? Why, I've got some Diskon records at home!"

"Yes. We're Diskon all right. It's quite a small company you know."

"Benny you astound me. Imagine you in big business! But how exciting!"

"Look, I must get back to poor old Grumman, Felix. He seems a bit put out. But before I go—you didn't say whether you were married or not."

"No. No I'm not married. Are you?"

"No. I'm not either."

"Oh. Neither of us. How strange. Must be something wrong with us. I mean, all our old friends. . . ."

"Have you heard anything of Laura?"

"Laura? No I haven't seen her since—well, when I last saw you. Don't you know either?"

"Oh a little. Nothing really. But you're sure—I mean you haven't seen anyone from Aylsbourn who would have known her?"

8

"My dear chap, I haven't been near Aylsbourn for thirteen years either. Oh, I believe I went through on my way to the coast one day. But no, I haven't heard a word of Laura for thirteen years. She might be dead for all I know."

"No. She's not dead."

"You've heard from her then?"

"In a way. I know she's not dead."

"How——?"

"Felix, I really must go. Poor old Grumman. I'll see you at Diskon next Tuesday then. A quarter past one all right?"

"Yes. Yes that's fine, Benny. Goodbye. I'll see you then. Awfully nice to see you again."

"Goodbye, Felix."

Jeremy Grumman watched them as they talked. Before him lay the slice of cold beef and the pickles, the cold potatoes and the beetroot he had chosen from the exiguous menu. The two tankards of beer stood untouched. There were not many people in; a handful of benchers and some black men. It was not the ideal place to bring Benedict, but on the other hand it saved a lot of expense. It was unlikely to cost him more than fifteen shillings for the pair of them. Really, he should have taken Benedict somewhere else, somewhere more lavish. No, it wouldn't do to try too hard. In any case, Benedict hadn't seemed to mind.

He sighed and took a swig of cold bitter beer. The need to get out of this soul-destroying occupation had grown to an obsession with him. It was too bloody ironic : he came from a celebrated legal family and was himself one of the most respected men at the Bar. People said he made fifteen thousand a year. Really, it was a good laugh. Last year he had in fact nearly killed himself with overwork and had cleared about two and a quarter thousand. In his twenty-five years at the Bar he had saved about two thousand; his wife had four hundred a year on trust. Even so, with three sons to educate, it was getting ridiculous. None of them was particularly bright, and their education was going to take a big bite out of his savings. He came in by tube from Moor Park every morning, and caught a bus from Baker Street. He worked like a dog, but the truth was, the majority of his time was still taken up with trifling cases. Yet he had what they called a first-class financial brain. His work on Company Law was supposed

9

to be the best. Maybe: at the moment it had only one possible use in his mind. It might help him get a job with Benedict. Perhaps even a directorship! It was a hell of a big business for any one man to carry on his shoulders.

He was reliably informed that the Diskon turnover was already £460,000 a year, and a good slice of the labour was unskilled. It would be no real hardship to pay him a regular three thousand out of that. And he would be able to put his feet up and watch the television play when he got home in the evening.

Benedict needed new blood! It would be a fine career and he'd be out of the treadmill for good.

There should be a pension at the end of it; perhaps an expense account even! It all depended on Benedict. A slight sense of antipathy ran through him, a glancing shiver of resentment. He watched Benedict talking; he seemed unusually animated. He was a cool customer normally, but sometimes you couldn't help wondering....

No doubt about it, though, a big man. One of the quickest new capital formations since the war. Now there might be a question of forming a public company, of floating a lot of shares. Well, Grumman was the boy for *that*.

A good man, Benedict. A very sane man indeed.

Weston was thinking as they talked: I wonder if he has forgiven me? I wonder if there is anything to forgive? I wonder if he is altogether sane? I wonder if it's possible that she *was* responsible for his failure? Because all this crap about Diskon doesn't make sense. At least, it makes all too excellent sense. Diskon is a monument to his failure; it's a by-product of all the spilled-over love, all the years of useless and wasted longing. What waste there is in romantic love! What a waste, oh what a bloody waste! Because we were friends once, good friends; and it's not as if I even took her away from him. What did I do that was wrong then? Was it merely that on that very still night thirteen years ago when we sat on the jet-black rock, unreal in the moonlight, with the lukewarm sea lapping at our feet, I told him the truth about love? Or did I tell him just the truth about *her*? Or the truth about himself? Or the truth about me? And isn't it true that nothing's gone right since that day on the jet-black rock? Because he may have a chef to save him bothering to go to the

Mirabelle, but has he got anyone who can look after his mind and heart? Why does he stare at me so as we are talking now; with fear and sadness in his eyes? And it's all so long ago now anyway and I truly don't know what happened to Laura. But it is absolutely typical of Benny the lover and the dreamer that he should know something of Laura even now; even if it's only that she isn't dead. I sometimes wish I could believe in love as he does; because what else is there? Yet what has it brought him but pain and emptiness? And what has not believing in it brought me? And what is there common to our condition but the knowledge of Laura? And why do I keep thinking of Laura, turning her name over and over in my mind like an amulet? Why do I, if I don't believe in her, or in love, as Benny does?

Benny is a nice fellow, only stark, stone bonkers. How he stares!

"I'm terribly sorry about that, Jeremy. It's a very old friend of mine—a school friend in fact. Felix Weston. He's a member of your Inn."

"Oh really? I don't recognize him."

"He's new here. Do you know it's thirteen years since I last saw him?"

"Really? It looked as if you were making up for lost time."

"Yes, I suppose so. I'm sorry. But I've arranged to meet him for lunch next week. Then we can go back over all those old times. A terrible mistake, but hard to resist."

"Oh, it's nice to meet an old friend."

"Yes. But the funny thing is, I've always hated his guts."

"Always . . . ?"

"No, not always. For a long time. I'm glad I've met him. You can't go on hating someone like that."

Benedict paused and for a moment seemed at a loss.

"It would be good—it would be a good thing if we could be friends again."

Benedict left Grumman cordially at about ten-thirty. They shook hands outside the Inn and went their separate ways: the one to the underground, Moor Park, his semi-detached house, his anxious wife, his next day's brief, and his tremulous hopes; the other on foot to his flat in Upper Brook Street near the business he had built; profoundly troubled by the chance that had brought him face to face with his own past.

He walked because he loved to go on foot through London at night, because the air was cold and crisp, the shop windows laden and glowing, the coffee bars jangling with youth and excitement, the old men loitering in the streets, just ejected warm and protesting from their snug boozers; Long Acre, Leicester Square, Lisle Street—he floated with the tide, past the hamburger stores and the hygienic stores, his tall, slightly stooping figure encased in a heavy black overcoat, his hands in his pockets, no hat on his head, and his head cast down as he sauntered along; oblivious to the oyster bars and the hell-fire preachers and the buskers and the whores, the news-vendors, the shoe-shine boys, and the narrow plush-carpeted pink-lit doorways leading down to hell. He was thinking about Felix Weston.

"GOOD old Felix! Well hit, Weston! Come on, Benny! You've got time for another!"

The voices carried over the years clear and fresh and the sunlight was quicksilver again. It was the old hot nineteen-thirties sun; the sun, Benedict reflected, that had shone down on Hitler at Berchtesgarden, on the men going out to die in the Thetis, on Jesse Owen's flashing legs, on the matinée theatre-goers blinking as they came out of *French Without Tears,* on his heroes McCorkell and Arnold as they batted all afternoon for Hampshire.

On this day though, he and Weston were merely giving a lusty impersonation of their idols. Valhalla Preparatory School needed a mere six runs to beat their old enemies Locks Priory with six wickets still standing; it was really only a question of who was going to make the winning hit. They took two runs and Felix Weston faced up to the bowling again. Benedict leaned on his bat and wiped the sweat off his face, glancing at the mighty Margrave Brewery scoreboard. He could hardly believe his eyes, yet there it was. Opposite batsman number one (that was Felix, he always opened for Valhalla) stood the figure 53. Batsman number six—Benedict—was credited with the incredible, the perfectly fantastic total of 48 runs. Valhalla had scored 112 runs altogether; he and Felix must have made a stand of getting on for 90. He couldn't quite believe it.

The snub-nosed, sandy-haired Locks Priory bowler began his run and Benedict crammed his handkerchief hurriedly away. His bat trailing, he took two or three steps in consonance with the bowler as he often watched McCorkell do, so that he would be already on the move if there was the chance of a run.

And there was. Weston cut the ball stylishly out towards point, and they took a quick single. Now Benedict faced the bowling. He was unconcerned; he had thoroughly played himself in and the ball was looking about the size of a pumpkin. He thumped a new centre and took guard.

The ball pitched short and Benedict had plenty of time to get his bat to it. He hit it with a rather ugly cow-shot but well in the centre. He felt that strong sensual pleasure as the spring took the shock, and then he heard applause run round the roped boundary. He wiped the sweat off his face again and self-consciously banged the end of his bat at an imaginary spot in the pitch, his head down. The applause continued, and he realized the Locks Priory boys were clapping too. With shyness, he raised his cap, as he had been taught to do, in acknowledgement of the applause. It was the first triumph of his life; he was thirteen and a half years old.

Felix Weston came half-way down the pitch for a conference (just as McCorkell and Arnold used to). He was a dark, good-looking boy, with curious black rings already forming under his eyes, as if he were an embryo debauchee. He grinned as Benedict approached.

"Good show, Benny," he said, "a lovely half century. Now don't do anything rash. You don't want to get bowled now. If you're not out it'll do your average a power of good."

"O.K., Felix. I'll block the rest of the over."

"O.K."

They separated to their respective ends.

The sandy-haired boy ran up again, and pitched up a fast, straight one. Benedict blocked it with respect and it began trickling down the pitch back towards the bowler.

Suddenly Weston shouted: "Come *on*, Benny!" and began to run hard. Benedict took three steps, realized his mistake, and yelled, "No!" He was too late. The bowler scooped up the ball and flung it hard at his wicket. His heart sank as he heard the clatter behind him.

Weston ran up as he began his dejected walk back to the pavilion. "Benny," he said, "how can I apologize? It was just an impulse. For goodness sake, forgive me."

"That's all right, Felix," Benedict said. "We're going to win. That's all that really matters."

Benedict's father was standing up as he came into the pavilion. He was clapping dementedly.

He was a tall, stooping, ruddy, excitable man, lean, his hair grey but his face still young and full of enthusiasm. He was forty years old. A fervent patriot, he had enlisted in the Hampshires in the first world war. This had not embittered him; on the contrary he had noticed only the courage, the comradeship, the

14

nobility of war. He had many good war stories. Keith Margrave, heir to the great brewery business, had been his platoon commander, and after the Armistice he had asked Mr. Benedict to come in as a traveller. This Mr. Benedict had agreed to do with his usual enthusiasm, and he had done very decently at the job. He had a wide territory—Hampshire, part of Sussex and Surrey, and he rattled cheerfully from one pub to the other in his brewery van. Where the publican was a Margrave licensee, his task was relatively simple: to encourage and incite, to note shortages and rectify complaints, to keep the supply of Margrave's celebrated bitter flowing freely to all who desired it. The hard selling came in on the soft drinks side. It was Mr. Benedict's duty to build up the sale of Marfrute in restaurants and groceries throughout his territory. He did this loyally, but without conviction. He had only three great loves that ruled his life. They were his beer, his cricket, and his son. He was a widower. He lived in a small house adjoining the "Thorn and Sceptre", a Margrave inn which served the inhabitants of Ashdale, a village just outside Aylsbourn. Mrs. Sampson, the landlady of the "Thorn and Sceptre", provided father and son with their evening meal and Kate, one of the barmaids, cleaned and laundered for them. The boy had lunch at Valhalla during term time and in the Margrave staff canteen during the holidays. Mr. Benedict made breakfast for them both himself. It was a pleasant life that the two had made for themselves.

Mr. Benedict had few outside interests. He enjoyed his job and indeed was an authority on the beer for thirty miles around. He was a keen cricketer and turned out regularly for the Brewery second eleven. He did little serious reading, though he studied the sports pages of the *Daily Mail* each morning. He read an occasional Cronin novel, but his evenings were generally spent drinking bitter at the "Thorn and Sceptre", in reminiscing about the curious people he had come upon in his thousands of miles as a traveller, and in entering for crossword competitions. He had been doing these for nineteen years now, and save for a guinea postal order one Christmas, he had met with little success. He was sure he would win one day.

"We'll go to Switzerland," he used to say to his son, "and stay at the Chalet Bisque in Lausanne, where your mother and I went for our honeymoon. Marvellous hot croissants we used to have for breakfast every morning. Monsieur Blanchisseur—he is the *patron*—will serve us personally. Great big jolly fellow, he was, red face and walrus moustache; we were favourites of his; he couldn't do enough for us. And we'll have some Chocolat Meunier with the croissants; marvellous stuff, like black honey. We can't make chocolate here, you know. The Swiss beer's not up to much of course; like gnat's pee, to put it vulgarly. That's the only thing I'll miss, the beer. But we'll go one day, son, you can bet your life on that."

Then beaming and enthused with nostalgia, he would bend his attention to the simple linguistic permutations that by a perennial hairsbreadth eluded him. He would never give up trying. And he would never give up loving his son.

"Well done, well done!" he cried embarrassingly, as the boy approached from the wicket. He shook his hand in an access of paternal pride.

Mr. V. V. Varley, headmaster of Valhalla, joined them. A large florid man of sixty, he stood six feet one inch and (as he was fond of telling his boys) swung the scales to just on eighteen stone.

No one knew exactly where Mr. Varley came from. He was called "Colonel" in the "Thorn and Sceptre", where he drank port and lemon each night, but malicious people in the town said he had promoted himself. It was even rumoured that he had been a sergeant-major. There was no way of confirming or denying this, for no one dared to ask Mr. Varley himself.

He had come to Aylsbourn in 1922, and bought Valhalla, a large ramshackle Victorian house, for what he jocularly called "a hundred down and chase me for the rest". It had once been a prosperous brewer's residence: basement, spacious ground floor, two floors above, maids' rooms, box rooms; the whole thing highly impractical to run even in the comparatively spacious nineteen-twenties.

At first people had been wary of the preparatory school which Mr. Varley had opened there. He seemed to have few academic qualifications, and the mauve and gold school uniform which he designed himself struck the population as flamboyant. On the other hand, he soon gathered round himself a legend for discipline. In consequence, he soon had an impressive row of successes in the Common Entrance examination. In the seventeen years of its existence Valhalla had prospered, till now it could boast a hundred and twenty boys, each of whose parents willingly paid fifteen guineas a term for the privilege of wearing the hideous mauve and gold cap. Mr. Varley was a great man, an institution in Aylsbourn.

He had black hair, still thick and wavy, which he brushed back severely. In the winter he wore a heavy black raglan coat with a white silk scarf, and carried a swordstick. For cricket, however, he wore a loud regimental blazer over crisply-laundered white flannels, with a white silk scarf knotted and tucked jauntily in at the throat.

"Well done, Benedict," he boomed. Then, turning to his father, he observed: "You must be a very happy man, sir."

"I most certainly am, I most certainly am." Mr. Benedict nodded several times with emphasis. They beamed down at the boy, who swung his bat awkwardly and stared at the floor. He was struggling with an unfamiliar problem: how to succeed gracefully. It was for this kind of skill that parents paid the fifteen guineas a term.

"What about a drink, eh?" Mr. Varley suggested.

"Never say no," Mr. Benedict claimed.

They turned into the pavilion, redolent still with the aroma of sawdust and oil lamps. The boy bashfully followed them.

"Lucky there's a club licence, what, Mr. Benedict?" chaffed Mr. Varley. "What's it to be—a pint of that excellent Margrave Ale of yours?"

"No better beer made," Mr. Benedict affirmed seriously.

"Right," said Mr. Varley. "And what about our hero— lemonade or ginger beer?"

"Lemonade please, sir."

"Rightyho. Two pints of Margrave Best Bitter and a pint of lemonade," roared Mr. Varley to the barmaid.

It was the best lemonade in the world, Benedict thought as he raised the pint tumbler to his lips; a cold acid-drop yellow liquid made with a liberal base of crystals that left a sharp citric flavour on the tongue; there could never be a drink in the world to match it. Not even Margrave beer, which was his father's livelihood. He drank half a pint of lemonade without pausing, while the two men watched benignly.

"Good lad," said Mr. Varley as Benedict lowered his glass

17

with a gasp. "Chip off the old block, eh, Mr. Benedict?"

"He certainly is," Benedict senior confirmed with a beam of universal euphoria. "Your very good health, Mr. Varley."

"And yours, sir."

Just then an extra-long burst of applause told them that the game had ended in victory for Valhalla. In a moment the pitch was clouded over with small boys in white.

Mr. Varley frowned out of the window and finished his beer at a gulp. "Discipline," he said firmly. "Excuse me, please."

As he strode across the grass, the boys divided before him. He took a silver whistle from his blazer pocket and blew spiritedly on it. The chatter died away. "*To me, Valhalla,*" he called.

"Excuse me, Dad" Benedict said, and trotted briskly towards the throng of small boys who were scrumming tightly round the centripetal figure of Mr. V. V. Varley. The Locks Priory boys watched gobstruck.

"Valhalla," Mr. Varley boomed, "have just won a fine victory. It was a good clean game, with plenty of give and take, and a thoroughly sporting occasion from start to finish. Now then, I want you to show your appreciation of the gallant show put up by our old rivals. School, three cheers for Locks Priory. Hip hip . . ."

The cheers rang crisply in the warm summer air. Like garish targets in a shooting range, the violet and gold caps bobbed up and down as if on invisible currents of air.

"As you know," Mr. Varley continued, "it is not the Valhalla custom to pick out boys for individual approbation. We believe here in the team spirit first, last, and always. But I will break a rule today. Weston and Benedict made a magnificent stand. Without my reference books I cannot say if it is a school record, but whether it is or not, it was an achievement of which every Valhallian can be proud. School—three cheers for Weston and Benedict. Hip hip . . ."

And again the shrill cheers echoed over the brewery pavilion.

"Once again, we near the end of the summer term," Mr. Varley continued. "I shall expect every boy punctually on parade for nine o'clock drill as usual on Monday. If you behave, you should be away for your summer hols, reports signed, by twelve. But you know me well enough to remember that I am quite capable of flogging the whole school at the slightest sign of indiscipline, last day of term or no. Bear this well in mind. Happy weekend, boys."

"Happy weekend, sir," came back the crisply-drilled chorus, and the caps bobbed once more into the air. It was the valedictory at the end of each Friday afternoon. The tight concentric circles of violet and gold split and sundered in all directions. The boys walked smartly in groups of two or three, exemplars of decorum, at any rate till they were out of Mr. Varley's sight.

Mr. Benedict came over and put his hand on his son's shoulder. He smelt faintly—and pleasantly—of beer.

"I must get along, son," he said. "Have to deliver twelve dozen Marfrute bottles over at Little Welcaster. I'll be back by six. Are you having tea at school?"

"Not today, Dad. Felix has asked me home."

"Oh." Mr. Benedict frowned. "Bloody young fool, getting you run out like that."

"It was just over-keenness."

"I suppose so. Anyway, you got your fifty. Ah here's the rascal now."

Felix Weston raised his cap politely as he approached them. He still looked crestfallen. With his jet black hair and his black eyes set in the dark face, he looked like a small Spanish pirate.

"Good afternoon, sir," he ventured deferentially. Then in a rush: "You must think me an awful tick, running Benny out like that. I just seemed to lose my head."

"Never mind, Felix," Mr. Benedict was in a forgiving mood. "It was a historic partnership. You'll both be playing for Hampshire, I'll take money on it."

Not only did Mr. Benedict believe this with every fibre of his uncomplicated and affectionate soul; he could envisage no higher ambition for either of them.

The boys grinned and exchanged glances. Fathers could be a blasted embarrassment.

"Anyway," Mr. Benedict added, "I'm off. Back at six, son."

"O.K., Dad." Benedict found it hard to conceal his relief.

The boys sauntered over to the railings, mounted their bicycles, and pedalled slowly out of the Margrave Brewery ground. A few minutes later, a small Margrave Brewery van, driven by Mr. Benedict, rattled by them. He honked his farewell and disappeared.

The two boys cycled slowly down the main road until it began to merge into Aylsbourn High Street. They did not speak. It was a moment of peace between them. They floated in a slight inter-regnum between the past and the future; this moment was the end of childhood, the overture of youth. They had played their last game for Valhalla, taken their last cold bath and—subject to good behaviour on Monday morning—been beaten for the last time. It was Weston who broke the silence first:

"You know, Benny, I'm going to miss you terribly."

"But I haven't gone into Shallerton yet."

"You will. Easily."

The next morning Benedict was to sit for his scholarship to Shallerton Oaks, the nearest public school. The fees, £150 a year, were far beyond Mr. Benedict's slender resources. Indeed he felt that he had had a good year when he made £500 with commission and expenses. It paid, in 1939, for a fortnight at Brighton for both of them, covered the rent of the house, met the upkeep on the Morris Eight, enabled him to buy a round of Aylsbourn bitter at the local, to give his son a new cricket bat on his birthday, to clothe him in grey flannel suits and even fork out the fifteen guineas a term for Valhalla. Quite evidently, though, it would not run to the £150 a year that Shallerton would cost.

But there was a scholarship; a benefaction of Margrave's Brewery worth at the moment about £135 a year. There was only one of these scholarships, and it was awarded on an examination, together with an interview. Mr. Benedict knew Ross-Tayfield, the headmaster of Shallerton, well, and consequently had no doubt that his son was going to win the scholarship. His evidence for this was in fact rather thin. He had button-holed Ross-Tayfield at the Margrave Sports, where the latter was an unwilling guest. Ross-Tayfield was a tall, gaunt, gloomy Scot, whose leisure was devoted entirely to ornithology. His idea of a treat was to give the school a lantern lecture with his latest slides of rare birds. Mr. Benedict had persuaded Ross-Tayfield to drink a pint of Margrave bitter with him, and had sung his son's praises. This would have entirely ruined the boy's chances, had not Ross-Tayfield already heard from Mr. V. V. Varley that the young Benedict had the makings of a really useful stand-off half. The only ambition in Ross-Tayfield's life was to see his school trounce Wargrave Castle. Since Ross-Tayfield had become headmaster of

Shallerton, his school had in fact drawn twice with the Castle and lost four times, the last occasion forty-seven nil. He had sacked his rugby master and redoubled his efforts. Hence if this Benedict boy made any sort of show with the papers, he would have Ross-Tayfield's active support at the interview. Of course there was competition. Half a dozen boys a year went in for it, but luckily it was restricted to the sons of Margrave employees, and Benedict, beside being the best footballer of his year, was reliable, if not brilliant at English. So, if only his maths paper were not too bad. . . .

Weston sighed. His father hated public schools, even small ones like Shallerton Oaks. This was especially annoying, because he could quite easily have afforded to send Felix there. The Weston money came from a Midland chain store business. Weston's grandfather had begun life as a grocer, and built up his trade until he had thirty shops. He had made the mistake of sending his only son, Gerard Weston, to Cambridge. Here Gerard had fallen in with a group of left-wing intellectuals, and, to his family's horror, had become an ardent communist. He had retired from the business, though prudently retaining his share in it. The stores were now run by a small consortium of managers, and Weston, since he had come back from Spain, had retired to the country to write a history of the civil war, to donate large sums to his party, to inflame the local peasantry with speeches and posters, and, perhaps pre-eminently, to brood. His first wife, Felix's mother, had died, and his second wife, a stunning artist's model, still only nineteen, now lived in the elegant Georgian house in the High Street which unflaggingly displayed communist slogans at by-elections.

So there was no question of Felix going in for the entrance examination, let alone the scholarship. He was going to Aylsbourn Grammar School. It was incongruous, Benedict thought; Felix belongs naturally at Shallerton; I belong to Aylsbourn. For once, he reflected, I have the edge on Felix; poor old Felix.

He turned impulsively towards him. "I could always fail tomorrow Felix. You know I can't go unless I get the scholarship."

Weston pulled up sharply and grabbed Benedict's bicycle by the saddle, hauling him to a halt too. He stared at Benedict hard, then his Mediterranean-dark face broke into a generous grin.

"Benny," he said, "you know you're nuts, don't you?"

"I don't really care about Shallerton Oaks. It's a good school, but—well I feel I belong here."

"You mean you think you're too bloody humble to go there?"

"Good Lord no. But I like it here. Don't you? I—I think I'll be a bit lost at Shallerton."

Weston stared at him again in affectionate disbelief.

"You really like this one-eyed hole? I'm longing to get out of it."

"I don't understand you, Felix. Do you know, I'd like to settle down and live here."

"Whatever for?"

"Well—it sounds silly I suppose, but I love the smell of the place."

"The smell?"

"Yes. It's a mixture of the Welcaster pond smell, and the dusty smell of the chalk in the air at Valhalla, and the blossy smell on the new books at Strether's shop, and the warm smell of the fresh doughnuts in Miller's bakery and—even the grass has a sort of——"

He looked at Weston shamefacedly.

"I suppose it sounds screwy."

Weston nodded solemnly. "Benny," he said. "You really are nuts. Anywhere—or anyone—can smell like that if you want them to. For heaven's sake remember that or you'll come a terrible cropper one day. But look here. Promise me one thing. Promise me you'll do your damndest on Monday."

Benedict grinned.

"O.K.," he said. "I'll do my damndest. After all, Shallerton is only eight miles away. I can cycle over to see you in half an hour."

Weston shoved Benedict's bicycle forward in a gesture of affectionate despair and they pedalled on dreamily again, each lost in his own thoughts. They turned down Brewer's Lane, which ran parallel to the High Street and just behind it, and banged the back door in Mr. Weston's garden wall noisily open. It was a small garden, but it had run to seed. In the kitchen window they saw the large, beneficent features of Mrs. Duncher, the Westons' housekeeper. She beamed when she saw them.

"Come along you boys," she called. "I expect you're hungry and thirsty."

In the drawing-room it was cool; the venetian blind was still down. For all his progressive thinking Mr. Weston was not a particularly sociable man. He and his wife had gone on one of their periodical day-trips to London. He would be attending a communist committee meeting in the East End while she went shopping at Harrod's; they would meet for lunch at the Savoy Grill and part again for the afternoon. She would go to the hairdresser's, he to the London Library. At six they would meet for a drink at the Fitzroy, and they would generally go to the theatre in the evening. They caught the last train, the 10.55 from Waterloo, back to Aylsbourn, and took a taxi up the hill home again. They would be indoors by a quarter to one. The Aylsbourn stationmaster said that Mr. Weston was often drunk when the train drew in.

At any rate, the house was now empty and cool. The sober works of Hegel and Marx fought for space on the bookshelves with the Hemingway novels, Gollancz yellow jackets, and the latest copies of the new magazine *Picture Post*.

It was (as Mrs. Duncher knew) Benedict's favourite high tea: veal and ham pie set in a huge dish of green salad, lettuce, cucumber, radishes, tomatoes, and cold potatoes. There was a thick, dark fruit cake and a monster pot of tea. The boys sat at each end of the long table and ate with gigantic zest. Benedict had six cups of tea, Weston five. They spoke little. The warmth and torpor of the summer day enveloped them. At thirteen it seemed hard to think about the past: even harder to cast the mind forward into the future. At length Weston said: "Come up to my room, Benny. I've got something I think will interest you."

Weston's room was at the top of the house, in what had once been a maid's room. His bookshelves provided an interesting comparison with his father's. There were Neville Cardus's *Cricket*, C. B. Fry's *Batsmanship*, and W. W. Wakefield's *Rugger*. There was a book by J. N. George called *English Pistols and Revolvers*. There was Auden and Isherwood's *The Ascent of F.6* and Macneice's first volume of poetry. There was a book by a man called Malinowski entitled *The Sexual Life of Savages*. But it was not books that Weston had brought Benedict to see. On the table under the gable window stood a small turntable, and under it a stack of records.

"I've got a new one, Benny." Weston grinned like a pirate returned to treasure trove. "And I know you're going to like it."

Gently he placed the shiny black disc on the turntable, wound the clockwork motor, and lowered the steel needle on to the track. There was a loud hiss and then the melancholy strains of the Basin Street Blues filled the little room.

Benedict listened entranced. Though the music was tinny and distorted, he though he had never heard anything more moving in his life. He had only a remote idea where Basin Street was, yet he felt as if he had walked its pavements. They would be drowsy and sun-sluiced and the hot, rich, boozy, jazz would float up from the tenement basements as you wandered along them. . . . He closed his eyes and drowned his senses in the music. He had never met an American, let alone a negro; but he felt he understood instinctively what the singer was trying to say.

"Play it again, Felix," he said. "It's superb."

They played it a dozen times, then some of their other favourites. So far Weston had only a score of records; the vogue had only just begun to filter down to them from the nineteen-year-old layer of English society that year. They had the Benny Goodman Trio playing "Avalon", and the Quartet playing "Moonglow"; they had Bob Crosby's "Royal Garden Blues" and Louis Armstrong's "Save It, Pretty Mama"; they had Muggsy Spanier's "Big Butter and Egg Man", and King Oliver's "Dippermouth Blues".

Already the earlier records were looking grey and old. But it seemed they would never tire of them.

Benedict watched his friend with anxious affection. Weston lay curled up in a basket chair, his feet tucked under him. His eyes were closed in concentration, his lips pursed to an imaginary trombone, his left hand holding its valve to his lips, his right executing elegant glissandos on the slide. Dear Old Felix, the imperturbable! But Benedict had something on his mind now which he felt Weston simply had to know.

The record ended and Felix began to re-wind the motor. It creaked as he ground away energetically. Benedict half opened his mouth to speak, drew in his breath sharply, and said nothing. Felix looked up, grinned and said: "Bloody marvellous the first four or five times. Then it gets tiring. Have you heard Goodman's 'Lonesome Road'?"

Benedict shook his head.

"It's great. I'll play it next." He put it on, set the needle

24

down, released the catch; there was the familiar excitement of the little hiss and the kick of the opening bars.

Benedict decided to speak over the sound: perhaps it would be easier.

"Felix," he said.

He had not spoken loud enough. Felix had closed his black-ringed eyes once more. Ecstatically, he accompanied the great Goodman on an invisible bass violin, plucking huge chords from its vibrating strings.

"Felix," he said again.

Weston opened his eyes. "Yeah, man?" he asked flippantly. To all intents and purposes he was in New Orleans.

"Felix, I've got something important to tell you."

"Speak on, friend."

It was a little difficult above the strident jazz, but Benedict plunged manfully on.

"It's about Arabella. She's going to have a baby."

Weston opened one eye, but showed no further interest. Arabella was his father's second wife.

Benedict felt a sense of anticlimax at his friend's apathy. Felix was a damnably cool cove! He waited with exasperated affection till the last bar of the record had faded away. Then Weston carefully took the record off, dusted it with his handkerchief, and put it away.

"Who told you?" he asked casually. A shade too casually; he was deeply interested.

"My old man of course. He heard it from Keith Margrave. I suppose your old man must have told him. What do you say, Felix?"

Felix pondered. His face was set in an expression of almost comical gravity.

"When's it due?" he asked.

"Not till February."

Felix did a quick calculation with his fingers. "Seven months. He hasn't wasted much time spreading the glad tidings."

"It'll be odd, won't it, Felix? I mean to have a brother or sister and you old enough to be its father. Well almost I mean."

Felix reflected. "It'll be a damn nuisance," he observed tetchily.

"Why?"

"Well, the old man gets quite broody enough over her as it is. Imagine the state he'll be in for the next seven months. He'll be even more under her thumb than he is now. You know she has him twisted round her little finger."

His young face was dark and clouded with complex and private griefs.

Benedict had a question he had wanted to ask for a long time. "How did they meet, Felix?"

"Oh at that bloody old fool Bantinglow's."

"But Bantinglow is one of our most distinguished painters."

"That's as may be. He's certainly a slavering old lecher. Arabella was his model."

"A *model*. Crikey!" It was the world before the war, and in Aylsbourn, which was fifty years behind the times anyway, the word could have only one connotation: free love!

"Yes, his model. And his mistress of course." Weston flung the intelligence off lightly, but he knew the effect it would have on his romantic and idealistic friend.

"Felix, you don't mean Arabella and that old reptile of eighty. . . ."

"Sure I do. Nothing the old swine likes more. I can't blame him though. Arabella must be pretty hot stuff in bed."

"Yes, but surely, Felix, you don't think your father married Arabella just for *that*? I mean quite frankly I find it hard to imagine him and Arabella. . . ."

"Do you? I find it the easiest thing in the world. What do you think they go down to the caravan every weekend for?" This was a particular source of irritation to Felix. Already he was developing sophisticated tastes. The idea of weekending at Torquay was mysteriously delightful to him. But a fat chance he stood of making up a threesome with his father and Arabella! He didn't know which of the two he resented more. He picked up a pencil and began to chew the end savagely.

Benedict sat struggling to order his jumbled emotions. He shook his head.

"Felix, I just can't understand you. First of all, I don't believe what you say about Arabella and Bantinglow. She's so—so *young* and, well, beautiful."

"Neither," replied Weston drily, "has yet been thought to disqualify one from lechery."

"But what would *she* get out of it?"

"The same as him. That's why I shall have a middle-aged mistress as soon as I'm old enough. They say you can play some good tunes on an old fiddle."

"I know they do, Felix, but that's just folklore. I don't believe that's *all* there is between people like your father and Arabella; not an *intellectual* like your father." The word intellectual figured frequently in Benedict's conversation: it was the greatest compliment he could convey.

"My dear old boy," Weston explained superciliously, "intellectuals are the biggest rams of all. Haven't you ever heard my father talk about the orgies at Cambridge when he was an under-..."

"Arabella married your father because she loved him," Benedict blurted out. It was his entire confession of faith; the gospel and the apostles.

"Because she loved him," echoed Felix, mocking Benedict's reverent voice. "Look, Benny, my father's worth a hundred thousand. That's point number one. Secondly, he's a randy old goat, with lots of experience gained in all the brothels south of the Pyrenees. Don't you think he's a better bet for Arabella than some doomy young bearded penniless painter from the Slade? Anyway," he added thoughtfully, "she can always pick up someone like that when he's dead."

"But your father isn't all that old, Felix."

"He's forty-five if he's a day."

"Yes, I suppose he is pretty old."

"And remember my mother is already dead."

"They didn't get on, did they?"

"No. She used to drink. Can't say I blame her. Always at the gin bottle, even before breakfast. There used to be some really gorgeous rows between them. Of course it was useful from my point of view."

"Why was that?"

"Well, as you know, I want to be a writer one day. I'm already keeping a journal. I've never told a soul this before, Benny"—and here Felix gave his most appealing smile—"so keep my secret for me, please. I know I can trust you."

"Of course you can, Felix. But what do you put in it?"

"Anything. Everything. Snatches of conversation, ideas,

27

sketches, tram tickets. But the stuff between mother and father was the best. Boy, it was fruity!"

Weston closed his eyes and beamed to remember.

"Wasn't your mother very famous?"

"She was a chorus girl in the nineteen-twenties. God, she didn't half use some ripe language when she felt like it. She was a slut, you have to face the fact."

"But she was your *mother*, Felix."

"Yes. And a slut. But tell me, Benny, why do you look so shocked at the idea that my father and his gorgeous model should live together in lust? Isn't that what everybody else does?"

"No. At least I don't think so. My father was terribly in love with my mother."

"Was he? He gets maudlin about her when he's got four pints of Margrave Best inside him. What were they like when she was alive? Didn't they row like all other married couples? Weren't there moments when they wished they hadn't set eyes on each other?"

Benedict hated his friend at that moment. Weston was a cynical swine. There was more to life than that, he was certain.

"Maybe they didn't row," Weston went on meditatively. "Maybe they had just grown into vegetables. That, I suppose, is what most of the peasants in this town do."

Benedict got to his feet. Weston looked up in surprise. "Off so soon, Benny? Why don't you stay to supper and see the radiant pair come home tonight? I can see them already: him with that shifty look in his eyes he always has when he's made a quick tax-free thousand on the Stock Exchange; her with that cow-like look they all get as soon as they're in the family way. Ugh!" He made a terrifying face, full of hate and renunciation.

Benedict had recovered himself; he smiled affectionately down on his friend.

"When did your mother die, Felix?"

"Three years ago. Nearly four. Of course *he* didn't bother to see her; hadn't seen her for years. It was just me and Mama and the nursing home."

"Felix, you'll get over it. It's your mother dying that's upset you, I'm sure of that."

"You think I shall grow used to the little trollop?" He sighed resignedly. "I suppose we grow used to everything in the end."

28

"One day, you'll fall in love, Felix, and then you'll understand and forgive."

Weston made an impatient movement. "Benny, unless you destroy this romance in you you'll destroy yourself. There is desire. There is conquest. There's comfort. There's resignation, dislike, and in the end quiet desperation. That's all love is!"

"Beside all these things," Benedict said softly, "there is love."

"How do you know? Have you ever been in love?"

"No. But when I do it will be with everything I've got: heart and mind and guts. . . ."

"Haven't you left something out?" enquired Weston drily.

Benedict laughed. "Yes and that too. But that's only the beginning. If you never get any more than that, you've only got dust and ashes."

Felix uncurled from his chair. He grinned at Benedict, his young black eyes glistening with affection and pleasure at what he saw. "Oh my poor Benny," he said. "What awful pain lies ahead for you."

The clock was striking seven in the hall as they passed through. Benedict put his head round the kitchen door and thanked Mrs. Duncher for his tea.

"Do you think the old battle-axe knows?" Felix asked.

"No. She'd be—sort of agog. You know how women are."

Felix dug his hand deep in his pockets as Benedict mounted his bicycle.

"I know what women are," he said solemnly. "The only question is, Benny, do you? And will you ever learn?"

"We'll see which of us is right," Benedict said good-naturedly. "Good night, Felix."

"Good night, Benny. And good luck in the examination tomorrow. I really mean that."

"I know you do, Felix. I'll do my best."

"That, unfortunately, Benny, is what you'll always do."

The High Street ran through the town from west to east, and he lived right at the eastern end, down Hop Field Lane. The simplest way home was along the High Street. But this evening something made him turn right and climb towards the long ridge of the Hampshire Downs which ran along the southern boundary of Aylsbourn. It was called Windmill Hill at its western end, and Cromwell Hill at the eastern end. A narrow lane ran along the top

29

of the hill, serving the well-fed houses on the top which looked down the Cressbrook valley. He could get home this way; it was longer, but it was quieter. For some reason he did not understand, he wanted to go this way. It was a tiny decision, but his own choice; and it altered the course of his whole life.

Windmill Hill was steep—as much as one in six in places. For much of its way it was bounded by a high privet hedge; then the hedge divided for the gates of the Grammar School. It lay back in a hollow, built in 1582 and extended in the eighteenth and nineteenth centuries. It was a small school, with hardly more than two hundred and eighty pupils, girls and boys. It was impossible to see very much of it from the road. Benedict had never had cause to go inside.

The school was just over the brow of the hill, and Benedict was going to coast down the other side; he was no longer pedalling, still drifting in the warm emollient wash of the evening air, drifting with the mood, with the day. As he was about to pass the school gates, two cyclists were emerging, and he pulled up to let them go by.

They were a boy and a girl; the boy was about sixteen, the girl looked a little less. The boy wore a pair of heavy-lensed glasses. He had a curious, wedge-shaped face; strong yet with humour in it. He wore a green blazer over white tennis clothes, and there was gold lettering under the breast pocket badge.

The girl wore a lime-green summer dress, open at the throat. Her arms were bare, and she carried a tennis racquet: she wore no hat and her fair hair was combed down to her shoulders.

They wheeled right as he drew up to let them by, and as they did so she half-turned and smiled to thank him. She had wide-apart green eyes and a pale skin; perhaps a few freckles. Then they sped down the hill and the boy said something which made the girl laugh. Then they were gone.

Benedict cycled on for a while, but he was in a trance. He had never seen anything so—perfect. That fellow—he was an intellectual of course!—anyone could tell. But, an athlete too. And that girl—she must have been *his* girl! These two, each perfect, each suspended at this moment in time, he had surprised in their happiness. *Perhaps they were in love!* He stopped altogether and stared down the long lane that wound down the other side of Windmill Hill. *They must be in love,* he thought. How could any other emotion between them be possible? Benedict tingled with pure, unentangled happiness. He was happy because they so evidently were happy too. He had no wish to intervene. He was grateful merely to have been there. There would be no coming back to this moment, but equally no taking it away. It was his moment and theirs. Nothing could ever alter that.

A voice calling in a ripe Hampshire burr recalled him; it was a labourer telling his children to come into their tea. He pedalled on again, but was in no mood yet to speak to anyone. A little lower down the lane there was a stile on the right, below a green notice-board which said simply "To Westaker Farm." Benedict threw his bicycle down, vaulted over the stile, and followed the path along the edge of the field.

There was a high fence on his right, behind which lay the little bungalows of the Sir Jonathan Rexcoth Hospital: the Aylsbourn air was so good that there were several famous hospitals built on its hills. Then the path turned right, and began to climb again; and as he came over the brow he knew he would see his secret view.

It was a wonderful view by any standards; yet no one had noticed it but Benedict. Six miles to the south-east he could see the great beech range of Oakhanger, where Garnett had written his famous natural history. From that side, the view was famous; there had been a half-page picture in *The Times* of it once.

This side, though, nobody knew; and Benedict thought it was a better view. He was looking down the Cressbrook valley; it was not particularly deep, but it lay like a long saucer down to Oakhanger and beyond; and the little hills of the Hampshire Downs cupped it in so gently that it was impossible to see the hard-limned horizon. The most distant woods lay in a haze of purple turning lime under the declining sun; in the middle distance the ploughed earth stretched away, biscuit-coloured and dry as meal.

There were no more than three buildings in the whole huge saucer; he was looking down on ten thousand acres of pure farming land. There were half a dozen cottage-loaf haystacks at Westaker, and beyond the grey slate roofs of the outhouse he could count the white windows in the side of the orange brick farmhouse. There was no sign of another living thing; only fields beyond number tilting at crazy angles and sewn together by the little hedges; yellow-green fields, then pea-green and then a sudden splash of coffee-brown soil. And some of the ploughed fields were bone white.

Not all the buildings were old; he could just see the silver glint on a modern metal granary in Oakhanger village.

He lay on his back and stared up, his hands behind his head, a straw in the mouth, feeling the hard, dry earth cradle him against the shoulder blades and hips; and he stared up into the sky.

There was no cloud; only a hard blue infinite lid over this bone-dry saucer which was his favourite and secret piece of earth. He allowed his mind to drown in the sky's empty and timeless and pitiless enormity.

They must have been in love, he said out loud; and the loudness of his own voice frightened him.

He lay there a long time, until the Aylsbourn mist began to gather. Then he scrambled up and ran down the path till he got back to the stile. Here he halted, and putting his hand on the crossbeam he said very quietly, but with the greatest possible solemnity: "I shall never forget today."

Then he vaulted over the stile, jumped on his bicycle and pedalled swiftly home.

Mr. Benedict peered at his son over his glasses as he came in; he was reading the *Daily Mail* sports page in the yellow light; a pot of tea under a cosy and two mugs stood at his elbow. He had taken off his shoes and put on felt carpet slippers through which his toes protruded; he had taken off his jacket and hung it behind the door. Blue pipe smoke filled the little room; he needed only his son.

"Hello, boy!" He greeted Benedict with his accustomed enthusiasm, throwing down the paper in a gesture of renunciation. "Here, I've just made another pot of tea, have some with me."

"Thanks, Dad." Benedict sank into the armchair opposite his father.

"Well," said Mr. Benedict, pouring with care, "that was some innings, son. If you go on like that you'll be playing for Shallerton first eleven in two or three years."

"I haven't passed the scholarship yet, Dad."

"You'll get it, don't worry, boy. Mr. Varley is prepared to take money on it. He knows a good thing when he sees one."

Benedict grinned. "Varley would bet on the date of his grandmother's funeral." Then he went on more seriously: "But tell me, Dad, why does it matter so much that I should get in to Shallerton?"

"Because it's a fine school!" cried Mr. Benedict. He passed over the mug of tea and began to pace up and down the room. "A *public* school. You'll be a public school man, Benny, think of that!"

"But isn't it going to cost you an awful lot of money?"

"Not if you get the scholarship."

"But the incidentals—clothes, books, pocket money. . . ."

Mr. Benedict dismissed them all with an impatient wave. "Worth every penny!" he cried.

"The other boys will be much better off than me."

"Don't worry about that. A gentleman never worries about your means. The main thing is to play the game and not be afraid to take your punishment like a man. They'll like you, Benny. A man who can bat like you today has nothing to fear at Shallerton."

"But is that the only advantage of being good at cricket? I play for fun, not so that people will like me."

Mr. Benedict seemed for a second to be losing his usual tolerance. Then he checked himself and went on patiently: "Benny, I'm hoping you'll go on to Oxford. You've got the brain, I know. You could be a blue: think of that—a cricket blue. Maybe even a double blue!"

"Sure, that would be nice, Dad. But it's not an end in itself, is it!"

"Of course not. Let me tell you son"—he leaned forward confidentially—"an Oxford blue can go anywhere in the world. He is welcome in any club; and take it from me—he never wants for a job. Why, the City will give a blue a job any time! And do you know there are three Blues on the board of Margrave Brewery at this very minute?"

"Yes, but two of them are members of the family, and the other married into it."

"But don't you see, son"—Mr. Benedict seemed genuinely pained—"*it all goes together*. A man with a blue is a man with a passport. He's a gentleman, and a scholar and a sportsman. What more can you want?"

"Why a scholar? Don't a lot of Blues fail their degrees and get sent down?"

Mr. Benedict paused as he filled his pipe and winked broadly. "Where there's a will there's a way. The varsity has never lost a good man yet. There's always the pass degree. You've got to be an imbecile to fail that."

Benedict decided to change his tack.

"So I'm to go to Shallerton to get a Blue. Surely I could get by going through the Grammar School?"

Mr. Benedict frowned.

"It's a question of contacts you see, son—friendships and connections. If you look through the history of Shallerton you'll be astounded at the great men it has turned out. Soldiers, statesmen, company directors—all united by this one bond." Mr. Benedict was lyrical now. "You'll love it. And I shall be proud to think a son of mine is there. It's—it's a question of *tradition* you see. You can't beat tradition."

Benedict pulled a large book called *Aylsbourn Antiquities* from the shelf, consulted the index, and turned the pages.

"Do you know when Shallerton was founded, Dad?" he enquired.

"Oh heaven knows. Hundreds of years ago."

"It was founded in 1841. And Aylsbourn Grammar School"— he flipped the pages again—"was founded in 1582. Robin Lazenby, the Elizabethan poet, went to school there; so did John Garnett, whose natural history is probably one of the hundred greatest books in the world; so did Benjamin West, the man behind the Reform Law agitation"—but he stopped as he saw Mr. Benedict's evident distress.

"I've nothing *against* the Grammar School, son," he said quietly. "I just want the best for you. I want you to get on, to be a success. I want you"—he hesitated in embarrassment, then plunged on desperately—"to have the best this country can give you; and I want you to learn how to give it back again. That's all."

There was a silence between them. At length Benedict closed the book with a bang and grinned.

"All right, Dad," he said. "I'll get that ruddy scholarship."

"That's the boy. You're not swotting tonight, I hope?"

"Good Lord, no." Mr. Varley was a crafty examination tactician and it was a cardinal rule in his campaign that the boys should relax completely the night before. "No—I think I'll read for a bit. Something really good." He glanced along the bookshelves, past the collected Caxton Shakespeare, the set of Dickens collected with three hundred newspaper coupons, the A. J. Cronins in their yellow jackets, the crossword companions and the standard works on brewing. No, there was nothing there. He pulled his small case on to his lap and rummaged inside it till he found what he wanted.

"I think I'll read H. G. Wells," he said.

"Ah that Red," observed Mr. Benedict without passion. "Wells and Shaw. As bad as one another. You'll get past that stage."

"I'm reading him for fun," Benedict explained. "You've no idea how exhilarating he can be. It's one I haven't read before— *The Food of the Gods*. It's terrific."

"Well, if it takes your mind off the exam tomorrow, I shan't complain."

Benedict read for an hour, while his father sat with his feet up and smoked his pipe. Not another word was spoken till, at half-past nine, Benedict got up and bade his father good night.

As he undressed he realized how stiff he would be in the morning; already there was a pleasing ache as he moved his hips. He picked up his bat and stroked the oily yellow wood, then swung it a few times, feeling again the lovely springing thump of the ball as it whined away to the boundary, and he heard in his imagination the indolent ripple of applause again for his fifty runs. Then he knelt on the bed and looked out of the window. There was no moon, but there was no wind either; the Aylsbourn earth lay breathless and expectant beneath him; and every star was in the sky.

There was a good smell in the air as if wood was burning; it was the rich, special, unmistakable smell of Aylsbourn. "One day," thought Benedict, "I really must find out what that smell is." As his eyes grew accustomed to the dark he picked out the low line of the Hampshire Downs, lying like a fat black porker against a backdrop-blue skyline.

Then Benedict remembered the encounter on the hill, and he

said to himself out loud: "This is the happiest day of my life."

Then he jumped into bed, and opened his book by H. G. Wells and read till it slid from his hands; and so ended his happiest day.

He awoke to find himself a prisoner in a platinum-tinted cage of light. He jumped out of bed and ran to the window, gulping in the air in case he had forgotten how good it was. But the smell was still there: heavy, rich and—now he thought about it—saddening, because there was in it an element of decay.

His legs were now full of their sensual, athletic ache, and he squeezed the calf muscles voluptously to loosen them again, one leg after the other, his left hand still holding the window sill. Perhaps he could find some mushrooms!

It took hardly thirty seconds to dress: shirt, trousers, a pair of running shoes. He straightened up from tying the shoes and caught his reflection in the old-fashioned oval windows of his dressing-table. He saw a rather tall boy, with a long, pink, serious face, and solemn caramel brown eyes. How odd, he thought. What an odd fish I am! And how can such an odd fish know eternity? For he thought he smelt eternity in the Aylsbourn air: no less.

He picked up a towel, stole silently down the stairs and ran to the end of their garden, vaulting the rhubarb pots and the low hedge which separated them from Twenty Acre field. There was dew still on the ground, marvellous, giving back the silver morning light, and the grass was fresh, still, and pure under his scurrying feet. His ankles were wet with dew; he ran without seeming to touch the ground.

The Cressbrook stream ran across the bottom of Twenty Acre, limpid, clinking and muttering. There were always three boulders he crossed it by and he leaped over them—one, two, three—without hesitation. After that the ground began to rise sharply towards that part of the Downs called Cromwell's Hill, where a skirmish was fought in the Civil War.

This hill flanked the farther side of the Cressbrook stream and was thickly wooded; but you could get over the fence easily and climb up through the undergrowth, seeing the sky above you only here and there through the thickets. Here the chalk had been thrown up nearly to the surface; you trod on pieces as you climbed and there were great white vertical cliffs in the hillside where the sparse earth had been washed entirely away by the rain.

He climbed up through Cromwell's Hill, taking a well-known path, picking at creepers till his hands were smeared a vivid green, brushing the soft morning cobwebs from his eyes.

Once over the top of the hill the wood ended abruptly and the land ran down again to Bailey's Farm. Here he thought there would be mushrooms.

He trod carefully over the springy field, avoiding the cowpats as he went, and then he saw his first mushroom, its white bulbous head peeping shyly through the grass. He tested it (as he thought) to make sure it wasn't a toadstool; but it peeled quite easily, it was all right. And what a whopper! There ought to be some more. Then he saw a little crop all together, and no sooner had he snapped them off by their spongy white stalks than he saw another three or four of the little white domes, dotted about like Maginot entrenchments in the grass.

Soon he had as many as he could carry. "Marvellous!" he said out loud.

It took only two minutes to scramble down again through the wood. At the edge of the Cressbrook he paused, glanced casually round and, assured that he was alone, threw off his clothes and dived cleanly in at the part where the stream opened out into a wide running lake. He slid through the green water, naked between the reeds, and only a line of silver bubbles showed his progress; then he broke the surface noisily, splashing and shaking his head like a dog, and struck out in a lazy crawl to the other bank. He touched it and turned, rolled on his back and threshed his legs in the air, blew water from his mouth and nostrils and gulped in the cold morning air. The sun shone on him through a filagree of fine branches.

He pulled himself ashore and rubbed himself down roughly till his young pink body glowed and steam rose from the bare flesh. He dressed again in thirty seconds, towelled his hair carelessly, scooped up his precious mushrooms, leaped his three boulders and in another minute was home again.

His father was up now, moving about the kitchen in his shirt-sleeves, his collar not yet put on, a front stud hanging carelessly in the button hole. He hummed as he made the tea.

"Hello, son!" he said. "What a load of mushrooms! Oh ho! We are in luck!"

Benedict laid the mushrooms on the kitchen table for his father to see. "Masses of them, Pop!"

"Not half bad," said Benedict senior appraisingly. Then he turned his attention back to the teapot. "But let's have a cuppa first. We can brew a fresh lot for breakfast."

They sat at either end of the kitchen table over the ritual, sipping the strong, hot sweet tea with little gasps of appreciation. Mr. Benedict had the *Daily Mail,* as usual, in front of him. There was a lot of unpleasant war news on the front, but he ignored it, and turned at once to the cricket scores.

"McCorkell 66!" he cried triumphantly. "What a hell of a grand bat he is, Benny! I hope he's in form on Sunday."

"Gosh, yes," Benedict agreed. "I'm longing to see McCorkell play again."

Margrave Brewery promoted a special gala cricket match for charity once a year. Many Hampshire cricketers came down for it, and there were always some celebrities; people like the Western Brothers, and a sporting columnist or two. The crowd came in their thousands, so many that beer crates were pressed into service for them to sit on; and the sun always seemed to shine. Benedict and his father were regulars at the game.

"Well," said Mr. Benedict, "this will never do. Let's get down to the mushrooms."

He cooked them with particular care, peeling them meticulously and frying them gently in butter. Soon the whole house was full of their unmistakable and delicate aroma.

It was the first sophisticated smell Benedict had ever known.

Then Mr. Benedict picked up some brown eggs, still mottled with little pieces of straw, and broke them into the pan. Benedict made the second pot of tea. Within five minutes they were sitting down to what Benedict and his father believed to be the best breakfast in the world.

It was still only ten past eight when they had finished and Benedict was due at Valhalla by nine sharp. He went up to his room, peeled off his old clothes, chose a new white shirt and his best grey suit, tied his mauve and gold Valhalla tie with care, polished his shoes and brushed his damp hair down into place. His father met him at the foot of the stairs and held out his hand.

38

"Good luck, boy."

"Thanks, Pop. It'll be all right, you'll see."

In the back yard of Valhalla School, the boys who were taking entrance and scholarship examinations to Shallerton Oaks that day were already arriving. Some were usually quiet, others boisterous. Benedict leaned against the fence, his hands in his pockets, watching the little groups of boys, at peace with the world.

Today he thought, *I shall win the scholarship. It's my day.*

Suddenly the bulking figure of Mr. V. V. Varley materialized at the top of the ironwork steps leading into the big classroom. He, too, seemed specially polished for the occasion. His black wavy hair was freshly brilliantined and his huge, red, knobbly, terrifying face shone in the morning sun. He wore a grey chalk-stripe suit, cut cleverly to accommodate his great belly. His boots (for he never wore shoes) glistened like black glass. He took out his whistle and blew a loud blast on it. Every boy in the yard stiffened to attention. At a second blast they doubled into lines, right arms stiffly extended, heads at the eyes right, shoes shuffling expertly as they formed two straight ranks, tallest boys at each end, shortest in the middle. At a third blast from the whistle they came to the eyes front. They drilled like guardsmen, and rather enjoyed it.

Mr. Varley passed slowly along the ranks. As he came abreast Benedict could smell the mysterious adult male aroma of lather, tobacco, and alcohol, so close was Mr. Varley to him. The knobbly face had been newly cut by a razor, he now saw, and a fresh piece of white cotton wool hung from the massive chin. Then his headmaster was by, and Benedict sighed under his breath. Mr. Varley was not easily satisfied. Two boys were sent inside to polish their shoes again, and another boy was set to work frantically cleaning a spot out of his tie. But in ten minutes the solemn little platoon was ready and Mr. Varley addressed them again.

"Valhalla," he boomed. "Right turn. Forward—*march.*"

They swung along, arms moving briskly, and Benedict allowed himself to sink mentally into Varley's world. He was all right, the old bounder, as long as you jumped to it; as long as you played the game. But Benedict played *that* game, as well as other games, easily and well.

They swung into the station yard and marked time till Mr.

Varley brought them to the halt and gave them permission to fall out. Each boy bought a return ticket to Shallerton and they streamed on to the platform to await the train. Still Benedict was in a dream. He sat alone on a station seat, the hum of the railway telegraph lulling him into an endless, mindless euphoria.

"Well, Benedict." The boy started and jumped to attention. "At ease, Benedict." Mr. Varley was in a relaxed mood this morning. He had drilled his boys ruthlessly the whole of this last vital year, but he knew when to take the pace off. "Going to get that scholarship today?" he enquired genially.

"I very much hope so, sir."

"I'm sure you will. And I know your father shares my view. Remember, don't rush at the questions. Read them right through, even the ones that you don't think you can do. Spend a couple of minutes thinking about each one if you like. Make notes on your rough paper. Be orderly. Don't ramble. Don't try to show off. Come to the point quickly, say what you have to say, and finish. Remember the examiner is only human. Make his job as simple as you can. And write legibly, Benedict!"

"Yes, sir."

"And another thing—when you come out at one, go to Dickins, the newsagent in the High Street. I have an account there. Order what you like in the way of chocolate and tell them to charge it to me."

"Oh *thank* you, sir." Benedict was deeply impressed with this evidence of a wider, adult world; he was intoxicated with the conception of credit *carte blanche*. Suppose he and the other boys *went off their heads* and bought the whole stock? What a scandal! And would Mr. Varley go bankrupt? Or was he limitlessly rich?

His dream-line was broken by the far-away thrum of the electric train. It was their train, coming to take them to Shallerton, to the future, to the unknown. Nothing could stop it now. He leaped aboard with his friends, bagged a corner seat, noted with relief that Mr. Varley was two doors down, and dozed in the cradling rhythm of the carriage wheels all the way to Shallerton.

Shallerton was a bigger and altogether smarter town than Aylsbourn. It was only fifty-nine minutes from Waterloo by fast train, and was therefore popular with men making between two and five thousand a year in the City. A hundred and fifty years ago it had been the central market for the English corn trade; the Georgian farmhouses built then had been snapped up and tarted over with white paint. Running water, central heating, electricity and telephones had been installed and the drives freshly gravelled to accommodate the big tyres of Bentley saloons.

But there was plenty of indigenous money in Shallerton too; although an economic spasm had carried the market away, it had not taken the rich farming land with it. There were squat, comfortable shops down Shallerton High Street that still catered for the local farmers; shops selling guns, saddles, stoves and boots. There were lending libraries for the farmers' wives, and small scented dress-shops selling tweed suits and twin-sets; there were three or four coaching inns, some estate agents and accountants, four banks, a solicitor, and one mysterious window behind which sat an old gentleman called the Commissioner for Oaths. There was a garage which sold bright red tractors and one reasonably good teashop which sold home-made shortbread.

It was a warm, friendly town that always gave Benedict the impression of self-indulgence. It was a town that seemed to do itself pretty well. It was a worldly and sophisticated place compared with Aylsbourn, whose air always seemed keener and thinner, yet somehow more pure and exhilarating.

Benedict felt content in Shallerton; but he felt alive in Aylsbourn. He loved both towns unaffectedly.

The boys tumbled out of Shallerton station and fell in again under Mr. Varley's booming orders. "Valhalla," he thundered. "Fall *in*." People stopped and stared at the tiny drill-parade in the station yard with amusement, and one or two local urchins shouted rude remarks; but the Valhalla boys were used to that and ignored it.

"Right *turn*. Forward *march*."

They swung up Station Road with Mr. Varley at their head. At the junction with the High Street he stepped out into the middle, raising both arms like a policeman, and imperiously halted the coast-bound traffic. Benedict was always deeply impressed by this; it was either enormous cheek on Mr. Varley's part or great moral courage; either way, it was admirable. Secure under his billowing black gown, they marched solemnly across the High Street, impervious to the frenzied honkings from the column of cars they had so brazenly halted. They wheeled

41

left, and marched up the High Street, then right and climbed the hill towards Shallerton Oaks School.

Here was their severest test. For as they marched up the school drive, they could see little knots of boys from other schools standing about informally. Every eye turned on the brave little column from Valhalla as it swung along. Benedict gritted his teeth and kept his eyes to the front. What did it matter what these other bastards thought? Perhaps they thought Valhalla soft. In that case, they should come and try one of Varley's cold baths some freezing morning. That would teach them.

"Valhalla *halt*. Left *turn*. Stand at *ease*. Stand *easy*."

Mr. Varley then marched forward and almost, but not quite, saluted Mr. Ross-Tayfield, who had watched the whole farcical scene with scarcely concealed contempt. No doubt, he reflected, all these blasted Valhalla boys would pass the entrance exam as usual. It was extraordinarily hard to fail the little swine. As for the scholarship—his eyes lingered on the languid, dreamy figure of Benedict—well, that had its compensations. The boy's father was dreadful, and so was his headmaster. The boy himself seemed half asleep most of the time and painfully gauche the rest. Against this, he was going to be a really beautiful scrum-half. . . .

Mr. Ross-Tayfield smiled thinly as he recalled the day he had surreptitiously come over to watch Benedict play for Valhalla the previous autumn; he recalled the long stride and the wriggle in the boy's hips and the ghostly dummy he had sold to six opponents in a row; and Mr. Ross-Tayfield smiled at this. Yes, he could put up with Benedict.

He clapped his hands sharply. "Scholarship boys, this way," he called.

Half a dozen boys detached themselves from the groups and followed Mr. Ross-Tayfield. Benedict joined them. They were led into a classroom full of chalk-dust and sunlight.

A young assistant master rose as his headmaster entered. He was reading a novel.

"Here you are, Johnson," said Mr. Ross-Tayfield. "The six Margrave scholarship candidates. I leave them in your care."

"Right, sir. Sit where you like, boys. You'll find writing paper on each desk." They scattered over the empty seats. Benedict chose a seat right at the back.

The young master strolled round with the printed examination papers, one of which he placed face down on each boy's desk. Benedict stared down at it. He was feeling drowsy after his early-morning swim; the morning sun was tempting him to close his eyes. He pulled his fountain pen mechanically from his breast pocket, tested it to be sure it was full, and wrote: BENEDICT: VALHALLA in the top right corner.

"Now then, chaps," said the young master. "It's two minutes to half past. I'll tell you to turn over at half past precisely. It's a three-hour paper on English Language. No talking, of course; and if any boy wants to go out he must raise his hand and I'll ring for someone to escort him. Don't rush at the questions, think them over for a few minutes; I think you'll find it pays. Well, good luck, everyone. Begin."

In a daze, Benedict turned his paper over. The words swam at first and he could not focus on them. Then they cleared and leapt up from the page with the dramatic super-reality of obscenity or news of death.

The minutes ticked away, and a boy dipped his pen into the ink with a sigh and began to write. Then another followed; and another; within six minutes each head was bent over the work—except Benedict's. He floated in the appalling enormity of the occasion. *This* was the moment that he had been trained for all his life, *this* was the moment when his future must be decided, *this* was the moment when his destiny must be hammered out. He had only to reach out now and take success by the throat; his stars were high in the sky; even Ross-Tayfield had smiled on him.

Yet just *because* he was free to choose, some entrenched perversity made him delay while the minutes ticked away. He was still in a trauma of delight from his encounter the night before on Windmill Hill: over and over he repeated to himself: it was my happiest day.

He sat staring out of the sun-slotted window, impassive, motionless.

It was fifty minutes before the young master noticed that Benedict was not writing. He watched him for some minutes then softly closed his book and tiptoed up.

"What's the matter, old boy?" he enquired kindly. "Not feeling well?"

Benedict jumped at the sudden voice. "No thank you, sir. I'm fine. I was just thinking."

43

"Oh, Well, don't leave it too long. You've just over two hours left."

He tiptoed away and Benedict looked down at his paper. The first question asked candidates to discuss a stanza of poetry:

> *You say there is no substance here,*
> *One vast reality above;*
> *Back from that brink I shrink in fear*
> *And childlike hide myself in love.*

Benedict stared at the lines desperately. At length he wrote on his answer paper:

"The poet is right. There is only love."

Then he methodically screwed up his fountain pen and walked out. It was a few minutes after eleven. The school drive was deserted. All the other boys had gone into their classrooms for the entrance exam. Mr. Varley was on his way back to Aylsbourn, where he was looking forward to his first port of the day in the "Thorn and Sceptre".

Benedict walked down the drive, each step in the gravel magnified by dry-mouthed fear. He passed between the iron gates and said to himself: I shall never go to Shallerton now. Then another thought struck him; I shall spend the rest of my school-days in Aylsbourn.

He lifted his dream-racked head and gulped in the rich air. Then he sauntered along to Dickins and bought himself a two-penny bar of milk chocolate. He drifted along the High Street, munching it absent-mindedly as he went. He felt no fear or shame, only a great lightness under him, as if he were exempted from the cares of gravity. Now I shall see them both again, he thought.

Sunday

There was a fine mist over the fields next morning. Mr. Benedict sang as he made the early-morning tea; this was one of the great days of their year and the sun was going to shine for them both once again. His son read the *Sunday Dispatch* in bed. Fortunately, no hint of the examination débâcle had penetrated; he had come in at six as if he had completed both papers, answered Mr. Benedict's eager questions non-committally, and gone to bed early with a book. Still he felt no remorse for what he

44

had done. Indeed, he was not quite sure if he remembered properly what had happened the day before. Was it possible that he had written only eight words altogether? Surely not: it must be a trick of the imagination: he had been too tense, too over-wrought. Of *course* he had answered all the questions!

The game did not start until two; so father and son could go to church as usual in the morning. Mr. Benedict was not a religious man, but he felt, like many Englishmen of that generation, that he ought to go to church before he went into the "Thorn and Sceptre" for a pint of bitter. "It always seemed to go down better after a service," he used to say. "I suppose it's all that singing; it gives you a real urge to wet your whistle."

Mr. Benedict was no drunkard. But he loved drink. "I often wonder what the vintners buy," he would declaim each evening in the "Thorn and Sceptre", "one half so precious as the goods they sell."

By the time the last hymn was announced that morning, Mr. Benedict was clearly very thirsty indeed. He sang loudly and with a good grace, but he fingered his stiff white collar nervously. That always meant, Benedict knew, that it was time his father had a beer.

All the same, the hymn seemed to have an added poignancy that morning, singing as it did of simple human endeavour:

> *There's no discouragement*
> *Shall make him once relent*
> *His first avowed intent*
> *To be a pilgrim.*

"Let us pray," intoned the Rector, and as he delivered the final blessing: *Oh God,* Benedict prayed, *don't let it be true that I wrote only eight words. I don't care for myself, but it would hurt my father so much.*

Mr. Benedict hummed a tenor accompaniment to the organ as they filed out past the Rector. "Good morning, Mr. Benedict," he said. "No doubt we shall meet at the game this afternoon?"

"We certainly shall, Rector."

"There you are," added Mr. Benedict as soon as they were out of earshot. "That's what I call a really sporting parson. I bet he wouldn't mind a beer after preaching all that time. I've half a mind to go back and ask him."

"You can't do that, Pop." The boy was terrified that his father would be rebuffed.

"No, I suppose not." Mr. Benedict was for the moment downcast. Then he cheered up again. "But I know what I can do. I can buy you a shandy."

"What exactly *is* a shandy, Pop?"

"A shandy is a mixture of beer and ginger beer generally; sometimes beer and lemonade. A marvellous thirst-quencher. We used to drink it on route marches during the war."

"But I can't drink *beer*, can I Pop?"

"Why ever not? Got to start sooner or later. And I wanted to celebrate that fifty of yours on Friday too, son. Oh yes, this is definitely the day for you to have a shandy."

"O.K., Pop. Whatever you say." The boy sat on the bench outside the "Thorn and Sceptre" as he always did. His father reappeared with a pint of bitter and a pint of ginger beer.

"Now then, son; drink a bit of that up and I'll pour in some real beer for you. That's it. That'll do for a start."

The boy had drunk some two inches, and this Mr. Benedict gravely refilled with Margrave bitter. The boy took a deep breath. He wasn't sure if he would like it. Suppose he was sick—how disgraced his father would be!

"Cheers, Pop."

"Cheers, lad."

That first taste—how it still lingered; bitter and clean through the fizz!

"Well?"

"Not bad at all, Pop. Let's have another."

"Another!" Mr. Benedict was greatly amused. "Another. My goodness, we'll make a drinker of you yet. All right, just this once."

He went inside and the boy leaned back against the whitewashed wall. So this was beer; this mysterious elixir on which his father's whole philosophy floated!

They drank two pints each, then went round to the back door for their Sunday dinner. A new linen cloth was laid in the parlour because it was Sunday.

They ate, as they always did, roast beef, roast potatoes and green peas, with apple tart, sugar and cream to follow. Then came two very big cups of strong sweet tea, which they dispatched very much more quickly than usual.

"Right son!" said Mr. Benedict, putting down his cup with a clatter. "The cricket match!"

The Margrave Brewery cricket ground was already crowded as they clocked in through the turnstiles. Inside was the scene that never failed to thrill them both.

The pitch, newly rolled and watered, stretched away, emerald and silk-smooth before them. The celebrated Margrave beer crates lined the boundary, forming an extra row of seats. A large white marquee had been erected beside the pavilion, and already gave off that unmistakable, English smell of canvas, grass, watercress and light ale. The Brewery Silver Band had been playing a selection from Gilbert and Sullivan to entertain the crowds, and was marching off just as the Benedicts arrived. They were just in time to get two of the crates to sit on side by side. They took off their jackets and rolled up their sleeves. They bought a scorecard each and took out their pencils. An avuncular sun beamed down on them from a cobalt sky.

There was a small spatter of claps as the captains came out to toss. Hampshire won and decided to bat first. Two minutes later, Arnold and McCorkell appeared side-by-side from the pavilion and began their slow gossiping amble to the wicket. The Brewery field fanned out further for Arnold, five men curved in a tight crescent behind the wicket.

Arnold took guard and Benedict took in a quick quarterlungful of air to help his heart cope with the delight.

It was spectacular cricket to watch, for the Hampshire men were unconcerned with championship points and opened their shoulders like Guinness-full coal-heavers. Fours and sixes fell like mortar-fire among the spectators. Wickets began to fall quickly as the county players took wilder and wilder risks, and soon the tail of film and radio celebrities had to be winkled out of the Brewery pavilion bar. The crowd guffawed at the droll contrast between the lusty professional hitting and the wild daisy-cutting antics of the amateurs, and there was a general susurrus of approval when Hampshire were all out in two and a half hours for 123 runs. Everyone then stopped for the tea interval, and Mr. Benedict led the way into the marquee.

It was always the tea of the year: soft white sandwiches filled

47

with cucumber and egg, boxes of strawberries and cream, and thick white cups of strong tea, with plenty of beer for those who preferred it. Benedict ate two boxes of strawberries, dipping each red and luscious fruit first in the cream and then in the sugar. His father had two bottles of beer and a number of sandwiches, then strawberries and finally a large cup of tea. It was a delicious ritual which everybody in Aylsbourn loved. It was cornucopia; there were so many boxes of strawberries that stacks of them still stood unopened at the end of tea. Margrave Brewery never stinted its guests at the annual cricket match.

They settled back on their crates at five and waited for the Brewery to bat. "Sir Keith is opening again this year," Mr. Benedict said. "He'll be good for a few runs. What a sportsman he is! And a brave man: I'll never forget him in the trenches. A major was watching the enemy from an observation post with a pair of binoculars and was shot through the head by a sniper. Died at once, poor devil. Keith Margrave stepped straight into his place without hesitation. He was nineteen then, a second lieutenant. That's real courage for you. Cool as ice, he was."

"A bit reckless, wasn't it, Dad?"

"You can call it that if you like. But where does courage end and recklessness begin? Ah, here he comes now."

Keith Margrave was coming out to bat. He was putting on weight, and his blond hair was thinning a little on top. But he still looked like a rather plump and overgrown sixth former. He wore an I Zingari cap. Benedict strained to see who it was accompanying Margrave to the crease as the other opening bat. The slim shape and the thick spectacles seemed familiar. Then the batsman lifted his cap for a moment to wipe his glasses, and Benedict saw that it was the Aylsbourn boy he had seen last night. He glanced eagerly down at his programme. Yes, that must be him, No. 2: HAMMOND, A. R. D. He flipped the pages to the notes on the two teams:

"HAMMOND, A. R. D. Tony Hammond at sixteen is one of the most outstanding schoolboy athletes of his generation. He is already in Aylsbourn Grammar School's First XI and First XV and has been given several games this season already by the Hampshire Colts. We understand the County Cricket Club are also taking an interest in his progress. He will be representing his county again this year in the AAA Southern Junior Championships and is much fancied to win. He is the son of that famous Hampshire athlete of yesteryear, the late Colonel John 'Stingo' Hammond."

Benedict read with hypnotized excitement. So this was Hammond! He had of course heard of his feats even at Valhalla. But still, it was an honour to open for the Brewery with Sir Keith, even if you were Tony Hammond!

The two batsmen held a parley in the middle of the pitch, a slightly comic contrast in silhouettes, then returned to their separate ends. Margrave was to take first knock and he faced up to the bowling professionally. He had a nice stance and though obviously a little out of training had no difficulty in presenting a plumb-straight bat to the first three balls from the Hampshire opening bowler, who was putting them down with a lot of zip. Then Margrave cut a loose ball through the slips and they took two runs. Mr. Benedict applauded. "Good old Keith," he cried. "He's away."

Soon after this Margrave was dropped. It was a fairly simple catch and it was impossible to say whether the Hampshire fielder had missed it deliberately by way of courtesy to such a generous host or whether he had genuinely muffed it. At any rate, Margrave made no more mistakes and hit a clean and solid forty-four runs before he was bowled, trying to lift a ball over the pavilion. He raised his cap modestly to the applause as he trotted into the pavilion, evidently well pleased with his day's work.

Meanwhile Hammond had been playing with cool elegance at the other end and had quietly collected thirty-one. With two extras, the Brewery needed forty-seven to win. Hampshire crouched ferociously: the game had suddenly taken on a piquant note of challenge.

Unfortunately the rest of the Brewery side seemed overawed. Two of the best wickets fell with only another six added, then a stalwart bottler blocked heroically for half an hour before finally snicking one up to the wicketkeeper. With six wickets to fall and fifty-five minutes left to play, the Brewery still needed thirty-one runs to win. Benedict sat on the edge of his beer crate, biting his knuckles with suspense.

Hampshire now had entirely woken up. The skylarking was discarded and even the comedians in the outfield trained their eyes ferociously on each ball. Number five just managed to survive to the end of the over.

Now Hammond had the bowling. He glanced round the field nonchalantly, then squared up to the Hampshire fast bowler, who had come back on after a rest. His first ball was a trifle short, and Hammond cut it imperiously for four. The ball rattled up against the crates only a few yards away from where the Benedicts sat.

"A very useful bat, this young fellow," said Mr. Benedict.

The next ball was very fast and straight and Hammond blocked it respectfully. He turned the next stylishly to fine leg and they took two. The next ball kicked high and smashed his spectacles into pieces. Little pieces of glass lay glinting in the sun.

Benedict half rose in his seat, breathless with anxiety. But miraculously Hammond had not been hurt. He handed the remains of his glasses to the square leg umpire and boldly took stance again. But hardly before the ball had left the bowler's hand he was running down the pitch to meet it with a most uncharacteristic swipe.

"Probably can't see an inch in front of his face," said Mr. Benedict. "But what guts!"

The ball rose in a very high parabola and fell with neat certainty into the hands of mid-on. Hammond had not stopped running and he wheeled to trot into the pavilion, raising his bat to acknowledge the hero's ovation he received. He had made forty-eight and the Brewery needed only twelve to win. It was too much for them: whether the heat or the beer or the occasion was responsible no one knew. But in the upshot Hampshire won by nine runs.

By now it was half-past six. The spectators rose and stretched themselves pleasurably. Then they began to move towards the pavilion, where it was the custom for Sir Keith Margrave to make a short speech. He appeared on the balcony in a blazer and Old Hanovarian tie and raised his hand to end the cheers.

"Ladies and gentlemen," he said when the noise had died down. (He had a pleasant voice with no trace of Hampshire in it, but on the other hand with little class affection either. It was not what Mr. Benedict would have called a "posh" voice. On the other hand, it was clearly different from the way his employees spoke.)

"Ladies and gentlemen," he said, "thank you all so much for coming along today to this game." ("Hear hear," said Mr. Benedict.) "It's been enormous fun, and how we managed to get as many as we did against Hampshire I shall never know." ("You got forty-four, sir!" called Mr. Benedict. His son blushed and looked down in case anyone noticed his connection.) "May I say once again how very much we appreciate the way these splendid Hampshire players give up their Sunday each year to make this match possible." ("Hear hear!" again from Mr. Benedict, but not so loud. He had noticed his son's embarrassment.)

"And now—let's get down to the dancing. I want you all to stay right to the end and remember—all the beer is on me tonight." ("Hear hear!" from everybody.) "I want you all to enjoy yourselves as much as I know Lady Margrave and I will. And don't go before the fireworks! We've got some quite sensational ones for you this year. On with the dance!"

There was another round of applause, and the strains of "Blue Skies" could be heard floating out from inside the pavilion. The young Brewery men and their girls began to move inside, hand in hand, humming as they went.

Mr. Benedict began to push his way through the crowd. "Come along, son!" he cried. "We must meet Keith Margrave."

But the boy hung back, overcome with awe and embarrassment. "No, please don't, Pop," he pleaded. "I'm sure he's busy."

"Nonsense! I often speak to him about you. He'd love to see you again!"

The boy followed with immense reluctance. His father jostled eagerly through the crowd which had now gathered round the Chairman and his wife, trying to catch his employer's eye.

At close quarters Keith Margrave was larger and older and pinker. His cheeks were already mottled a bonhomous red through over-indulgence and drops of sweat stood on his face. But there were kindly wrinkles round his eyes. Yet still the boy prayed: *Oh God, don't let me have to talk to him. Let him not notice my father.*

"Sir Keith!" called Mr. Benedict, over several heads. "Sir Keith!"

"Oh hello, Benedict," said Margrave with easy upper-class charm. It had cost many thousands of pounds to teach him that particular kind of graciousness; but he had learned the trick well.

"Good evening, Sir Keith. Do you remember my son? I've often told you about him."

"Hello young Benedict." The kind blue eyes stared down at him with mild and amused interest. "I hear you're quite a useful man with a bat. You'll have to play for us next year."

"He scored fifty on Friday for Valhalla against Locks Priory," Mr. Benedict said proudly.

"Jolly good show! So you're at Valhalla, are you?"

"Yes, sir."

"Jolly good. A splendid chap, old Varley. And where are you going when you leave Valhalla?"

"To Shallerton, sir, on a Margrave Scholarship," Mr. Benedict put in with a beam. "He took the exam yesterday."

"Shallerton, eh? Good school. And on our Scholarship? Capital. When d'you know the results?"

"In about a fortnight, sir," said the boy. What would Sir Keith Margrave say if he knew what that answer paper contained? There is only love—but of course he was dreaming; he must have written more than that!

"Well, cheerio, Benedict," Margrave was saying. "I must get in to the dance. See you both there, eh?"

"You certainly will, sir," said Mr. Benedict. "You certainly will." Then, when the great man was out of earshot: "There! It wasn't so terrible, was it?"

"No, Pop." But he still wished his father hadn't done it.

They began to move into the clubhouse with the high-spirited shoals of Margrave employees. "This way, son," called Mr. Benedict. He pulled open a side door marked "Changing Rooms", and they both slid in through it. Immediately Benedict was assailed by the warm adult male smell of sweat and embrocation. There was a huge communal bath in which seven or eight young men were splashing noisily. They had a sort of phallic splendour: majestic in their hirsute nakedness, lordly and insouciant. Benedict remembered this bitter-sweet moment always; it lay complex in his memory, a touch of happiness for its insolent carelessness, a tang of sadness for its haunting reminder that all men, however noble they may seem, are merely animals that must suffer, procreate, decline and die.

But that was only a moment; then they were through the changing rooms and into the clubroom. Mr. Benedict fought his way to the bar, jocularly exchanging wisecracks with his many friends and amiably introducing his son : "This is my boy. Scored fifty for Valhalla against the Priory yesterday. Play for the Brewery? He's going to play for *Hampshire*." Then at last, when he had reached his haven, he turned, beaming with pleasure and pink from the sun, to ask: "What's it to be, son? Another shandy?"

"Yes please, Pop." The boy was caught up in the mood, exhilarated by the infectious happiness of the great Margrave clubroom. Like his father, he was gregarious by inclination.

Mr. Benedict ordered his customary Margrave Bitter and handed the boy the long, tan-coloured, fizzing shandy. "Well, cheers, son. Here's to the future."

"Cheers, Pop. And thank you."

Through the great noisy gusts of bonhomie, like cream running over Gaelic coffee, there slid the soft seduction of saxophones playing "Sweet Lorraine". The young men glanced up, looked at their wrist-watches, straightened their ties, and finished their drinks.

"The dance is beginning, Dad."

Mr. Benedict looked down at his son, and for a second there was a trace of fear in his benignant eyes.

"The dance? You're a bit young for dancing, aren't you, son?"

"Oh, I don't want to *dance*. I just wanted to watch and listen. I've never seen a dance before."

"All right. Let's go into the dance." Mr. Benedict could refuse his son very little.

The dining-room in the Margrave clubhouse had been cleared, and at one end the Margrave Serenaders, an ensemble recruited for the occasion from the personnel of the Silver Band, played dreamy, inoffensive dance music. After "I'm For Ever Blowing Bubbles" came "Red Sails in the Sunset", and then "Little Man You've Had a Busy Day". The couples shuffled round languorously, cheek to cheek, the young men in Brewery cricket blazers, the girls in summery print dresses. Sir Keith Margrave was dancing with Miss Maddocks, his secretary. She was forty, and had been harmlessly in love with him for nearly twenty years. Everyone knew, nobody cared, except possibly Miss Maddocks herself. She had a lean, noble face and grey hair drawn severely back. Few people knew that she had taken a good degree in economics at London University, and could have been earning six times as much in retail business by now had she wanted.

The boy did not know the story; but he thought Miss Maddocks was enchanting. Indeed, to be fair, he thought every girl there enchanting that night.

His father went off to get another round, was detained and away gossiping for twenty-five minutes. Benedict did not care. He sat in a corner, mesmerized. He was outside time and dimension, floating on the deep content that had settled over the room.

Then the M.C. stepped forward, and took the microphone. "Ladies and Gentlemen," he said. "Tonight we have a very special attraction for you. You may be surprised to hear that Mr. Tony Hammond, hero of today's game, is also a jazz trumpeter of no mean ability. He has recently formed his own jazz band—the first ever formed, I believe, in Aylsbourn. Ladies and Gentlemen—Tony Hammond and his Original Dixieland Jazz Band!"

The curtains swung back, to reveal Tony Hammond still in white cricket flannels and shirt, but wearing too his green first eleven blazer. He now wore an old pair of glasses held together by sticky tape. Behind him were a trombonist and clarinet player, both of whom Benedict recognized as having played in the game that day, a boy of sixteen or so with a banjo, a bearded man of thirty on the drums, and a young negro bass-player. There was a whistle of surprise from the Brewery employees. No one had seen such a bizarre assortment of people gathered together in captivity before.

Tony Hammond raised a yellow, much-battered trumpet to his lips and struck his left foot smartly flat on the floor twice, then four times at twice the speed: one, two—*one-two-three-four*. And so, as they swung into "The Jazz Band Ball", the sleepy Hampshire town of Aylsbourn heard the music of New Orleans for the first time.

Benedict was transfixed. Though he had heard Felix's records, the music on them seemed to be coming from thousands of miles away. Now it was in the room with him: urgent, driving, and full of joy.

Benedict knew that only one thing was necessary to complete his happiness: the girl. His eyes wandered over the room; she was nowhere to be seen.

Tony Hammond played with his eyes closed, his head tilted slightly back, his glasses glinting in the light, his strong brown fingers moving expertly over the valves. He played with a tearing, gay virility that took Benedict's breath away. At the end of his solo the clarinet took over, pure and liquid after the rasping brass, and after that the sonorous trombone caught up the melody and worked long improvisations into it. Then they were playing gloriously together, while the bass thumped sonorously behind them and the drums limned their music in a tight rhythmic framework.

As the sound died away everyone applauded. Benedict jumped to his feet and clapped for all he was worth.

Now Tony Hammond led his band into a slow, melancholy tune; like the first they had played, it was famous, a cliché of jazz, but Benedict, on that summer day in 1939, had heard it only once before in his life, the previous day, in Felix Weston's house. It was the Basin Street Blues, slow, sad, haunting. . . .

> *Where all the dark and white folk meet*
> *In Basin Street, land of dreams,*
> *You'll never know how nice it seems*
> *Or just how much it really means.*

Benedict let his attention wander once more over the crowded floor. This tune—could it have significance for them too?

Then he saw her; perhaps in answer to the incantation of the blues, perhaps by the merest chance, she had slipped into the room while the music was playing, and now she stood watching as Tony Hammond took up the story on his trumpet again where the negro had left it.

She was wearing a white dress and her hair was still combed down to her shoulders. She was smiling to herself as she watched Hammond play, a little private smile, and Benedict was able to confirm now that her eyes in truth were green and that there were one or two little freckles on her face; her nose was small and turned up at the end with a tiny arrogant gesture. She was a little above the normal height for a girl of her age and she conveyed a marvellous sense of coolness and grace. Benedict was only a dozen feet away from her. He was bewitched; he could not have moved if he had tried.

After the second chorus Tony Hammond laid his trumpet

gently on a chair and strolled across the floor, threading his way between the shuffling couples in the crooning haze with certainty to where she stood watching. She smiled at him; he held his arms out, and in a moment they were drifting on the floor, melting into the mood and the moment. Benny was spellbound. Her small left hand lay, not decorously against Hammond's shoulder blade, but round his neck, and her fingers moved gently in the short hair just behind his ears. Benny felt for the first time in his life, a small stab of sensual longing; but his principal emotion was one of simple excitement and delight. The rhythm section, holding the fort while the brass and reeds had a quick drink, now changed their style again, and broke into a quick one. Benny hummed the melody—it was one of those Fred Astaire things—what was it now? Ah yes, "Cheek to Cheek"—and how apt! How beautifully they danced, he reflected wistfully; they moved on the floor with the ease and sophistication of very old and bored lovers.

They passed out of view in the swirl of the dance and another, much larger couple swam into range. Benny started: it was his headmaster! Yes, it was Mr. Varley all right, in his well-pressed cricket flannels and blazer, swinging along in a brisk, business-like quickstep. And the woman in his arms was—surely not!—yes, it was Madam.

Benny had never listened to the stories about Mr. Varley and Madam. As far as he was concerned, Mr. Varley was the fountain of all honour. Why, each morning he addressed the whole school, drawing some moral instruction from a story in the morning paper. His code was simple and rigorous; the Ten Commandments covered it pretty adequately. There was nothing in the Commandments about not drinking port and lemon. Apart from this one, and in Benny's world, quite forgivable lapse, Mr. Varley was decorum personified. "Listen to the story of this wretched little worm, boys," he would declaim from his high stool. "He was only a chandler's clerk, but some designing woman got her claws into him. Result? He steals twenty thousand from his employer over a decade; but is eventually and inevitably apprehended. Now he is doing seven years' hard labour in Wormwood Scrubs—and never were they more richly deserved. Mark that well, boys. Lust is the root of all evil." He would then rake the little room with his liquorice-black eyes while the boys sat rigid with terror. Did the headmaster know about *them*? Would he one day find them out? And if he did, what unimaginable punishment would follow?

Yet here was Mr. Varley, nimble as many another fat man on his twinkling, well-polished toes, steering Madam round the floor; more than that, holding Madam in his arms!

Madam was the housekeeper at Valhalla. None of the boys knew what her real name was. She was a big, terrifying woman of about fifty-five, with a jutting bosom and iron-grey hair swept straight back in a severe bun. She smoked Balkan Sobranie cigarettes and drank pink gins. Her voice was loud, clear, rasping, and "posh". According to one story, Madam was the daughter of a famous county family who had employed Mr. Varley in his youth as a butler. It was Lady Chatterley's Lover all over again. According to another version, Madam had been a mistress at a famous girl's public school. Mr. Varley, stationed nearby as a regimental sergeant-major, had won her heart and spirited her away. Now she was Mr. Varley's mistre—— But Benny could never bring himself to pronounce the word, heavy as it was with cabalistic undertones of adulthood, corruption and experience. Dash it all, the stories might have been true; but if Mr. Varley had fallen in love with Madam, why had he never married her? This, for Benny, solved the whole conundrum. The stories were untrue and Mr. Varley was a man of honour.

However, it could not be denied that he was now circling the dance floor with Madam in his arms; and they both seemed to be enjoying themselves.

Madam wore a red brocade dress and three rows of choker pearls. She wore no wedding ring but several others; they were all large, ornate and, it was thought locally, genuine. Her face was pink with excitement and perhaps one or two gins and she threw back her head, laughing alarmingly in her massive contralto at one of Mr. Varley's sallies. They both looked—thought Benedict —though it was faintly ridiculous to use the term of two such very old and formidable people—they both looked *radiant*. Then Benny had a flash of insight. He saw the whole thing. *They had just fallen in love!* After all those dull and wasted lonely middle-aged years, each a stranger to the other in the musty schoolroom world, heavy with chalk-dust and the smell of old plimsolls, they had found each other. Suddenly perhaps, meeting in a corridor at dusk, when the day-boys had gone and the emaciated boarders were settling to sleep in their hard narrow beds, Madam and Mr. Varley had passed in the corridor and their eyes had met. Mr. Varley would have stopped dead in his tracks and she would have paused, a little timorous for once, and asked if he wanted her for anything. And he would have said no, unsure of himself for half a historic moment, and then he must have said, in a rush of confidence, "Madam, may I escort you to the 'Thorn and Sceptre' for a nocturnal pink gin?" And she, her upper-class training showing at once, would have taken the invitation in her well-bred stride: "But how kind, Mr. Varley. I should be enchanted."

That was it all right, thought Benny; and it's only happened a day or two ago; that's for certain. They are in love too.

They passed out of sight, and for a little he saw no one who was close to him; though he knew everyone at the dance by sight at least. But a few minutes later, he saw, with a leap of the heart, Felix's father and stepmother dancing an elegant tango.

Mr. Weston was a short, dapper man, with well-groomed black hair and a small, neatly-trimmed black beard. He wore heavy spectacles. His political beliefs had not noticeably affected his weakness for clothes. Tonight he wore a white tuxedo; in his breast pocket was a red display handkerchief, and he wore a pair of black suède shoes. These last particularly offended Benny's father. "Bloody brothel-creepers," he used to murmur, whenever he saw them.

Arabella Weston had certainly not grown tired of her husband yet, despite Felix's gloomy forecasts. She was quite a little girl, with her hair parted down the middle and simply brushed; she was brown and wholesome as a new-laid egg. She wore a simple rust-coloured dress and danced very close to her husband. Benedict tried hard to master the reality of the news; these two who now embraced on the dance floor, moving with practised ease over the polished floor, were also consummated lovers whose congress had been sanctified by the rites of the local Register Office. At one anonymous moment some eight weeks ago this experienced middle-aged intellectual and this fresh young girl had, in the endorsed privacy of their marriage bed, conceived a child, which, even as they circled the floor in a gay beguine, she carried for him in her womb. What enormous joys they must know! And what extra edge was given to the excitement by the notion that she was almost a child herself; not all that much older than he was! And yet at some moment unknown, she had crossed over from innocence into knowledge. How this legislated adult happiness beckoned him on! How wonderful it must be to long for love and find it!

"Another shandy, son?" Benedict came back from his long reverie with a click of guilt. His father had returned at last, bearing the best peace-offering he knew. The moment of dissonance between them, his father's first hint of fear at parting and his own answering resentment, had gone. They were friends again.

"Oh hello, Pop. Thanks very much. Cheers. Tell me, what sort of chap is Tony Hammond?"

"A really fine lad. I don't know him well, but of course I knew his father, old Stingo. Charming chap; such a damned pity he took to the bottle."

"What actually happened, Pop?"

"Well, like so many of these athletes, he made the mistake of going into the wine trade, into one of Keith's subsidiaries in fact. Everything went fine for a while; he was one of the most popular men in the county I suppose, and whoever went to see him had to stay for a drink. Well that was all right, but one day Hammond found he couldn't do without a drink, even if it meant lifting the wherewithal from the till. Keith had no choice, really, but he just had to sack him. There was no question of calling the police. The D.T.s did the rest."

"What happened to the mother?"

"She went off to South Africa and married again."

"So who looks after Tony Hammond?"

"An old clergyman over at Bales Whitney. There's no money left at all; I think Keith contributes a bit."

"Then why didn't Hammond go to Shallerton?"

"He's a very stubborn boy and he refused. Said he was going to repay Keith Margrave anyway, and the less it cost to educate him the sooner the debt would be paid. He's an extremely independent young man."

"What'll he do when he leaves school?"

"Why, go to Cambridge of course. He's a dead cert for a Double Blue and a good job in the City."

That, as far as his father was concerned, was the ultimate satisfaction a business career could offer.

"What a sad story, Pop."

59

"Life is full of sad stories. But what's so very terrible about Tony Hammond's life? The world is at his feet."

And the girl was in his arms; they danced by, deep in conversation, and Benedict's father seemed not to notice or to comprehend the wonder and excitement of it. Soon Mr. Benedict was gossiping with Brewery friends again and the boy slipped gently away. Quietly he edged his way through the bar and out into the open. He strolled across the cricket pitch, his hands deep in his pockets, content. It was quite dark now, and moonless, but the stars gave back to the earth a strange luminosity. It was, in the literal sense, very silent, and yet the pitch on which he walked, scuffed from the heroics of the great day, seemed to contain the faint echoes of the cheers and laughter. It was as if he was walking along the soft floor of some mighty sea-mollusc, hearing all round the murmurs it had trapped over the centuries. The air was warm and—yes, there it was once more—the mysterious and bitter-sweet Aylsbourn smell. I shall remember the smell, he thought to himself, when every other memory has gone.

He didn't recall how long he stayed out alone in the darkness; it seemed a very great time, but it was probably not more than half an hour. He was disturbed by the doors of the clubhouse balcony being thrown suddenly open, and by the sudden burst of noise and laughter from the revellers. People came pouring out on to the balcony and Benedict realized it must be time for the firework display. This was the climax of the Cricket Match; Keith Margrave loved fireworks in a secret way and was said to spend five hundred pounds on them each year.

Benny hurried back and joined his father. Soon there was the huge whoosh of the first rocket, the exploding radiance of its green stars in the sky, and for a moment every upward-turning face, caught in its glow, was battle-pale. The boy felt a sharp snatch of pity for this plangent reminder of their common humanity. Then the crowd gave a great "Ah!" as it burned away and a great "Oh!" for the next rocket with its crimson stars and soon the whole horizon was stained the long gamut of the spectrum as Catherine Wheels spun in their silver spirals and the Golden Rain cascaded into the gunpowdered air. They were all children again; the pyrotechnical magic seemed to renew their forgotten innocence. Benedict wanted the delight never to end, but for the shadowy Margrave employees crouched behind the set-pieces to fill the sky with multi-coloured light till dawn. But all too soon it was time for the great finale, the illuminated set-piece of the King and Queen, with GOD BLESS THEIR MAJESTIES in letters of fire beneath, and as George the Sixth and his consort sputtered and glowed in effigy, they all rose to sing the National Anthem. Benedict noticed, in the weird refulgence, that Tony Hammond stood just in front of him and that the girl was still beside him and that her hand was in his.

Monday

Each day at Valhalla—even the last day of all—began with prayers. At nine-fifteen precisely the whole school assembled in the main hall (it was in point of fact the drawing-room of the old house, its many layers of chocolate paint kicked bare by hundreds of boys' shoes) and Mr. Varley himself conducted the service. He swept in that Monday morning, Benny remembered, fearful as ever, his great black gown billowing behind him, his enormous red face shiny and knobbly and perennially terrifying.

Mr. Varley's views on religion were so eccentric, and the phrasing of his prayers so idiosyncratic, that many parents simply did not believe what their sons reported on the subject. Those who did might well have been tempted to take their sons away, had not Mr. Varley attained such a reputation as the best crammer in a fifty miles radius. Those boys who simply could not make their parents believe that they were telling the truth about the shape and content of Mr. Varley's morning service often got cuffed for blasphemy. Mr. Varley's service was certainly unique. One distinctive feature was the movements that accompanied it.

Mr. Varley closed his eyes that last morning as usual and said: "Let us pray." A hundred boys bowed their heads and closed their eyes. To have been caught with them open would have been inviting Mr. Varley to fling an inkpot across the room at the offender. More than once a boy had been carried out unconscious after being struck on the head.

Having got through the Lord's Prayer at drill-ground speed, Mr. Varley launched into his own prayer:

"Oh Lord, help us to remember the sufferings of thy son Jesus Christ. Get those arms up in the air," he barked in a military aside. A hundred small pairs of arms rose to a horizontal position. The room seemed to be suddenly filled with little scarecrows.

"Now just keep them up. Keep them *up*, Weston, if you want to get away on your last day without a beating. See how it hurts. Now think how our Lord must have felt. Keep them up!"

The boys gritted their teeth. It was not a bad game, a sort of battle with your own will, and you gradually got used to the pain.

"Right! Lower them."

The arms thudded gratefully down.

"Help all doctors and nurses," Mr. Varley continued, his eyes still tight shut. "And guide thou the surgeon's knife."

A mighty crash shook the room as a hundred small hands came down on the desks in front of them. With the expertize of long practice, the hundred fists slid down the desk lids, performing an imaginary incision with a scalpel.

"Bless all cashiers"—the boys doled out imaginary cash across a putative counter—"with their special temptations. Bless all sailors and those in peril on the sea"—the boys paid out imaginary anchors—"Bless all teachers and parents" [no action for this] "and bring us all in thy good time to thine abode. Amen."

Mr. Varley then instructed the boys to sit. This was usually the moment for his little homily. Today was no exception.

"Today," he began with great solemnity, "you are about to break up for the long vac. Many of you are saying goodbye to Valhalla for the last time. Many of you, indeed, thanks to my coaching methods, are going on to fresh fields and pastures new. As you know, Varley of Valhalla is not given to idle boasting. But you can all be proud of the fact that this school is sending one of its number on next term to one of England's most famous public schools; in fact to Sedbergh."

There was a murmur of approval at this. Most Valhallians were died-in-the-wool snobs. In the past Varley had sent very nearly all his boys to Shallerton Oaks, which was known to be a fourth-rate public school. But Sedbergh, that was something!

"Some of you are going to Dartmouth and so will at once be faced with all the manifold temptations the world has to offer. I need not specify. Some of you, after a brief apprenticeship, will be entering your fathers' businesses. To these I say a special word: remember that other people's money is sacred, even your fathers'. Remember the parable of the talents. That talent I have tried to make you live, eat, and breathe in this school."

62

He's done that all right, thought Benny. He quite liked old Varley at that moment.

"But to every boy leaving Valhalla this term," Varley continued, "I have this special, final word to say." He inclined confidentially over the desk.

"What I want to talk to you about," Mr. Varley continued, "is constipation." There was a little murmur of relief round the room.

"No boy should tolerate constipation," Varley continued, "for a moment. In a fit, active youth, the motions should be as regular as clockwork. Once, twice, or even three times a day."

He paused, and frowned.

"However, even on the most conscientious of us constipation may lay its dread hand. If it does, it must be rooted out at once." He leaned forward. "Take a laxative boys. Never be afraid to take a laxative. As you know, here at Valhalla we believe in Epsom Salts for normal cases, and castor oil for the obstinate ones. Whatever your predicament, boys, never shirk your duty. Take your medicine like men! And the stronger, the better."

He paused again, and looked round the room.

"Never fear the consequences of being taken short in the street. If it happens, approach the first respectable door you see, raise your cap, and ask to see the lady of the house. When she appears, raise your cap again and state your business briefly but succinctly. Once the matter is over, thank the lady of the house, leave sixpence for the maid, and take your leave."

Benny had heard this speech five times now, at the end of each school year, but it never failed to fascinate him. He was sure that it would be etched into his brain when he died.

Mr. Varley then appended his valediction.

"For those of you," he said, "going on and out into the world, this is a moment of joy and sorrow mixed. Temptations as well as opportunities await you.

"Some of you, I do not doubt, will climb the Ladder of Success. Some of you will slide down into the Slough of Despond. Some will falter, some will founder. But remember this. You are always welcome at Valhalla. Varley of Valhalla is always good for a loan. No Old Valhallian need ever go hungry. Many a Valhallian have I helped over the stile. Many an old boy has come to me penniless, and not one has ever been turned empty away. Many a temptation has laid an Old Valhallian low. Sometimes it has been drink,

63

sometimes gambling; sometimes"—and here Mr. Varley fixed the school with his black, glassy eyes—"it has been a woman who has brought an Old Valhallian down to perdition. But whoever has come to me, I have in no wise cast out. The price of a dinner, a glass of decent wine, a cigar—these no old Valhallian has ever asked of me in vain. Nor ever will. To paraphrase Belloc's beautiful lines:

> *Valhalla made me*
> *Valhalla fed me*
> *Whatever I had, it gave me again.*
> *And the best of Valhalla loved and led me——"*

Mr. Varley paused, then in a voice resonant with emotion concluded:

God be with you—Valhalla men.

At this there was a spontaneous applause, but Mr. Varley quickly checked it with uplifted hand. He nodded to Madam, who sat rigid and unmoved at the upright piano in the corner. She lifted her heavily beringed fingers and the school stood to sing the traditional valedictory hymn: "Lord, Dismiss Us with Thy Blessing."

Benedict sang, as always, with gusto. It was a solemn moment, for, despite the appalling rigour of Varley's régime, he had quite enjoyed being at Valhalla. In a way it was a little disquieting to realize that he would never come back to face those liquorice-black eyes again. He could, of course, come back as an Old Boy to enjoy a port and lemon with his old headmaster at the "Thorn and Sceptre" one day. Only—would Mr. Varley have forgiven him, even after the lapse of years, for the disgrace he was about to bring on the school? There is only love . . . He still couldn't believe he had done it.

The hymn ended and the boys resumed their seats. Now came the prize-giving. The boys leaned back pleasurably. It was an enjoyable ritual, for Varley always concealed the names of the winners until this moment.

There were a number of prizes at Valhalla. Varley had a liking for honour, and he had created a number of his own decorations. There were bronze and silver medals for the best performances in each sport, and silver cups for the victorious houses. There were four houses at Valhalla—Foch, Kitchener, Pershing, and Hindenberg—and Benedict, as Captain of Kitchener, went up proudly twice to pick up the trophies his boys had won. But the supreme prize at Valhalla was the Varley Award for Endeavour. It was won on an elaborate points system, kept by the headmaster himself, with marks allotted for industry, honesty, courage, and a number of other virtues. Benedict had always secretly hoped he would win it, and now his chances seemed high. His academic work had been sound, and his house was in good shape. That fifty last Friday might just tip the balance!

The Award for Endeavour took the form of a small golden Ganymede, naked on a plinth. One or two parents of boys who had won it had sent it back as unsuitable for display in their drawing-rooms. However, there it stood again this year, glistening on the headmaster's desk.

Mr. Varley cleared his throat. "We now come," he said portentously, "to the principal award. As you know, this is the greatest honour our school can bestow. I make my selection each year only after the most careful thought. This year the choice has been particularly difficult. Two boys have been outstanding and there is virtually nothing to choose between them. Their names are Weston and Benedict."

Many eyes turned curiously to regard the two friends, now thrown into an unexpected antagonism, and Benedict felt cold with suspense. Weston leaned back, unconcerned.

"Unfortunately," Varley continued, "there is only one trophy. So in the end I came to a very simple decision. I tossed a coin—heads for Benedict, tails for Weston." He paused and gave the two boys one of his rare and formidable smiles.

"It came down tails. Come up, Weston."

Felix uncoiled lazily from his desk and strolled up to the front, loudly applauded on all sides. His sophistication and cynicism had endeared him to his contemporaries.

Benedict felt ill with shock and disappointment. What a way to decide! Trust Felix to come off best! Would life always treat him as the runner-up?

Weston lounged back to his seat, looking thoroughly bored. He placed the little golden Ganymede on the desk in front of them. "I don't know where the hell I'm going to put it," he muttered to Benedict. "It's too damned vulgar for my study. What do you think it'll fetch melted down?"

But before Benedict could answer, Mr. Varley raised his hand for silence.

"The coin's decision was swift, but entirely arbitrary. So of course I have not forgotten the runner-up. Benedict, come up. I have a little consolation prize for you."

He rose and went forward. What on earth had the headmaster got up his sleeve now?

Mr. Varley picked up a small white box that lay before him. "Well done, Benedict." He beamed down at the boy and suddenly the great face was no longer terrifying. "I'm sorry you couldn't have the Ganymede, but I went to the jeweller specially to get you this." He handed over the box; Benedict opened it, and saw that a half-hunter watch lay in the cotton-wool. It was gold. He couldn't believe it.

"Turn it over, Benedict."

He turned it. On the back there was an inscription. In flowing italic, two words had been etched out of the polished metal: *Honoris Causa.*

"What does it mean, Benedict?"

"It means for the sake of honour, sir."

"Yes, as a mark of honour. I hope you'll keep it always."

"I will, sir."

Benedict went back to his seat. Felix looked at the watch without interest.

"Second-hand I imagine," he said. "What's the scribble on the back?"

Benedict showed him and Felix snorted. "Bloody rot! That proves it's second-hand. I mean not even Varley would write crap like that on the back of a watch."

Benedict never discovered whether Mr. Varley had put the words on or not. He looked at the watch several times more during the course of the morning.

At twelve-thirty the bell rang for their last school lunch. They queued up down the stairs leading into the basement. In this dingy and subterranean area, Madam cooked food of frightening inedibility; frightening, because no boy was allowed to leave a mouthful. Small boys were sometimes seen chewing on with agonized determination a quarter of an hour after the plates had been cleared away. Boys had smuggled out pieces of meat and subjected them to scientific tests; seeing if they could be melted

66

in hydrochloric acid or severed with a hammer and chisel.

Mr. Varley stood at the door of the dining-room with a large hairbrush in his hand. The boys waited docilely to have their hair brushed unceremoniously before they went in. As his face was pressed for the last time into Mr. Varley's waistcoat and he felt the rough motion over his scalp, Benedict felt another pang of loss and nostalgia. It would never happen again.

Madam had turned up trumps for their last day: it was cottage pie and beetroot followed by sago pudding. The boys ate in silence at a long gloomy table. Mr. Varley sat at their head eating a hot and nourishing stew. He never tired of telling his boys that as a grown man, he needed more calories than they did; a lot more.

But at last it was done, and they were released up into the sunlight. They cleared out their desks, returned their books to the store, and shook hands one by one, a solemn little file, with Mr. Varley at the front door. "Goodbye, Benedict," said Mr. Varley when his turn came. "Or rather, *au revoir*. I'm sure we'll see a good deal of you when you're at Shallerton. You'll play for the Valhalla Old Boys of course?"

"Of course, sir."

He sighed as he pedalled away with Weston. "You know, Felix," he said, "I shall miss that old scoundrel."

"Of course you will, Benny," said Felix sardonically.

"Won't you?"

"I hope I never set eyes on him again. And with a bit of luck I won't have to, judging by the state of his blood pressure right now."

Benedict laughed. How cold and refreshing Felix's cynicism was! What a healthy corrective to his own optimism!

They cycled lazily out of Aylsbourn towards Welcaster. Felix had been given five shillings. Despite his misanthropic pose he was generous-natured and had suggested a celebration tea in Miller's cake shop.

To get there, they had to leave their bicycles by a fence and cut across a meadow. As they were crossing it, they saw two boys approaching from the other side. Both were wearing the yellow and green blazers of the Grammar School.

When they were clearly within earshot Felix said offensively: "I suppose these are the sort of peasants I shall be living with next term."

The two boys obviously had heard, for they halted, blocking the pathway. Neither was much of a beauty: one boy was tall and gangling, with jug-handle ears and a strangely bent nose. The other was short and square, with a homely potato face. He carried a cricket bat.

The taller one spoke. His voice still had a trace of Hampshire in it, but he spoke with authority and precision.

"Would you kindly repeat that?"

"I said," Felix repeated clearly, "that you were the sort of peasants I should be living with next term.

"We look forward to the pleasure of your company," said the taller boy levelly. "Obviously Mr. Varley has not been able to teach his young gentlemen very good manners. However, we have ways of knocking them into shape."

"We're getting an extra supply of Lifebuoy soap in at home," Felix informed him. "My people are anxious that I shouldn't catch anything infectious from the lice-ridden proletariat."

The two grammar school boys exchanged glances. "I wonder if it would be any help if we gave him a preliminary doing now," said the small, square boy reflectively.

"No, Ken," said the other shaking his head regretfully. "This problem must be tackled at leisure. Let them by."

He stood to one side with elaborate courtesy and made a small bow.

Felix went to walk by, but the tall boy's long leg shot out like an adder's tongue and tripped him. Trying to save himself, Felix grabbed at him as he fell, and in a moment they were rolling on the grass, locked together and punching each other savagely.

Benedict sprang forward to pull them apart and saw too late that the potato-faced boy had swung back his cricket bat. It was as if somehow he had always known what was going to happen. He tried to duck, but there was no time. Even as he saw the bat scythe through the air he felt in anticipation the horror of the moment. He never quite got rid of it.

And then the bat hit him, with all the boy's force behind it, right across the face; across the bridge of the nose and the right eye. For another second it seemed as if his body simply could not believe it; then the pain scooped him up and encapsulated him. As the light died away there was a sound in the back of his head like a great gong being struck somewhere deep beneath the level of consciousness. He sank slowly to his knees and the last thing he remembered was the hot, wet blood running down his face.

He was out for probably no more than fifteen seconds, but when he came round he saw three anxious faces staring down at him. His nose was swelling and unreal; he could see it mushrooming from his left eye. But—oh the terror of it—he could not see at all from his right eye. He opened and closed the bruised eye-lid, but there was only a red haze, whichever he did.

He sat with his head bowed, holding both hands to the injured eye. "Felix!" he cried. "Oh Felix! I can't see!"

All anger had melted away. The boy who had hit him knelt down beside him. "Let me see," he said quietly. He moved Benedict's hands gently away and Benny always afterwards remembered his grave face, white with shock, close to his, studying the grisly damage with solemn concentration.

At length he got to his feet.

"We've got to get him to a doctor," he said. "Where's the nearest?"

"Mackay," Felix put in. "That's his house over there."

"Anderson is my doctor," Benedict said mechanically.

"Too far. We can't take you all that way. This may be urgent."

The three boys stared down at Benny in concern. There was blood all down his shirt now and the eye was coated with a red film.

"Benny," Felix said. "You've got to get over to Mackay's. Come on, we'll help you."

They helped him gently to his feet. His legs trembled, but he could walk, supported on each side.

It seemed a long way to Mackay's house.

Felix rang the bell and stood back. The three of them were crestfallen and awed by the enormity of what they had done.

There was a long silence. "Oh my God," said Felix. "Don't say they're not in."

He rang the bell again; and at last they heard footsteps.

"Thank goodness," whispered Felix. His precocious assurance had melted away.

The door opened. It was the girl; she was wearing the same lime-green dress as when he had first seen her. Even in his misery, though, he felt a quick thrust of disappointment that she should be as tall as he was; even in low heels her eyes looked straight into his.

Her eyes were the same colour green, her skin pale and a little freckled as he so vividly remembered, her blonde hair drawn back and cascading luxuriantly in a pony-tail. On her arms was golden down and her young figure was sweetly full; she was, in nature, a woman already, and despite his stricken condition, Benedict was desperately and poignantly aware of it.

He was a horrifying sight. Already a huge aubergine-tinted bruise was spreading, while the blood ran without stint down his chin and his shirt was blotched crimson. His hands were red as a butcher's and trembling.

But she had evidently seen blood before and she did not hesitate.

"My father and mother are out," she said. "But if you'll come into the surgery I'll do what I can until they get back. You boys can wait in here."

She indicated the waiting-room, and led Benedict by the arm into her father's surgery.

Benedict always hated surgeries; especially he hated the display of steel instruments in glass cases. But today, for all his distress, he didn't mind.

She quickly took out a sponge, gauze, and bandages, and held the sponge under a cold tap. She glanced over her shoulder and saw that he was still standing.

"Sit in that chair, please," she said briskly. He sat heavily; his knees were trembling too.

She was ready. For a moment she studied the battered face, frowning seriously. "It won't hurt," she said. "It'll just be cold." And she placed the sponge gently on his face.

After the first shock, it was very comforting. The cold water seemed to draw the aching bruise right from the bone. He gave a little sigh.

"Does it hurt?" she asked quietly.

"Oh no, thank you. It feels wonderful now." And having said that he suddenly found himself shaking and sobbing violently. The tears poured down his face, mingling with the blood. "I'm sorry," he gasped between sobs, "terribly sorry."

She bit her lips. "It's all right," she said. "Don't worry about it.

You've got shock, that's all. It's quite natural. It always happens. Here; come and lie down."

She lifted him from the chair and gently led him to the couch. "Lie down," she commanded him. She tucked a blanket over him and he felt suddenly warm and protected. But as she resumed the sponging, he began to shake even more and his teeth chattered alarmingly. She came to a quick decision: she sat down herself on the couch and lifted his head on to her lap. He turned and lay with his face against the cool lime-green cotton of her summer dress and was at peace.

It seemed a very long time before Dr. Mackay came home. But at last the surgery door opened.

"Hello, Laura. What have you got here?"

Laura: it was the first time he had ever heard her name.

"This boy has been hit in the eye, Daddy. I've just sponged the blood and covered him up. He's got shock."

"Dear, oh dear." Benedict detected, in the articulation of those three words, a faint but attractive remnant of Scottish, and it was strangely comforting.

Mackay went to the sink and meticulously scrubbed his hands. Then he came over and said: "Let's have a look, young man."

Benedict always remembered the doctor's face staring intently into his injured eye, the tiny tufts of beard where he had not quite shaved thoroughly in the morning, the odd lines of grey in his black hair, the St. Thomas's Hospital tie, and the gold signet ring on the little finger of the hand that gently held the damaged eye open.

Finally he stood up. "You're very lucky, young fellow," he said. "It's just a bruise. In twenty-four hours you'll see as well as ever. I'll bandage it up for you and give you something for the shock. Now what's your name?"

"Benedict, sir. Peregrine John Benedict."

Mackay laughed at this. "Bit of a mouthful, isn't it?"

"Yes, sir. It was my mother's idea, that Christian name. Everyone calls me Benny."

"Any relation to John Benedict at the Brewery?"

"He's my father, sir."

"Is he now?" The doctor beamed with pleasure and Benedict felt an enormous surge of relief. It was nice to have people smile

71

when they heard your father's name. With all the old boy's faults, he was really quite a charmer.

"Then you must be the young Benedict who hit fifty for Valhalla on Friday."

"Yes, sir." How on earth did he know that?

"Quite a famous young man, Laura," the doctor observed as he worked on the eye. "Mr. Varley was telling me all about him. A pity he's going on to Shallerton, or Tony would have been interested to meet him."

"Oh, sir, but I'm not going to Shallerton," Benedict blurted out. "I've failed the examination. I'm going to the Grammar School."

"Good gracious, you're a little pessimistic, aren't you? The examination was only this weekend, wasn't it?"

The doctor was evidently well informed on all local affairs.

"Yes, sir, but I know I've failed."

"Nonsense. You've just had a nasty sock in the eye and it's upset you. You'll be right as rain in the morning and ready to hit your first century."

Father and daughter smiled down at him.

"Now where do you live, Benny?"

"At the other end of the town, next door to the 'Thorn and Sceptre'."

"Yes of course you do. I'll run you home."

The three boys rose in crestfallen silence as Doctor Mackay and his daughter gently shepherded Benedict through the surgery door.

"Is he all right, Doctor?" asked Felix anxiously.

"Oh, it's you is it, Felix? He's bruised the eye, but he'll see again in the morning."

"Thank God for that," said the potato-faced boy. "I'm afraid it was my fault, sir."

"No," said Felix. "I was to blame."

"We all were," said the tall boy with jug-handle ears.

"Well I'm glad to hear that. You must all be good friends, eh, Benny?"

"No, sir, not exactly; at least——"

"We've never met I'm afraid," said the potato-faced boy. "I'm Kenneth Heppel and my friend is Milo Johnston."

"Ah." They were now at the car. The doctor settled Benny in

72

beside him and Laura sat on Benny's left. "Well, you'd better jump in too and explain yourselves to Benny's father."

They scrambled into the back and the doctor's Railton moved smoothly off.

"If you're Milo Johnston" remarked the doctor, to the jug-eared boy, "I imagine you're a relation of Johnston the Physics master?"

"Yes, sir, he's my father."

"And you" (to the potato-faced one) "must be a relation of Will Heppel at the garage?"

"He's my father, sir."

"Well, well, it's a small world. And you say you're not friends?"

"We didn't know each other before," said Benedict. "But I think we are friends now."

THAT was the end of that long summer weekend in 1939; four days whose every minute he seemed to recall with perfect clarity. Then it all became confused again, and he remembered only in snatches and fragments, irrationally, as most people do. He remembered:

One afternoon in the summer of 1939

Kenneth Heppel and Milo Johnston called to see Benedict. He was in his favourite place, suspended in a hammock strung up between an iron hook in the wall of his father's cottage, and a branch of their greengage tree. Lazily he dipped into a bag of greengages while he ploughed steadily through a library copy of *Those Barren Leaves*. This, as far as Benedict was concerned, was the nearest he would ever get to heaven. It had been a warm day again; there had been that delicious ankle-deep mist on Twenty Acre when he first looked out of his window that morning; and now the great warm patriarchal sun was descending slowly over the elms. Soon it would be time for his evening glass of shandy, carried foaming to him by Kate from the back door of the "Thorn and Sceptre". He lay, at peace with the world, transported in his imagination from the gentle market town of Aylsbourn to Mrs. Aldwinkle's sunbaked castle above the glittering Tyrrhenian Sea.

He was disturbed by the rap of the front door knocker. Sighing, he laid down the novel; it was physical distress to him to be recalled nowadays to the real world.

The two boys stood sheepishly in the front porch.

"Oh hello," said Benedict.

"Hello," said Kenneth Heppel. "We just came round to ask about your eye."

"Oh. That's very good of you. It's all right now thanks. I can see just as well out of it as ever."

The battered eye had now indeed receded very nearly to its normal size, and only the faint lingering discoloration of the gargantuan bruise remained.

74

There was an uncertain pause. Then Benedict said: "Why don't you both come in? There's no one here; my father's still out and I'm just reading."

He led them through into the little kitchen garden at the back, found them deck chairs and brought one out from the woodshed for himself.

"What we wanted to do," said Milo, choosing his words carefully, "was to talk to you about your friend Felix Weston. We had a few words with him after we saw you home the other day, and we decided that he wasn't quite such a creep as we thought. Still, it was really his fault, you know, that you got that sock in the eye."

Benedict grinned. "I nearly always carry the can for old Felix," he explained. "But you know, really he's a very amusing fellow. And he has some family troubles which make him act like a screwball."

The two visitors exchanged glances.

"You mean," asked Heppel, "Arabella?"

Benedict was startled.

"You mean you know Mrs. Weston too?"

The two visitors grinned. "Of course," Milo said. "After all, it was in all the papers, wasn't it? I mean about her being Bantinglow's model and all that."

"In fact," said Benedict, "I don't think it's Arabella that really worries Felix. It's his father."

"It's two halves of the same problem," said Kenneth. "But we wanted to tell you that whatever he's suffering from he'd better watch out when he gets to Aylsbourn in September. We've agreed to leave him alone; but we can't guarantee the behaviour of all the others if he comes out with any more of that offensive class-war stuff."

"He doesn't mean it, you know. It's only a reaction because his father's a communist."

"The last time we had a boy from Valhalla," Milo said, with a little relish in his voice, "he was carried home the first day with five stitches in his head."

"What on earth did he do?"

"He asked the fellows when lunch would be served."

"I'm sorry. I don't follow."

The two boys smiled grimly at each other.

75

"It's just as well you're not coming to Aylsbourn," said Kenneth. "You'd get carved up too. Midday, we eat dinner."

"That's a bit fierce, isn't it? I mean to belt a boy just for saying that?"

"If Weston calls the chaps peasants," said Kenneth, "we can't be responsible for his safety."

Benedict laughed. "It was a bit much. But I'll be there to look after him."

"Surely you're going to Shallerton?" asked Milo.

"I think you'll find I've failed to win the scholarship."

"Well, won't your father pay for you?"

"Good Lord, no! He's not a millionaire."

"Isn't he? We thought all those Brewery executives made a fortune."

"I don't suppose he makes any more than your father."

"Well," said Heppel, "he certainly makes more than mine."

"I think we ought not to quibble about this," said Benedict. "There's only one man in Aylsbourn who makes any money, and that's Margrave. What does it matter whether your father makes eight pounds a week or ten pounds a week? Margrave is worth a hundred thousand."

"I think you'll find," said Heppel, "that Weston isn't worth much less."

"Look," said Benedict. "I've got an idea. Why don't we go up and see Felix now? He's really very amusing company."

They looked at each other. "All right," said Heppel. "Perhaps we can see the gorgeous Arabella at the same time."

But there was no sign of Felix or Mrs. Weston when they rang the back bell of Felix's house ten minutes later. Mrs. Duncher opened the door.

Perhaps, Benedict thought, she's been admitted to Arabella's secret. Her mild blue eyes seemed to have an unusual gleam in them and she show unaccustomed animation. It was as if someone had just passed a high electric current through her dumpy body.

"Felix isn't back yet," she told them. "He's gone out shopping with Mrs. Weston."

"The lucky sod," muttered Milo Johnston.

"Tell you what though," said Mrs. Duncher. "They'll be

76

back for tea soon. I expect I can find you boys a cup if you'd like to wait."

"Thanks very much, Mrs. Duncher," said Benedict quickly. "It is rather important that we see Felix."

Over the fireplace in the drawing-room was a creamy nude by Bantinglow. The model had her back to the artist, but there was something in the delicious flow of her back and buttocks that seemed familiar.

"Christopher!" exclaimed Milo. "It can't be!"

"It is," said Benedict.

"Fancy letting that old lecher see you starkers!"

"Nothing to it," Benedict said casually. "Bantinglow—even at eighty is a man of the world. He would be far more exciting to a girl like Arabella than some doomy poet."

"Yes," said Milo. "He might have more small talk. But just imagine. . . . ."

"Ah," said Kenneth, who had been peering out of the window, bored by this exchange. "Here they come."

The three boys jammed themselves into the window-seat and stared down. Arabella was coming along the High Street arm in arm with Felix. He was carrying her shopping bag and they were deep in conversation.

"Just look at that lucky sod!" breathed Milo.

Benedict knew as soon as he set eyes on them what had happened. Arabella had told Felix her news. That was why she was going out of her way to be nice to him. They made, Benedict reflected, a rather charming couple; Felix was already the same height as she. They looked happy and insulated, like young lovers.

In another moment they heard the key in the latch, the sound of their voices, the answering voice of Mrs. Duncher, and then the drawing-room door opened. The boys rose to their feet awkwardly.

Arabella came in first. She seemed to Benedict to be in bloom, like an early-morning rose. Her face was a little flushed and her eyes shone. She wore, Benedict always remembered, an olive green corduroy suit, and a russet-coloured blouse. Felix followed. When he saw the visitors, he tried hard to wipe the expression of serenity from his face. He was too late; Benedict, for one, noticed.

"Well, boys," said Arabella. "This is a nice surprise."

"I don't think you've met Milo and Ken before," Felix said to

77

Arabella rather ungraciously. And then, to the boys a little grudgingly: "This is my—— This is Arabella."

Good God, thought Benedict, he's actually shy about her.

"You must all stay," said Arabella, "and have some tea. I'll ask Mrs. Duncher to lay it here in the drawing-room."

"Look," said Felix, "why don't you all come up to my room? I've got some marvellous new jazz records. My father bought them for me in London yesterday."

"Does Mrs. Weston like jazz?" asked Benedict doubtfully.

"Heavens yes," said Arabella. "But I don't know much about it. When I was rushing about in London we always used to go crazy about Harry Roy."

She realized from the boys' faces that this could not be right. Felix explained to her. "Harry Roy is not exactly *jazz*, Arabella," he said. "I'll play you some real New Orleans music and you'll soon see the difference."

"I'll go and see what Mrs. Duncher can cook up," said Arabella. "You boys go on up and get something really hot for me to hear. I want to learn."

It was mysteriously delightful to all four of them, the thought of this little assignation with Arabella in Felix's room.

Gerard Weston had certainly turned up trumps. A keen believer in the sentimental, folklore aspect of jazz, he had gone to town and bought Felix some treasures. He had got some Parlophone Black Labels and some of the Brunswick Sepia series. There was Jimmy Noone's "Way Down Yonder" and Gene Krupa's "Three Little Words"; Louis Armstrong's "Muskat Ramble" and Johnny Dodd's "Bucktown Stomp".

In ten minutes Arabella was back with Mrs. Duncher. Both women carried large trays; they had made a splendid high tea. There were scrambled eggs on toast and Devonshire splits and toast and strawberry jam, and a plate of Huntley and Palmer's chocolate biscuits.

Mrs. Duncher withdrew, and Arabella sat at the top of Felix's table and poured out large cups of tea. Felix turned the gramophone off till after they had eaten, so that they could concentrate on the music later.

"Well, now," said Arabella, "I hope I'm not inhibiting your conversation. I'd like you to treat me as one of the gang."

"The trouble is, Arabella," said Felix, "that normally we talk

78

about only sport, which wouldn't interest you, and sex, which you know all about anyway."

"That's not fair, Felix," Arabella reprimanded him. "I'm madly interested in cricket at the moment. I adored that game on Sunday. And as for sex: truly, I'm a complete beginner."

Benedict stared at her, mesmerised. He had never heard a woman say such a thing in his life.

"You can't," said Milo, "be quite such beginners as we are."

Arabella gave a little chuckle at this. It was a sound which riveted Benedict in his chair. "Now boys," she teased them, "this is too modest of you. I've heard of all the affairs between the boys and girls that take place under dear old Sandy Macpherson's unwitting nose. You all spend your time falling in and out of love with each other. You don't know how lucky you are. I was brought up in a convent. I didn't kiss a young man until I was seventeen."

The boys stared at her with respect. She had certainly made up for lost time!

"Could you tell us, Mrs. Weston——" began Benedict. But she gently interrupted him. "Please call me Arabella. After all, I'm not very much older than you. And I'm certainly not old enough to be your Mum."

She was clearly enjoying her little flirtation with them. Benedict cleared his throat and began again rather shyly: "Could you tell us, Arabella"—it was delectable, the unwonted, the previously forbidden pleasure of using her Christian name—"what it is like to be a girl?"

They all laughed at this one, uproariously. "Oh, Benny," cried Felix, "you really are priceless."

"No," said Arabella smiling gently at Benedict when they had subsided, "it's a perfectly good question. But it's a jolly difficult one to answer. I mean, I have no comparative experience. How does it feel to be a boy?"

"Awful, quite often," said Milo, unexpectedly. "I mean, you're so unsure of what you can do."

"But," said Arabella in mock surprise, "that's just what it's like when you're a girl. Truly. You're full of strange dreams and fears and hints of future delights and little shiverings and portents of romance. You're so—*vulnerable*."

"Did you ever want to be a boy?" asked Kenneth Heppel boldly.

"Oh passionately, especially when I was small and I couldn't do the things my brothers could do. It's hateful to be told that you're soft and delicate"—here a shadow of vestigial resentment flitted across her face—"when you want to be out climbing trees. You feel—sort of second class. But eventually, when you get to about fifteen—when you become conscious that you're a woman —then it has its compensations."

Benedict was fascinated. He had never heard any woman speak so—frankly—before.

"What sort of compensations?" he asked. His voice sounded odd to him: it was an almost histrionic whisper.

Arabella looked at him for a second and then said: "The usual things; the fun of wearing a new dress. Colours, sights, smells; being given flowers. Having men look at you in the street in a certain way."

"You mean you *enjoy* that?" asked Benedict incredulously.

"Yes. Why ever not?"

"It doesn't strike you as—crude?"

"No. It is part of life. My dears: this is my philosophy. All people can be divided into two great categories. They are the life-diminishers and the life-enhancers. Now, as for me, I'm pro-life, one hundred per cent. So if a man looks at me in the street and his look says I like you—then I'm glad. It's as simple as that."

The boys digested this novel intelligence in silence.

"Suppose," said Milo, "I saw you in the street. In London one day; suppose we passed in Charing Cross Road. Suppose I looked at you and realized that you were the only girl there could possibly be for me——"

"You'd be wrong," Arabella interrupted him drily. "There are lots of girls for all of you. Maybe in this town, maybe on the other side of the world; maybe they're hardly toddling about yet; maybe they're already dreaming about you; but believe me; there is no one and only girl."

"But suppose——"

"Ah yes; in Charing Cross Road. To me, as a member of the Pro-Life Party, it would be a shame—no, much worse—a scandal and a crime—if you allowed her to pass you by."

All the boys began to speak at once. "Oh, I know," she conceded, "there are the big conventional forces against you. But they're only inside you. The girl wouldn't mind. On the contrary, she'd be delighted. Isn't that what a girl is waiting for all her life? If you don't speak, you may be cruelly wasting that girl's life—taking away her one real chance of happiness."

"I'll tell you all something now which I've never told anyone," said Milo with unusual animation. "One day I was going up to London in the train. And there was a girl in the compartment with me. She got in at Shallerton. She was truly beautiful. As beautiful as you Arabella"—a strange nearness had fallen over the little attic room as though the people in it had been friends or lovers for years—"and you know I did the most reckless thing."

"Milo," said Kenneth with mock concern, "think carefully before you speak."

"I suddenly said to her," Milo blurted out, "I said—'I bet you wouldn't kiss me.' And she did."

"All the way to *London*?" asked Benedict.

"Yes. She wouldn't tell me her name, and of course I've never met her again. She ran away from me at Waterloo and disappeared in the crowd. I've never forgotten that," he concluded sadly.

"And she won't forget you," Arabella comforted him. "You know, Milo, that kind of thing happens all the time. Even in jolly old England, where it's not supposed to. It even happens here in Aylsbourn."

Great heavens, Benedict thought. Who would dare suggest a thing like that to *Arabella*?

"Yes," Arabella went on, evidently enjoying the little scandal she was creating. "There's at least one distinguished gentleman in this sleepy old town who makes passes at other people's wives—and quite a distinguished citizen too."

Great heavens, thought Benedict. Surely not Macpherson? Or Sir Keith Margrave? Surely not Doctor Mackay? Not—perhaps —*my own father*? But Arabella wasn't saying. "Boys," she went on, with a touch of remorse, "I've already been frightfully indiscreet. Let's keep it within these four walls, shall we?"

They all nodded. "But," Milo persisted, "Arabella, how *could* you meet a girl you just passed in the street?"

"Good heavens," Arabella chided him. "That's up to you, Milo. Pity the poor girl. She can't very well waylay a man she likes in the street. Not in this civilization, in this century, anyway. Of course, she can make it pretty plain in all sorts of ways that she's not averse to being approached."

"A glance would do?" asked Benedict.

"A glance would do," said Arabella seriously. "Or better, you should see to it that your fingertips touch as you pass."

"What do you look for in a man?" enquired Kenneth Heppel.

Arabella considered this question. The boys waited in a torture of uncertainty. What on earth would she say now?

"I think first," said Arabella slowly, "arrogance. Yes, I definitely put arrogance first."

The boys listened in respectful and awestruck silence.

"Then I look for something a little indefinable. I think I shall have to call it—appetite. Not in the literal sense of course; I mean appetite for life; joy in being alive." She paused. "You must think me a very wicked woman. I mean what about kindness, generosity, patience, tolerance—all those things you read about in women's magazines? Well, I've nothing against them except that I don't believe in them and they bore me. I'd never *look* for them."

"What else?" asked Benedict.

"Oh," said Arabella casually, "the right smell. A man can be an angel, but if he doesn't smell right it's no good."

She laughed. "If you boys could see your faces! But now, this is rather unfair. What do you boys look for in a girl? Come, Benny, you are the only true romantic here. What do you look for?"

Benedict realized that everybody was watching him curiously. He racked his brains. The answer seemed to come up from a long way down in his sub-conscious memory. It was as if he had always really known what he was going to say, but had never dared admit it to himself. He cleared his throat nervously.

"Magic," he said.

Once again they all collapsed, as if knifed through with laughter. Even Benedict joined in this time. At length Arabella took out a little handkerchief and dried her eyes. "Oh Benny," she said, "you have such delicious miseries ahead of you!"

"Tell us one more thing, Arabella," pleaded Felix. "Benny and I have often argued about this. Is there really such a thing as love?"

There was a silence again in the attic room; not an absence of sound but a taut stillness, like the interval between a sliver of lightning and a clap of thunder. Benedict noticed that now

Arabella had gone very pale. Even her lips had lost their usual vivid colour. The question had evidently distressed her.

"I think," she answered thoughtfully at length, "that love is possible between two people; just as I believe that it has occasionally been possible in history for mystics to communicate directly with God. It's of that order of probability—and that order of importance."

"But for most of us," urged Felix, "there is only flattery, sex, habit, despair?"

"Oh, but besides all these things, Felix," said Arabella, but she was speaking to herself, "there is love."

Benedict often found himself wondering why, at that moment, she looked so pale.

That awful day
When his father heard about the scholarship. They hadn't had the grace just to say he'd failed; no, there had to be a consultation between Mr. Ross-Tayfield and Mr. Varley, and then another consultation (in the relative comfort of the "Thorn and Sceptre") between Mr. Varley and Mr. Benedict, and then that excruciatingly embarrassing interview with his father when neither quite liked to look at the other.

"They seem to think, son," his father had begun shiftily, "that there may have been some mental—er, some nervous trouble. Let's see now, when did you get that sock in the eye?"

"Two days after the exam." It was no good trying to give his father that easy let-out.

"Yes. Well, they seem to think it would be a good idea son, if" —and here his father's face was in an agony of self-consciousness —"you went and had a chat to the doctor. I mean, they feel you must have been definitely ill on that day. Would you mind doing that for me, old chap?"

"No. Not a bit. But I'm afraid you'll find there's nothing wrong."

There had in fact been nothing wrong—nothing that the doctors could put their fingers on, anyway. Anderson had called in Mackay, and they had both sent him up to see a specialist in London, who had asked him several hundred questions and hit his nerve-centres with a small rubber hammer; but it all came to nothing in the end. Later there was another harrowing conversation with his father about taking the Shallerton scholarship again;

83

the boy had been adamant and his father had finally given in. But he had been mystified and hurt: clearly there was more to his son than met the eye. And any variety of off-centre behaviour made Mr. Benedict instinctively uncomfortable.

Benedict was desperately sorry about his father's distress and often racked his brains for an explanation. But his own behaviour was as big a mystery to him as it was to the doctors. The night he had heard the news first, Benedict always remembered, his father had got drunk at the "Thorn and Sceptre", a thing he had never done before. Four pints of Margrave best bitter had always been his father's mellow limit; but that awful night he had gone on to neat whisky, and been sick in the kitchen. They both had tried to forget about it, but the memory was still there between them.

Mr. Varley had taken it in quite an unexpected way. He had asked Benedict to come and see him one evening soon after. The boy had found his old headmaster sitting in the high chair in his study. The room was illuminated only by one small reading-lamp, and there were long shadows on the walls, casting an eerie glow on the groups of cricket and rugger teams and the long line of silver cups.

"Benedict," Mr. Varley had said with surprising gentleness, "I am very sorry indeed to hear what has happened. I understand and I sympathise. I know how you must be feeling. You see, I have had the experience of mental trouble in my own family. My poor younger sister was a stranger to us for many years, and they finally had to take the dear creature away. There are moments in all our lives, I sometimes think, when sanity seems to hang by a thin thread. I know that has been my own experience. If that ever happens to you again, you must go to your best friend at once and pour your troubles out. Never bottle it up inside you. The brains, my dear Benny, are only like rather complicated bowels. They must never be allowed to clog."

"Thank you, sir. I'm truly sorry to have let you down."

"Don't ever worry about it, Benny." He noticed that his headmaster had used the affectionate diminutive. "I'm still convinced you'll be a credit to me. You're still only a very young fellow. There'll be plenty more chances in your life. You've lost a battle, you haven't lost the war. Oh yes, Valhalla will be proud of you one day."

"I wish I could believe that, sir."

84

"You've got to believe in yourself, Benny. Until you do, nobody else will believe in you."

"I'm afraid no one else will ever believe in me, sir."

Mr. Varley smiled. "I'm not much of a betting man, Benny, but I'd take money on you."

"That's very good of you, sir. I'll try not to let you down again."

"You haven't let me down, Benny. You don't think all this"—he indicated the roll of honour behind him, on which his boys' successes were inscribed in gilt—"means a thing to me, do you? That's only for the parents' benefit! It's the boys themselves that matter. You know"—and here his voice took on a slightly dreamy quality—"it's sometimes the biggest rascals one's most fond of. Yes, the biggest rascals." He was smiling to himself. "You know," he added, "I used to be a bit of a rascal myself."

They parted good friends that night; friends in a way they would never have been if he had won his scholarship.

But that was Mr. Varley's reaction; his father was made of very different stuff and would never really get over it.

September 3rd 1939

The Rector had rigged up a wireless in the church, so they knew it was pretty serious. God, what a beautiful day it was! The leaves were pancake yellow and toffee brown, the sun spun gold in the branches, and the air so crisp and thin that it made you want to run, your feet never properly touching the ground.

The Rector turned on the wireless after the Magnificat and they sat listening to that flat, gentlemanly voice. Years afterwards, one saw this moment recalled by the movie camera, captured from a thousand different angles: the crowds in London, somehow shabby and old-fashioned, the women with their embarrassingly short skirts, and even the men somehow skimped in their suits and ludicrous, not moving jerkily as they did in the first world war films, yet unmistakably out of date, belonging firmly to another age.

". . . I have to tell you that this country is at war with Germany."

Benedict gazed down from the choir-stall at the rows of stolid English faces. War with Germany, war with Germany. It was

85

tautologous: whoever else would one be at war with? Benedict had never known war at first hand, but he had read about it in the encyclopaedias and he had seen the ghastly frieze in the War Museum which showed blinded soldiers groping along patiently, one behind the other; he had seen all the boys' books and worshipped all the normal heroes; and all this vicarious experience had left him with one over-riding notion: war and Germany were one and indivisible.

Yet he felt no hatred of Germany at that moment; only a love for his own people so ferocious and proud that the tears came and he cursed himself. He looked at the faces again, but more carefully now, trying to see not one large friendly blur but sharp individual portraits. There was his father of course, wriggling in his stiff white collar and best blue suit and already eyeing his watch carefully to see how long it was to drinking time. There was Mr. Varley, vermillion-faced and gigantic, bulging from his check suit, both big hairy hands on his stick, leaning forward intently to hear Chamberlain's words. There was Keith Margrave, mottled and patriarchal and upper-class in his Old Harrovian tie, and next to him poor patient Lady Margrave in a navy blue suit and sensible shoes. And then there were the Mackays. Laura's father and mother did not normally go to church and presumably had come today merely to convey a sense of solidarity. Benedict studied them with interest. Dr. Mackay, he estimated, was about forty. He wore a tweed suit and suède shoes, and a red woollen tie with a large knot. He looked like an economics lecturer at a small provincial university. But to Benedict he was an intellectual, a man of reason, and hence almost beyond criticism. He had never seen Mrs. Mackay before. She wore her blonde hair like Laura's, though a little darker, drawn severely back over the ears, emphasising, to Benedict, the *spirituality* of her face. She was small, with little well-scrubbed hands and a plain gold wedding-ring. Benedict stared down at her with awe: she was Laura's mother.

Laura wore a biscuit-coloured coat with a high collar, and a yellow silk scarf, and she had snuggled down into it like a squirrel; her hair was brushed down to her shoulders and held in place by an Alice band. Occasionally she turned the pages of the Prayer Book absent-mindedly, and the thin gold bangles on her wrist glistened in the sun. Once she turned and looked quickly behind her at the solemn rows of parishioners, as if she were looking for somebody.

What did war mean to Laura? A succession of absurdly romantic cameos flowed through his imagination. If the Germans ever got to this church, he would fight them right the way back to the pulpit, just as, in the Civil War, a Cavalier Officer had fought off a dozen Roundheads from it till finally one of the swine had got behind and run him through. He would give his life gladly for Laura, he reflected; if this new war needed justifying, then for him Laura was its complete justification. And then, just then, Laura saw him, and remembered, and smiled. And to his amazement, she put her hand up to one of her marvellous green eyes, made a face, and dropped it down again into her lap, as if to indicate that she remembered that terrible, blood-soaked summer's day. Then she looked seriously down at her Prayer Book again.

The broadcast ended, and there was a sighing and stirring in the little church. "Let us pray," said the Rector. He prayed that Britain would win; and after that Benedict remembered that they had sung a beautiful anthem: *God is a spirit, and they that worship him must worship him in spirit and truth*. Benedict was never deeply religious, yet this music and these words seemed to him always afterwards to represent the quick of the mystery; for if there *were* a God, then he must, Benedict reflected, be infinitely mysterious and unknowable. Why should a God who was omniscient and omnipresent, eternal and infinite, be also loving? For loving was a human condition, in altogether a different bracket from all the divine attributes. It was like one of those exam papers in logic. Pick out the word which does not belong: beauty, truth, justice, pudding; omniscient, omnipresent, eternal, infinite, loving; *that* was about how difficult it was. The lines rang in Benedict's head, mocking him as they often did, but never more ironically than now: "Back from that void I shrink in fear, and childlike hide myself in. . . ."

Only a mysterious God would do then, one infinitely incomprehensible, unclutchable, unknowable, unheeding. And what point was there in worshipping a God like that? Yet how tranquil and liberating was the old Judaic invocation at the end of the service: *this* God, whom the Jews had invented and the Christians had borrowed, *this* family patriarch was *somebody*: "The Lord bless

87

you and keep you; the Lord lift up the light of His countenance upon you, and give you His peace."

Then the Rector rose and said rather self-consciously: "Today I am sure we would like to conclude by singing our National Anthem together." The organ pounded out the simple and sad little tune and everyone rose to sing it. But today the odd thing was, they *did* sing it, even the mumblers like his father opened their mouths and their chests, proclaiming for all they were worth the naïve and jingoistic sentiments with unusual gusto:

> *Send him victorious,*
> *Happy and glorious,*
> *Long to reign....*

Benedict stopping singing in the middle of the line, and gripped the carved wooden choir stall to steady himself. He closed his eyes in disbelief, then opened them again. It was true; it was no nightmare. Tony Hammond was in the congregation; right in the back, and he had noticed him merely because, while everyone else stood, Hammond remained in his place. Benedict already knew that Hammond was an unbeliever. Why then was he in church that morning? Was it God or Laura he wanted to be near? And now, had he found God or——Benedict could not bear to formulate the question, even to himself. For as they all sang together, with such wonderful and unwonted gusto, calling God the infinite and unknowable spirit to their country's aid, Tony Hammond remained seated in his place.

●

Christmas 1939

Or rather a few days before Christmas; the last day of term at Aylsbourn Grammar School. For that was where he now belonged. There was no snow, but ice, and a hard frost. Benedict walked to school with a long gold and green woollen scarf swung round his neck and woollen gloves; but no overcoat. In those days he never seemed to need one. He hummed as he strode along. It had been a happy term. He had never touched the ecstacy of the summer again, but he had been content. He had been disconcerted at first by the teaching at his new school. Before, he had been crammed with information; now he found he was expected to have ideas. He was expected to argue and think for himself. Before, he had been drilled with machine-tool precision; Mr.

Varley asked no higher virtue than obedience. Benedict had picked up the new technique quickly; in the green exercise book which he carried under his arm there were already several A minuses. He had worked hard, responding eagerly, and now it was the last day of term, and three weeks of delicious idleness stretched ahead.

The whole school was to assemble in the Old Hall. This was a long low room, part of the original Elizabethan building, into which the whole school could cram if necessary. Normally the girls occupied the new building on the other side of the road. Today they filled the whole of the right-hand side of the Hall and, perhaps because they were girls, they were there first, row upon row of them in green woollen sweaters, white blouses and grey skirts. They were chattering among themselves, then as the boys hurried in, eyes met across the room. There was a curious tension in the room as it filled; it was full of love. Yes thought Benedict, this room is full of love. The chatter increased, and the laughter; the room was gaily decked with winter flowers and paper chains; there was a sense of holiday in the air.

Abruptly the common-room door in the extreme right opened and the staff filed in. First came the Headmaster, old Macpherson. He was Scottish, a fisherman's son, a tall, bald man in pince-nez with a rich deep voice full of good round vowels. Boys from the Cressbrook Valley, whose train was sometimes so late in the morning that they missed prayers, would congregate of their own will outside the middle door of the Old Hall, which was just behind his dais, so that they could hear his beautiful bass voice rise and fall in sonorous melody with the hymn. He built Latin and Greek into his boys' minds with the expertness and solidity of a craftsman, so that they never forgot: *Quiss multa gracilis te puer in rosa perfusus liquidis urget odoribus grato, Pyrrha, sub antro?* The lines would run through Benedict's brain all his life, rooted there for good; and all the grammatical apparatus of the languages stayed with him too, like Government debentures, faithfully bearing interest, but rendered ridiculous by inflation. He was destined to remember all his life the gracious feel of his blue book of Horace's Odes, the forbidding shining green of the Livy, the fat, friendly red of the Tacitus. It was all part of Benedict, useless as the memory of a broken romance; but cherished perhaps for that very reason.

Macpherson was a scholar, a dry kindly old man whose wife was an invalid and whose only son had died in infancy. He gave all his considerable gifts to his school without question and without stint. He did not understand politics, but wanted only to conserve things as they were. He read minor Latin poets for fun and had published an edition of Catullus. He kept a pet tortoise in his garden. He went once or twice a year to London to attend meetings of the Horace Society and would attend a Bach concert in the evening if he could. He lived in the School house, which was part of the original Elizabethan structure, and, to Benedict, the most gracious building he had ever seen. No one ever knew for sure whether Macpherson believed in God or not. Certainly he sang the morning hymn in his beautiful bass voice every day, and read the prayers with resonant piety: "Lord of the seedtime and the harvest, grant thy blessing we beseech thee to this thy school. May there be from these human hearts an abundant ingathering. . . ." But he did not go to church, and read Voltaire for pleasure. He was the most serious man Benedict had ever met, and the most considerable. There had been one memorable morning when, because the master concerned was ill, Macpherson had taken them for English.

"Now boys and girls," he enquired amiably that day: "which poem shall we read this morning?"

No one had any ideas, so Macpherson made a proposal. "Have you ever read Milton's sonnet On His Blindness? No. Then we shall study that today."

They read it first straight through, then line by line, Macpherson interpolating and explaining as they went along: " 'Ere half my days', boys and girls. Can ye imagine what it meant to the poet to be blind before he was thirty-five? . . . 'Fondly.' Now that doesn't mean lovingly, as it would today. It means foolishly. 'I fondly ask'—he sees that it is foolish to question God's will even as he does so. 'Thousands at his bidding speed and post . . .' Now that doesn't mean they post letters, boys and girls. It means that they travelled by post-carriage, the fastest there was in that time. So post means to ride at express speed. And so to the great affirmation of the final line: 'They also serve who only stand and wait.' Now, that doesn't mean to stand and loiter. It means to wait at the Lord's table. A perfect line of poetry and deservedly part of everyday English usage. Now boys and girls, let us say the poem again out loud, but this time trying to give every word its true meaning." And together, accompanying their headmaster, they began again:

> *When I consider how my light is spent*
> *Ere half my days in this dark world and wide*
> *And that one talent which is death to hide*
> *Lodged with me useless, though my soul more bent*
> *To serve therewith my Maker, and present....*

Always the lines came back to Benedict without effort, and the sound of the chanting voices, Macpherson's grave and deep beneath, and the calmness in the room, as if the spirit of Milton himself had filled it. Benedict had never consciously learned the poem; after that hour with Macpherson it was his for ever. Now another such moment was about to be born.

Macpherson mounted his dais, his firm old face illuminated in the buttery light of the December sun, his ragged gown lending him mysterious dignity; the rest of the staff filed along and stood to each side of him. The whole school rose and there was exhilaration in the air, a sense of occasion. It was the end of the year; the old exercise books, replete with errors and blots and crossings out, would be thrown away, and new ones started next term. It was a moment of lightness and hope.

"Today," Macpherson's Scottish voice rang round the room, "as is our custom, we sing a Latin Christmas hymn, 'Adeste Fideles—O Come All Ye Faithful'." The piano banged out the first few lines, paused, then began again, the whole school singing at the top of its voice:

> *Adeste fideles, laeti triumphantes,*
> *Venite, venite, ad Bethlehem.*

The tears came into Benedict's eyes at the beauty of the hymn. Already he had lost his precarious faith; but he was too full of the world's awe ever to lose the overwhelming emotion the melody conjured up in him. Always, whenever after he heard it, the crowded school-room came back, and all the voices singing:

> *Natum videte, regem angelorum.*

And then there was the simple but, to Benedict, quite marvellous choral device: at the next line the girls stopped singing and the boys' voices were heard alone:

Venite adoremus ...

And then the girls alone:

Venite adoremus ...

Benedict looked along the rows of girls, until he saw the only one who mattered; and he saw with joy that Laura sang with the best of them.

Then together again, with the basses and tenors among the masters and senior boys weaving a joyful counter-melody into the climactic final line. And Benny saw that even Tony Hammond was singing:

Venite adoremus,
Dominum.

Then the next verse, and the next: the singing was glorious; Benedict wanted it never to end.

The afternoon of the Christmas Party

It was the custom at Aylsbourn that each House had a party on the last day of the Christmas term. Benedict was in Johnston's House, so called after Milo's father, and to his great delight he quickly discovered that both Laura and Tony Hammond were in Johnston's too. Milo was in Johnston's for family reasons, and Kenneth Heppel was in the house as well, though only by chance. Felix was in Parkinson's House—they had decided it was not fair to put two of Valhalla's most talented athletes together—so he was the only member of the group who could not be present at the Johnston's party. He claimed not to care tuppence: "I'm only interested," he told his friends, "in women of forty."

Looking back on it later from the adult world, Benedict often thought what an enlightened little society it was. It was accepted that everyone would want to have a partner at the house party, and for days beforehand there was a heightened excitement in the air. It was always known that Mr. Johnston had a list of every boy and girl in his house and would do his best to see that each went with the partner he or she wanted. The intrigues, the whisperings in corners, the notes to and fro, the heartaches this modest list entailed each year! Yet in the end everyone was paired, and the few broken hearts were soon mended.

Benny decided he would ask Constance Pickering. Though he still worshipped Laura from a distance, he realized in his more rational moments that she was nearly two years older than he; an enormous gap at their age—and in any case he knew she would be going with Tony Hammond. But Constance; she was within the ambit of what was just possible; indeed she sat only five feet away from him each day. She was a curiously proud girl, and she customarily held her head very high; she walked with great grace even though her dress always seemed rather racily short. Anyway, her legs were worth looking at, Benedict always thought. She spoke rather softly and had a slightly cynical sense of humour. She was exceedingly bright, and the boys often had some difficulty in keeping ahead of her. By long and unwritten convention at Aylsbourn, the boys did as little work as they could—until a girl got to the top in a particular subject. Then the boy who was thought to be best in that field would have to set to and work until he had got to the top again. Constance was unnervingly good at unlikely subjects like mathematics and physics: Milo was thought to be the expert in these subjects and he often used to curse at the way she made him sweat to stay ahead. However, it probably did him a lot of good.

Constance lived at Welcaster, a hamlet just down the main road from Benedict's own village of Ashdale. She had no parents, but was looked after by a rather elderly and strict couple called the Hayleys. It was thought that her parents had been split up by the war. Constance had little time for flirtation; she worked hard and took a noticeably cool view about romantic attachments. Benedict, however, was undeterred by this rather unpromising set of facts; since they had talked to Arabella, he and his friends had developed a new confidence. To have called it arrogance would have been exaggerating; but Benedict was certainly less easily diverted by thoughts of his own inadequacy than before. He decided to sit down and write Constance a letter asking her to be his partner. All the same it took him nearly a week before he could both work up his courage and write exactly what he meant to say. During this period, he kept glancing at her across the room; but there was never a hint of her intentions on her proud and beautiful face.

93

In the end he wrote the note: "Dear Constance, Would you please come to the Christmas party with me?" It was not a very complex communication; but it was his sixth shot.

He sent it across to her in the Larousse dictionary. This was the way all amorous communications were exchanged at Aylsbourn; the convention was so prevalent that the staff must surely have known about it. But nothing was done to prevent it. Indeed, the whole school lived all the year round in a higher octave of excitement because it was mixed. It was normal, as Arabella had suggested, for each boy to fall in love with most of the girls of his generation in turn before he was eighteen. Indeed, romance was not unknown in the common-room. It was said that Mr. Parkinson, the squat, dark Welshman who had taught himself chemistry in between shifts at the mines to get out of his native valley, had been seen with Miss Aliss, the faintly soignée if now grey-haired geography mistress on his knee one afternoon. It was rumoured that Miss Collins, the biology mistress, though at least fifty and no oil-painting, had a crush on Mr. Johnston, despite his married status and jug-ears. It was even known that old Macpherson himself had been seen walking arm-in-arm with Miss Dindale, breathless and fresh from Somerville with her good second in English. . . . But it seemed to be pretty innocent; and in all his time at Aylsbourn, Benedict heard of only one scandal. That, though, on the afternoon of the party, was still a long way into the future.

"Please pass on to Constance," he had written on his note. "Private." No one had been known to break the strict conventions of the game, and Constance was the first to read his private message.

She read it, then without hesitation took out a sheet of paper and wrote carefully on it. He watched the Larousse come back across the room with suspense and longing.

The note was neatly folded. On the outside she had written: "Please pass to Benny. Private." He opened it in sharp and delicious terror.

"Dear Benny," she had written, "it is sweet of you to ask me. I don't quite know yet what my plans are. Someone else has asked me but I may say no. Can you dance? I don't mean are you an expert, but can you get round the floor without the usual excruciating flounderings?"

Benedict was in despair. He deliberated for a long time before replying. At length, though, the ponderous Larousse went back across the room with his reply in it.

"Dear Constance," he wrote, "I have to tell you the truth. I can't dance. And yet I sometimes feel as if I'm almost dancing. This is especially so when I'm listening to jazz. I feel I could learn quite quickly. I wonder—is there the slightest chance that you'd teach me? Just enough, I mean, to get by without disgracing you."

He watched for some hint of emotion on her face. There was none. She wrote busily:

"Dear Benny. Yes, I'll teach you. I'm not sure if I'll go with you yet. It rather depends how you get on. Love Constance."

It was the first time any woman had ever sent him her love. He was transported. And whenever he looked back to this little exchange over the years, he reflected that, though he had forgotten every damned word in the Larousse, he had learned something far more useful: that no woman ever says yes; at least not just like that.

It was arranged that the first lesson should be in the library that same evening. There was a radiogram there, and after the librarian had finished dispensing books it was tacitly understood that the room could be used for social purposes. Benny looked round nervously as he hurried in; fortunately, however, none of his friends was to be seen. He had made a weak excuse about having to check some points in the reference section and the others had gone off unsuspectingly to gossip in Miller's teashop. He opened the door gingerly and saw with a thumping heart that Constance was already there. She sat in a corner, legs demurely crossed, reading the *Oxford Book of French Verse* with somewhat studied detachment.

"Hello, Constance," he said. "How nice of you to come."

"Hello, Benny. Don't be silly. Every boy should be able to dance. Did you bring any records?"

His spirits sank. "No. I'm afraid not. Aren't there any here?"

"Not really. I've had a look and there only seems to be a rather cracked recording of the New World Symphony."

"Oh hell." He rummaged about anxiously.

"Ah, what's this. 'Dinah.' Will that do?"

"Yes. It's a quickstep. Aren't there any more?"

"Don't seem to be."

"O.K. Put it on then."

His fingers shook rather badly as he placed the needle on the well-worn disc. The music brayed suddenly and with unnerving volume.

"Isn't it a bit loud?"

"Sorry." He turned the volume down. "Dinah" became a whisper.

"Now I can't hear anything."

"Sorry." He fiddled nervously with the knob.

"That's better. Come on then."

So the actual moment had arrived when he had to take the delectable Constance in his arms. Surely she couldn't be *serious* about this?

But she was; she stood in the middle of the library floor, waiting for him. It was quite dark outside, and inside the library the reading lamps in their amber shades cast a discreet light. Her face was half in shadow. She noticed him hesitate, and smiled. He could hardly believe it. Suddenly she didn't look quite so proud and unattainable.

"Come on, Benny," she said. "Don't be shy."

He placed his left arm diffidently round her waist. It was a slim waist and the manoeuvre presented no difficulty. Now that it was done, it seemed the most natural thing in the world. He took her hand in his. It was a small hand, and a little less warm than his own. Her fingers closed gently but deliberately round his. Now it was her turn to hesitate.

"You know, Benny," she said, "we shall never be able to dance unless you hold me a bit closer."

"Closer?"

"Yes. It should be possible for us to dance holding a record flat between us."

"You're not serious?"

"Of course. You are a duffer, aren't you? Didn't you know that?"

"I'm afraid not. But there isn't another record, except that Dvorak. . . ."

She laughed. "I don't think we need to put it to the test. Hold me a bit closer. I'll tell you when you're close enough."

He tightened his hold a minuscule.

"A bit tighter. I won't bite you."

96

He held her, as it seemed to him, recklessly tight.

"That's better. Now we can dance."

"Well tell me what the steps are."

"Just move your feet after mine. It's a bit difficult because I'm supposed to follow you. But just follow."

They began to move round the floor in a simple geometrical progression. After six or seven steps, he nearly tripped.

"Sorry."

"It's all right. Now then—'Dinah, is there anybody finer, in the State of Carolina . . .' "

The minutes passed in a mindless flow of unimagined delight. Constance danced lightly, and soon he fell in to her rhythm. They played the record again and again. Benny wanted the lesson never to end. Finally, however, she stopped, her cheeks a little flushed with the exertion—or perhaps even with a little of his communicated excitement—and said: "I think that'll do, Benny. You can dance—enough for the party anyhow."

"But what about the tango and the slow foxtrot and all that?"

"Oh you'll pick those up easily enough now. Anyway, they only play quicksteps."

She stowed the *Oxford Book of French Verse* away with some other books and papers in an old string bag.

"Then we can go together to the party?"

She didn't look up. "Yes, I think so."

"Your other arrangement has fallen through?"

"Benny, why are you so tiresome? I said I'd go with you."

"I'm sorry, Constance. It's just that I've never been to a thing like this before."

"Oh well you'll enjoy it. Now are you going to see me home?"

He could hardly believe his ears. "*May* I?"

"It would be more polite if you had offered first."

"I'm sorry. Of course—I mean there's nothing I'd like more."

"Come along then."

Once they were out in the dark road, to his terror and delight she slipped an arm through his. They walked in silence. It was a marvellous Aylsbourn evening, with that unmistakable sharp tang of decay in the cool air.

"Tell me about yourself, Benny. You're rather an odd boy you know. I can't make you out."

"Why ever not? I'm extremely ordinary."

"No, you're not. You're very dreamy. Often you look as if you're miles away. And you're dreadfully sensitive too. If anyone says anything unkind to you, you look as if you're about to burst into tears."

"It's because," said Benedict in a sudden mad access of confidence, "I really *feel* like crying. I wish I were as tough as my friends; I mean people like Felix."

"Oh, but you're much more interesting than they are."

They walked on in silence.

"Tell me, Benny," she asked after a while, "what do you want to do when you leave school?"

"I've never given it a thought. I'm so—sort of intoxicated —with being alive that I can't think ahead. I can't imagine that anybody would ever *pay* me. I mean I'm so hopeless at all practical things. I'm sure I shall be very poor when I'm old. But—what about you, Constance?"

"Oh I'm quite certain. I'm going to be a biologist. I'm fascinated by it. I shall go to Southampton University College—maybe even Cambridge if I work hard enough—and when I've got my degree I shall do research. I'm positive about it."

"Will you ever—marry?" It was an impertinent question; he wished he hadn't asked it even as he said it.

"I expect so, Benny. People usually do, don't they? Probably some excruciatingly dull chemist."

"You don't believe in love, then?"

"Not really. I am a biologist you see; and once you've studied biology at all thoroughly, romantic love seems rather ludicrous."

"I dare say it does." Unhappily they had arrived at her guardian's house. There seemed no good reason for prolonging the delectable conversation any longer.

He remembered, though, that as she said "Goodnight, Benny" they seemed suddenly to be shaking hands in a rather formal way. Yet she had squeezed his hand with what seemed like affection. Only he must have imagined it.

And now it was the day of the party.

Milo's mother had asked him to bring home one or two friends to lunch first. The fact that later in the afternoon she would have to feed fifty starving adolescents seemed not to deter her. Possibly the experience she had gained over the years in trying to quell Milo's gargantuan appetite had inured her. He was without question the hungriest boy in Aylsbourn. He had grown six inches in the last two years and it seemed that he would never have enough to eat. He was badly spoiled by his mother and two sisters; if he wanted something he usually got it.

It must, Benedict always thought wistfully, be fabulous to live surrounded by women as Milo did. Mrs. Johnston was a plump brisk woman of forty and a bit, who seemed to revel and thrive on the many cares of her young family. She made, Benedict always thought, the best home-made jam in the world: plum jam, apricot jam, strawberry jam, blackcurrant and apple jam, melon and ginger—there were always fifty gleaming jars of the stuff standing on the big shelf in her larder, each with a neat white label and white paper cap. She also made home-made wines with a kick like neat Scotch—Milo had already surreptitiously, as an experiment, drunk himself into a stupor on them. All through his life, Benedict remembered the vivid taste of the vegetables from the Johnston's garden—the new potatoes, sweet and fresh from the earth, the smooth broad beans, the soft green peas, the pure green-edged-with-white of the crisp young lettuces. As far as Benedict was concerned, Mrs. Johnston was the best cook the world had ever known. And even when, in later life, he had eaten at the Mirabelle, he didn't really change his mind.

Milo had an older sister called Joanna, and a twin sister called Tessa. Neither daughter, unfortunately, had much natural beauty. Mr. Johnston's spectacular jug-ears had been heedlessly transmitted by the life-force to all his children. Joanna was a mysterious girl, who said very little, but was thought to be unusually clever at mathematics. Mr. Johnston planned to send her one day to London University. A very tall, leggy creature, she was naturally gifted at games, and was the best runner in the school. Because Johnston's already had so much athletic talent, she had been put in Parkinson's House. In her bedroom, so Milo reported, there were several dozen photographs of Cary Grant. She was quite uninterested in boys of her own age, and had accepted with amused contempt an invitation from Felix to go with him to Parkinson's Christmas party. Her acceptance had secretly delighted Felix: "I don't know what it is," he had confided to his friends, "but I can only take an interest in women older than myself." Joanna was some fifteen months his senior.

Tessa was quite different. She wore her hair in a page-boy cut and had an appealing gentleness. She seemed incapable of expressing an opinion or finishing a sentence. Benedict thought her a trifle boring, but luckily Kenneth Heppel had asked her to come with him. Milo himself had invited a round-faced little girl from London called Doreen Pepper. She was wildly unpopular with the other girls because of her relatively sophisticated London point of view and her precocity at languages. Even the boys found her snatches of French—"Quel ennui" and "Espèce de merde" were her two favourite expressions—a little overpowering.

All the Johnston children and their partners were at lunch that day, and so were Benedict and Constance. With Mr. and Mrs. Johnston, that meant that there were ten people seated round the long farmhouse table in the kitchen. This seemed positively to inspire Mrs. Johnston; Benedict always remembered the huge dish of steak and kidney pudding she made for them that day, and the blackberry tart which Tessa had made, and the sarcasm which Milo had levelled at it, pretending that he was unaware of the tart's authorship.

"Good Lord, Mum," he said after the first mouthful. "This tart is a bit heavy, isn't it? Not like yours at all."

"Don't be so unkind, Milo," said his Mother. "You know perfectly well that Tess made it."

"I certainly didn't," cried Milo, "or I'd have had some of the apple dumplings instead."

Tessa blushed and looked as if she might cry.

"You do talk rot, Milo," Benedict put in. "It's the most delicious tart I've ever tasted."

"Trust Benny," said Felix sarcastically, "gallant as always."

"Strangely enough," said Kenneth, "I'm sure he means it."

"Of course I mean it," Benedict said indignantly.

"You mean to say," asked Milo incredulously, "that as a matter of scientific fact, it's the best tart you've ever tasted in your life?"

"Certainly."

"Benny, you see," said Constance, "is a special kind of maniac. What he wants to believe, his senses make him believe."

"A psycho-somatic," put in Mr. Johnston.

"Oh, is that what he is?" said Felix with mild interest. "I always knew he was a screwball."

"I think Benny was just being polite," said Mrs. Johnston.

"A virtue we don't hear too much about in this day and age," added her husband.

"I wasn't being polite," Benny insisted with some heat. "I mean it as a cold, sober fact."

"You may take it as a cold sober fact," Joanna Johnston echoed sardonically to her younger sister, "that your tart is the finest Benny has yet tasted in his journey through this vale of tears."

"Quel espèce de bavard," interposed Doreen Pepper. The others looked at her with distaste.

Tess had not spoken. She still seemed on the brink of tears. Instinctively Benedict reached across and put his hand on hers. "Don't you worry what they say, Tess," he reassured her. "I'll still maintain it's so till my dying day."

The table rocked with laughter. Benedict blushed and bowed his head quickly, concentrating with unnatural ferocity on the disputed tart. Then Tessa really did cry. She jumped up from the table and ran out of the room. Benedict half rose in his chair to go after her, but Mrs. Johnston motioned him to sit down. "I'll go," she said.

"God, what a milksop I have for a sister," grieved Milo. "Can't even take a little honest criticism."

"One day," said his father, "you'll discover that it's very hard to take."

"But I take it every day," expostulated Milo. "From you, from my friends. . . ."

"But never," said his father, "about anything which has meant the slightest heart-ache to you. You've never done anything that meant as much to you as that tart did to Tess."

"Good Lord, Daddy," said Joanna. "What nonsense you do talk! Such a fuss about such a little thing!"

"Not such a little thing," her father insisted. "The great proportion of mankind are concerned with things as small. The luxury of leisure for abstract thought is the prerogative of only a fraction of one per cent of those who live on the earth's crust."

Benedict looked at him with new interest. He had never quite understood what Mr. Johnston remained in Aylsbourn for. He had got a first in physics at London; he could have gone into research or industry; why had he buried himself in this somnolent Hampshire backwater? There was nothing in his outward appearance to explain it; he was a gangling, skinny man with a round head perched on the end of a long neck. The remarkable jug-ears lent him the curious appearance of a human water-pitcher. He wore old sports jackets with leather patches in the sleeves and corduroy trousers. There was no doubt though in Benedict's mind that he was an *intellectual*. That, for Benedict, excused almost everything.

Tessa and her mother came back into the room.

"I'm sorry, everybody," Tessa said.

"We're the ones who should be sorry," corrected Kenneth. His responsibility as her partner at the party later that afternoon had dawned on him rather late in the day.

"Yes," said Milo. "I'm sorry I ever tasted your confounded tart."

"It was all a storm in a teacup," said Mrs. Johnston comfortingly. "Really we should be ashamed of ourselves. After all, we've all got so much to be grateful for."

Yes, thought Benedict looking round the room, she's right. Shall we ever be so happy again? He let his gaze slide slowly round the room. All his friends were here: Kenneth Heppel the tough boy from the poor side of town, Milo Johnston the thinking machine, Felix the precocious man of the world: his closest friends. And although the only girl who would ever matter in his life was not there, well, he would see her later in the day, and in the meantime it was comforting to have the proud and cynical Constance sitting next to him: so close indeed that their legs seemed to touch under the table; and the odd thing was, Constance didn't move her leg away. Come to think of it, they'd been sitting like that for ten minutes. But Constance showed no sign of concern or indeed excitement; she ate her blackcurrant tart with nonchalance. That, thought Benedict to himself, is what biology must do for you. However, he didn't move his leg either.

And now, at last, it was time for the Christmas party. They walked down from the Johnston's house to the school in the early December twilight; Constance had a scarf over her head, Benny always remembered, and she wore a cherry red coat over her party dress; and as they walked along he remembered her saying how idiotic such parties were: "You know, Benny," she said, "while we are bursting balloons people will be dying."

"Where?"

"In the war, you moron."

"But there's precious little war going on."

"Oh, but there will be, Benny. You'll see."

"Do you think we'll win, Constance?"

"No."

"No?"

"That's what I think. We're so hopeless. We're so amateur. We only just won last time, didn't we? And we haven't got America this time. Look what Hitler has done in Poland. Did you read what happened to Warsaw?"

"Yes, but they were stabbed in the back by the Russians."

"Who's to say that's the end of the Russians in this war?"

"You mean they might try to carve us up too?"

"I don't know. But I should like to know what Felix's father feels about Russia now."

"I don't think he takes the pact very seriously. If doing a deal with the Germans will help communism, then it must be done. The end always justifies the means."

They walked a few yards more in silence. Then Benedict said: "What do you think will happen to us if we lose the war?"

"You'll be shot," said Constance with what sounded suspiciously like relish. "And I will become the mistress of a lieutenant-colonel in the SS."

"Will you mind that?"

"Not as much as you'll mind being shot."

They were at the gates of the school. Members of Johnston's House were arriving in little knots, gossiping, laughing. Benedict felt the communicated excitement in the air. Perhaps they were doomed; if so, all the more reason to be happy while they could!

The tables were already laid for tea, with small white cards at each place. Benny and Constance found themselves at the head table. The other names, he saw with a catch at the heart, were Mr. Johnston himself and Miss Dindale, Tony Hammond and Laura.

The room began to fill up. There was a pleased buzz of anticipation as each couple worked out where they were to sit. Mr. Johnston and Miss Dindale threaded their way through the tables to their place. Miss Dindale shone with enthusiasm and what appeared to be Lifebuoy soap. Mr. Johnston, now that he had changed into a suit, looked almost respectable. He greeted Benedict, though they had only just been together, with kindness. "I thought you'd like to sit at my table, Benny," he said, "as this is your very first term with us."

The minutes passed. "Trust Tony Hammond," said Mr. Johnston good-naturedly, "Late as ever."

"Oh but he has other virtues," said Miss Dindale rather dashingly. She had a soft spot for Hammond too.

"Ah," said Benedict, "here they are."

Hammond and Laura stood in the doorway, looking for their table. He was wearing his characteristically off-hand clothes—a pair of corduroy trousers, a red shirt, an old cable-stitch fisherman's sweater, suède shoes. Laura, as if in sympathy, wore a black sweater and red check skirt. She still wore her Alice band and her honey-coloured hair was as usual combed down to her shoulders. By Aylsbourn standards they looked pretty avant-garde. Mr. Johnston waved, Laura saw him and touched Hammond's arm. Then they both smiled and began to make their way across the room. They made a pleasing pair.

"Here come the young Marxists," said Constance.

"Who isn't a Marxist these days?" Benedict said, half to himself. He couldn't take his eyes off Laura.

Tony Hammond was in a genial frame of mind. "Good afternoon, sir," he said to Mr. Johnston, squeezing his shoulder amiably before sitting down. What splendid arrogance! thought Benedict. Arrogance had become a key-word in his vocabulary. "Hello, Benny," he added, swinging into the seat beside him. "Mind if I sit here?"

"Not a bit, Hammond." They had spoken only two or three times altogether—imagine Hammond remembering his name!

"And I'll sit on Benny's other side," said Laura.

He could hardly believe his good luck. Now, for the first time, since that terrible day in the surgery, he would have a chance to talk to her.

"What have you got for us today, sir?" Hammond asked politely.

"We've a couple of one act plays, then a few carols, then tea, and then dancing."

"Quite a programme. Who's doing the plays?"

"Oh, it's the Cressbrook Gang."

The Cressbrook Gang was an institution at Aylsbourn. The river meandered some twenty-five miles down the valley before debouching into the Southampton Estuary. Along its banks there were one or two scattered villages which were almost unbelievably secluded from the twentieth century. Often for days on end they would be cut off altogether by floods or snow. The people who lived in the Cressbrook villages tended to be dark and volatile; so much so that one local historian had even advanced the theory that they were still pure Celts. They were a clannish and talented people : musical, eloquent and extrovert. The Cressbrook children came up to Aylsbourn each morning on a branch line, and stuck very much to each other. One of the Cressbrook Gang, a very poor boy called Aelfric Gates (and where the devil, Benedict used to think, had he got *that* name from, if there was nothing in the Celtic theory?) was thought to be potentially the most brilliant in the school. Though he was only a few months older than Benedict, he already understood differential calculus. He had written and was producing the two short plays. As the lights went down, Benedict leaned back with a sigh of sheer content.

Aelfric Gates certainly knew his stuff. Both plays were a riot. Benedict rocked with laughter at a most palpable imitation of Milo's father. When the lights went up even Mr. Johnston was wiping his eyes. "Well," he said philosophically, "it's a sort of fame."

Next Miss Dindale went to the piano and they plunged with whole-hearted pleasure into the carols. Benny sang with gusto, and was pleased to notice that Tony Hammond and Laura both sang too. Hammond supplied a bass melody while Laura had a light, pleasing contralto voice.

At last it was time for tea. "My goodness," said Mr. Johnston, "that was thirsty work!"

"Not so thirsty as playing a trumpet," said Hammond.

"Tell me about this jazz," said Miss Dindale. "Is it just a passing phase? Or is it here to stay?"

"Miss Dindale," said Hammond with mock seriousness. "Once

we've had you out there swinging on the floor you'll never look back. You'll *know* that jazz is here to stay."

"Are there any special steps you have to learn?"

"You can do a quickstep to it. But there's a new sort of dancing just beginning in America. It's called the jitterbug. Rather a vulgar title I'm afraid—they'll think of something neater soon— and this new dancing goes perfectly with jazz. It's quick, intricate, elegant—a kind of galvanized gavotte."

"Can you do it?" enquired Constance.

"Yes," said Laura. "Tony and I can do it. We can show you when the dancing starts." Then to Miss Dindale. "If you have no objection."

"Good heavens, no," said Miss Dindale. "I'm fascinated. But have we got any suitable records?"

"Yes," said Benny. "I've brought a lot of Felix Weston's. They don't have any dancing at Parkinson's party."

"Good gracious," said Miss Dindale. "Then how do they pass the time?"

"Oh," said Constance, "a lot of adolescent games. You know."

Laura suddenly turned to Benedict. "Well, Benny," she said with affection and mischief in her voice. "And how's that poor old eye? I've never seen a sight like it in all my years as my father's unpaid nurse. You know, I felt quite faint myself."

"Well you certainly didn't show it." But Benedict's voice sounded unreal to him—thick and high in his throat. He was talking—at last—to Laura!

"Yes," said Hammond with sudden interest, "that reminds me. Benny, I've watched you play a couple of times this term and I'd like you to come and practise with the School Colts next term."

Benedict could hardly believe his ears. The Aylsbourn Colts! This was success beyond his most extravagant dreams.

"Now there's something else I just don't understand," complained Miss Dindale. "Can anyone explain the point of this rugby football to me?"

"Yes," said Laura, "I can. It's one of the biggest kicks I know in life, watching the boys play. That, and jazz."

"Is it?" Miss Dindale looked a little taken back by this frank revelation. "Do you often watch, Laura?"

"I never miss watching Tony play," Laura said simply. But

she was not looking at Hammond; she seemed to be staring into the middle distance.

"We're not just thugs you know, Miss Dindale," said Mr. Johnston. "Benedict is an Aldous Huxley fan, so I hear."

"*Are* you now?" said Hammond with new interest. "What have you read, Benny?"

"Oh," said Benny, embarrassed, "not much I'm afraid. Things like *Those Barren Leaves* and *Eyeless in Gaza.*"

"Haven't you read *Brave New World* yet?"

"I'm afraid not."

"Then I must lend you my copy. It's one of the great books of the twentieth century. And what about *Point Counter Point*?"

"Afraid not."

"You shall have that too."

"Aren't you," asked Laura with mock concern, "putting rather advanced ideas into young Benny's head?"

"Impossible," said Constance, "Benny will never be a cynic. He is a romantic."

"And what," asked Mr. Johnston, "do you mean exactly by that? I mean, is he a romantic in the purely literary sense—or does this romanticism permeate his everyday life?"

"In every sense," said Constance with a trace of contempt.

"Only in the sense," Benny heard himself saying, "that I believe in love."

Laura and Hammond exchanged a glance. Then Laura smiled at him. "Benny," she said, "there's more to you than meets the eye."

"There's more to all of us than meets the eye."

"Leave him alone," said Hammond. He was interested. "What about Evelyn Waugh, Benny? Read any?"

"Sorry, no."

"Oh. Then you must have my copy of *Decline and Fall*. You haven't lived till you've read that. What about Hemingway?"

"Sorry. . . ."

"He's an American writer. Superb. You must read *Death in the Afternoon* and *The Sun Also Rises*. Here"—he took out his diary—"I'll make a note to look them out for you."

"That's awfully kind, Hammond."

He studied Hammond surreptitiously as they talked. He had

never been quite so close; now he could analyse his appearance in some detail.

It was a curiously wedge-shaped face; very strong, with a sharply defined cleft in the chin. The eyes were a mild bluish-grey; his hair the colour of straw and very thick. He wore a pair of heavy horn-rimmed glasses with thick lenses; he was known to be as blind as a bat without them. He had a pleasing, if slightly derisive, smile. His voice was deep and musical. There was a scar across the bridge of his nose from an old football injury. He talked in a natural and relaxed manner, which did not change whether he was in conversation with Mr. Johnston or Benedict or indeed Laura. There was nothing gallant about him; he didn't go out of the way to pay compliments. He was a trifle under six feet tall, but very slim in the waist. The most surprising thing about him were his hands. They were rather terrifyingly big; square and very strong.

To Benedict, Hammond was the epitome of the complete man. He had played stand-off half for the Hampshire Colts, and was quite certain, Benedict thought, to win an Open Scholarship to Cambridge. He read authors like Huxley and Hemingway, and had written three, to Benedict, exquisite short stories about the Spanish Civil War, which had been published in the *Cressbrook Review*, a highbrow Hampshire magazine. He had had a poem published in the *Poetry Quarterly*. He played a swinging jazz trumpet. Over and above all these things, though, he had won the love of Laura.

By shifting his position slightly, and pretending to be engrossed in the conversation, Benedict could study Laura too. It was her green eyes, he decided, that were the most riveting thing about her; he had never seen anything quite so startling. Her skin too was striking in its paleness; she looked as if she might be Scandinavian.

Her hands—the hands he remembered so well—were small and the nails neatly kept; squarely cut without fuss or adornment. She still wore the thin gold bangles she had worn in church the day war began. Her wrists were almost touchingly thin. She listened a good deal and laughed quite a lot. Her favourite expression, he noticed, was "Gee *whiz*!" with all the emphasis, used ironically, on the whiz.

"Now for the dance!" decided Mr. Johnston. Quickly the

chairs and tables were stacked and soon they were launched into a set of old-fashioned dances, beginning with the Sir Roger de Coverley. Benedict trembled with anticipatory pleasure each time it was his turn to link arms with Laura. She danced so deftly that those moments passed all too soon.

When they had tired of traditional dancing, Mr. Johnston decided they could play some quicksteps. The school radiogram bounced out the naïve melody of "Dinah", and the young couples launched themselves tentatively on to the floor. Benny found himself opposite Constance. They smiled at each other, remembering their travail in the library in preparation for this moment.

"Come along, Benny," said Constance. "And don't forget what I told you about the gramophone record."

In a moment they were moving round the floor, looking quite expert against some of the others.

"Look at Hammond and Laura," said Constance. "It will interest you."

Benedict glanced round and saw that Laura had one arm twined affectionately round Tony Hammond's neck. She was not behaving in quite the uninhibited way she had at the Margrave dance; still it was, to Benedict, a novel spatial relationship.

"That," said the knowledgeable Constance, "is called the college clutch."

"It looks quite fun."

"You think so? Let me try it on you.'

Benedict was horrified. "Don't be so outrageous, Constance. People might see us."

"They can see Laura."

"Yes. But she——"

It was too late. Constance was bent on experimenting with the college clutch and he was part of the essential apparatus for the experiment. To his surprise, he found himself enjoying it. His sense of decorum soon ceased to trouble him.

"You know, Constance," he said, "I've never met a girl quite like you before."

"I bet you say that to all the girls."

"I've never talked to any other girl. Except Arabella Weston."

"I expect she told you a thing or two."

"She certainly did. You know she said a most extraordinary thing."

"What?"

"Well, I really can't repeat it here. It will interest you though. As a biologist, I mean."

"I can hardly wait to hear."

"Oh look, Constance. That must be the jitterbug."

Tony Hammond and Laura were jiving with relaxed elegance in the centre of the floor. They looked insouciant and beautiful. Benedict and Constance stopped to watch.

"You know," said Benedict, "it must be marvellous to be in love like that."

"They're not in love," said Constance definitely.

"How on earth do you know?"

"I know."

"Well, how on earth . . . ?"

"Don't be tiresome, Benny. I'll tell you why some other time. When you tell me what Arabella said."

"I don't know if I could repeat——"

"Benny, some day a woman will have to take you in hand."

"Perhaps you."

"No. It won't be me."

"How can you be so sure?"

"It's a question of chemistry. Valencies and all that stuff. You're too nice to appeal to me."

"I suppose it's no secret to you that——"

"You dote on Laura? No secret at all."

Benny swallowed. "Do you think it's obvious to other people?"

"No. You see I'm the only one who's bothered to make a proper study of you, Benny. You're a very interesting psychological specimen. In fact, one day, I shall probably win my Ph.D for a thesis on you. I can imagine it now: 'P. J. Benedict—A casebook in romantic psychopathology.' "

"I shall be pretty flattered. I mean, it's my only chance to become famous."

"Nonsense, Benny! People who are as nuts as you generally end up in the headlines."

"You think I'm nuts too?"

"No. I think society is nuts."

A few minutes later, Mr. Johnston called for silence. "Before we conclude tonight's most enjoyable party," he said, "I'm going to call, by general consent, for a Ladies' Excuse Me."

Constance rose. "I shall be back, Benny," she said.

"Who are you going to ask?"

"Mr. Johnston. I'm ambitious, you see."

Benedict sat bemused. What an astonishing girl! And what on earth did she mean by saying that Laura and Tony weren't in love? If that wasn't love, then what in the name of heaven. . . .

He was disturbed by a shy voice. It was Tessa Johnston. "Benny," she said, "would you like . . . ? I mean. . . ."

"Tessa, I'd love to dance with you." To his shame he had forgotten all about her. She seemed to tremble slightly as he put his arm round her waist, but she followed very easily as he launched into his newly acquired steps.

"Thank you, Benny," she said, "for what you said today."

"I meant it, Tessa; truly I did."

"I know you did. That's why I shall never forget it."

In the summer of 1941

Old Macpherson retired. He had not been well for some time, and now his heart was showing definite signs of weariness. He was in any case sixty-seven and his normal retirement date had been postponed by the war. He told the school he was going without fuss on the last day of the summer term. No one could quite believe it. Macpherson and Aylsbourn had become interchangeable symbols. But he said he would continue to live in the town and he hoped they would all keep coming to see him. Then came even more startling news.

"You may well be wondering, boys and girls," he said carefully, "who is to take my place here. Our governors have gone into the matter very carefully, for as you know, they always have your welfare very much at heart. I think they have found you a new headmaster who will give you the very greatest intellectual stimulus." He paused. It was not easy for him. "Your new head, boys and girls, is to be Mr. Christopher Ilex."

There was an audible stir among the senior school. Ilex the poet, spokesman of the left and ardent educational reformer! Coming to Aylsbourn of all places!

"This," muttered Felix, "is my father's work."

Gerard Weston had been appointed a governor of the school

before his extreme political views had become well known locally. The fact was that, like all communists, he was extremely conscientious in public service, and had probably done more good than harm to the school over the years. But Ilex . . . this indeed was a *coup de théâtre* that Weston had engineered.

Ilex in 1941 was still only twenty-eight. The son of an Anglican bishop ("Always a bad start," as Felix remarked), he had had a remarkable academic career at Winchester and Oxford. He got a crashing first in history, won the Newdigate Prize, was President of OUDS, and had been offered a Fellowship. Just then the Spanish Civil War broke out and Ilex immediately went out to join the Republicans. He published a long volume of poetry which became a rallying-point for his generation, was badly wounded, returned to England in 1939, resigned from the communist party over Poland, though maintaining his Marxist views, worked in a publisher's for six months, then got a job as an assistant master at Eton. His second book of poetry had been published that spring and showed even greater achievement than the first. And now he was coming to Aylsbourn.

"You should be a happy man today, Benny," said Ken Heppel with affectionate irony. "Aylsbourn has acquired another intellectual."

"Maybe even Stephen Spender will come down to talk to us," Felix mocked him. Ilex was known to be friendly with the Auden/Isherwood/Spender/Warner axis.

"As long as he doesn't scrub science altogether," Milo Johnston said. Ilex was an ardent defender of the humanities.

"But what does he want to come *here* for?" Benny asked.

"That's obvious. Because he can be the boss. He couldn't treat a big public school quite so radically. But us! We're perfect material. Peasants' sons, noble savages; you can imagine how his dim idealistic mind works."

"Tell you something else," said Milo. "It'll be the first homosexual Aylsbourn has ever known."

"Well," said Felix, "*vive le sport*. Only you'd better watch out, Benny. Those liquid brown eyes of yours will probably appeal to him."

"Maybe," said Benedict absent-mindedly, "he'll write some poetry about Aylsbourn."

"I can just imagine it," said Ken Heppel. He thought hard,

screwing up his homely features in concentration. "It'll start:

'Enriched with Aylsbourn dung my peasant mind . . .
'Swings on its rusty hinges glory's gate.' "

"The trouble is," said Benedict, "that you're all secretly jealous. I can't help it if I have an ambivalent appeal, can I?"

This canard about Benedict was based on the slimmest possible evidence. He had that February received a Valentine card couched in clearly homosexual terms. Felix, however, was thought to be its anonymous author.

The scandal received powerful support when it was heard that Ilex was bringing with him Martin Hennessy, also a poet member of the new left. The word ran round that Hennessy was Ilex's boy-friend. Then the scandal-mongers had a set-back. It was discovered that Hennessy had just married a rich American woman, whom he had met during a research year at Princeton. It was said that she was old enough to be his mother, and was a close friend of Ezra Pound.

"You have to admit," Benedict told his friends, "that the old place is looking up."

Ilex's first public appearance was something of a disappointment. When he emerged from the common-room door into the Old Hall on the first day of the new term, he looked rather unimpressive. He was a small man, no more than five feet three, but he had a very large head, rather like a tadpole's. He wore a very well-cut dark grey worsted suit and sandals. When he spoke, however, his voice came as a shock. It was enormously deep and fruity and not in the slightest bit revolutionary. The girls looked at him with especial interest. "If he's what you say he is," said Constance later, "I think it's a cruel waste."

"I've already decided on my plans," said Joanna. "I'm going to seduce Martin Hennessy from that rich American wife of his."

"You'll never succeed," Tessa said firmly. "Anyone can see that he's incorruptible."

Incorruptible perhaps he was; but beyond a doubt he was inexhaustible. The first morning he was to teach them, he came bounding into the room in his dinner-jacket, stretching his arms over his head. "I've been up all night at a party in London," he told his mesmerized audience. "There was a perfectly ghastly air-raid, so we all moved down into the cellar. I went for a row on the Cressbrook at six a.m., then had some bacon and eggs at the 'Wheatsheaf', and now I'm bursting to do some Roman History with you. Anyone here ever read a book by Robert Graves called *I Claudius*? No. Well I'll start by telling you about that. . . ."

"You know," said Felix afterwards, "you sat through that as if you were in a trance."

"It's just," said Benedict, "that I've never seen anyone wear a red bow-tie with a dinner-jacket before."

"I've got a feeling," said Ken Heppel, "that we haven't seen anything yet."

One day in January 1942

Mr. Benedict received his call-up papers. He opened the official envelope at breakfast with evident excitement. Benny knew—or divined—what it contained and he was afraid. Why did his father have to go? He was getting on for fifty and he had more than done his bit in the last war. It would leave him entirely alone in the world. Something like panic seized him. Then the emotion passed away; he couldn't resist the pleasure so obviously written in his father's face. For Mr. Benedict, war meant life with the throttle wide open; he was never a hundred per cent alive in peacetime. And the Army was the best club he knew.

"It's a training battalion, Benny," he said excitedly. "Just the thing I wanted to do."

There had been an element of estrangement between them ever since that awful day when his father had heard about the scholarship. This made it seem all the more intolerably poignant to Benedict that his father should be leaving him now. It was all very well to talk of a training battalion; but just suppose his father were posted overseas and killed before he had had a chance to make it up! He felt the tears not far away. This was terrible; he couldn't disgrace his father further by crying in front of him.

"That's wonderful, Pop," he made himself say. "When do you go?"

"In four days. Not very long. But I've one nice surprise for you, Benny. I've arranged for you to go and live with Milo. His father and mother are both very fond of you, and they've agreed to look after you for the rest of the war. We'll keep the cottage on and of course you'll be able to come back here so that we can spend my leaves together. Keith Margrave is being very generous and making up my pay, so don't worry about the financial side. I'll pay Mr. Johnston for your keep."

"But they're such a large family already. . . ."

"You know how it is in life, Benny. To them that hath shall be given. There's nothing they like better than young people in the house. Won't you enjoy being there?"

"Oh yes of course—if you're quite sure——"

"You'll see, old chap. They'll love having you."

It'll be odd, thought Benedict, to live in a house where there are women again. It softened the thought of his father going more than he he would have thought possible.

One night in February 1942

Benedict was awakened from his sleep by a very gentle tapping on the wall. He had been living with the Johnstons for a month, and was happy in a way he had never known possible. The family, as his father had promised, had received him with open arms, and he relished all his life their long rambling discussions round the big kitchen table: what dress Tessa ought to buy, whether Joanna ought to go to Cambridge, what was wrong with Milo's football; religion, politics, gossip; it was all grist to their mill. He had an attic room at the top of the house, divided by only a thin plaster and lath partition from Tessa's room; they could—and did—talk to each other through it.

At first Benedict thought he was dreaming, but as he opened his eyes he heard the sound again—a very gentle but persistent knocking on the partition. He sat up.

"Is that you, Tess?"

"Yes. I—I'm sorry, Benny. I feel frightened. Can I come and talk to you?"

"Yes of course."

There was a full moon, the colour of Wensleydale, throwing its pallid light across his room. There was a little knock at his door and then Tessa came in. She was wearing an old red flannel dressing-gown over her striped pyjamas. Both had been handed down from her elder sister. Her hair was pulled back in a knot, emphasizing her large, saucer-like eyes, and odd little ears. She was trembling slightly.

"Oh, Benny, you must think me dreadful."

"Of course I don't, Tess. Come and sit down."

She sat on the edge of the bed.

"Now tell me what the trouble is."

"I shall feel such a fool in the morning. Suddenly the whole world seems terrifying. It's so—big and somehow indifferent to us."

"It is big—but you're one of the luckiest people in it. Very few girls in the world have the sort of family you've got—I mean so much security and fun and affection."

"I know. I know it sounds ungrateful but—well, they won't always be there. Won't it be terrible when we're on our own?"

"There'll be other people. After all, your father and mother didn't always have each other."

"I know I shan't ever be as happy as they are."

"That's a pretty sweeping statement. Why on earth shouldn't you be?"

"I seem to make such a mess of my life. You know Ken Heppel is very fond of me?"

"No, I hadn't realized."

"He's written me letters. One every day. They're so sweet. And I feel dreadful because I can't feel the same way about him."

"Don't worry about it, Tess. You're too young to feel like that about any boy."

"That's not true, Benny, you know that."

"Well, of course sometimes we *think* we feel. . . ."

"You're in love with Laura, aren't you?"

"How did you know that?"

"I know."

"I don't think we ought to use this word. It's such a big word, and we're so young to use it."

"But tell me truthfully, Benny, will you ever feel about any other girl the way you do about Laura?"

"I can't imagine it. No, I can't think what it would be like. You see, basically, Tess, I'm a one-girl sort of person. I'm very romantic. I put this one girl on a pedestal. . . ."

"Poor Laura!"

"Yes, but she doesn't know." A frightening possibility crossed his mind. "She *can't* know, can she?"

"I don't think so, Benny. I think she's far too wrapped up with Tony Hammond to notice anyone else."

116

"That's the funny thing, you see. I'm happy for her to be with him. It seems so right for them both. Don't you agree?"

"Of course I admire him. But I couldn't feel about him the way Laura does."

"Tell me, as a girl, do you find Laura beautiful?"

"Of course I do. She's the most beautiful girl in Aylsbourn, everyone knows that."

"Do you remember when she fell off her horse and broke her arm? And then went out riding again when it was still in plaster? That's when she really looked superb. It was such an—an arrogant thing to do. It really seemed to knock all the breath out of me when I saw her ride up our lane that day, very straight, one arm in a sling, but still sort of—disdainfully in command, if you know what I mean."

"One thing about you, Benny—you do appreciate a girl."

"But isn't being alive so exciting that you've got to be crazy about it? That's how I feel. I get so excited sometimes I can hardly speak, and when I run my feet don't touch the ground."

"Aren't you ever afraid?"

"Of course I am."

"You never seem to be. I'm afraid most of the time."

"Whatever of?"

"Oh, everything. Of death, for instance."

"Well, everyone's a bit afraid of that, Tess."

"But not as much as I am."

"Have you ever read the *Life and Death of Socrates*?"

"No. You know I'm not very clever."

"You don't have to be clever to read that. It's beautifully simple writing. I think I've never felt really afraid since I read it."

"I don't think reading would help me, Benny. It's just a feeling in my case."

"Yes, I understand. Then the only answer to that is that you must have someone whose hand you can reach out and touch— not necessarily in the literal sense. That's why all our little jealousies and rivalries and pushing and struggling for power always strike me as so tragic. There's only one real enemy and that's death; just as there's only one great sin, and that is waste of life. We're all on the same side in this battle, and death plays a confidence trick on us when he pretends he's an ally."

"Will you be a conscientious objector?"

"I don't know."

"Ken will be. He's a complete pacifist. He says he won't take a life under any circumstances, whatever they do to him."

"You know, Tess, if you travel all over the earth you'll never find anyone who has more goodness than Kenneth."

"I realize that, and that's why I feel so dreadful that I can't return his love. Because that's what it is, isn't it?"

"Yes, I think it is. To tell you what I honestly feel, I think we can love now in a way we shall never be able to again."

"Then why don't older people understand? I mean, they'd think we were absolutely crazy if they could hear us."

"Perhaps they do understand. Perhaps they're just trying to protect us."

"But you said we only had each other."

"That's what I believe, Tess. Look, you have me, for example. I'll always be your friend."

"Will you, Benny?"

"I promise you. And you know I never break a promise."

"I believe you, Benny. I shall be able to go back to sleep now. But, please, never tell anyone I've been here will you? It sounds so—brazen."

"You, Tess? Never!"

"One day I might be."

"Tess, don't try to shock me!"

"Does it shock you?"

"Of course it does. You know I put all my girls on a pedestal."

"But you said you were a one-girl man."

"I can't always live in a dream, Tess. Perhaps it's just as well that the ideal thing should always be out of reach. I'll have to find another girl one day, a real flesh-and-blood one, not a dream-girl like Laura."

"I hope you do, Benny."

"And you'll find somebody too, I know you will. Then you won't be afraid any more."

"I'm not afraid now."

"That's good. I'll see you in the morning."

"And when we meet at breakfast. . . ."

"No one will ever know, I give you my promise."

"I believe you, Benny."

118

Christopher Ilex lost no time in stamping his personality on the school. Felix reported that Ilex had confided his secret ambition to his father: it was to take an ordinary grammar school and, with the ordinary material available, by sheer dint of personality make it so good that parents would actually hesitate between sending their sons there or to one of the big public schools. Soon distinguished poets, actors, writers were staying in the school house, organizing concerts, speaking, lecturing, arguing, debating. It was intoxicating: but there was something hothouse about it. "I sometimes get the impression," grumbled Milo, "that we're just his bloody guinea-pigs."

However, everybody began to respond. Ilex had so much energy and so much fire in his own teaching that it was hard not to catch his enthusiasm. He gave them a series of lectures on Greece and another on modern architecture; he formed a small dining club from the senior school and actually got a cabinet minister down to it that first winter as well as an air marshal, a trade union leader and the head of an Oxford college. The squeeze was on: Aylsbourn was going to get its name into the Open Scholarship list or bust.

Ilex also showed an unexpected interest in sport. He was sufficient of a realist to know that athletic achievement still counted in England and he was determined therefore that Aylsbourn should triumph in sport too. Martin Hennessy had played wing forward for Cambridge and he was put in charge of the school fifteen. Four nights of the week they went out running and this secretly to Benedict was one of the sharpest pleasures life could afford. There was the long trot through the thick November leaves down to Welcaster pond, with the air coming into his lungs in great rasping gulps that seemed to make him drunk; then the long climb up Cromwell ridge with the calves aching and the ribs tightening; then the glorious run along the top of the Downs, with all Aylsbourn lying in soft silhouette beneath; then the final agonizing sprint down the Brewery Hill and into the school's hot baths. All the four friends played for Aylsbourn: Felix and Ken affected to despise the game, Milo and Benny openly loved it. Milo, in fact, was already playing full back for the school; with his dangling arms and meat-plate hands he was a natural for the job. "Besides," as Felix pointed out, "it doesn't matter how much he gets kicked in the face. It can't get any worse than it is."

This was Tony Hammond's last season; he had been playing for the school for four years now and he would soon be nineteen. He had only one remaining ambition: to trounce Shallerton before he went. The trouble was to persuade them to play; when Hammond had written challenging them to a game they had sent an offensive note back offering to send their second fifteen. Ilex quickly changed all that. He and Ross-Tayfield belonged to the same London club, and one telephone call quickly clinched the matter. Shallerton said they had of course a full fixture list, but, seeing that Ilex was now in charge, they would be glad to send over their first fifteen for a trial of strength on the first Saturday in December.

This was Tony Hammond's great challenge. It seemed to matter more to him than even his newly-won place at Cambridge. He soon became fast friends with Martin Hennessy and together they trained the school relentlessly evening after evening.

Hammond had always played stand-off half himself; he was a thrusting, ruthless player and Benedict could make himself almost sick with excitement to see Hammond carve his way through an opposing pack, leaving them sprawled on the grass like a row of ninepins. But now Hammond had a better idea. He brought Ken and Benny up from the second fifteen as a pair of halves. Ken was a natural scrum-half ("It's his working class background," Felix used to say. "He's used to being trodden on.") and he and Benny had developed a remarkable understanding. Kenneth would sling the ball out time after time without so much as a glance behind, and somehow Benny always managed to be there to scoop it up. They played mock games at enormous pressure, stopping every quarter of an hour for a breather and a talk. Hennessy played too; Benny felt a faint sense of lèse-majesté the first time he brought him down, but Hennessy didn't seem to mind. They all grew hard and fit, keyed and tuned to a pitch they had never before experienced. The tension as the fateful Saturday grew nearer set their teeth on edge.

Even the girls caught the sense of excitement. Tessa became an expert with the embrocation bottle; even her brother thought she might find her life's work as a masseuse. With her gentle hands she had an instinctive knack for easing all the bruises and aches out of them. Joanna, an instinctive athlete, probably understood what they were trying to achieve best; night after night they used to sit round the fire planning their tactics and drawing diagrams. Sometimes Hammond himself would join them; then, when they grew tired of football, they would all sit round the big kitchen table and the talk would go on into the small hours. Hammond talked of the books he was reading, of the Cambridge college to which he was going next autumn, of jazz, of his hopes and plans for the future. (He had swung round completely in the previous two years about the war; and now he badly wanted to fight. But his eyesight was hopeless, and he was turned down on medical grounds.)

Constance claimed to hate all violent sports; but she said she would come to the game to see what it was they all got so excited about. All the Mackays were coming and Felix's parents, and Sir Keith Margrave would be there for sure.

On the great Saturday the Shallerton coach rolled through the school gates and Benedict felt his nerves contract in the pit of the stomach as they got out. They wore chocolate and cream jerseys and looked thoroughly bored.

Hammond went up to meet their captain, Gervase-Jones. He was a very dark, offensive young man of eighteen, with black wavy hair and thick lips, who tried hard not to look as if the whole outing was a most appalling chore. He knew Hammond; they had played for the Hampshire Colts together many times. Hammond disliked him cordially.

"So this is your little place," Gervase-Jones began with monumental diplomacy. "Amazing what you can get for nothing these days, isn't it?"

When Shallerton came out on to the Margrave Brewery ground they faced a wall of hate you could almost reach out and touch. Benny looked round and felt a quick stab of simple happiness to see all the people he loved best lined up together for the fight: Milo, at full back, looked almost comically grim, but Benny knew that no one from Shallerton could get by him while he remained on his feet; Ken Heppel, small, bouncing and tough, like a rubber ball, was just in front of him; Hammond was on his right, his curious wedge-shaped face serious but very calm; Felix out on the wing, lean, very fast and nonchalant and somehow extremely comforting; Aelfric Gates out on the other wing, pawing the ground like a long, delicate hare. These were his friends and his people, and those bastards from Shallerton would cross their line over his dead body.

It was a perfectly crisp late autumn day and the air was absolutely still; chimney-smoke rose straight into a Gillette-blue sky and the grass had a deliciously rough spring in it. The last thing Benny remembered clearly before Gervase-Jones kicked off was Laura standing on the touchline, her hands deep in the pockets of her coat and he bit his knuckles to restrain his joy.

It was a perfect kick; the ball climbed slowly up into the crisp air, turning lazily over and over then plummeting down into Hammond's safe hands. He swung the ball out clean and true to Felix, who dropped it. They scrummed and Shallerton got it out. Gervase-Jones gave it a mighty punt and with an upper-class cry of "Follow up, School", headed at full speed for the point where Milo was waiting to receive it. The three met at the same spot together and went down in a heap. Only Gervase-Jones got up. Milo lay where he was. Only one leg rose and fell to show he was conscious.

Hammond turned him over. Milo's ugly battered face was pumice coloured. It did not take long to diagnose the trouble. "I'm afraid, old chap," said Hammond, "that you've bust a collar-bone."

They carried Milo off and Hammond dropped back to take his place. In the next forward rush he went down on the ball in the absolutely lion-hearted way he always did, and was kicked very hard on the head. He lay on the grass, still, with the un-troubled expression of death on his strong face. It took him half a minute to come round and Dr. Mackay ordered him to be taken off. "No more football for him today," he said firmly. After that it was a shambles. Shallerton won by forty-four points to nil, and at tea afterwards Gervase-Jones talked quite openly about cancelling the return game.

The day of the second great game

After that Hammond lived for nothing else but the return game. He had willing allies. Even Felix had taken the strongest exception to Gervase-Jones. The contest between the two schools had in it the hard bitterness of class war. They drove themselves remorselessly all through the next three months. Ilex himself referred to the return game the day before it was due to be played. "As you know," he told them, "we had appallingly bad luck last time with accidents. But Johnston, I'm glad to say, is absolutely fit again, and Hammond is none the worse for wear. I shall be present myself tomorrow and I expect every single person in this school to be there too." He looked down the serried rows and repeated carefully: "Everybody."

When they got over to Shallerton their hearts sank. It was a big, ugly Victorian building, but imposing, and all their five hundred boys were there to see the slaughter. The Aylsbourn supporters—boys and girls—stood along the other side and Benny couldn't help thinking how much more decorative they looked.

They kicked off into a cold wind and for the first half they were seldom out of their own twenty-five. It was desperate defence; tackle, loose scrum, kick for touch, line-out, tight scrum and then the same again. Every time Hammond fell on the ball Benny's heart was in his mouth. But though he was kicked black and blue he somehow stayed on his feet. He lent them all a super-addition of courage.

As the minutes passed Benedict felt his spirits rising. The truth was, man for man, fifteen men for fifteen men, they were as good as Shallerton; neither side could make an impression. And it might be that the Shallerton men would tire first.

As they sucked their crescents of orange greedily at half-time Hammond grinned at them. "You lovely bastards," he said. "You know something? Today we're going to win."

Gervase-Jones kicked off for the second half and the roar from the crowd took on the ugly baying sound which the audience at a big fight make when they want to see a kill: a high fluting noise like a wind in tall trees. Only a minute later came the chance Aylsbourn had been waiting for; Ken Heppel got out a very hard clean straight one to Benny who took it at full tilt, then had the absolute satisfaction of handing off Gervase-Jones with a thump that might have been heard a mile away. The ball went down the three-quarter line like a hot potato to Aelfric Gates. He made for the right corner with the entire Shallerton pack after him, then just as it seemed he must go down, Hammond whipped across behind him, at an angle of ninety degrees, snapping up the ball in a beautiful scissors movement that they had practised a thousand times. Felix was coming down the blind side sly and jet-quick and he took the ball from Hammond absolutely flat out; and nothing, Benny was sure, on God's earth could have stopped him then. He streaked over the Shallerton line, but not satisfied with that, cut into the centre and put the ball down right between their goal posts, ending up with four men on top of him and all the wind knocked out of his body. But the shout of pure joy from the Aylsbourn line made it all worth while. Hammond converted and Shallerton came back as if berserk. But it was no good now; Aylsbourn were not going to give an inch. Hardly one of them escaped without some sort of injury, but when the final whistle went their line was still unviolated.

The Shallerton boys were quite nice afterwards. They showed their guests round the school, which now seemed even more ugly and cold than before and stank of carbolic soap. On the way home in the school bus they sang their hearts out.

When they got to Aylsbourn High Street and the bus had stopped, Ilex got up and announced: "Gentlemen, I am proud of you. It has been one of the happiest days in my life."

"Do you know," said Felix later in disbelief, "old Ilex was actually blubbing when he said that? I was right next to him and as he sat down he took out his red silk handkerchief and wiped his eyes."

One day in late February 1942
—he could never think which, he was going up to Shallerton in the train, and he had forgotten why he was on his own. He had wandered on to the platform and saw that Hammond and Laura were already there. Hammond was wearing a dark lounge suit and looked as if he might be going to a party. She on the other hand, was rather casually dressed in a sweater and skirt. It was a mild morning, with just a hint of spring in the air. He tried to avoid them, but they both saw him and looked pleased.

"Hello, Benny," called Hammond. "Are you coming to Shallerton with us?"

"Well—I was going. But I don't want to inter——"

"Nonsense. We'd like you to come with us. Wouldn't we?"

Laura nodded. They both looked relaxed and happy, yet somehow—conspiratorial.

They got into a third-class coach. "What are you going for, Benny?" Hammond asked.

"Oh, just to get some books."

"Very sensible. There's a much better selection up there. Laura's going shopping; why don't you go together?"

Benedict could hardly believe his ears. "But what about you, Hammond? Aren't you——?"

"I'm visiting some friends. We're only travelling on the train together, aren't we?"

Laura nodded seriously. "Do keep me company, Benny," she said.

Benedict swallowed back his astonishment. Here was a thing! He looked from one to the other. No, there was definitely more in this than met the eye. But what? It was utterly baffling. Perhaps they wanted people not to know they were together. But if so, why *set off* from Aylsbourn and then part company at Shallerton? It didn't make sense.

Hammond talked easily all the way to Shallerton. He seemed to bubble with high spirits. He had got a place at Cambridge for September, he had defeated Gervase-Jones; ahead of him lay one more carefree term's cricket and perhaps a trial for Hampshire. He had received an encouraging letter from the Editor of *Penguin New Writing*. Everything was coming easily to him. Benedict studied the strong, wedge-shaped face with awe; there was no limit to what Hammond might achieve. He might even be Prime Minister one day! After the war there might be a communist government. Or he might be the Auden of the nineteen-fifties, or England's answer to Hemingway. . . .

Laura listened. But now that he watched her intently she seemed not to be listening properly. Her thoughts were miles away. Where?

Outside Shallerton station Hammond waved them a cheerful goodbye and made off with long energetic strides up the Castle Hill. They watched him disappear. Then Laura turned to Benedict. She looked at him for a moment as if she had only just realized he was there.

"Well, Benny," she said, "let's go shopping."

"Where do you want to go, Laura?"

She gave a little shrug. "Oh, I only wanted some stockings. We can get those anywhere."

Then why come to Shallerton for them, thought Benedict.

They spent a blissful hour together buying books, and then they went to buy her stockings, and there was still time for them to catch the 12.57 back to Aylsbourn. Laura said nothing all the way home. She sat in a corner and stared out at the hedges and fields racing by the window. And as he watched her beautiful face a sudden thought came to Benedict: maybe Constance is right after all. Maybe they aren't in love. But if they're not . . .

He turned the problem over often in his mind after that; but there was no solution.

One day in April 1942

Benedict was sitting reading a book in front of the kitchen fire. He had a bad cold, and Mrs. Johnston had told him to stay in for the day. The family had gone out; it was a perfect spring day and Mr. Johnston had taken them all for a drive to visit relatives at Winchester. Joanna, however, had asked to be excused.

She came into the kitchen and sat down in the rocking chair. "Hello, Benny," she said.

He glanced up. "Hello, Joanna. Didn't you want to go with the others?"

"No. I feel—rather upset."

Benedict put down his book with new interest. Joanna was usually such a withdrawn girl—she must have something important on her mind.

"Whatever is the trouble, Joanna? It takes a lot to upset you."

"I discovered today that Tony Hammond is leaving."

"Yes, that's right—at the end of the summer term. An alarming thought crossed his mind. "What; not *now* . . . ?"

"Right now. To tell you the truth, he's been given the push."

"*What?*"

"Ilex has told him to go. He's going to take a temporary job in London until September."

"But whatever for? I mean he's the most brilliant chap we've ever had. . . ."

"I don't know. It's a scandal of some sort. It may even be political. Your guess is as good as mine."

"Is it——?"

"No." Joanna shook her head and permitted herself a little smile. "No, it's not your beloved Laura. I'm sure of that."

"How do you know?"

"I heard Daddy talking on the telephone. I couldn't help it—I picked up the extension upstairs when he was in the middle of a telephone conversation with Ilex. He realized I'd heard them talking and made me promise not to tell a soul."

"Then . . ."

"Why am I telling you? Because I must tell somebody. You see I was rather fond of him myself."

"Well we all were. But how do you know Laura wasn't involved?"

"Because I asked Daddy. He looked rather embarrassed and said it was nothing like that at all. I know he wouldn't lie to me."

"Then what on earth can it be?"

"I haven't the slightest idea. He left this morning, so we can't ask him. All I know is that he's gone. Perhaps"—and there was a sadness and loss in her voice that Benedict never forgot—"we shall never see him again."

In early September 1942

Milo went up to Cambridge to try his hand at a scholarship paper. He was not yet seventeen and there was really no chance of his winning anything for another year; still, Ilex wanted him to have the experience. His three friends took him to the station and put him on the train.

"And don't forget," Benedict shouted as the train drew out, "to write and tell us how it's going." Milo was the first of them to try his strength in the outside world.

Milo beamed out of the window. "You'll get the first gripping instalment tomorrow," he assured them.

Nothing, however, appeared in the next morning's post; nor Wednesday's. On Thursday, however, Benedict came down in the morning to find a letter in mauve ink and in Milo's familiar flowing hand awaiting him. It was his usual inimitable style:

Dear Chums:

As it is my custom to commence with the most important items, I'll give you a list of what I've eaten to date. I arrived at Cambridge station and reached Trinity College at about 3.20.

I was shown my rooms and mooched about until dinner came up at 7-0 p.m. We all sat down in a huge hall very much like Westminster Abbey and numerous waiters passed round: (1) tomato soup (2) stewed meat (assorted) and dumplings, potatoes and parsnips. Coffee cream followed.

For breakfast this morning we had porridge, fish, toast, butter, jam, coffee, plenty of sugar etc. For "luncheon" at 12.15:— Bacon and eggs on toast, with potatoes and leeks, followed by chocolate cream and wafers. (Of course new bread and water are always present.) For dinner tonight:— oxtail soup, roast beef, Yorkshire pudding, roast spuds, and spinach, suet pudding etc.

All the waiters are in evening dress at dinner but wear shoddy (e.g. tweed suits) at other times.

A woman wakes us up at 7.45 with hot water, cleans our shoes, lays the fire and makes our beds.

The college is like Windsor Castle and Hampton Court rolled into one. Physics this morning was the easiest scholarship paper I have seen but even so I could only do one question.

The crackling from the neighbouring women's colleges—Girton and Newnham—is terrific but unfortunately Cambridge abounds in R.A.F. aircrew and Americans.

About 300 blokes are sitting for Natural Science Schols alone; however a week here is worth the 9/- a day they charge any time.

Tuesday 7.30 I got some matches and we've lit the huge fire. I discovered some more of Trinity: huge masses of cloisters and courtyards etc. on the other side of the road. Two of the courtyards over there are known as the billiard table and the spittoon.

I hear there is a roof-climbing society which operates during term nights.

Needless to say the paper was awful again this afternoon (I did one question in Chemistry—the wrong way). Still there's worse to come—tomorrow is pure maths.

Around the dining hall are pictures of the great men of Trinity—Isaac Newton, Francis Bacon etc. Pity Milo Johnston will never adorn the wall.

Wednesday 7.30 I've just seen that bastard Gervase-Jones. It seems he's coming up this year and has come up a few days early to do some rugby practice. He recognized me at once, but pretended not to. Dinner tonight was celestine soup, fried fillet of haddock, parsnips, potatoes, blackberry slice. Our written exams finished at 12 noon and after "luncheon" (savoury pastie, greens, potatoes and bread pudding) I went to see Eric Portman in "Escape to Danger". Afterward I had tea in Lyons (sausage, egg and baked beans on toast, tea, cake etc. etc.).

The tutor gave me another interview tonight and said that if I win anything he'll send me a telegram and if not he'll write to say why not.

Our physics practical is to be held in the Cavendish Laboratory of all places and for this I have to stay till Monday mid-day. I'll be home about eleven, and Benny, please ask Mum to have something ready because I shall be bloody ravenous.

Till then chums,
Your old pal,
Milo.

Milo failed to get a scholarship, but Ilex's strategy worked, for the next year he won himself a place at Trinity—provided the county would support him, which they quickly said they would—for September 1944. Benedict secretly believed that one day Milo's portrait really would hang in the Trinity hall.

New Year's Eve 1943

Ilex was giving a dinner party for his staff; Mr. Johnston unwillingly struggled into his old-fashioned dinner jacket with its high wing collar and drove off with his wife at seven o'clock. His wife was not really looking forward to the occasion any more than her husband; she would have preferred to be at home with her family and in any case found Ilex rather trying company. To make it up to her children, she suggested that they ask one or two friends in for the evening. "I'll make you some mulled claret," she promised, "and a cold supper, and you can see the New Year in and enjoy yourselves."

"Which is more than we shall do," grumbled her husband.

The Weston and Mackay families were going away together to Torquay for Christmas. Benedict felt ill with jealousy, but Felix reassured him. "You may take it as read," he said, "that I have got my eye on one of the maids at our hotel. There's nothing I like better than a bit of low life. But I'll keep my eye on your lovely, languorous Laura for you. There's always some keen young R.A.F. officers down there. Now surely you'd rather me than them?"

Benedict reluctantly agreed that this was so. "But promise me," he begged, "that you'll write to me if she falls for anyone else. Don't keep it from me. I must know."

"If the worst comes to the worst, you shall be told," Felix promised solemnly. So far, however, there had been no word from Torquay and Benedict—who knew Felix could never resist the opportunity to transmit a little scandal—began to breathe more easily.

Though the New Year's Eve party would lose some of its spice without Laura and Felix, it was still fun to work out whom they should invite. Ken would come of course, and Constance; and they decided they would ask Aelfric Gates, of whom they were increasingly fond.

That made seven. For even numbers, they needed one more girl. Milo had a suggestion. "Why not," he asked, innocently, "Doreen Pepper?"

"Oh really, Milo," said Joanna. "Is that the best you can do? She's such a common child."

"Yeah, but sexy," said Milo with deliberate vulgarity, rolling his eyes saucily.

"I'm surprised that you haven't got better taste, Milo," said Benny, "but if you have this *nostalgie de la boue,* I suppose it's got to be satisfied."

"You said it, man."

"I think," said Tessa, "that Milo doesn't give a jot about the Pepperpot. I don't think he cares tuppence about any girl. He's just doing it for a joke."

"Oh *ask* her," said Joanna, who was technically in charge. "We'll see who gets tired of her first. Us or Milo."

"I am insatiable," said Milo greedily. The others looked at him with interest. Was Milo joking after all? One never knew for sure.

Benny was up in his room shaving as the Johnstons' majestic old bull-nosed Morris rolled down the drive. He hummed as he worked. Shaving was a new experience in his life and was still hardly necessary to him more than once a week. But for a special evening like this, a special toilet was required. He was disturbed by the now familiar tapping on the wall.

"Hello, Tess."

"Hello, Benny. I say, Benny."

"Yes."

"Could you zip me up?"

"Of course."

He wiped his face clean, and went into Tessa's room, knocking carefully on the door first. Tessa was wearing a charming dress of primrose yellow which was especially flattering to her dark complexion. From the front it looked complete, but when she turned her back towards him he saw that it was unzipped down to her waist. She lifted both hands in a movement of instinctive shyness to her face and said:

"I don't know what I'd do without you here, Benny."

"I'd expect you'd have to zip it yourself."

"Don't be beastly, Benny. You know perfectly well that's pretty well impossible."

"I'm glad to hear it. It makes a very agreeable duty. There— is that right."

"Thank you, Benny." She leaned slightly backwards, and to his surprise he found he had to hold on to her so that they both kept their equilibrium. His hands joined quite naturally round her waist. Looking into the mirror, he thought they made a slightly idiotic couple—she with her hauntingly large eyes and painfully thin body, he with his intense and liquid brown eyes and excessively earnest expression.

"Benny," she said. "I'm going to wear scent tonight for the first time in my life. The scent you gave me for Christmas."

"It was a very small bottle. Are you sure you want to waste it on an occasion like this?"

"What better? Benny, it was kind of you. It must have cost the earth."

"It cost six and six as a matter of fact. I bought it from the money I got for fire-watching."

"Benny, you must learn never to tell a woman exactly how much a present cost. Then she can always delude herself that it was much, much more. Not that it matters in my case. I thought

131

it was sweet, whatever it cost. But tell me, why did you buy me *scent* of all things?"

"I just thought you'd—enjoy having it."

"It's a very *special* present for a man to give to a girl."

"You're a very special girl."

"Do you think the scent will attract Ken Heppel?"

"I don't think it will exactly restrain him."

"Have you tried it yet?"

"I sniffed it vaguely in the shop."

"I'll put some on and you tell me what you think?"

She dabbed some on to the back of her hand and proffered it.

"I think Ken Heppel will go berserk."

"You know, I like him a little better. At least, I always liked him. But now . . ."

"Now you feel maybe . . ."

"Yes." She dabbed the scent behind her ears.

"You know, Benny," she said, "tonight for the first time I feel like a woman."

"To me you are a woman. The one I know best in the whole world."

"Is that really so, Benny?"

"Who better? Laura bewitches me and Constance——"

"You're sure you haven't got a soft spot for Constance?"

"No—not exactly. I don't feel—close to her, the way I do towards you."

"She's a very sophisticated girl."

"You mean you don't like her?"

"Certainly not. I do like her. But she's rather frighteningly intelligent."

"I agree. Also she's slightly—well outrageous."

"You mean—fast?"

"I don't know. All I know is, she does this college clutch in a rather embarrassing way."

"But I could do that, Benny."

"Yes, but you wouldn't."

"I might."

"Well try it on Ken Heppel and see what happens."

"Oh I wouldn't do it to Ken."

"Why ever not?"

"It might encourage him."

"Tessa, I shall never understand women."

"There's nothing to understand."

"Listen. There's the bell. Someone's arrived. The party's beginning."

Mrs. Johnston had excelled herself: her cold supper was delicious and the mulled claret very quickly had its effect; they sat round the kitchen fire drowsily, talking in small groups of two or three. Benedict found himself unexpectedly next to Aelfric Gates, and in half an hour had found out more about him than ever before.

By now Gates was very nearly six feet tall, alarmingly slim, but built like a thoroughbred greyhound. His shy faun's eyes lent credence to the idea that he was some gentle animal that would scamper away when you stepped on a twig in the forest. It turned out that his father was in fact a forester.

"So what do you want to do when you leave Aylsbourn?" Benny asked him.

"I don't care. As long as I can read philosophy."

"Philosophy?"

"Yes. Whitehead. And Russell. Have you ever read *Principia Mathematica*?"

"Can't say I have."

"It's a fabulous book. Intoxicating."

Benny studied Aelfric with interest. He thought he could almost see what Ilex got out of his new job; what Felix called his "intellectual orgasm from watching raw intelligence spawn out of the earth". Aelfric was now far and away the cleverest boy in the school; he churned his way through all the books in the library with contemptuous ease; he soaked up languages like a piece of blotting paper, and he ripped through mathematics papers like a child tearing newspapers.

"But if you want to be a philosopher, why are you specialising in history?"

"Because Ilex talked me into it. You see, most annoyingly, my highest marks in the Cambridge exams this summer were in history. Ilex said I might be the first boy to win an Open to Oxford or Cambridge from Aylsbourn. And he made the point that in Hennessy we have one of the best modern historians in the country."

133

"But it meant giving up mathematics."

"Well, he advised me to. It hurts me to remember it sometimes. I read on my own. But mathematics is a funny thing. Unless you keep in top gear, you can go rusty quite easily. And a lot of the big schools have real assault courses on the Open Scholarships in Maths and Science. Ilex is a bit contemptuous of our science teaching here."

"But Milo's father is quite good at teaching maths, isn't he?"

"Ilex doesn't think he's up to teaching scholarship stuff. He may be right."

Benedict turned this conversation over many times in his mind afterwards. He had suffered a similar disappointment. His own marks in the Cambridge that summer had shown a strong bias towards science. This, he was convinced, was due simply to his friendship with Milo and the specially good teaching of Mr. Johnston. As it happened he was most keen to take English. But Ilex had been against this.

"Frankly, Benny," he said on the day they discussed his future (Ilex had latched on to all his boys' nicknames very quickly), "I don't see you as a prospect for an Open. But you might well win a County Major or one of those local awards. Only you must be sensible about it."

"But I like English best, sir."

"It's not a question of what you *like* best, Benny. It's a question of what's going to get you furthest. In two years' time when your age group leaves here, I want a dozen scholarships at Oxford and Cambridge. You're part of that plan. Now tell me—would you rather read physics at Cambridge or Eng. Lit. at some grubby provincial university college?"

It was on the tip of Benedict's tongue to say the latter; but he stopped himself; it wasn't true. For one thing, he wanted desperately to stay with his friends, and Ilex had already launched Milo at Cambridge. Ken Heppel and Felix Weston were both hopeless at science, and would have to take an Arts course. But in any event, they were not going to end up in a grubby provincial university college. So Benedict had acquiesced. He was quite enjoying science, but now and again he had a sharp stab of regret that he would not read English.

The time passed pleasantly, but by half-past nine Milo became restive. He looked at his watch and realized that his parents

134

would be back in roughly ninety minutes' time. He had a clear notion how he wanted to fill in the intervening period.

"Well now, folks," he announced, "I think the time has come for a game of Murder."

"Haven't you got over those childish games yet?" Joanna asked.

"It's not childish the way I play it."

"Who wants to play Murder?" asked Joanna.

"I do," said Kenneth promptly. He looked at Tessa shame-facedly out of the corner of his eye. The only advantage of the game as far as he was concerned was that it would provide a legitimate opportunity to be alone with her.

"I'm all for it," said the Pepperpot. The other girls looked at her. They had not been in any doubt about *her* views.

"I'd rather go on talking," said Aelfric.

"Benny?" asked Constance.

"I'm happy. Whatever the others want."

"Constance?"

"Yes. Why not?"

"Tessa?"

"I don't know. At least I think——"

"That's it then," said Milo unceremoniously. He got out a pack of cards and shuffled them expertly. "Now you all know the rules. Ace of Spades is the murderer. Keep quiet if you get it. A gentle squeeze round the throat means you've committed the crime. The victim must count ten before screaming to let the murderer escape. Everyone must stay where they were when they hear the scream. Jack of Spades is the detective. He can ask any number of questions but only accuse one person of being mur-derer. O.K.?"

He doled out the cards. "Oh," said Joanna. "I'm the detec-tive."

"All right. Stay here and put your feet up. You'll have work to do later. Everyone else scatter over the house. I'll turn the lights off at the main switch."

Benedict felt his heart begin to thump harder as the whole house was suddenly drowned in darkness. He had played this game too often not to knew its curious and minuscule tactile pleasures. He moved quietly through the darkness and began to creep up the stairs. On the landing he tripped over what felt like a sack of runner beans on the floor. He reached out a hand and felt to see what it was.

"Go away," said the sack. His hand encountered a well-shaved male neck, and a female hand round the neck. It was Milo; and unless he was much mistaken, the Pepperpot. He prowled on up the second, narrower flight towards his own room. Near the top of the stairs he stopped. Someone was in the way, he was sure. Again he groped. His hand closed on a bare arm. He slid his fingers down to the wrist, seeking identification. Still there was no move or word from the darkness. Then the problem was solved for him. A light scent, which had cost him six and six a few days ago, was in the air.

"Is that you, Tess?" he whispered.

"Yes. We're not supposed to talk are we?"

"No. Are you the murderer?"

"No. Are you?"

"No. Let's hide from the others. I hate being murdered."

"Where?"

"Your room is nearest."

They tiptoed in and closed the door gently behind them. Benedict steered her gently towards the bed. She resisted a little.

"Benny, do you think we ought? I mean, won't people talk?"

"I'll go when they scream."

They sat side by side on the bed. Only their hands touched. They heard a bump and laughter downstairs.

"Do you know who the murderer is, Benny?"

"Yes. Milo."

"How do you know?"

"I've seen him do it before. He gives himself the ace so that he can control the length of the game. No one can turn the lights on till he's done the murder. It may take anything up to half an hour."

"Do you think he's really a sort of Casanova?"

"I think he thinks he is."

"You're not a bit like that, Benny."

"Only because I'm too nervous."

"Even of me?"

"Yes."

"What do you think of my Tropical Sin."

"Your *what*?"

136

"The scent you gave me, you idiot."

"Oh. Pretty good. That's how I knew it was you."

"You recognized me by the scent?"

"Yes. You know, according to Aldous Huxley, there are some very disgusting things in scent. For instance——"

"Don't, Benny. You're spoiling it for me. Tell me, does this scent tempt you at all?"

"Yes. As a matter of fact it does."

"But you're too shy to do anything about it."

"No I'm not."

"Obviously you are."

Even Benedict realized that this was an open invitation. He slid his left arm round Tessa's waist and put his right hand gently on her neck, turning her face in the pitch darkness nearer to his. He could feel the large vein in her throat bumping under his little finger.

"What are you waiting for, Benny?"

"Nothing." The next moment their lips met, slightly asymmetrically, but with unhurried gentleness. He never forgot the innocence of that kiss. It seemed to go on for a long time.

Tessa put both her arms round his neck and very slowly slid her lips away. "Oh Benny," she whispered. "That was the very first time."

"It was for me too."

They kissed again. Benedict's mouth was as dry as if he had just escaped death and his heart pumped recklessly. It was as if he had just finished a five mile race. To his great surprise, he found he was shivering. And so was Tessa.

She took her mouth reluctantly away from his.

"Benny," she said. "This is awful."

"Why?"

"Well I mean, we live next door to each other. Where will it stop?"

"Don't be ridiculous, Tess. There's nothing immoral in a kiss."

"Yes, but suppose my mother discovered we were making love right under her nose?"

"I could ask to move into Milo's room."

"Oh no. I couldn't bear that."

"Then we'll just have to be strong."

They kissed again and she ran her thin fingers through his hair.

"Where did you learn to do that?"

"In a film."

"I wonder what people did before films. I suppose they just taught each other. Do you realize that the knowledge of love is the one subject that's passed on from generation to generation with almost nothing being written down?"

"Benny, why are you so serious? Kiss me again."

During their fourth kiss there was a horrifying scream from below.

"That's that awful little bitch Doreen Pepper. She's been murdered. I'd know her voice anywhere."

Tessa jumped up, turned on the light, and began to arrange her hair in the mirror.

"Quick, Benny," she whispered.

He tiptoed out, slipped quickly into his room, and was lying on the bed reading a Penguin when Joanna came in on her tour of inspection.

"Well," she said sarcastically. "Here's a new talent. Reading in the dark."

"It was only while I was waiting."

"I've seen enough, thank you. Here," she handed him a handkerchief from a pile of newly laundered linen on his dressing-table.

He sat up and looked in the mirror. There was a large red smear on his face and another on his collar.

"Good heavens!" he said feebly. "How on earth did that get there?"

"That's what I'm going to find out," Joanna said with mock iciness. "Come downstairs."

It took her only thirty seconds to discover that Milo, a poor liar, was the murderer. He shuffled the cards enthusiastically again. As he did so the boys and girls eyed each other with heightened interest. He dealt the cards out.

"Oh!" said Tessa, and the disappointment was sharp in her voice. "I'm the detective."

Benedict's eyes met hers across the room and said: Don't be sad. There'll be plenty of other times. She recovered herself, smiled, and said, "Off you go then. And behave yourselves."

Benedict decided to follow the same strategic plan as before. He would make his way stealthily up to his room and sit in the darkness there, away from everyone, trying to re-create the delight he had just experienced.

He edged his way cautiously up in the darkness, each sense needle-sharp, aware that other lives were expanding near his in response to the beauty of sharp new tactile sensations. He reached his room at last, and softly opened the door. He tiptoed across the little room and reached out to discover exactly where his bed was. But all his groping hand encountered was something warm, curving and silky. He withdrew his hand sharply. It was a girl's leg!

"Hello, Benny," said a languid voice. He recognized it at once.

"Hello, Constance."

"Is this your room?"

"Yes."

"I thought it must be. Am I taking all the space?"

"No. Oh thanks."

He sat on the edge of his bed. Somewhere beside him in the darkness Constance was delectably stretched out, apparently entirely at her ease. It was enough to give a chap the creeps!

"Are you the murderer?" he whispered.

"No. Are you?"

"No. And it can't be Milo again. He wouldn't give himself the same card twice, would he?"

"Oh so it's fixed, is it? I thought it might be. Why doesn't he take the Pepperpot out into Twenty Acre if he wants to smooch with her?"

"I think he doesn't quite know how to set about it. But in the dark, everyone seems to lose their inhibitions. Have you ever noticed that?"

"No."

"No?"

"Not in your case anyway, Benny. You must be the slowest male in the county of Hampshire, unless you count that old tortoise in Macpherson's garden."

"I'm nothing of the sort. I'm just not—er—promiscuous."

"Oh is that what it is? There is only one overwhelming passion in your life?"

"You know there is."

"It must be a bit boring though. Will you be able to live on

139

Platonic love for ever, Benny? Rather in the way some inventors thought they could find an engine that ran entirely on air?"

"Of course not."

"The funny thing is, you would make a good lover. You're so absurdly pure."

Benny felt a slow sense of shame rising inside him.

"I'm not all that damned pure!"

"Oh really? You surprise me!"

To his mortification he heard her give an overt and rather theatrical yawn. Suddenly he felt wildly angry. He half-turned, and swung his legs up on to the bed beside Constance. He put his arm right round her waist and pulled her roughly until she was tight up against him. Their faces were now side by side on the counterpane. He could feel her quick breathing.

"Say that again."

"What?" She sounded a little frightened, or perhaps excited.

"What you just said."

"I said you surprised me."

"Before that."

"I forget. Benny you're hurting me."

He hadn't noticed that he had dug his fingers hard into her arm. He relaxed them as if he was going to get up and leave her and then changed his mind and kissed her quite viciously. She stiffened for a second with the shock, then relaxed completely and put both arms round his neck. She half opened her mouth and, to his astonishment, bit his lower lip, though quite gently. He took his mouth away, more in surprise than anything, and to his further surprise she slapped his face quite hard. The sound rang out in the darkness and for a moment he felt slightly stunned.

"What in hell's name did you do that for?"

"Because you asked for it."

"Why do you talk such nonsense? I can't make you out at all. First you ask me to kiss you and then——"

"I didn't ask you."

"Well you invited me to."

"The trouble with you, Benny, is that you're so inexperienced. You've probably never kissed a girl before in your life."

"Oh yes I have," Benedict said confidently, secretly thanking his lucky stars that he had lived through the last half hour.

"How many?"

"Plenty."

"That's a likely story. I can tell that you're a beginner from the way you kiss."

"I wouldn't like to say what I can tell from the way *you* kiss."

"I expect you've never been kissed properly before."

"Who taught you to kiss like that, Constance?"

"My priest."

"*What?*"

"My priest. You know I'm a lapsed Catholic?"

"No I didn't."

"Well that's what made me give it up. I told my confessor that a boy had kissed me, and he asked whether it was with the mouth open or shut."

"And that put the idea into your head?"

"Yes. Don't you find it pretty exciting?"

"Yes."

"I must say you don't show it."

"I'll show you."

They kissed again. Benedict found it an intoxicating, though alarming experience. He had never been in such proximity to a girl in his life. There seemed no part of Constance that was not pressed very hard against him. An extremely naïve thought passed through his head: if there were a Creator, then what artifice he had shown, what divine imagination in shaping men and women in such a deliciously complementary way! How marvellous, for instance, that a woman's hips were made so invitingly wide, so that——

Just then all the lights went on.

"Cave, everybody!" They heard Milo calling. And then there was the sound of the Johnstons' bull-nosed Morris coming slowly up the drive.

They stared at each other, not quite believing that they had just been locked so impetuously together. Constance took a small handkerchief from her bag and carefully wiped Benedict's face clean. Then she nonchalantly put on some lipstick, and straightened her hair in the mirror. Next, she put her arm through Benedict's.

"I'll tell you a secret, Benny," she said. "It was the first time for me. The first proper time the way the priest said. I'll always be grateful to that priest."

"So will I," said Benny.

That night it was his turn to tap on the wall. Tessa was awake.

"Yes, Benny."

"Tess, I must see you."

"Come in, Benny."

He pulled on his dressing-gown and tip-toed through. It was a moonless night; he couldn't see her face.

"Come and sit down, Benny. What's the matter?"

"I can't sleep."

"Why not?"

"I feel such a—so unfaithful to you, Tess."

"Why? What did you do?"

"I—I kissed Constance."

"But I don't mind, Benny. After all, why shouldn't you?"

"I wanted to remember this evening as something special between us. Completely innocent and yet—memorable. And then I have to spoil it by misbehaving with Constance."

"But you didn't *misbehave*, did you?"

"Oh no of course not. But she's a very passionate girl."

"I like her. She's different from any other girl I know. Do you like her very much, Benny?"

"She frightens me a bit. She's fascinating and tough and very nice all at the same time."

"Maybe she has reasons for being tough we don't know about."

There was a silence.

"Tessa, do you think your parents realized what was going on?"

"Of course they did."

"They didn't mind?"

"No—they know we wouldn't do anything really bad."

"Why did the game go on so long? It seemed hours, that second time."

"Because Milo took the Ace of Spades out of the pack. I saw him. If there's no Ace there can be no murderer and no murder. So the game goes on indefinitely."

"Trust Milo! And is that why he made you detective?"

142

"I think he thought I was not likely to like that sort of thing."

"Well, he was wrong, wasn't he?"

"Not really. It was only because it was you, Benny. I wouldn't with just any boy."

"That's why I feel so awful. I mean first you and then——"

"Oh don't worry about it, Benny. All men are like that."

"Are they?"

"Yes. Men are naturally polygamous; women are monogamous."

"Well I'm not. Not really. I was just——"

"Led astray? But that's always the trouble, Benny. Everyone sets out with the best intentions."

"Tessa, do you think I'll always be like this? I mean unable to resist temptations? I do so want to love only one person."

"If it's Laura, I think you'll be all right."

"But she's right out of reach."

"Not any more—not since Tony Hammond went away."

"But I'm sure they're still in love."

"No they're not."

"How can you be sure?"

"Something. I don't quite know. Anyway, he's in Cambridge now; probably he's met all sorts of exciting girl undergraduates. You know what, Benny? You ought to ask Laura out. She's awfully lonely, anyone can see that."

"Oh, but I couldn't Tess."

"Why ever not?"

"First, it would be so dishonest. It would look as if I was trying to steal her behind his back."

"You won't steal her unless she wants to be stolen."

"And anyway, she'd never go out with *me*."

"Why ever not?"

"Well, she's a year older for one thing."

"But you're both in the senior school now."

"I'm sorry, Tess. Of course I'd like to, more than anything in life. But I won't—not while she belongs to Hammond."

"Poor old Benny! You are faithful. No—not faithful—honourable."

"That's almost an insult these days. Do you know what Constance called me?"

"No."

143

"Pure."

"And you were upset at that? But it's the nicest thing anyone could say about you, Benny."

"I'm not pure. I'm only human, Tess."

There was a long silence. At length she said:

"Benny?"

"Yes?"

"Have you ever thought what it would be like to kiss Laura?"

"No. At least—not in any clear way. You see it's such an unlikely thing. . . ."

"But suppose it happened. What do you think it would be like?"

"I just can't imagine. It would be indescribable."

"Shall I tell you something, Benny?"

"Yes, please."

"It would be just like kissing Constance or me."

"But——" He paused. He couldn't hurt her by saying how infinitely separate those two experiences were. And yet—perhaps she was right. Perhaps she would combine all the sweetness of Tessa with all the passion of Constance!

"What is it, Benny?"

"Oh nothing. Just that everything is so baffling. And wonderful. Do you honestly forgive me, Tess?"

"There was nothing to forgive, Benny."

"And we're still friends?"

"We'll always be friends."

January 4th, 1943

was the day Felix was due back from Torquay. Anxious to see his old friend again—and in particular anxious to know what news there was of Laura—Benedict set off early along the High Street to call at the Westons' house and ask Mrs. Duncher what time the family were expected. To his surprise, however, he saw Felix walking down the High Street towards him. He was surprised on two counts: that Felix was back so early, and that he should bother to start walking towards Welcaster to call on Benny—for there was nowhere else he was likely to walk. As Felix drew near, Benedict realized that Felix had some news for him. His dark face gleamed with unusual excitement.

"Benny," he said as soon as they had greeted each other. "I've got news for you."

"What is it?"

"Not here. Let's go into Miller's."

They settled themselves in their favourite corner, well out of earshot, and ordered coffee. Benedict watched his friend's face anxiously.

"Well, how was Torquay?"

Felix made an impatient gesture of dismissal.

"All right. Benny, I've discovered why Hammond left in such a hurry. But you must give me your word of honour never to tell a soul. I found out through reading something I shouldn't, and no one must ever know."

"I give you my solemn promise."

Felix waited till the waitress had brought the two coffees and withdrawn. Then he leaned across the table and said, very slowly and distinctly: "Because he was having a love-affair with Arabella."

4

BUT all that, thought Benedict as he let himself into his flat had been a long time ago; seventeen years ago, to be precise; he had lived as much life again since that astonishing January morning. He was just twice as old as that boy whose heart had seemed to stop when Felix broke the news to him. For a dream had been destroyed in that moment, and another planted in its place. He would never admire Hammond in quite the same way again; but suddenly, as the mystery of Laura's relationship with him had become clear, a long avenue into the future had seemed to open. He had not known whether to cry or laugh that morning; he had been born into a new world. The moment of truth over the coffee cups in Miller's had sliced his life neatly in two. And what could he say of the seventeen years that had followed after?

He crossed his drawing-room and went out slowly on to the balcony. As he breathed the London air, he remembered suddenly that he had not been really alive since the day he left Aylsbourn, for the simple reason that always afterwards he had felt subconsciously as if he were choking a little. It would be good, he thought, to breathe that marvellous air again. It had been—what?—thirteen years now since then, and a good deal of it he did not care to remember.

And yet—was he so very different from the Benny his friends remembered? Let's see, who was he today? Did a different personality entirely inhabit that same mortal shell? Today he was P. J. Benedict, Managing Director of the Diskon Company, a Fellow of the Institute of Directors, with seventy-five thousand five shilling shares in his own company. What would Benedict, the boy, the dreamer, the lover, say to *that* lot?

What would he say to P. J. Benedict, proprietor of two paintings by Kokoschka, a drawing by Picasso, a nude carved by Butler, a first edition of *The Masters*, signed by the author? Not much; it was too damned studied, the front he presented to the polite world. What, then, of the *Collected Poems of Auden* and the *Journals* of Stendhal that he kept—and conscientiously read—in the lavatory? Still pretty suspect.

What would he say to P. J. Benedict, tenant of an eight-room apartment off Upper Brook Street, weekender at a cottage in Rye, skipper of a Dragon Class yacht, proprietor of a 110 m.p.h. Bristol 406 costing £4,500? Mm—not much.

And what about P. J. Benedict, shopper at Fortnum's, connoisseur of château-bottled claret, whose shirts were made in Jermyn Street for five guineas each and whose suits were made in Dover Street at fifty? What would he say of Benedict, habitué of the Ecu de France, the Caprice, the Mirabelle? Thumbs down, for sure.

Finally then, what would he say to P. J. Benedict, member of the Reform Club, earnest Liberal voter at election times, aficionado of the *New Statesman*, donor of a hundred guineas a year to Christian Action? So-so; he'd think it pretty standard, a stereotype do-gooder set of reflexes.

No, Benny the boy, the lover, the dreamer, would have had one hard, unnerving question for his yet unknown older self, a question that P. J. Benedict did not like to face, even in his imagination. You seem to have done pretty well, Benny would have said; you've been lucky and you've got quite a lot. *But what have you given back? What in God's name have you given back?*

5

How on earth could one have explained to Benny at seventeen, except by transporting him forward through time? It was all so unimaginably different, and all so long ago. Benedict went over to his writing desk and opened it with a key from the heavy bunch on his chain; stigmata of the capitalist through the generations. Under the photograph albums and the account books there was a thick volume bound in good green leather: it had been his Christmas present from Tessa. He had begun writing in it a few days after Felix broke his news; it had taken a few days for him to assimilate the shock; he had begun to write on—he opened the book—ah yes:

Friday, January 15, 1943

Today—my seventeenth birthday—I start to write this chronicle of my thoughts and experiences. I do so with very mixed feelings. It will never seem anything but naïve when I look back on it one day; yet it is the only way I know for a man to look at himself objectively.

I hope it will teach me something about myself. Above all, I hope it will help me to come to terms with the strange and troubling new turn my life has taken—which makes me tremble even now as I try to write about it. I shall really go stone bonkers if I try to contain my emotions any longer. Better by far to lay them out and dissect them; to do the job thoroughly with a sharp surgeon's knife.

It's Laura, of course. Where else but here would I dare to confess that I haven't really had a quiet moment since I first saw her more than three years ago? And how, Benny, people would say, can anyone of *your* age possibly know what it's all about? Well, I wish the people who say those things could be put through the torture I've been through. Then they'd know. I know now as certainly as I sit here that I shall never love anyone else quite as I love Laura. I don't have the experience, unfortunately, to cope with a situation quite so alarming.

I suppose I was a fool not have guessed about Tony Hammond. After all, Gerard Weston has always been his great mentor in politics; the two of them as far as I know, form the entire communist cell in Aylsbourn. (Ilex? Who knows?) I remember so vividly in retrospect those long evenings *chez* Weston, the marvellous and incongruous vintage port circulating round the table (Gerard Weston was too sensible ever to have thrown away *that* bourgeois bequest of his father's), Felix and I spellbound by our elders, G. W. and Hammond always talking and arguing, setting the world to rights on Marxist principles, while Arabella sat watching them at the end of the table, her lovely eyes resting gently first on one, then the other. And I remember one evening as we were listening to the Mozart Clarinet Quintet round the fire that I saw a look pass between Tony and Arabella, just a glance, but they smiled at each other and I ought to have guessed.

Felix says that according to the letter he found—a recent one— his father seems to have forgiven Arabella and they are going to carry on; Hammond had promised never to come back to Aylsbourn; Gerard took it pretty well—a man of reason and all that crap—but of course he was smashed by the shock. It was his self-esteem which took the worst beating. I asked Felix why she didn't run off with Tony if she loved him; he says he doesn't know how serious it was on Tony's part and there's also Felix's little half-brother Timothy to consider. He'll be three in a few days, and though it nearly killed her having him she dotes on the dribbly little wretch. In common sense, how could she go off with Tony? Would she live in digs in ecstatic poverty just to be with him while he was still just a student? How would he react to that kind of responsibility? No, obviously, she has to stay where she is. I feel so sorry for all three of them. Felix says the only surprise to him is that Arabella stuck his father for so long.

It's now clear that Laura was merely acting as an extremely decorative and efficient decoy for this affair; a strange and not very pleasing role for her. But she did it beautifully, as she does everything.

So Tony Hammond has passed out of all our lives—presumably for good. I confess to myself that the world is just that bit greyer without him. I shall always be grateful to him for teaching me as no one else could how sweet it is to be alive. I shall remember him best the night of the great game, after we beat Shallerton.

Hennessy gave a party for us at his place—the Tithe House, about a mile down the Cressbrook. It's an old Queen Anne sergeant's mess of all things, but done up, of course, and one odd feature is the threshing barn, a long low building which the previous owner meant to convert into an annexe for a married couple to look after him. But he never did, so it's still in its original state. It's immensely old, and big, but still just a barn. By the time we got there Hennessy had got the place rigged up like a night club—as I *imagine* a night club—with tables and trestles and candles stuck in bottles. Mrs. H. had just got a splendid food parcel from America. She cooked us some southern fried chicken and there was a barrel of Margrave bitter which some of us drank straight for the first time. We got there at about eight-thirty after changing and having a hot bath and a shave to coax out all the aches and bruises. There were about twenty-five of us altogether. The band was already there and just as we got there Tony Hammond got up and led them into their opening number, The Original Dixieland Onestep. And whenever I hear that old tune now I feel a sense of joy so fierce that it seems to be strangling me. It crystallized the miracle of the day.

I wish it had been possible to record him that night. No, strictly I don't, because of course it would have been dreadful in retrospect; ragged I dare say, and naïve. But at the time it sounded out of this world. Tony plays with that hard, low, driving snarl that you hear when Spanier blows, and I suppose he's learnt a lot from the Spanier classics. The beauty of jazz is that it's never the same two nights in a row; each occasion is unique. That night, to me at least, he seemed to play as if it were his last night on earth.

All the girls looked enchanting that night—to me anyway—even Tess had somehow made herself look touchingly pretty—but I was waiting for Laura. She arrived at about ten, wearing that biscuit-coloured coat which always makes her look a bit like some delicious squirrel, and when she took off her coat she was wearing a dress of black and gold that seemed to glow in the candlelight. Hennessy asked her jokingly if she'd like some beer and I always remember the special little grimace with which she refused, and then, damn Hennessy, he asked her to dance and I was gibbering with jealousy.

It took me four beers to get up the courage to ask Laura to

dance. I don't know how I got up or went over or what the hell I said or how I said it, but I know she smiled and said of course, and the next thing I knew we were dancing.

She's nearly as tall as me and as I looked at her I realized once again that those astonishing green eyes are her secret; they're quite wide apart; I once read that if a woman's truly beautiful, you can put another eye between her two eyes, and absurd and mechanical though this explanation sounds, it does apply in her case. It gives a quality of serenity. I don't know. We talked about the great game and she said it was the most super thing she'd ever seen in her life. I know this sounds ridiculous in cold print, but she uses schoolboy words and somehow succeeds in making them sound madly sexy. Of course she's being ironical; just in the way that she says Gee *whiz* when anybody says something particularly pompous.

She danced with Tony Hammond when he was taking a breather between tunes and I danced with Tess and Constance. It was a fabulous party and they didn't play "The Saints" till about one—and then he took about nine extra choruses till we all went wild. It was the most un-English thing that ever happened in Aylsbourn.

That very night I ought to have realized about Tony, or seen that something was wrong, because he said he had to drive over to Shallerton to stay with friends. Why he should want to do so at that hour of the morning never occurred to us; in fact he and Arabella were borrowing a flat over there which belonged to a friend of hers, an artist. She was supposed to be in London. So Tony Hammond asked me if I'd see Laura home. Would I!

There was a monstrous moon, orange in the Aylsbourn mist, and an iron frost; the frozen puddles crackled and clouded as we stepped on them. The Cressbrook Valley was wallowing in a calm, Wellsian, lunar radiance. If the Martians had come that night, I don't think any of us would have turned a hair. The earth seemed specially blessed. You could see for many miles. Laura took my arm.

I can't record what we said. I can't remember what we talked about and if I could I wouldn't. It would break the spell.

Saturday sixteenth

I had to stop then, partly because I was so damned tired,

151

partly because I couldn't think how to circumscribe in words the strange thing that has happened to Laura and me. I can't now.

Last Thursday evening—it was a soft, caressing, January day, with already a faint murmur of spring in the earth—the kind when Aylsbourn always looks its haunting best—I happened to have to go back to the library to get a book. It was about seven-thirty. As I walked along the High Street I realized through a chink in the blackout that the light was on and I couldn't help wondering if perhaps somebody hadn't broken in. I let myself in (Ilex has given us all a key to the front door) and tiptoed up. I confess I was pretty damn scared and there was no saliva left in my mouth by the time I got to the top of the stairs. I pushed the door slowly open. Laura was sitting there all alone, her head buried in her arms at the long table where we all work. She was crying.

I tried to mutter some excuse, but she said it didn't matter. "Please come in, Benny," she said—how can I ever forget it? —"you're the only one I could stand seeing just now."

So I sat down and said nothing for a long time, and then after a bit she dried her eyes. I thought I should be horrified to see her cry—after all no girl looks her best with red eyes—but oddly, it only accentuated her desperate wistfulness and for once I didn't feel she was unattainable at all. I felt only that I'd like somehow to protect her—whatever it was that she needed protecting from.

"Oh Benny," she said at last, "you must think me an awful idiot. It would be more sensible if I could offer you some explanation. But I can't. I'm just crying because life is so intolerably sad."

"Is it?" I said. "Usually I can hardly stop myself jumping in the air because I'm so doomy and glad to be alive."

Then she smiled at me and said: "Good old Benny. You know, I'd trust you to the ends of the earth."

"Well then," I said, "trust me to the end of the High Street; let me see you home."

She looked at me for quite a minute, and then she said, rather under her breath, yes. It was as if she'd seen me for the first time, and I truly believe that was the explanation of her strange expression.

We walked very slowly and after a while she put her arm through mine as she had that night in the Cressbrook Valley and we didn't say anything. Dr. Mackay and his wife were playing bridge with some friends. She asked me to come in—odd I'd never been back there since that terrible day in 1939—but I said I wouldn't. Instead I asked her if we couldn't perhaps meet the next day and to my astonishment she said: "Oh that would be particularly nice; I'd so much like to talk to you."

I still don't know for sure why she was crying.

Sunday 17th

Yesterday Laura and I went to London. My father had sent me a pound for my birthday; I've never had so much money in my life. Ilex and Hennessy have made us ravenous to catch up with all the books we've never read. In Charing Cross Road we searched all the small shops for anything by D. H. L. or Havelock Ellis or a new Huxley. We finished up with the Penguin *Psychopathology of Everyday Life* and also *Totem and Taboo*. Then we went into Soho and had lunch together. "Isn't it wonderful," she said, "to feel we're really grown up?"

We came back on the fast corridor train and walked up to her house from the station.

Now here is a strange thing: from that haunting encounter in the library till last night there had been no *physical* relation between us even of the most innocent sort. Yet, last night, at her gate, she suddenly put her arms round me and began to cry again. That was all that happened; nothing more; not one kiss. She is a most mysterious and enchanting creature.

There was a terrible air-raid down in the Portsmouth area tonight. Owing to the odd shape of the Downs we can see all the way there on a good night, and hear the guns and see the fires. It was unearthly and hellish, but it had a perverse beauty. It seems to heighten the intensity of each passing emotion between Laura and me.

Monday 18th January

For a year and three months now Milo and I have been committed to science—he gladly and I with dragging feet. I hope Ilex is right. We have Constance with us and little Tess, who's not very bright but is trying her damndest to keep up with her brother. Ken and Felix are on the Arts side with Laura—who is of course a year ahead of us—and this fellow Aelfric Gates who's been shooting up through the school ever since Ilex took over. Aelfric, it's now definite, is to be our very first guinea-pig for an Open Scholarship; he's very tall and shy, a bit like a rabbit. The fact that his father is a forester, says Felix, gives the project added piquancy for Ilex, an ardent socialist and cousin of a lord.

However, the significant thing is that, though Laura and I read different subjects, we can meet every day in the library, which is reserved now strictly as a sort of common room for the senior school. We sit there playing records and talking. Laura is now nearly eighteen and she still doesn't know what to do with her life. Sometimes she thinks she'll read medicine like her father, other days she wants to work in an antique shop. It hurts me to see this beautiful creature so lost, and there's nothing—not yet anyway—that I can do to help.

Yet this is the difference she had made to me: my actual perceptions seem keener and stronger, and sometimes I quite genuinely have difficulty to stop myself jumping in the air with excitement. I'm on a new level of experience, I seem to live in a sharper, clearer air.

Tuesday 19th January

Walking home tonight Laura said suddenly: "I'm sure my life will be very unhappy." It was quite comical, like the girl in *The Seagull* whose first remark is that she's in mourning for her life. But Laura really believes it. I said, what about her own parents; they were perfectly happy, why couldn't she be? She said no, although they looked so solid and cosy together, they hadn't always got on, and for a period when she was quite a child they'd lived apart. This was news to me. Then she made a very simple declaration of faith; I suppose any woman could subscribe to it; yet it was quite moving. She just said: "I love beautiful things; trees, water, flowers, scents, sounds, colours; I hate ugly things."

I wouldn't bother to record what appears such a banal statement, except that I am sure in her subconscious mind she was referring to Tony Hammond, and very deep down she doesn't think that what he did was ugly.

Wednesday 20th January

Laura came this evening to my Gramophone Society for the

first time. It was, I'm afraid, not a very distinguished programme, but I shall always remember Laura curled up in the armchair. She looks so serene sometimes that I can hardly bear to look at her. Holberg Suite good. Greensleeves always drives me almost nuts with happiness; that arcadia in the dawn of everything before corruption and lust and jealousy got hold of us.

Thursday 21st January

I find myself surprisingly attached to physics despite everything. It's entirely due to working with Milo. He's my catalyst. It sounds ridiculous (all this journal will one day) but it's true.

He *looks* like a piece of lab equipment. Maybe it's because his father teaches us physics. Milo is the thinnest man I've ever seen and his ears are at right angles to his head. He is also the funniest man I've ever met and, come to think of it, the hungriest. He eats like a bloody horse. I've seen him eat three lunches one after the other at school, including the rice pudding, and anyone who can do that has a worm.

Milo doesn't have emotions; he just works and eats. I only have to come within his magnetic field and I start working too, like a bloody fiend. He's a Jesuit among scientists. I'm sure he'll be a great scientist one day.

About being an instrument. When there's a German bomber going over, he turns his head from side to side, using those big bat-like ears like home-made radar. Then he stops with his funny bent nose pointing at a certain angle and says: "That's where the bastard is coming from."

He gets up at six every morning to work.

A really shameful incident this evening. It's one of the strangest things that has ever happened to me. I was coming out of the library when I saw Felix talking to Laura. Though I desperately wanted to stay and talk I saw the Shallerton bus coming and jumped on it without saying hello. I had the curious premonition that if I did stay there would be some bitter consequence one day. It must have seemed extremely ill-mannered. I didn't even appear to recognize Laura.

Friday 22nd January

I went with Kenneth Heppel to see *In Which We Serve*. It helped me sort out the curious and very mixed feelings I always have when condemning England to my friends. I now see that I do love England even though I object to the principles and policy of its government. This should really have dawned on me before. How could I, loving the Cressbrook Valley as I do, ever hate the country of which it's a part?

Afterwards Ken and I went into the coffee bar in the High Street. Mrs. Duncher, the Westons' daily woman, was in there and she told us that a German plane had come down low that afternoon over Bales Whitney (her village) and machine-gunned the children. No one was hurt, luckily, though there are deep grooves from its cannon shells right across the road. Mrs. Duncher said that if she were an R.A.F. pilot she would go over Germany and shoot every German man, woman, and child on sight. Neither of us agreed with her, though for rather different reasons.

Ken Heppel is a pacifist, but a real hundred per cent one. He will never fight and never change his mind. I suppose he's the nicest chap I've ever met. He's small and rather knobbly, with a working-class face. This sounds a pretty offensive thing to say, but he'd laugh.

Class is a strange business. I don't think we know much about it here in the Cressbrook Valley. We have enormous local rivalries, such as our hatred of Shallerton. The fact is that in this small community, we range through just about every social class. Tony Hammond's mother is related to the original family who built our school and who were given a peerage under George the Third. The present Lord A. is a pasty little snurdge of fourteen. However, they're authentically upper-class all right; there are members of Hammond's family buried in the churchyard four hundred years back.

Laura is upper-middle class. One of her grandparents, she says, was a famous Edwardian surgeon, another was some relation of Tennyson. Felix's father is upper-middle class, communist sub-division. Milo, I think, is middle middle.

I am lower middle, and Ken seems to be in the upper slice of the working class. His father is a mechanic, a trade unionist, militant Labour man, skilled, who spent a long time on the dole and took part in the General Strike. Mr. Heppel works at the Alysbourn Garage; goes in each day in overalls and comes home each day covered in oil.

The Heppels live in a council house on the poor side of town up by the graveyard.

There are also people at school whose fathers are unskilled labourers. Aelfric is the cleverest; how wonderful it would be for us all if he did win an Open. I wonder what will become of us all?

But this all started because of the German machine-gunning. Ken flatly disagreed with Mrs. Duncher on straight Lansburyan grounds. I disagreed too, yet I fully accept that we can't have any squeamishness if we are to win the war. But against this, if we use their methods we lose our own ideals and become no better than they are. We have already lost. It's an appalling dilemma.

It was such a lovely night that I walked home with Ken. He asked me about Tess, and I said I thought her quite enchanting. He then said something very reckless: that he would never love anyone else quite as he loved her. He asked me if she ever talked about him. I said yes, sometimes, and always with affection. I hope that wasn't too encouraging.

We were talking so hard, and so intoxicated with our talk, that he then walked back with me, and then I walked half-way back with him. God, though, it was fun. Bed at 1.30 absolutely exhausted.

Monday 25th

We went to Miller's as usual. We always order a dozen cakes and a large pot of tea; then we can sit there from four to five-thirty. When Laura poured tea for us, still flushed from the cold air outside, her tongue between her lips in concentration, she looked suddenly very young. I felt a ridiculous tenderness for her.

She says that the bracelets she wears are a hundred years old. I watch her quick fingers as she pours the tea with fascination and awe.

This afternoon I went to hear Ilex taking them for Greek. They work in the library. It was marvellously snug up there; the fire was piled high with wood and the wind whistling outside only accentuated the sense of safety. I listened spellbound. They're reading *The Frogs*. I can't understand much but I enjoy the sound of the Greek, especially when Ilex reads a bit. We are indeed lucky to have him. Perhaps in Ilex we see the dawn of the new era in education. In his two years here he has opened our lives to the world outside the Cressbrook Valley.

Tuesday 26th

After the incessant rain the Cressbrook flooded today in a way I've never seen before. The water rose to within six inches of the archtop under the Watermill and great waves were rolling across Twenty Acre. The wind, I estimate, was gale force. Laura and I stood on the parapet of the Watermill and watched the water froth and boil in the weir. Truly it was exhilarating to feel the force of that strangely warm wind in the face and to be sprayed by the fine rain.

Wednesday 27th

We went to see one of the most plainly told screen stories I've ever come across: *Wake Island*. We got talking about films afterwards and decided to put this in our gallery of great pictures: *Fantasia, Gone With The Wind, In Which We Serve,* and *Citizen Kane.*

Thinking of these films for which I have a special affection reminded me of many other things which I shall always hold as beautiful. First, always, the day when I first saw Laura. Then, two poems by de la Mare: "The Listeners" and "I Sit Alone". Then, the memory of the first concert I ever heard; even though it was only the New World Symphony in Shallerton Town Hall, a thing you can always sell to a semi-literate audience.

Today I add two more things to my list. The first is a poem by D. H. Lawrence called "Snake". The other was the sky tonight as we walked home along the top of the Downs. Though it's so early and the nights are still long, it had a premonition of Spring and this despite the cold; a smoky duck-egg blue with that curious and special tang in the air; you gulp it down and it makes you feel tipsy.

Thursday 28th

A baffling experience today: Keith Margrave asked me to lunch at the Brewery. I've grown up with the smell of it. I know it will one day be Proustian in its power, wherever I am, to throw me back in my imagination to Aylsbourn. He showed me over and I saw the entire operation. They use enormous copper vats and the yeast on the top is thick and frothy, the colour of milky coffee whipped up. The one thing they fear like the plague is what they call ropey beer—it means some bug has got into the system and it can take two years to get out. When this last happened to a brewer, Margrave told me, all the others rallied round to help him out. There are still quite a lot of craftsmen working there, especially the coopers who make the barrels; but I noticed they're using electric tools now and to hell with the old hand craftsmanship. When there's a really good froth on the beer they call it a rocky head. Margrave gave me some Russian stout to try; they bottled it originally for the Czar of Russia and my God it's strong. Frankly too strong for me. We had an excellent plain lunch in the boardroom—roast beef and apple tart. There were just the two of us. He asked me how my father was and I said he seemed to be enjoying life enormously down at Salisbury. He asked me a lot of questions about my work and hopes and I told him I had no clear ideas yet.

I told Laura about it this evening and she said I am a clot; obviously Margrave wants me to come into the Brewery. I think he was just trying to be kind to the son of one of his favourite men. It is true that he has no children of his own.

Friday 29th

Ilex came into the library today when we all were sitting about. He looked upset and with reason: poor old Macpherson had had a mild stroke. Worse, though: apparently some small arteries behind his eyes are hardening and his sight is rapidly going; what little there is left mustn't be taxed. We would be able to imagine, Ilex said, better than he, what it would mean to the old fellow not to be able to read, for it is his greatest pleasure in life. Would any of us, he asked, volunteer to read to him? Needless to say everyone of us, even Felix, volunteered at once. I remembered that day when we read Milton's sonnet "On His Blindness" with Macpherson. As soon as I could I got out and walked for half an hour trying to get used to the cruelty of it, but it was no good.

Monday 1st February

Tonight we had the first evening this year of the Eccentrics, a club that Hennessy formed when he first arrived. Since then we've had some intoxicating discussions: free will, free love, and this evening communism. It was the most riveting evening I've known, the intellectual excitement of it was indescribable.

The conversation turned to the civil war in Spain. Hennessy was out there, on the Republican side of course, but an ambulance driver because he's also a pacifist. He read us some short stories he wrote during that period. One or two seemed good to me. One especially was haunting: about a young wounded soldier lying in a shell-hole and whistling "Frankie and Johnny" to keep his courage up.

The news from Russia had been marvellous. Last week the German Sixth Army, commanded by von Paulus, surrendered at Stalingrad. Mr. Johnston says that one day we shall see that their scientists are every bit as good as ours. One or two of our best scientists went there before the war and came back saying this, but weren't believed. I find it hard to believe myself.

I could swallow communism more easily if it didn't mean disloyalty to England.

Later we got talking about dreams and I was fascinated to see what Laura would say about hers. But they turned out to be fairly conventional: dancing by a moonlit sea (with whom?), being chased (by whom?), falling over a cliff, and getting married (we asked her to whom but she could never see). Later I asked Ken Heppel if he thought she really didn't know and he said she certainly wasn't telling us the whole truth. I can't be sure. But this I do know: there is a lot about her I don't understand properly yet.

Then we got talking about extra-sensory perception and taboo. Mr. Johnston said there was a rational explanation for all the strange phenomena one reads about—the Versailles apparitions and Borley Rectory.

I wish there were a little more magic in the world.

Tuesday 2nd

Laura took me home this evening and we had supper with her parents. I don't know quite what they make of me; on the whole I imagine they think I'm harmless, and on the whole they're right. Dr. Mackay knows Auden; he has books all the way up the stairs of the house. He and Laura's mother used to leave every summer and travel for two months before the war; sometimes

Spain or Yugoslavia or Greece, but they've been as far as North Africa. To me they look perfectly happy; but Laura insists they parted once. Moreover, she says all married people do, metaphorically at least unless they've become complete vegetables with no feelings left. I can't accept this. My own parents were perfectly happy, I'm sure, though of course I only have my father's evidence.

The Mackays accept that there was nothing between Laura and Tony but a curious hero-disciple relationship; she has talked to me about it now. She says that Tony was often at their house because his father and the Mackays were once good friends; that Tony always treated her as a favourite younger sister, taught her tennis and all that, but there was nothing else. He used to tell her all his secrets and she got a vicarious sense of adventure from his relationship with Arabella. When I asked her what she thought about him sleeping with Arabella, she made a typical wisecrack: "Who *wouldn't*?"

Wednesday 3rd

Laura took me out riding with her this afternoon. I'm a complete peasant in this, but she's an expert. I'm bound to say it's quite agreeable when we're just moving at a very slow walk, but anything faster puts the wind up me. She has a mare, a bright chestnut, which stands just over fifteen hands and is seven years old. She's fairly well built to my layman's eye, part Welsh cob, part thoroughbred. Laura's been schooling her for two years now and jumping in local and novice competitions and small shows. She's won several prizes, though not as many as she'd have liked because Rosie (that's her mare) refuses at walls painted red. Laura has even—and this I don't like to mention too much in front of my friends—hunted.

Everything about Laura—even her bloody horse or mare or whatever it is—fascinates me. I can never hear enough.

Monday 8th February

Laura and I went to the Classic to see Jack Benny and Ann Sheridan in *George Washington Slept Here*. It was one of the funniest films we've seen in years. We walked home; there was a gibbous moon and a little mist. But again, there was an enticing touch of spring in the night air; how odd that you can feel it so early in England. I wonder what sort of summer we shall have and where we shall all be eighteen months from now? Soon it will have been four years of war. I'm unable to believe in the war in one sense. I know those poor sods are dying by the thousands in Russia, and I know all about North Africa. But here it's so damned peaceful; we're cradled in this valley and in a way the horror we see in the sky over Portsmouth only seems to accentuate our own womb-like safety. Of course it's an illusion. Once or twice already bombs have dropped in the Cressbrook Valley; usually because the pilot's lost his way; but on one famous occasion because the German captain was a Wykehamist and couldn't bear to drop his cargo—or so the papers would have us believe—on his old *alma mater*. The Germans could do with a few more Wykehamists.

Tonight nothing happened; it was utterly still and moonshot and the whole town seemed to be only just breathing. There's hardly any traffic ever now even on the main road to London. We often walk down it four abreast. I long sometimes for the day when it'll be full of old Fords bumper to bumper and heading for the sea, the families disgorging their empty packets of Smith's Crisps and Tizer bottles on us. This just shows how bad the ache for peace can be and how hallucinatory this false peace in which we're all so seductively lulled. It's often said but it's true: war brings happiness to many people, just as it brings misery and pain and death to many more. One day soon it will take us all out of the Cressbrook Valley. I go for my medical this April. I shall be seventeen and a quarter then, the minimum age to volunteer for aircrew. I've never had any doubts or misgivings about this.

Tuesday 9th

We went to the market at lunch-time today; Laura wanted to buy a rabbit for a small male cousin of hers. I'm bound to admit here privately that though I should hate to work on the land I do get a kick from the bucolic dung-imbued ambience of the place. We went into the "Wheatsheaf" for lunch and bumped into Mr. Varley. He's looking almost mauve now—much worse than the small veins on Margrave's face—and really not terribly healthy. Also, I noticed that there are some grey streaks in his glossy black hair. I introduced him to Laura and he treated her with almost exaggerated gallantry. He insisted on buying us both a shandy. Afterwards I asked Laura what she thought of him. She said he had the particular enticement that all former criminals had. I asked her what on earth she meant and she said that she had no evidence that he'd been inside at all, it was just a hunch. How astonishing if she were right! She usually is.

Afterwards we strolled through the market again, inspecting the porkers, the cutters, the baconers, the capons, the cockerels and rough-plucked hens. Laura found two charming little rabbits.

This afternoon I did my best afternoon's work in chemistry this term: two whole volumetrics (oxalic and H_2O_2 with $KMNO_4$) and preparation for a third (iron in ferric alum).

Wednesday 10th

Today chemistry was dull, so in the afternoon I eaves-dropped on Hennessy's class in American History. I truly believe he could make any damned subject on earth interesting. He has a long lean face, thick lips, slightly protruding blue eyes and a bow tie. There are still occasional suggestions that he and Ilex have a homosexual relationship. It may be that they do but only, I think, a Platonic one.

I looked over Laura's shoulder and saw that he had given her an alpha minus query minus. I've never heard of such a complicated mark before. I don't quite know what it means but sometimes I wish science were amenable to that sort of imprecision.

Hennessy came to the Gramophone Society tonight—"Love of Three Oranges" was best—and stayed on afterwards telling us about the Fabians and particularly the Wells-Belloc literary battle (Mr. Belloc objects and Mr. Belloc still objects). Also the Chesterton-Shaw debate, G.K.'s weekly, and the Belloc-Selfridge debate. All this was new and fascinating to us. We got on to Freud and H. said Freud was over-inclined to attribute everything to sex; recommended us to read Adler as a corrective, but warned us that he went to the other extreme and attributed everything to desire for power. I'm pretty sure F. is right in saying that this lust for power is basically sexual.

Laura says her father takes a cool view of Freud. He says that his case histories give an exceptionally biased view because many of his clients were bourgeois Jewish women brought up in a rigid

163

and conventional framework—hence all the neuroses and repressions.

Pretty well an ideal day. My leg is still painful from last week's football injury so they told me not to play today. Instead I went alone to London on the fast train to Waterloo. I walked—or rather sped—up Villiers Street and Charing Cross Road and bought a Pelican by Waddington called *The Scientific Attitude*. In Foyles I made two fairly routine purchases: *Opera*, a Pelican, and Joad's *Guide to Modern Wickedness*. I walked for half an hour trying to find this new gramophone exchange place, but no luck. I cursed myself for not making a note of the address. In Villiers Street on my way back I was disturbed by what I thought was the slow, dull beat of dive-bombers; it turned out to be just the air-conditioning plant of the underground.

I got home at seven and found to my great delight that my father would be here tomorrow on his way north to a new posting.

After supper Tessa, Joanna, Milo and I played Louis Armstrong records. T. and J. find his voice coarse and a little shocking, but we tried to explain to them the feeling he puts into even the most corny little piece. I really believe we have no right to run down negro music; especially not right now, when you look at what white civilization has achieved in central Europe.

I looked at Joanna while the music was playing and thought to myself that though she will never be a beauty she will appeal to somebody. When you're not talking to her and she doesn't realize you're looking, she looks sometimes dreadfully wistful. How our faces give us away if we don't keep our guard up! She has a pleasing shape too. Milo is rather coarse about her pectoral developments; she pretends to resent it, but I think secretly she quite enjoys it. Poor little Tess will have to wait another year or two before we start making fun of her on that score.

My father came in time for lunch. He looked marvellous; absurdly young and good-looking in his second-lieutenant's uniform. There's no doubt that he's one of the men who blossom in war. To him it's just a rather good game, with strict rules of conduct to be adhered to on both sides. However, he is not such an idealist that he has any illusions about the Germans—how could he after spending three years as a prisoner in their hands? He talked amusingly about the Army and the astonishing people he meets. We put him on the train at five with several jars of home-made jam in his bag. Tessa said this evening that as he was so attractive it was a shame he didn't marry again. I had never thought about this before, and now she's raised the possibility I find it distressing.

Tuesday 16th

Today Milo nearly killed himself. He added thio-cyanate to hot dilute acid and collapsed from HCN fumes.

Wednesday 17th

Although Ilex doesn't understand science he realizes its importance. He's badgered the county into converting some old workshops into a new laboratory. Considering it's wartime, this is an achievement; but I'm sure they're right. One day it will pay dividends. We move in next week—quick work considering they began work only a month ago.

Saturday 20th

Frankly the leg is all right, but I played truant from football because Laura wanted to go to London. We got there early and booked seats for the evening performance at the Saville. Then went to the Shaftesbury Avenue Gram. Exchange and bought the Italian Symphony. But we couldn't get "Bach Goes to Town"—our new favourite. We lunched in Glasshouse Street on Spaghetti Bolognese and half a carafe of ordinaire. It cost six and two. Laura went halves.

When we came out it was foggy. It was strange to walk across Waterloo Bridge and hear the rumbling of the engines without being able to see them. Laura said Limbo would be just like that.

When I'd said good night to Laura I waited under her window until her light came on. She sat at her dressing-table and brushed her hair for about ten minutes. Then she did her nails or something. Then she got up and drew the curtains and I waited for another ten minutes before the light went out. I wasn't—at least

I hope I'm not—becoming a voyeur: but I just can't take my eyes off her.

Milo wanted to go down to the High Street this afternoon so I said I'd go too. He didn't look very pleased and I couldn't understand why, for he was only going to buy chocolate with his sisters' ration cards—the hungry-gutted bastard. Afterwards he wanted to go into the library to hear some records. He's an odd fish. He seems cold sometimes, yet he was moved almost to tears by "Slaughter on Tenth Avenue". We jawed about jazz and philosophy. I told him about Louis Macneice, whom I've just discovered, and he threw bits of Whitehead at me.

At about six-thirty all became clear: the Pepperpot appeared wearing a lot too much lipstick and eyeshadow. She wore a tight blouse and a skirt with a slit of about four inches in the side. I don't know what Milo sees in her and nor do his sisters. I decided to beat it, but they said to stay a bit and play a few more records. This gave me a good chance to gauge her mentality. I put on a Goodman record and she said it was terrific—whose record was it? I said it was hers. She was quite gobstruck; apparently there's a favourite of hers on the other side and she had never turned it over. Soon after that I left them to it.

Milo came in at about ten-thirty looking sheepish and gave Tess his handkerchief to wash. It was covered with the Pepperpot's vile lipstick. However, if it makes him happy.

Monday 22nd

Working late in the lab tonight I did a colorimetric (Lovibond comparator) for iron which Constance checked. We got exactly the same result. This shows that, by co-incidence, we have the same red colour sensitivity. It sounds incongruous, but I felt in the lab this evening as if I belonged there, and was not just an intruder.

On the way home Constance asked me about Laura; was she missing Tony? I said I thought so; she had a card at Christmas, otherwise the only news we've had came when Ilex told us he'd had a university trial. He didn't make it this year, but he's almost bound to next. I asked C. what she thought of Laura. Constance made a very odd reply. She said: "Laura has a greater capacity for disaster than any other girl I know."

I'm liking calculus a lot lately. Milo is more persistent than I am at it though. If he doesn't understand something he goes on and on asking until he's got it right. He has an absolute fixation about space flight. He spends all his spare time designing rockets. They frighten me. I am sure they will kill a lot of people before we eventually hit the moon; but Milo's the sort of moonstruck fool who would volunteer to go the first time. In a weird way, I think he would like to die in outer space.

Went into Shallerton early this morning to buy Felix a present for his seventeenth birthday; finally settled on John Buchan's *Augustus*. I think Felix and Augustus have this in common at least: neither would ever let any woman deflect him. This evening there was a little party *chez* Weston. Arabella is looking perceptibly older, her adventure seems to have coarsened her face slightly and she smokes about forty cigarettes a day; there is a nicotine stain on her charming little fingers which I hate to see. But she is terrific fun still and the most outspoken woman for sure in the Cressbrook. She sat next to me in a corner and talked about her son, Timothy. She seemed to glow with the excitement of having made him; in fact she said several times: "He's very well *made*—all legs at the moment but the head is very fine"— rather as though he were a piece of sculpture.

We discovered an astonishing thing tonight—she is only *twenty-four*. Constance said rather coarsely that this was no doubt the reason for Tony Hammond; that Gerard was getting past it. He looked old tonight, though he's only just fifty. He drank a lot and got very excited about Russia. Now we could see, he exclaimed, whether they were serfs or not; would serfs have defended Stalingrad like that? He and Arabella appear to get on, but if you watch carefully you do notice little asperities between them sometimes. That sort of thing must leave its mark, even on men of reason.

Felix was in fine form. He said he would fight in this war, but only because it's the safest thing to do. The best plan, he explained to us, is to be a staff officer fifty miles behind the front lines billeted in a château well stocked with Veuve Cliquot and a lonely châtelaine. Gerard enjoyed this; he's proud of Felix.

Everything comes easily to Felix. He should get a Classical Open to Oxford. He's the most *mature* friend I have. He doesn't carve me up quite the way he once did, though, I've got used to him and can carry on the debate with him on more or less equal terms. Constance says he will come to a sticky end. She is a profoundly pessimistic girl. In this way, she and Felix have a lot in common, but they don't get on well.

Later in the evening Arabella took me up to show me her son. He lay sleeping peacefully and I must say it was comical to see how like Felix he was, and yet not so at the same time; there were hints of Arabella in his little face. Arabella said something significant: "He makes it all worth while." All what?

Sunday 28th

I'm on edge, my nerves seem to be stretched taut like violin strings. For instance, I went into the lab to do some ferric reduction titrations this evening; it was very peaceful and I could work really fast, completing six titrations. Yet the hissing of the acid down the sink made my skin crawl, I don't know why. I feel as if something enormous is going to happen any moment. The tension is about as much as I can take.

Thursday 4th March

We went to the Classic tonight and saw the Glenn Miller film *Orchestra Wives*. Though of course many of my friends say Miller is corn, I suspect his music will give us all a Proustian throwback one day, and some of the corn—"At Last", "Perfidia", "American Patrol"—is charming in a light way. All sorts of dance tunes are threading themselves through our lives. I don't think I'll ever forget dancing with Laura to Artie Shaw's "Begin the Beguine"; it's a tune that seems to have been playing all through my young life. The same can be said of "That Old Black Magic". Very occasionally, as in "Smoke Gets In Your Eyes", the words rise above the usually abysmal level of banality. I dare say some earnest young American graduate will write a thesis about this in 2043.

Friday 5th March

At the Eccentrics tonight we discussed what education should be like after the war. Afterwards we played records till midnight.

Felix had a good story for us; apparently a girl who was at school a few years ahead of us, called Nancy Foster got married in Aylsbourn on Saturday. She's twenty and was a shorthand-typist in Shallerton; she left school at fifteen. Everything went well till the reception when her boss, who was giving her away, made a very complimentary speech about her. She then burst into tears and said she really loved him! (That is, the boss.) Confusion all round. Her friends managed to calm her down and finally she went off rather tearfully with her groom.

Laura then made a very curious remark. She said she was sure that many girls had similar ambiguities in their emotions when they married; the only difference about this girl was her appalling frankness. Constance said it was stories like that which convinced her she would never marry. Yet how strange women are: before the evening was out she said quite distinctly: "*When I'm married* I shall expect my husband to have a horse and a car." What sort of sense is that?

Felix remarked that forty was the perfect age for a man to marry. When pressed to tell us how old he thought his wife would then be he replied cryptically: "Either seventeen or forty-three."

I remarked how dreadful it must have been for the groom. Ken said what about the boss—he wouldn't feel too comfortable. Constance said on the contrary: for the boss it must have been a delightful experience—a public declaration of undying love from a woman and absolutely no obligation to do anything about it.

Milo, of course, brought the conversation down to earth by enquiring how they would have got on during their wedding night. Constance drily remarked: "Probably as well as most people." A very interesting discussion then developed about whether one ought to sleep with one's fiancée before marriage. Every single person there said yes, including Hennessy. Felix tried to pull my leg. He said he was disappointed—how could I seriously claim to be a romantic if I took this view? I said I thought far too much about the real importance of sex ever to entrust a delicate and important initiation of that sort to the hazards and leering, back-slapping, boozy heartiness of the wedding day.

I got some very heartening support from Laura. She said she found the ritual of a traditional marriage service nauseating—

all that white, symbol of virginity, and fertility-rite stuff with the rice and the shoes. She said that when she wanted to be deflowered no one would know about it. Tess said what a terrible waste; Laura would look terrific in white. Then, exasperatingly, Laura added absent-mindedly that she might get married in white after all if she had a really fabulous dress. How the devil can one keep pace with a woman's mind from one moment to the next?

Thursday 25th March

A fabulous film at the Classic, *The Magnificent Ambersons*, produced by the one and only Orson Welles. I said to Laura afterwards that it must be both marvellous and terrifying to have to struggle with a talent as Welles did; it would be a bit like having a Rolls-Royce engine in an Austin Seven, the enormous power of the talent would almost shake itself out of one's body with impatience. Then I asked her if she thought anyone we'd ever met had a touch of original creativeness, might, in fact, come to anything in the outside world. I was thinking of Tony of course. I shouldn't have asked her, because she could only give an evasive reply. But I wasn't expecting what she did say: "You're the only one we shall ever hear of again." For once, she's wrong.

Friday 9th April

I've got back from my R.A.F. medical. Everything went fine on the first day—I held up the mercury in the barometer and all that; but during the eyesight tests I could see they were worried about something. Finally the M.O. asked if I'd had a bash in the eye. I said yes—what else could I do? He said that though it was only very slight, one of my muscles didn't respond properly and I could never therefore be passed as a pilot. I could be a navigator—what about it? I was desperately disappointed for a moment; but even in the middle of my despair I remembered thinking that I must never tell anyone why I'd failed in case it ever got back to Ken Heppel—who would never forgive himself.

And then something Ken had said came back to me and made it easier to bear. He had been talking only a few days before about the emotive propaganda effect of R.A.F. uniform. Suppose,

Ken said, we were a really adult society, and that we had decided that for survival's sake we had to fight. Then the actual killers should be chosen by lot and dressed in a drab prison-grey uniform which buttoned up tight at the neck, rather like a Chinese peasant's; and this would be a perpetual reminder to them and anyone else of the evil thing they were being forced to do. For what is the reality of the matter? These glamorous R.A.F. bomber boys with their wings and gongs *are* killers, when all is said; their job necessarily involves eviscerating women, ripping little children limb from limb (how horrible even to write it down—but they actually have to do it). But by the accidental separation of cause and effect—you can't actually see your bombs gouge people's entrails out down below—you can maintain the illusion of romance. Of course that's why some men prefer being fighter pilots. But whether it's really any better morally to fill another pilot with cannon shells—rather than some German down below—I don't know. Anyway, I suddenly saw how little it mattered what I did in the war.

The difference between Ken and me is that I, while acknowledging the horror, believe it must be done to defeat a worse horror. He won't have anything to do with it. He is in for a rough time, I'm afraid.

I said yes to being a navigator, and already I'm rationalizing my disappointment. After all, the pilot is only the bloody driver. The navigator is the real brains of the outfit. But the moral responsibility is exactly the same.

Friday June 4th

Mr. Varley died this week, after a heart attack, and I went to his funeral this morning. I don't really know why. I wore a rose in my buttonhole—one of the yellow ones that came from his garden and which he wore every day through the summer. It was just a little hopeless gesture of defiance from life to death. The most harrowing moment came when the earth was thrown into the open grave; Madame (her name I've discovered is Mrs. Fitzherbert and she's a widow; there's not much doubt what she was to Varley) cried pitifully. There were a lot of O.V.s there. Most of them looked like car salesmen, but there was a fair sprinkling of offensive-looking R.A.S.C. subalterns.

Varley was in many ways a ridiculous person and yet I had a

lot of affection for him. The world is a little bit greyer without him.

There was a fascinating obituary notice in the *Cressbrook Journal* today. It turns out that he *was* a regimental sergeant-major. He came out after the 1914-18 war and got a job as a physical training instructor in a Borstal, before buying Valhalla on the never-never. Laura—as usual—was astonishingly prescient about him. He wasn't of course, a criminal, but he had lived with naughty boys. It's as if she's got a crystal ball she can nearly, but not quite, read.

Saturday 24th July 1943

Laura and I went to London to see the ballet at the Lyric. We were early so we walked across Hungerford Bridge. *Twelfth Night* was superb; in fact I'm afraid that in the terrific heat *Les Sylphides* was a bit of an anti-climax. Afterwards we went into the Coventry Street Corner House and ate waffles. Then a most astonishing thing happened. Suddenly Laura put her hand on mine. I looked up—needless to say I was just taking a mouthful of waffle—and saw her looking at me as if she'd never seen me before. "Benny," she said, "why are you so sweet to me?" I muttered something. "No," she insisted gently. "Tell me. Why are you always so good to me when I never give you any affection in return?" I began to say I didn't want anything, that to be with her was all I needed. But I couldn't express myself. And then the words came tumbling out and I told her all about that first time I'd seen her and how I'd loved her ever since and would never love anyone else in quite the same way.

All this in Lyon's Corner House—of all the places in the world to choose!

She didn't answer, but kept staring at me with a sort of gentle astonishment; she seemed to be searching every line in my face to see if I was joking. I don't think she could take it in at first. Then she put both her hands on mine as it lay on the table and said softly: "Hello, Benny." With those absolutely typical yet quite unexpected words, she committed herself to me. I think we have a love affair on our hands.

Sunday 25th July 1943

This morning we met early and went for a walk. I wanted to show her the exact route I'd taken that day, which changed my life. As we walked I even told her about the examination fiasco, a thing I thought I'd never tell another soul. At last we got to my secret view. It was a marvellous summer morning, and we sat in the grass looking out towards Oakhanger. It was absolutely still. Then she said: "Benny, why have you never kissed me?" And I said: "Because I never thought you wanted me to." Then she said: "Kiss me now." I could hardly believe it wasn't a dream. For a moment or two I couldn't have obeyed if I'd tried; my mind seemed to have ceased to relay messages to my body, so great was my surprise. Then I half turned and I remembered her face was very grave, just as Hammond's was at the beginning of that game, and in an absurd way the analogy is real, for to her it was the beginning of a more serious adventure. And then— how else can I put it down, except in plain words?—I found that I was kissing her, and her bare arms came slowly round my neck and drew me softly down into the grass.

It was quite different from anything I've ever experienced; neither quite innocent like Tess, nor wild like Constance. Instead, with unhurried gentleness, she let her kisses wander all over my face, as if she were on a voyage of exploration: she kissed my eyes, my throat, even my hair. In a little while I began to respond and in a few moments we were both trembling with the unspoken promises made by our silent lips.

Soon we drew apart and lay staring up into the sky, only our hands touching, for inexperienced as we both were, we could read the message in those kisses and we were both reluctant that we should in any way be hurried. We talked drowsily, like exhausted lovers instead of two young innocents brushed by the finger-tips of desire, and we had no wish for any other expression of our love. For that was what it was. If Laura never loves me again, I know she loved me just then.

I won't try to describe the rest of the day; as far as the world is concerned we passed it in a quite ordinary way; but every word and every look between us was on two levels of meaning: the world's and our own. We parted quite early because we were both incapable of any more emotion, and besides, by doing so, we will make the next day seem to come more quickly.

Wednesday Sept 29th

We're into our last year. Most of our futures seem fixed. Milo has his place at Cambridge next autumn, Felix at Oxford, though he will go into the Army first, Ken Heppel will almost certainly get into Southampton when he comes out of the mines. I'm definitely fixed at Imperial College, London. Laura is going to Art School next autumn, probably in Shallerton; Joanna is going to King's College, London, and Tess is doing a secretarial course. Poor little sweetheart, even Ilex couldn't win her a scholarship. Constance, cleverest of all our girls, has got into Somerville. Our great triumph is Aelfric Gates, who won an Open at Oxford right on schedule. Next summer Ilex will have fourteen university places, eleven at Oxford and Cambridge. You can't begrudge the man his triumph; already they're calling it The Aylsbourn Experiment and odd-looking men from the Ministry of Education are coming down to give us the once-over.

Wednesday 9th February

The snow's been falling steadily in the Cressbrook Valley for two days and tonight we were out tobogganing. Milo has a sledge and we took it in turns to whiz down the side of the Downs in it two at a time. I took Laura down with me; she lay on top of me and with her arms round my neck was quite safe as we streaked to the bottom. We all felt like children again.

Thursday 10th February

Poor little Tess was rushed to hospital for an emergency operation today; how quickly happiness can go sour. It was acute appendicitis. However, thank God, it seems tonight she's going to be all right. The thing that touches me most, though, is that she asked for me first when she came round. The fact that she was so near death brought the old enemy into perspective for me again; it would be so bloody *annoying* to die now. By way of an amulet, I think I should make a note now of the people to whom I owe thanks; for since I can pay no allegiance to God I must offer my gratitude to my fellow-men and women. First then, to Laura, for the gift of love; next to my father, for showing me what is good; then my friends—Felix for shattering my dreams; Milo for giving me so many laughs; Ken for understanding me better than anyone else in the world; Tess for her tenderness; Joanna for her wistfulness; Constance for kissing me the way she did; Macpherson for teaching me what language is; Ilex for making me reach further than I thought I could; Hennessy for making me think; Arabella for showing me what a woman is; poor old Varley for teaching me how to put up with the world as it is; Mrs. Johnston for feeding me; Miller's teashop for harbouring me; the Cressbrook Valley for filling my lungs every day with its good air; Hammond for teaching me how sweet it is to be alive.

Wednesday 17th May 1944

Each day I grow more disillusioned with this course of science I so recklessly embarked on. It's all my own fault, I quite concede that; but I shall never be better than mediocre at it. The day of reckoning is very close now.

Friday 23rd June 1944

Mr. and Mrs. Johnston have gone to Bournemouth for a few days. Needless to say, this suggested to Milo that we ought to have what he calls an uninhibited party. It's to be tomorrow night; the girls are making some food and we're laying in a barrel of best Margrave bitter. How delightful to be eighteen, free, idle and in love on a summer's day!

Sunday 25th June, 1944

Well, it was quite a party. We played lots of records and danced to them: innocuous tunes like Tommy Dorsey's "I'll Be Seeing You", Glenn Miller's "Perfidia", Artie Shaw's "Begin the Beguine". Then we had some supper and sat around talking. Later, Milo put some Beethoven sonatas on the radiogram and turned the sound up to full bore. It's amazing how we never really listen to music when it's played as a sort of teashop noise; just as coffee is best strong, so good music is best loud. Then we turned off the lights and drew back the curtains. The garden was drenched in moonlight. The girls curled up on our laps. We drowned in the music. It seemed to lift one's imagination right out of its physical mountings, to use a rather crude analogy, and sent it floating away over the Cressbrook Valley. It was the kind of evening where when you wanted to speak you couldn't because the music had been quietly strangling you. Later we played the Brahms First Quartet—the thing it took him four years to write—and what an impact that has! You feel him carrying you along with absolute certainty. You feel that the music has been chiselled and hammered and polished till it has a hard glowing brilliant perfection. I can't imagine that life has any keener pleasure to offer.

No one noticed the time until suddenly Ken said, "Look—it's dawn" and we saw that very delicate, pale hint of light in the sky. Then we stretched ourselves and went out into the garden where it was very cool. There was a light dew on the grass and Laura cut a yellow rose off one of Mr. Johnston's trees with a pair of sewing scissors and put it in my button-hole. She knows I love them—a trait I picked up from old Varley. It was a very young bud and still closed, and there were little drops of dew glistening on it. I don't think there will ever be another night quite like it.

I've not tried to write down everything that's happened between Laura and me because I don't happen to have the necessary intellectual equipment to crystallize it in words; the dream is corrupted as the pen touches the paper. Also, I've no wish to record all the moods and subtleties and complexions and shadows of our love-affair because one day it may make bitter reading; I mean that everything else must seem an anti-climax. What I will do is transcribe in this journal one of her many notes to me; I am tearing all the rest in little pieces. They would never be understood by anybody else, and might not even be understood even by me one day; there is a lively possibility that the man who would read them in twenty years would be a stranger to me.

But I can't resist the temptation to transcribe just one note. The sight of her handwriting is the keenest pleasure I know. *My* name in *her* writing—P. J. Benedict Esquire indeed! And inside I found a casual prose sonnet:

Benny my dear:

I called to see you but found no one in. You were with the boys up in Felix's room. The light was on as we walked up from the station and I heard music. Needless to say, you were playing one of those very old Armstrong's. I felt warm and safe to think of you there. But, unexpectedly, I was too shy to knock. I should have wanted you to myself. London was awful without you. It was one of those female days: shopping and the hairdresser. My father was at a medical conference at the War Office; mama and I went to a place in Soho called Le Jardin des Gourmets; apparently papa used to take her there when they were, to use that blushmaking old word, courting. I looked at it with astonishment and a sort of prenatal recognition. I can't imagine them holding hands there any more than I can imagine—but you know what I'm trying to say. Benny, dear, I'm in bed now, in a demure white cotton night-dress (what a provoking little bitch I am) and I love you. Please take one special kiss to bed with you from me.

Laura.

Friday 21st July

Ilex called us all into his study—it was the last day of term and our last day there—and gave us all a glass of sherry. He then made a very touching little speech—that is to say he was touched, indeed near to tears. He said it had been the happiest three years of his life, that we had all done him proud (he didn't put it like that of course), and that he couldn't imagine life ever offering him any greater reward. Then came the usual drill about keeping in touch and coming to see him which old Varley gave. He didn't offer to pay our debts, but he did give the impression he'd be only too pleased to act as our Father Confessor. There've been hints for some time that he's going over to Rome.

Ilex is a man whose faults are written large all over his face, but he is a remarkable man all the same and we're lucky to have known him. Hennessy is leaving this term and going to America. He's the one I shall miss most of all.

And now we have three months left—three delicious months with nothing to do, no responsibilities, no duties, twenty-four hours in each day our own—before the world scoops us up and takes us out of the Cressbrook Valley.

★ 6 ★

THE summer of 1944 was, then, the last that Benedict and his friends were to spend together. It was unique for this alone, but it was memorable in several other senses. It was, first, a beautiful summer; not as good as 1940 but full of warmth and a new quality—hope. There was a sense of excitement in the world which had permeated even Aylsbourn. The allied armies had invaded Europe early that June and each day the boys would work out the advances on a large map with pins and coloured string. It was a timeless summer; they had absolutely nothing to do but wait. For its differing reasons the world did not require them till autumn; there was a formless vista of weeks stretching ahead of them without care. No one expected anything of them till then. They had little money, but they had something far more precious: freedom.

The routine for each day, therefore, was exactly like the one before. Benedict and Milo would get up at about eight, and read the morning papers over a long lazy breakfast. Then they would stroll round to fetch Ken Heppel from the council estate near the cemetery, and on down to the High Street to collect Felix, who was generally still in his dressing-gown. Then they would move on at a leisurely pace to Miller's where Joanna and Tess, Laura and Constance, would be having coffee. They would sit and talk idly for an hour and a half. Then they would drift down the High Street, stopping to buy a record or two, the antediluvian shiny black heavy ones which used to spin at seventy-eight revolutions per minute.

Then they would meander on up to the market square and into the "Wheatsheaf" for bitter beer. They all drank this, girls as well. Even Laura had grown to like it. Then they would eat lunch in the "Wheatsheaf's" back room. It cost in those days one and ninepence: meat and two veg. and a roly-poly pudding. After that they would walk out of Aylsbourn, each day by a different footpath. Usually they followed the Cressbrook. There was a compelling quality about its crystalline clarity and pureness; it was hypnotic to lie by it and let one's hand trail in the

178

cold, clean water. The pebbles were smooth and golden and the cress rippled in the tide. Sometimes they would swim where the Cressbrook widened out into the Mill Pond. Then they would lie on the bank, read the latest Koestler novel or a bit of Auden, gossip, lie on their backs, chase each other, sleep.

Sometimes they would take a portable gramophone up into the Aylsbourn Downs and play the latest Frank Sinatra or Glenn Miller records—never anything more complicated. Somehow, the one tune which seemed to emerge for Benedict as the theme song of that interlude was Tommy Dorsey's "I'll Be Seeing You". Though the lyric was naïve, it seemed to sum up their subcutaneous emotions, and the tune, though simple, was hard to forget. Often Benedict found himself humming it, as he strolled along the sun-poached pavements on those idle days of interregnum. It seemed to carry overtones of their own transitory situation:

> *In a small café,*
> *The park across the way,*
> *The children's carousel,*
> *The chestnut tree,*
> *The wishing well.*

And time without number, he danced to that hissing old record with Laura.

In the evenings they would go to the Classic, hoping always to see another *Citizen Kane* or *Le Jour Se Lève*, and even if—as nearly always happened—they were disappointed, it was part of the ritual of their life. After that, they would go to Felix's room and play poker tirelessly till one in the morning.

There was only one troubling interlude during those three months: Constance left suddenly to get a job at Portsmouth. No one ever got to the bottom of it; true, her guardian, Mr. Hayley, had become ill and had been obliged to retire from the Post Office; what puzzled her friends was that her parents, wherever they were, seemed to take no interest. Ilex was known to be furious. His cleverest girl not taking up a place at Somerville! There were angry exchanges between him and the Hayleys and it was still not quite clear what was to happen when she departed abruptly for Portsmouth one day in September.

They all went to see her off at the station. She looked adult and soignée in a tweed suit and appeared quite unaffected. They stood about not knowing quite what to say while the train made its preparation to go. Benedict began to feel a sense of sadness, bitterness and waste welling up inside him. He took Constance by the arm and walked a few paces with her.

"Constance, please, isn't there anything we can do?"

"Nothing, Benny."

"But you can't just give up a chance like that."

"I have no choice."

"But you had such great dreams—to be a new Madame Curie!"

"All dreams have to end, Benny, as you'll find out one day."

"Promise at any rate you'll keep in touch. Write to us."

"I can't promise. I may."

The guard's whistle blew. Her three pathetically small suitcases were stowed aboard. They all kissed her goodbye. As the train drew out, she didn't wave; in fact she turned her face away from them.

"You know," said Laura as they walked home, "it's a funny thing, but I never saw Constance cry before."

Mr. Benedict came home for a short leave late in September and stayed for forty-eight hours at the "Wheatsheaf". He still looked full of beans. Benedict took Laura to meet him at tea-time on Sunday. He seemed painfully shy at first, then realized she was on his side and talked too much, but was full of gaiety and hope. His cadets, he claimed, were the finest in England, far finer even than the young officers in the first war—fitter and more articulate and less snobbish. His mild blue eyes sparkled as he talked; Benedict found himself hoping, to his shame, that no bloody woman would snap him up; his father was too precious to share.

Laura came to the station with them. On the platform father and son disappeared into the Gentlemen's; it was not a very private place but it had to do. They stood side by side.

"Do you like her, Pop?"

"Of course I do. She's a sweet girl. Is it serious?"

"Yes."

A fleeting expression of loss and pain passed over his father's usually untroubled outdoor face. Then it cleared and he smiled.

"She'll be a credit to you, son. You have my blessing."

He waved vigorously till his train was out of view. Then Laura said: "What a poppet. If you ever desert me, there'll always be your father."

The dates fell close together: Ken Heppel had to leave for Durham on October fourth, Benedict went to his Aircrew Receiving Centre on the sixth, Felix reported to Aldershot on the seventh, Milo went to Cambridge on the ninth. They decided, therefore, that they would spend their final evening, October third, together.

They began to drink punctually at six in the "Thorn and Sceptre". The Margrave bitter seemed never to have tasted better. It was limpid and full of life. They sat on wooden trestles down each side of one of the pub's wooden tables, talking and laughing uproariously between long swigs. By eight o'clock they had finished four pints each. But they felt no effect whatsoever, until they went outside. Then the Aylsbourn air took its sudden, heady effect, and they were drunk.

It was a moonless night, but every star was in the sky. Benedict gulped in some deep breaths. "Tell me," he asked them, "what is it about this air?"

"It's the manure that excites you," explained Felix. "A simple case of coprophilia."

"It's the malt from the brewery," suggested Milo.

"It's the hay," Ken suggested. "Or maybe it's the Cressbrook. All rivers have their own smell."

"I think it's the wood," Benedict said absently. "All trees breathe. They give off a sort of sweetness when they're heavy with fruit."

"Or maybe," said Ken, "it's all these things."

"Whatever it is," Benedict said, "I shall never find it again."

"Any small country town could smell like this," Felix said.

"But not to me," Benedict replied.

"Hey," said Milo, "I want to show you all something. Have you ever tried spinning a dustbin lid? I've discovered quite by chance that if you throw one with a really good flick it'll spin for miles. It's something to do with its aerodynamic shape. Watch this."

He lifted the lid quietly off the dustbin outside the "Thorn and Sceptre". He leaned back, like a young Greek athlete, then whipped it away from his body with a quick horizontal movement. He was quite right. The lid rose, as if carried by a gust of warm rising air, and sailed away into the dusk, and out of sight. They waited for what seemed a month. At last there came a far off crash and tinkle of glass.

Doubled up with laughter, they trotted away. They worked their way steadily from one end of Aylsbourn to the other, drinking half a pint of beer in each pub, and skimming dustbin lids away into the night between drinks. By ten o'clock they were gloriously and uproariously tight, with the sort of euphoria which only very young men, with untried livers as clean as a whistle, could hope to achieve. Finally they found themselves marching out of Aylsbourn with a dustbin lid apiece, held in front like a breastplate, singing *Il Toreador* rather incongruously at the top of their voices. After half a mile a workmen's hut came into view. The road was up and the excavation was protected by a cluster of red lanterns. "Hey!" said Milo. "I've got a better idea. Bring one of these lamps each."

He picked up one of the red lamps in his long ape-like arms and trotted over the grass with it. The others followed. They were past caring. Milo led the way down to the edge of the Cressbrook. It flowed sweetly under them in the dark, chinking and muttering as it always did.

Milo leaned over and gently lowered the lid horizontally on to the water so that it floated like a shallow boat. Then he stood the red lamp on it and pushed the little home-made lightship out into the middle of the stream. It twirled once or twice, then set off downstream in the current, the lamp borne along erect on its float. The others followed suit. Soon the four red lamps were bobbing down the Cressbrook in line astern. They made a curious and beautiful sight.

The friends followed, stopping now and then to double up with laughter at Milo's bizarre device. In half a mile the Cressbrook flowed out into a much larger river and as they saw their brave red lamps swept out into the stronger current they became silent. They watched without speaking until the little pools of light faded from sight.

"By morning," said Milo at last, "they'll be out to sea."

It was Benedict's turn to tap on the wall.
"Is that you, Benny?"

"Yes. I'm drunk. Can I talk to you?"

"Of course."

He stumbled and nearly fell over as he came in.

"Oh sod it!"

"How much have you had, Benny?"

"I don't know. About eight pints I suppose."

"How can you hold so much?"

"You can't. We were all sick. Except Felix, and he was looking pretty green when we left him."

"Is Milo all right?"

"He was when we'd put his head in the horse trough. By the way, Tess, if you ever see the Pepperpot again, say it was all our fault."

"What was?"

"Well really it was Milo's idea. We posted sixpennorth of fish and chips through her parent's letter box."

"Oh Benny!"

"And we—oh Tess, never mind what we did. The room's spinning round and I can't see you."

"Lie back then."

She held him gently and felt his forehead with her hand. "Gosh you're hot!"

"Lay your sleeping head my love," murmured Benedict, "human on my faithless arm."

"I'll never be faithless to you, Benny. You'll always be someone special in my life. No one will ever quite replace you."

"I know that, Tess. Tess—I can only tell you this because I'm drunk and I can't see your face. . . ."

"Tell me, Benny."

"I'm afraid. Afraid to leave you and your parents and my friends. And to leave Laura. Tess, I'm afraid of leaving the Cressbrook Valley. I'm afraid I shall lose you all. And what else will there be? I don't believe in God. I believe only in men and women. We only have each other."

"You'll always have me, Benny. I'll write to you all the time you're away."

"Will you promise? You know I'm going abroad—probably to America or South Africa to start my training? Will you write to me wherever I am and tell me everything that's going on here?"

"Yes. I'll tell you everything I can. You know I shall only be home at the weekends—but I'll find out what's happened and write to you."

"Thank you, Tess. That will make all the difference. You promise?"

"I promise, Benny."

He had arranged to say goodbye to Milo and Felix the night before so that he could be alone with Laura at the station. It was an exquisite Aylsbourn autumn morning, with that characteristic catch in the early air. The autumn, thought Benedict, is the best season; it never lets you down. It makes no promises; it is beautiful but inexorable. As you get older it must become more and more the best season of all; rich, sad, elegiac. A season to say goodbye in.

Laura wore her old coat and scarf thrown loosely round her neck. She seemed to want to look as casual as possible. When the signal plonked down to announce that the train was due and the rails began to thrum quietly under its approaching wheels, she put her arms round his neck, despite the handful of early-morning passengers, and put her mouth very close to his ear.

"Benny," she whispered. "I'm sorry I've never slept with you because then I'd have a part of you that no one could ever take away. But please promise me, when you come home, that you'll take me away—maybe to that old pub at the source of the Cressbrook—remember?—where you can hear the water running underneath the window. And then we shall be able to make love properly, as no two people ever did before. I know we're young and don't understand very much about it, but we can teach each other. Will you promise?"

"Yes."

He loaded his cases, full of his life's belongings and Mrs. Johnston's home-made jam, into the rack and held her hands until the whistle blew. The train began to move very slowly and she walked beside him as long as she could, until at last their hands had to part, and he watched her until she vanished in a jumble of signal gantries. Then, no longer a boy but a man called by his country to fight for the Cressbrook Valley, he went and shut himself in the lavatory and wept all the way to London.

★ 7 ★

1764305 2nd/Lt. Weston F
GHQ SEALF
SINGAPORE
May 16 1945

SWEET SLOB:

How bloody pleased I was to receive a letter from you today. I was lucky to get it, for everything's had to be re-addressed twice. I must say I'm enjoying Singapore. First it is green. Second it looks like our accepted idea of a city—shop window-dressing is an art. Every variety of entertainment exists except dog-racing and even the tarts are mechanized. They follow one around the streets in what we call tri-shaws (a bicycle with a small carriage attached) and if you feel like it you can hop in beside them and are whisked off to the nearest knocking-shop.

The only trouble is that everything is so expensive. A cinema seat costs seven shillings. Fortunately alcohol is duty-free. Chinese girls are most attractive and, I am told, quite splendid in bed. I will write to you in more detail about this later. They wear a very seductive two-piece costume in a very thin material and I am curious to know what, if anything, they wear underneath.

It is ironic that whereas during my brief stay in India I left the women alone because they were so repulsive and pox-ridden, though I could well have afforded it, here the cost is so high that one simply has to save up—and I'm still afraid of catching pox. The 85% pox rate here is a legacy from the Japanese occupation.

You may be surprised to hear that I am commanding a company. The reason is simple: the real company commander is on a week's course, and I am holding the fort till he gets back. Of course I am only a figure-head who signs chits. However, it is comforting to think that, in principle at least, I hold the power of life and death over 147 men—up to seven days' CB or three extra guards or forfeiture of leave.

To tell you the truth, Benny, I have a notion that I may stay on in the Army. It is an ideally lazy life and there is no question of taking decisions. Moreover, I find the people very amusing. I am bound to say that I had a signal success at a concert the other night, when I sang our old song "Please don't burn our shithouse down" to an audience of three hundred men and twelve officers. You'd have been proud if you'd heard the applause. It just shows what the old alma mater can do for you. Oh, and I brought the roof down in the mess the other night with "There was a young girl of Antrim"—remember how Milo recited it to us that day in the library early in 1944? At last I see the benefits of a classical education.

Sorry this is such a short letter but I'm on duty as I told you. I send you my love you old slob and don't let the bastards grind you down.

Yours ever,
Felix.

Trin Coll Camb
June 28 1945

Dear old butch,

Thanks a lot for your last letter. I was glad to hear you're enjoying life out there and doing plenty of flying; don't get too homesick; the weather is appalling and there's a mood of frustration and bloody-mindedness in the air.

You're quite wrong in assuming that I'm just living it up in Cambridge. Didn't you realize that I had to face the Preliminary Examination of the Natural Science Tripos at the end of this term?

I started my revision just two and a half weeks before the great day. Two weeks before the first examination the Ministry sent round a charming little note to all tutors saying that the number of scientists at Cambridge must be reduced by at least 20%. These unfortunates were to be extracted from those in the age group born between April 1925 and September 1926 which as you know includes yours truly. My hair turned a touching birch-grey. I asked my tutor if he thought a second would do. He said that if the government wanted these boys they'd take them if they had starred firsts.

That night I did twelve hours work and went to bed at 4.30 a.m.

and was up early enough to do an hour's work before breakfast. A second year man kept me going with benzadrene. Believe me those two weeks were a hideous nightmare. I even gave up my place in the college tennis team; I couldn't have held the racquet. When I saw the Electronics paper my grey hair turned to a beautiful silvery white. The chemistry wasn't too bad and for physics I had revised the right things. For maths just the wrong.

By the end of it all I was convinced I had got a third and would shortly be on the way to join Felix in Singapore. To crown all, the college tennis matches against Girton and Newnham cancelled. Never in all my life did I need your moony old face so much to cheer me. However, my tutor has just written to me. . . . "Dear Johnston. Congratulations on your second class which was not at all far from being a first. Your marks were etc." So I have scraped my way back into Cambridge for another year.

Thanks for your queries about my sisters; Joanna is working hard at London and Tess seems to like her shorthand. Ken Heppel seems to spend all his spare time seeing her; I can't think what they see in each other. I saw Laura walking down the High Street when I was at home last vac. She looked terrific. We stopped and exchanged thoughts about the weather, the state of the world, Felix and (did you guess?) you, you, and you again. I don't know what it is about your pixilated old mug that inspires this devotion in her. But I confess I'd love to set my eyes on it too. My parents send their love to you.

Your old pard
Milo

Miners Hostel
Blackhill
County-Durham.

July 23 1945

Darling boy,

I just wanted you to know that I'm going to marry Tess. You will throw up your hands in horror I know but we're both quite sure about it. Of course I'm not twenty yet so it won't happen for two years at least, but we shall probably get engaged officially this Christmas.

Please don't ask me why. We just think we have an enormous chance of being happy. Also, between us, I'm afraid if I don't grab her someone else will. I know she's not a great beauty but she is the gentlest creature I've ever met or ever will.

Please send us your blessing.

Yours always
Ken

Fourth Training Group
"L" Divisional Headquarters,
Sebastopol Lines
Salisbury
August 2 1945

Dear Cadet Benedict,

It is indeed a most unhappy duty for me to confirm the telegram despatched yesterday. Your father had established himself as one of our most valued training officers, and his death is a severe blow to us all.

You may care for a slightly fuller explanation of how the tragedy occurred. As far as I can gather, Lieutenant Benedict had led his men on a training exercise over rough country some fifteen miles from here, and, as laid down in his orders, was instructing them in negotiating water at night. One of the cadets got into trouble when out of his depth, and your father immediately dived in to rescue him. I understand from the medical report that heart failure—probably caused by the shock of the cold water—was responsible for his death. The cadet in question managed to struggle ashore.

In view of the gallant nature of his act, formalities have been opened to make him a posthumous award. Though I do appreciate that this can be of little solace to you at this juncture, we all feel here that it is the smallest gesture we can pay to his memory. We are, all, believe me, mostly deeply grieved at this tragic waste of such a valuable life and at the loss of such a congenial and well-liked brother-officer.

Yours very truly,
J. P. R. O'Creasy
Commanding Officer

Dear Mr. Benedict,

I am writing on behalf of the cadets in "B" Platoon who were under your father's care to tell you how terribly sorry we are about his death. Lieutenant Benedict was not just an officer as far as we were concerned; he was like a father to us. If I may give you just two small examples; before our rooms were inspected he used to go round secretly putting an extra polish on our shoes in case we were charged with slackness. He always used to give us his sweet ration. These are very small matters, and perhaps, objectively, slightly ridiculous. I can only tell you that we did not look at them in that light. We are all more upset than I can adequately say. The fact that the man he gave his life for lived makes it all the harder to bear. Please accept our most heartfelt sympathy.

Yours faithfully,
F. J. Dean
Officer Cadet

From the Chairman's Office

My dear Benny,

We are all most dreadfully grieved at the tragic loss of your father. He was one of my oldest friends, and in the Brewery and this part of Hampshire he will never be replaced. A part of the old world has died. I do wish he could have lived just a few more days to see the end of this terrible war.

I'm not going to write you a long testimonial to the memory of your father; it would be an impertinence to someone who knew and loved him as you did. I do want to say just this: that if when you come out of the forces you want to join us here there will always be a place for you. It would be a delight and a consolation to me to have a Benedict with us once more. And I need hardly tell you that this is a business with a very solid future; I believe you could go a very long way in it.

As you know, I am your father's executor. You may be surprised to hear that he had never at any time cashed the Margrave shares which we pay to our executive staff at the end of each financial year. In consequence, he has left you some £700 of Margrave stock which I strongly advise you to keep. The brewery are going to double that for you.

He left all his books to me—as he rather touchingly put it, they were all too lowbrow for you! But after that you are of course the sole beneficiary.

The cottage, as you know, is Margrave property. It is yours, and we shall not let it to anyone unless you quite definitely do not intend to return and settle here.

It is very much my hope—and Betty's—that you will, though. She joins me in sending you her love and sympathy.

Believe me Benny,

Your old friend,

Keith Margrave.

GHQ SEALF
SINGAPORE
August 9, 1945

Dear Benny:

I've only just heard about your father's death and I'm writing at once. You won't expect—or get—a lot of maudlin clap-trap from me about it. But it did occur to me that perhaps you would be in a state of pointless remorse because you didn't fulfil the image he'd made for you. You could masochistically make out a case to show you had disappointed him. You didn't go to Shallerton and you never played for Hampshire and you didn't get a Blue and you haven't even got a commission yet (nor will you, if the war packs up in the next few days). You haven't fallen into his mould of "gentleman". And yet I am quite sure that the day you hit that thumping fifty for Valhalla (and I like a fool ran you out) made him as happy as he was ever likely to be. It's ironic what trifles will make some people happy.

I thought this might stop you moping. If not, please forgive your cynical old pal for interfering.

Yours ever,

Felix.

Benny my darling,

I'm sitting down now to write to you because we all needed you so terribly today and I can only begin to imagine how you must be feeling. Why they couldn't have flown you home I don't know. I suppose six thousand miles is a long way in wartime. All the same, it must have broken your heart not to have been here when your father was buried.

I won't distress you with a long account of the service; strange, though, like you, I haven't a vestige of faith left, yet there's still that odd emotive comfort in the words of the Prayer Book. It was a beautiful Aylsbourn morning; still quite cold, but with a sense of summer in the air. Everyone was there; Keith Margrave, and Lady M, my parents of course, the Westons even (the first time he's been in church in thirty years so they say) all the Johnstons (Milo came from Cambridge) all the Heppels—yes even Kenneth had come down from Durham, and Ilex. I was glad there were no women members of your family—when the earth is thrown down into the open grave it is truly a terrible moment for believers and non-believers alike and I don't think I've ever seen a woman who could stand up to the horror and hopelessness and futility of it.

The Rector was on his best form and spoke quite touchingly about your father; it wasn't even hypocritical as these speeches usually are. For he *was* a good man, in any reasonable definition of that over-worked term. He had no enemies and such a lot of friends.

I remembered what you always say about the life-diminishers; I always feel they come into their own at a funeral. So to show I was a member of the Pro-Life-Party I wore my gayest dress and I was delighted to see quite a few eyebrows raised. I know if you'd been there you'd have worn an Aylsbourn rose in your button-hole, which is your special and wonderful arrogance.

After the service we all came out feeling dry and somehow a little lighter in heart—odd, that lifting of the spirit you get after-wards—and some of us went into the Thorn and Sceptre to have drinks—which—to coin the old cliché—is what he'd have wanted, and as God is our judge, exactly what he'd have done himself. Then my parents went off to London and I shut myself in my bedroom and sobbed my heart out, for I felt as if I'd lost a little bit of you. Forgive this, Benny darling, I'm thinking of you continually and come safely home soon.

Laura.

★ 8 ★

(a)

BENEDICT sat in the sun and waited. His aircraft had landed him at Salisbury airport at the uncivilized hour of five-thirty a.m. and he had no idea when he would be collected. He had already been sitting there two hours. He didn't care. It was pleasant to bask in the sunshine and meditate. The great point about this life, he reflected, and the thing that must endear it to Felix so much, was that there was absolutely no decision to be taken, no responsibility. He unfolded for the twentieth time a worn piece of paper containing his orders. It was headed "Confidential" and said simply:

> "You will proceed to Salisbury in Southern Rhodesia, flying by BOAC flight 162 on the night of January 6/7, 1947. You will wait at the airport where you will be contacted by Squadron Leader Rupert Ripley D.S.O., D.F.C. You will be under his personal command from then onwards."

Benedict had been in some odd situations since that day he had left Aylsbourn, but none stranger than this. The letter had emanated from a section of the Air Ministry with an ominous and indeed phony-sounding title: "Department of Psychological Research."

However, who was he to worry? As long as it made the time pass more quickly till he saw Laura. . . .

A Humber shooting brake swung through the station gates. It pulled up sharply right where Benedict sat, and a scruffy young R.A.F. pilot leaped out. With his battle dress he wore a bow tie and a pair of flying boots. However, he wore the ribbon of the D.S.O. and D.F.C. Benedict jumped up and saluted.

"Good morning," said the pilot pleasantly. "I take it you're Benedict?"

"Yes, sir."

"Fine. I'm Ripley. Jump in."

He took one of Benedict's bags and swung it aboard. Benedict scrambled into the Humber and Ripley made as if to let in the clutch. Then he stopped and said: "What's your other name?"

"Other name, sir?"

"Yes. Christian names?"

"Oh. Peregrine John."

"Christ! What a mouthful. What do people call you?"

"Benny, sir."

"Benny. That's fine. My name is Rupert. For God's sake call me that and drop this sir crap."

"Right." He couldn't quite get the Rupert out the first time.

He watched his new commanding officer as he drove. He was very tall and at close quarters not so young as all that—at any rate not as young as Benedict. Twenty-eight? His limbs were loosely articulated and he wore a revolver in a holster, which, in Rhodesia, seemed a little eccentric. He had a humorous hawk nose, bushy eyebrows and black eyes. He was good-looking in a desperate sort of way. Benedict tried to recall what this particular variety of slightly piratical good looks reminded him of. Then he remembered: Felix.

"Well, Benny," said Rupert after a long silence. "This is the craziest one I've ever been in to date, and I've been in some pretty Fred Karno jobs in my time."

"I'm afraid I haven't a clue what we're supposed to be doing."

"Nor have I. Here." He swung the Humber into the kerb. "Let's have some breakfast. I imagine you haven't eaten yet. Then we can talk."

They sat down and ordered bacon and eggs and coffee.

"Now," said Rupert, "I suggest we start by exchanging brief biographies. Tell me yours first."

"There's not much to it. I volunteered for aircrew when I was seventeen and a quarter——"

"When was that?"

"April 1943. I was called up in October 1944 and came straight out here as a u/t navigator. I was within forty-eight hours of passing out and getting my commission when the Japanese war ended. Then they said either we had to sign on for three years or it was too bad. I didn't want to sign. So they made me redundant."

"And since then?"

"Absolutely nothing. I've made tea, swept out hangars, all

194

that kind of thing. Then I suddenly got posted down here."

"How old are you?"

"I'll be twenty-one in a few days."

"So you hadn't done anything before you joined up?"

"I was at school."

"What are you going to do when you do get out?"

"I'm going to read physics at Imperial College, London, specializing in electronics."

"Where are you from?"

"A small place in Hampshire. You wouldn't know it."

"I might. Tell me the name."

"Aylsbourn. It's a little brewery town in the Cressbrook Valley. About seventy miles from London."

"I know it. I've been through it on the way to sail at Buckler's Hard, haven't I?"

"You might have done, yes. Very few people recall it, I find."

"Sleepy little place with a nice High Street. Smells of malt if the wind's in the right direction?"

"That's it." He found himself warming to Rupert. A perceptive chap! He hadn't met anybody else in the entire Air Force who knew anything about his town.

"Right. Now I'll tell you mine. I got expelled from my public school at sixteen for laying one of the maids. My father, a stiff-necked old sod, a Presbyterian, a Scotsman, and a chartered accountant—if you can imagine a more diabolical combination —threw me out."

"What—out into the street?"

"Right. Bags and baggage. I didn't mind a bit. I never got on with the old bugger. So I made straight for Soho."

"You went to live in Soho at sixteen?"

"Yep. Why not?"

"Must have been pretty interesting. But what did you do for a living?"

"I got a job with an outfit called Crackerjack Films. I got £2 a week. My room was eleven and six so it wasn't as bad as it sounds." He smiled to remember. "The film industry before the war was a romantic place in a mad, broke way. I always remember the first day I went there. There were three Hungarians in the studio. They were singing 'Funiculi, Funicula'. I always remember the scene-painters. They used to fill themselves up with beer and work all bloody day and night. They got three to four quid a week. It was slave labour really. There were no unions, you see. It was pitiful. Anyway, the boss, Captain Yodel, took a fancy to me. It was my clean white collar that did the trick. He used to send me down to the City every Friday to get the cheque to pay the wages. I had instructions not to come back till I'd got it. I used to plead with them until they gave in. Then I'd dash back with it in a taxi and we'd pay it in at the back door of the bank."

"Sounds an unstable sort of business."

"It was. The people in it were so odd you see. We had a bloke called Llewellyn Williams. He had played rugby for Wales. He was mad as a hatter. He used to advertise a special device in the small adds which he said was certain to kill flies. You sent in sixpence and he sent you back two wooden blocks. I remember he used to take a sack of sixpences in to the Gerard Street post office every Saturday, laughing fit to bust."

"But wasn't that fraud?"

"People were simpler then than they are now. He had another one. Football pools were just starting and he had an add which said: 'Why face odds of a million to one when with our permutation you can reduce it to fifty-six to one?' "

"And could you?"

"Yes—for a stake of £1,984. But our creditors were the best value. At first when they called they used to send me out and I'd say that Captain Yodel was out and wouldn't be back. Finally they got wise to that and brought a mattress round. They used to sleep in our front office."

"You're not serious."

"My dear Benny, I am telling you the solemn truth. You have no idea what life was like in the hysterical thirties."

"Did you make any films?"

"Heavens yes. We had a vaudeville thing—Windmill type—and a serial. People liked half-hour instalments in those days. One of our salesmen had a bright idea. He joined twelve together and flogged it as the longest film on earth. It was too. It sold like hot cakes. The only trouble was, every so often the heroine would appear to be run over by a train only to be miraculously rescued the next second."

"What were the actors like?"

"Quite awful. But I and another boy used to have a lot of fun. We used to ring up bit-part actresses and say were doing a film test that evening. Then we'd buy a one and sixpenny bottle of cocktail mixture from the Regent Wine Company and shoot them some line about the camera breaking down and throw a party. You never knew your luck."

"But surely this didn't go on for ever? I mean what about the creditors?"

"Yes—all good things have to come to an end. It folded. Next day I answered an ad for a presentable, well-educated young gentleman who would earn £8 a week selling textiles. I turned up and was interviewed by a Wing-Commander Maxwell. He had two brothers, Lieutenant Commander de Winter and Brigadier Hazelwood."

"How on earth could they be brothers then?"

"Their real name was Alhambra. They were Egyptians. The ranks were equally phony; but it seemed to help in business before the war. Anyway, they took me on and the next morning I reported for work. I was shown into a room with about thirty other young men in it. De Winter was standing at a blackboard with two words written on it. One was BOXES and the other was WAKAZOO."

"I don't follow."

"Neither did I. We had to spell them out in a unified chant, like an American football crowd: B-O-X-E-S and W-A-K-A-Z-O-O. Boxes, it appeared, were what we sold—three pairs of silk stockings in each. We had to sell eight to ten boxes a day. Anyone who got over ten was called a hot-shot."

"What was Wakazoo?"

"That was just their war-cry. We had a song too. It went:

    'Psycho Silks are up-to-datest, WAKAZOO.'
    'Psycho Silks are up-to-datest, WAKAZOO.'

and so on."

"But that surely wasn't taken seriously?"

"Believe me, Benny, it was taken dead seriously. It was that or not eating. I remember I once lived for four days on a sample of dog biscuits I found in Norfolk Square. I've slept on Brighton beach several times."

"How much were the stockings?"

"Five and eleven and six and eleven. We got a shilling a pair on one lot, one and three on the other."

"What kind of people did this job?"

"We were an astonishing collection. There were defrocked priests, remittance men, Malayan tea-planters who'd come home to start a farm and lost everything, and public school wasters like myself. There were also one or two very amusing and talented people among them."

"Any women?"

"Oh Lord, yes. We had one old dear of eighty. She used to swoon on people's doorsteps and say she hadn't eaten all day. She made a packet. She used to sing us songs in a frail, genteel little voice. One, I think, used to go:

"What wonderful fish the sole is
What wonderful fish are soles."

He paused to light a small cigar. "One had the odd impression," he went on, "going round middle-class Britain in those days, that the place was loaded with neurotic and sex-hungry women. Sometimes a salesman would disappear for a week at a time. My greatest *coup* was in Bath. I was passed on from salon to salon for days on end."

"I suppose it all ended with the war."

Rupert sighed. "Yes. That was the end of it. I joined up, figuring it was the safest course, did half a tour, and then had the good fortune to get shot down. I bust a leg and got grounded. And so—here we are."

Benedict took a deep breath. "Well, Rupert," he said, "I'm afraid my story is pretty tame compared with yours."

"Nonsense! Everyone has a fascinating story to tell."

They got up. Rupert paid the bill. He grinned at Benedict.

"I've got a feeling we're going to get on, Benny," he said.

"Thanks," said Benedict. He wondered what his friends at home would say to all this. He was not sure how much to believe. On the whole he had already learned that there was no circumstance too bizarre for reality; it was only fiction that had to draw the line. He estimated that Rupert's story was about eighty-five per cent on the level.

When Benedict had changed he called at Rupert's office. He found his commanding officer smoking another cigar with his feet, still encased in flying boots, on the table in front of him. There were pictures of Betty Grable and Ann Sheridan on the wall.

"Ah there you are, Benny," cried Rupert. "Now sit down and I'll tell you all about our secret mission. It's this. We have to travel throughout the whole of the MEDME area, lecturing the troops on 'The World of Tomorrow' and answering their questions."

"*What?*"

"That's it. That's my brief direct from the Air Ministry. Here —you can read the letter if you like." He passed over a document headed "Most Secret". Benedict read it. Rupert was telling the precise truth.

"But what on earth do we know about the World of Tomorrow, Rupert?"

"I don't know what your information is, Benny, but I know sweet F.A. about it. No, don't worry, we'll tour the stations, get the chaps together, then I shall tell them a few of my better yarns and a few flying adventures and we'll push on to the next place."

"But what am I supposed to do?"

"Make a note of their questions and send them back to the A.M. They're trying to find out what's on the average serviceman's mind. I could tell them: one sharp short four-letter Anglo-Saxon word; however, if they're prepared to finance this Cook's tour for us, who are we to grumble? So don't be an awkward young cuss, Benny; help me draw up an itinerary. . . . "

That was Monday. Within a few days Benny had become enchanted with Rupert. His commanding officer was a man who had never heard of Angst. His motto was *carpe diem,* and he seized each day with an exhilarating zest. Benny began to unwind in his company, became less tense, moonstruck, dreamy and withdrawn. As their first weekend drew near, however, Rupert became broody.

"Benny," he said, "we have got to get ourselves organized with some crackling. Do you care for girls?"

"Of course, Rupert. I was brought up with them you see, and I've missed their company dreadfully."

"You can say that again. So do I; every bloody minute. But I've been doing a little groundwork in the two weeks I was here ahead of you. I've got a sweet little number lined up for Sunday called

Mimi Chimes. If you have no objection I'll ring and ask her to bring a friend so that we can make up a foursome. You'd like that?"

"Yes."

"It's as good as fixed then."

On the Sunday morning they were both ready at nine. Two large American cars rolled up to the door of their camp.

"Bit extravagant—two cars—isn't it?" asked Benny innocently.

Rupert stared at him in disbelief. "My dear old fellow, you don't believe in that *menage à quatre* lark do you?"

"Oh no; I just forgot how well-off people were here."

Benny's date was a fluffy blonde called Tootsie. She was nineteen and said she worked as a secretary. Her accent fascinated him; it was just as he imagined someone from Deep South in America would talk. She prattled away about her parents: ("Mah Deard and Mah Merm") told him about the time she thought she saw a ghost ("Ah was so skeered ah was paralahsed") and said how much she hated black men. However, it was certainly fun to be with any girl after so long. Soon she was questioning him about his own life: did he have a girl friend back in England?

"Oh yes," said Benny. "Her name's Laura. She's twenty-two, an art student. I'm afraid that doesn't convey very much. But I'm longing to see her again. It's been nearly two and a half years."

"You're lucky," said Tootsie. "Ah hev an unhappy lerv lahf. You see, Benny, ah'm in lerv with a married man."

Here we go again, thought Benny. But it was such a marvellous day, and the air so rich that he could almost imagine he was home again. They stopped at a place called Mermaid's Pool and picknicked there. The girls had brought a splendid cold lunch—cold meats, asparagus, amacunda pears, cream and bottled beer. It was poignantly nostalgic. Afterwards they lay in the sun and Tootsie volunteered to read his fortune from the palm of his hand.

"Ah'm afraid, Benny," she said, after a close study, "ah see a terrible ernhappiness in yoh lahf. But you hev good kahnd friends and yoh'll never be pohr."

When they drove back into town Tootsie invited him to stop at her parents' house for a glass of whisky. "Mah Merm and Deard hev gone away to Durban," she said, "so ah hev the place to mahself, which is kahnd of cosy."

"Thank you very much, Tootsie, but really I have to get back into camp by twelve." (He didn't, but it was the only excuse he could think of.) Tootsie seemed surprised. "Well, Benny," she said, "if yoh quite sure, ah'll understand. But ah will say this. They're aren't so many boys like yoh left. But yoh can kiss me good night, ah trust?"

"Oh yes," said Benedict. "I can do that."

Rupert beat his head against the wall in despair when he heard about it. "Handed to you on a plate," he kept moaning, "and you drop it through your butter-fingers. Oh Benny, I'm so ashamed for you. Please promise never to mention it again. I don't know what my friends would say."

"I'm sorry to be such a prune, Rupert. But I shall be going home in a few months and—well, Laura and I have got something special planned."

"She must be a dish if you can wait that long."

"She is, Rupert."

Early in March Felix wrote to say he was sailing for home. Was there any chance of seeing his pixilated old friend en route? Benedict took the letter to Rupert. He had told him much about Felix and he was curious to see how the two would get on. "I just wondered, Rupert," he said, "whether we might fly up to Malta next and meet Felix there. His ship stops there for a couple of days."

"No sooner said than done," said Rupert decisively. "There's a little piece of Maltese crackling pining her heart out for me in Valetta. Benny, my boy, arrange the tickets."

(b)

Odd, thought Benedict, how offensive a lieutenant's uniform can make a man. He studied Felix's appearance with disfavour. His cynical friend had grown almost nut-brown in the sun; he looked more Spanish than ever. The three sat drinking Chianti and exchanging reminiscences of their lives. Felix's researches into the social mores of the Chinese girl had been thorough; he and Rupert were soon busy exchanging notes. Benedict sat moodily. He felt left out of it; and Laura was still such a long way away. He blocked out each passing day in his diary; it was only a matter of weeks now and they would be together; they would go to that pub at the source of the Cressbrook. . . .

"Snap out of it, you moonstruck old prune," cried Felix at last seeing his friend's reverie. "You're missing the fiesta."

They had crossed to the Island of Gozo with a barrel organ playing in the little ferry boat and a Mediterranean sun beating down on them. It was one of the most peaceful places Benedict had ever seen. One day, he thought, Laura and I will come here.

The fiesta was charming in its innocence: procession, fireworks, and music. When it had passed by the three friends began to drink again. Then Rupert suggested that they should take a new bottle of Chianti and go and sit on the rocks looking over the sea. There was an enormous Mediterranean moon and they could sit with the warm water lapping round their bare feet. They drank steadily, passing the bottle backwards and forwards between them. It was their third bottle of the evening. The conversation was drowsy and desultory; Benedict was half asleep. Suddenly Rupert prodded him.

"Wake up, Benny," he cried jovially, "stop thinking about that dream girl back home."

"Dream girl?" enquired Felix thickly. He was very drunk.

"Yes," said Rupert, "Laura."

"Oh dear old Laura," said Felix. "The constant nympho."

Benedict sat up.

"What did you say, Felix?"

"I said the constant nympho."

"What do you mean by that?"

"Well, Christ, Benny, surely I don't have to tell you. Everyone knows she's the hottest little bitch in the Cressbrook Valley."

"That's right," said Rupert, not entirely understanding, "Benny's been living a life of monastic purity out here, dreaming of the day when he gets back to her. Must be some dish to be worth that kind of wait."

"I wonder how much waiting *she's* doing," Felix said.

"Felix I'm warning you. . . ." Benedict was angry now.

"Everyone knows she's been sleeping around since she was about fifteen. First there was dear old Tony Hammond, then of course she had to make that pass at me down at Torquay. . . ."

"That's a lie, Felix."

"Is it, my dear innocent Benny? And how the devil do you know?"

"Because I know Laura."

"Because I know Laura." Felix mimicked him. "Benny, you'll learn one day that no woman is worth waiting for. Love 'em and leave 'em. Especially when it's only a randy little whore like Laura. *Hey, Benny!*"

Benedict never quite knew what made him do it; it frightened him always afterwards to remember, for he had never lost his temper before. He recalled nothing for some thirty seconds, and then through a deep darkness, laced with exploding rockets, he heard Rupert shouting: "Let go, Benny! For God's sake let go. You're killing him!"

He opened his eyes. He was sitting on top of Felix with both hands round his throat. Felix's tongue was swollen and protruding from his lips. His face, in the unearthly moonlight, looked a brownish-purple. He was holding Benedict off with all his strength, and Rupert had both arms round him from behind. But it was several minutes before with their combined efforts they could prise Benedict off. Felix sat doubled over, getting his breath back in long sobbing lungfuls.

"For Christ's sake," Rupert said. "You nearly killed him, Benny. No girl is worth that much."

"This one is," Benedict said. He turned and walked back to the hotel, still shaking. He and Felix did not speak to each other again that night; and they parted company in the morning without saying goodbye.

Before he went, Felix said to Rupert privately: "For God's sake keep an eye on that maniac fool. He'll do himself serious harm one day."

203

BENNY MY DARLING

. . . It's just two years and a quarter since you've been away;
I remember as if it were yesterday walking home from the station
and—because I badly needed something to occupy me—doing the
washing up. There was a pile of brown string in our kitchen which
you produced at the last minute—remember?—to tie up some of
your things. In a way I'm glad we've had this long separation and
the chance to carry on our unending conversations in this way, it
can't have done anything but good. . . .

Benny my darling,

. . . I've just washed my hair and done some much overdue
darning—romantic pastimes both—and now I'm sitting down to
write to you. I am sending today's Observer off to you and you'll
see from it that Hampshire walloped Cambridge but I don't know
whether to be glad or sorry, what with Milo and everyone going
there. Incidentally, it appears that Joanna is having some fearfully
torrid love affair with a married man in London . . . they're all
awfully worried about it, but what on earth can they do? I did tell
you, didn't I, that she got a jolly good degree in June, not quite a
first but an upper second, and now she's working with the
American Air Force on some complicated problems to do with
rockets. All those Johnstons go the same way. No one knows anything about this man but I'm glad to say he's NOT an American.
Not that I'm anti-American but the distance would be an added
factor against it, if there were any hope of their marrying. Benny
it must be dreadful to see one's children growing up and having
to go out into the world defenceless against being hurt; yet what
can one do to help? I think we can only tell them how to live and
then leave it to them. I suppose our children will give us the same
heartaches. I find it hard to imagine exactly how it will feel to
have your children. . . .

I'm following your journeys on a map. You do get around
don't you? I hope Rupert is looking after you; he seems old

enough to be your father from what you say about him in your letters. And I do hope Transport Command is looking after you.

One of the students here asked me out to an oyster supper at some place in Soho, but I said I'd rather not. I couldn't bear Soho without you.

You are a darling to say you want to buy me some things; really you shouldn't bother, but since you so sweetly insist on checking my measurements, it's shoes five and a half, stockings nine and a half, and—maidenly modesty on one side for the moment—vital statistics, 34-25½-34. (The waist is the true figure—I could squeeze into something a little smaller, but it wouldn't be very comfortable.) One thing I *have* been looking for for ages is a pair of sandals with wedge heels, medium height, heelless and toeless, but you're only to buy them for me if they're cheap and *you* like them. ...

February 19th 1947

Benny my darling,

... I was so thrilled to get your long letter and the photographs. As you say, the camera didn't seem to be quite in focus but they are a joy to have all the same. Rupert looks quite harmless, now that I've seen what he looks like. Benny, I'm so worried about your lip. I love you to play rugger, you know that, but I do wish you didn't always have to be the one to be bounced . . . it must be awful trying to eat and drink. Do be more careful next time you play. I know that's pointless advice but I do worry about you.

We went to London last night, just my parents and I, to celebrate—you'll never guess—their *twenty-fifth* wedding anniversary. We went to Manetta's for a dinner dance and met some friends of theirs, a doctor who'd been a student with Daddy, and wife and a son of about our age. Let me tell you at once that he was an utter prune, a snurdge of the first water. I didn't feel like dancing without you—I kept remembering that unforgettable summer in 1944 which seemed as though it would never end, when it seemed we danced to Glenn Miller night after night after night. . . . Benny, I'm sure you'll be madly famous one day and that some ghastly little man will sit in the British Museum editing our love letters. I'm afraid mine will look so unintelligent to his fish-like eyes; I wish I were as clever as you . . . never mind him though, let's always write just for each other. You know I often wish I could post myself to you in one of these dull Forces parcels. One day I suppose we'll look back on this time and smile about it from our cosy, sanctified married state.

The snow's coming down deep and crisp and even and I ache unbearably to recall how we used to whizz down the side of the Hampshire Downs in Milo's toboggan, me hanging on round your neck like grim death and you always steering with what Felix so rightly called your "dexterous ferocity". You know, mention of my parents' celebration of their quarter century of (so-called) connubial felicity reminds me; I'm afraid the Westons' marriage is breaking up. According to that old gossip Mrs. Duncher, they're throwing plates at each other and it's pretty established he has a little piece of nonsense down in Southampton. Poor things . . . can you imagine us ever throwing plates, Benny?

March 19 1947

Benny my darling . . .

. . . Felix came home today and insisted on taking me out to supper at the Shallerton Arms. It's a new place, they've converted an old disused mill, and between you and me it's rather nasty. You get a lot of chaps there with Jaguars who've made a fortune out of plastic handbags and the wine tastes like vinegar . . . however, Felix obviously meant well; this was part of his disguise as the perfect *homme du monde* as you always call him. . . . He's a little plumper and quite good-looking in a spivvy sort of way but I'm bound to say he was the perfect "gentleman". . . . We talked a lot about you and though he didn't want to mention it I gathered there had been some enormous row between you. Anyway, he's quite forgiven you he says; I wonder if you've forgiven him? He wouldn't say what it was all about. I think under that cynical exterior he's really very fond of you. Shall I tell you a funny thing? I believe he's really very frightened of women. None of us know what effect it must have had on him to see his mother die when he was so young and on his own; and nice as Arabella is, no child can adjust easily to have his father marry again. . . .

March 27 1947

Benny my darling:

. . . I've just come back from Milo's twenty-first birthday party. It was enormous fun, but I did miss you. Everybody was there and you know I had a strong impression of how we're all growing up . . . there were four or five *couples* there, that is people going steady and pretty well engaged. Tess and Ken have fixed to marry in June; how wonderful if you could be back by then. The weather has been bitter; it's the worst winter in living memory and poor old England is just about at rock-bottom; we had all the electric fires turned off at art school the other day, you can imagine what it was like trying to paint. Oh and what do you think, one of the boys here who is studying photography has asked me to act as his model . . . if you don't think it too unrespectable I think I'll do it so that you can have a new photograph. He shot me a lot of stuff about my being very photogenic. I went to the hairdresser this morning and had my hair done in a new way for the party—I can't exactly describe it to you but it was piled up on top . . . but I felt sad because you weren't there to approve or disapprove. Milo was full of beans; he's a little more serious now and working hard for his degree in June; then it seems he will have to go into the army. He's in the university tennis team, did I tell you? And they'll be out practising as soon as this dreadful winter shows signs of breaking up.

Tess and Ken look completely out of this world and you know she is looking prettier every day. She's got a job with a solicitor in Shallerton which she'll keep after they're married; meanwhile they're looking for somewhere to live here. But as you know flats are pretty hard to find these days. Oh Benny, seeing all their plans and preparations makes me think such a lot about us. . . . You know some imes I'm frightened; we will have changed and we mustn't be surprised if it takes a little time for us to get used to each other again. Ken has a marvellous plan. He's buying an old M.G. on the never never—one of those four-seater ones, and he suggests that he and Tess and you and I should go on a tour of England in it this summer; wouldn't that be heaven? I send you thousands of unplatonic kisses. . . .

April 4 1947

Benny my darling:

. . . The most astonishing thing: Constance came back to Aylsbourn today. We had a long talk in Millers and I'm delighted to say she's going to live here again. But my dear, can you imagine —she's been married and divorced since we last saw her. Apparently only a few months after getting to Portsmouth she married an American naval officer. It seems he was a nice guy, but very young and they lasted six weeks. Six weeks . . . imagine Benny. I tried to get out of her why she rushed into marriage like that, she just shrugged her shoulders and said it was one of those things; but I'm convinced it was a bitter reaction from the disappointment of not going to Somerville. I still can't get to the bottom of why she didn't go. Can you imagine what she did in Portsmouth? She worked in a department store. Can you imagine Constance selling dresses??? She said it was the best way to earn money quickly, she was on wages plus commission and I imagine she could sell quite well if she put her mind to it. I asked her how it felt to be married, and she said she had never felt so imprisoned in her life. Oh I should have said that this naval officer, though a nice guy, was rather addicted to what Constance calls hitting the bottle; she said it was disconcerting to wake up in the morning and find that your husband couldn't stop shaking until he'd had a shot of Scotch from a bottle by the bed. I said hadn't she noticed that before she married him? She said no, they all drank a lot down there. I still don't know why her parents never helped her; I'm sure they're separated, because why didn't they look after her when her guardian died last year? The divorce isn't through yet; Constance cryptically said she could get one on three different counts. Poor Constance! And yet do you know she looks magnificent; even more proud than before, and she holds her head very erect as if to say "I'm Constance and don't you ever forget it." I asked her why she came back here and she said simply "it's home". She asked a lot about you. To be frank she said: "How is the pixilated old loon?" She is fond of you, I think. Now she's getting a job at the Brewery as a secretary; she's acquired shorthand. Oh but Benny, she would have made a wonderful scientist, what a criminal waste!

April 19 1947

Benny my darling:

. . . Nylons—what a heavenly present! You know really you shouldn't, you don't earn so much—7/3 a day isn't it? but what a thrill to receive them—I shall keep them and wear them the first day you're home. . . . Benny what do you think, Ken Heppel's father is going to buy the garage. As you know the owner died recently and Mr. Heppel has managed to raise an overdraft from the local bank, plus some small savings and a private loan from Sir Keith M. . . . I wonder what he'll be like as a capitalist? Even stranger, Ken wrote to Tess the other day saying he'd like to run it. You may think this an odd decision for such an idealist as Ken, but in fact I'm sure it's merely that he's utterly unambitious in a material sense and this will prove an unspectacular way of earning his bread and butter while he works at politics, which as you know is his first love. My God though, what an uphill struggle he's got to swing the Cressbrook Valley—it's been solidly and you could almost say maniacally Tory since the Reform Bill . . . still if anyone could do it Ken will. . . . I find it a bit ironic, do you remember that "garage proprietor" was one of his key words of contempt? "What will the garage proprietors of England say about *that*?"

Tess says one day they're going to build an entirely modern house on Cromwell Hill and it'll just have one huge piece of glass all along one wall so that they can look right down the Cressbrook Valley. . . . Benny I do envy them. . . . I've just bought a rather zippy new pair of slacks which I think even you, reactionary though are about women's dress, will love. They're a crazy colour, not exactly mauve but a sort of wine colour if you can imagine such a thing. . . .

May 15th 1947

Benny my darling:
. . . Tess and Ken were married today, and although as you know I disapprove intensely of the hocus-pocus, well, when it came to the point I rather enjoyed it. I meant to be strong-willed about taking part, but when Tess asked me to be a bridesmaid how could I refuse? Joanna was the other one and I must say Tess looked lovely. Milo was best man and need I tell you, it took Ken all his time to get Milo ready! Even I, sophisticated old cynic that I am, felt a bit tearful.

Tess had been hoarding her coupons for ages and bought a gorgeous wedding dress—heavy creamy satin with long tight sleeves and a train. Her headdress was a tiny coronet of pearls and Mrs. Johnston lent her own lace veil.

As for the bridesmaids! Our dresses were both the same—a lovely soft, pale apricot colour with heart-shaped necklines and very tight waistlines (I could hardly breathe) and romantically full skirts. Milo gave us both pearl necklaces as our bridesmaid's presents. It was the first time for ages that I felt really grand and not in the least "utility".

We drank quite of lot of Champagne *chez* Johnston afterwards and there was dancing; you can imagine how lonely I felt when that well-worn but splendid old radiogram of theirs began to thump out "Perfidia". . . . Oh and Benny, another wonderful thing, Aelfric came down specially for the wedding and he and Constance took one look at each other and that was that for the rest of the evening. Poor old Aelfric, I don't know whether Ilex pushed him too hard, but he hasn't been at all on form and they're rather worried whether he's going to get much of a degree at all this June. He looks so painfully shy and sort of *taut*. Isn't it odd; I don't believe Constance so much as looked at Aelfric before, but now they're both a bit lost and they seem to find consolation in each other. . . . Benny it's only a matter of weeks now before you're home again and sometimes I find it all quite terrifying. But it will work out for us, you'll see. . . .

June 1st 1947

Benny my darling:

. . . It's spring at long last, that terrible winter is over. I've just had another of your delicious letters, you know as I read them I can hear you talking to me. This evening I walked alone up to our secret view and remembered the first day you took me there . . . now it's only a few weeks before you'll take me there again. Marvellous news about Constance—Aelfric asked her to go up to Oxford for a Commem Ball. As you know he's poor as a church-mouse, but he'd saved up some money just for this last fling by working on the land in the vacations. Constance watched the Eights from the college barge, she was quite a sensation at the Ball. One awful little squirt, an old Etonian, even proposed to her! She's softened a little and responding, I think, to the security of being among her friends again. Felix was here on leave looking even more dissolutely dashing than ever and what do you think? He saw Tony Hammond! He went into a record shop in Oxford Street and there was Tony *serving behind the counter*! Of course they went and had a drink together and Tony rather made light of his job; he said it was temporary while he was waiting to hear from the B.B.C.; but Felix didn't believe it. After all, it's two full years since Tony left Cambridge, the brightest of our hopes, and what has he done? Not much apparently. He worked for a while in an art gallery in Paris, and got rather seriously involved with a married woman, and had to leave in a hurry. He went down to Spain and earned a very little teaching English, then he got a job on a yacht at Monte Carlo with some rich Greek. But what's it all for? What is his real strength? I could never make out whether he wanted to be Prime Minister or Poet Laureate or whether perhaps he didn't just want to drift along with the current. Oh he still plays that trumpet, by the way, twice a week in a small club. He's got a one-room flat in Cromwell Road. Felix says darkly that he believes Tony is paying a lot of attention to a German starlet of nineteen who's over here making a film. He is, Felix adds, wildly attractive in an unwashed way. Poor Tony!

July 7th 1947

Benny my darling . . .

. . . Rupert called tonight. What a character! My mother quite swooned though my father was less rhapsodical. He told me all about you, says you're the sweetest man he's ever met and quite unspoiled by living with *him* all the time. He brought your present for me—it was perfect, how did you develop such marvellous taste? I hope you haven't been talking to any strange women. . . . My mother admired it particularly and I shall be wearing it on my finger the day I meet you. Rupert stayed to dinner and told us about a plan you had to go into a partnership together—you as the technical man and he as the salesman—in the record business. It sounds terrific fun Benny, and perhaps I can be your receptionist; I'll wear a pair of severe hornrimmed glasses and frighten undesirable callers away. . . . But you will take your degree first won't you? Otherwise you'll always regret it. Of course I can understand you want to start earning money, so that we can marry soon, but we've all the time in the world and no one can take us away from each other. . . .

. . . I've had a long rambling letter from Tony Hammond. I don't know what to make of it, truly, it reads as if it's been written by a maniac. I hope he's going to be all right. Isn't it odd how the people one thought most of when very young usually come to a sticky end?

It's late Benny, and I must be up early tomorrow, I have a class at nine in Shallerton. I'm enjoying painting enormously and when you come home you shall be my first professional commission. The fee will be one of your kisses, the highest fee ever paid for a work of art. . . .

July 20th 1947

Benny my darling:

. . . Ilex left today and we all had to go to the gala farewell. You have to hand it to him, his public relations department is remarkable. He had the Minister down and half the county. The Minister said the Aylsbourn experiment would set the pattern for the British education in the next half century etc. etc. It appears that Ilex has produced—at any rate on paper—the best scholarship results (allowing for our small size) in England. And now he's off to be a high-powered university professor in California. Dear Ilex! He was (as usual) quite tearful when people said all these nice things about him. There's a new man coming to take over, from Lancashire, a rather bleak scientist, the first we've had in charge at Aylsbourn. Poor Mr. Johnston has been passed over. . . . Yet another crazy card today from Tony; you must try to see him when you're home; it's only a few days now. . . .

15th August 1947

Benny my darling:

. . . These last few days are the worst of all. *Please* come home soon, I'm so lost and miserable without you. Any day now I'm expecting a letter to say you're on the way. I do hope you can fiddle a plane, surely the R.A.F. can do that for you after keeping you from me for nearly three years. For all I know you may have sailed or already be somewhere in the sky, flying towards me at three hundred miles per hour. . . . I must sound quite daft, but I sometimes go out and look up into the sky to see if it has any hint of you, but it's always inscrutable. . . .

23rd August 1947

Benny my darling:

. . . Still no word from you and I'm getting so frightened. It's like calling out in the dark when you're small and afraid, and no one being there to reply. Do you know how many letters we've exchanged while you've been away? Nearly three hundred—I counted them the other night. . . .

24th August 1947

Benny my darling :

. . . Please come home quickly. I need you desperately. Only you can give me the sense of security and the sanity and the love I need. Please come home quickly. . . .

THE night, now that Benedict was saying goodbye to it, the Mediterranean night was one thing he would regret; its air clear as the Cressbrook and frigidaire-chilled; its sky like ace-black steel etched out with a billion silver-nitrate needle-points. He watched the waves sliding by below, mesmerized; indigo and creamy lace with, at night, a flash of phosphorescence on the edge.

In the early hours of the Wednesday, exactly a week after they had set sail, they passed Gibraltar and softly turned northward past the vivid bare Red Cheddar cliffs of St. Vincent. They looked, Benedict thought, like a foretaste of England; it might almost have been a piece of Devon; Torbay for instance, on a summer morning. He sighed. It was best not to think about it, to let the mind run free. . . . He had sent his last letter to Laura, number three hundred and twelve, and down in the hold of the ship were his homecoming presents to her; lengths of dress material from Alexandria, negro carvings from Nairobi, Israeli jewellery from Ramat Gan, an Italian handbag from Eritrea.

On Thursday morning they sailed purposefully up the coast of Portugal and the sea was still marvellously calm until they turned into the Bay; then it roughened as if by reflex action and the wind turned cold as the Cavendish Laboratory. A sister ship passed, southward bound, and they all crowded to the rail, glad to have even a fleeting contact with fellow-men on the unheeding sea. Benedict couldn't sleep that night; they were due in next day.

But Friday morning came at last and in disbelief he watched the termite life along the docks as they edged gently up Southampton Estuary. And now he was only thirty miles from home.

When his name was boomed over the tannoy an iron-fisted fear seized his heart; he ran to the signals room and ripped the telegram open with shaking fingers. It was from Rupert: GO TO THE SOUTH DOCK GARAGE AT ONCE WHERE YOU WILL HEAR SOMETHING TO YOUR ADVANTAGE. That was a typical communication trust Rupert; he'd probably arranged a crate of Margrave bitter. Or was it possible that Laura—but no; he'd written to say specially she wasn't to come; there would be all the drear formalities of disembarkation and form-filling and he wanted to be alone with her when they met. When they met at her parents' house in Aylsbourn. Especially as her parents were in Italy.

He got to the garage by nine. Rupert had certainly arranged a surprise; a note in his own hand which said: "My dear Benny, Knowing how struck you are on this girl I thought it would be nice for you to have this car for your leave. Don't worry, I didn't steal it; I bought it, or rather put down thirty quid on it and the rest on the never-never. . . . I've gone to Paris with a bit of crackling; it's yours till Friday fortnight—make the best of it!"

It was an M.G.—Rupert knew it was Benny's favourite car; he would not have put it past the old reprobate to have bought it just for that reason; to give his friend this special pleasure.

He stowed his luggage in the back, buttoned up his civilian overcoat, wrapped a thick woollen R.A.F. scarf round his neck, and let in the clutch with a sigh of unalloyed happiness.

The roads were strange at first; narrow and twisting and left-orientated; but his heart raced as he saw the familiar signs of home approaching: the Margrave Beer advertisements, the Southern Region stations, the Wessex buses, the corn stooks, the elegiac scent of hay, the scars of white chalk on the low rolling downs, the sight of the most crystalline water in the world as he swept over a bridge and saw the Cressbrook rippling underneath; and then, quicker and quicker, the sights and sounds and smells of home—the names of the villages: Bales Whitney and Ashdale and the green signpost which said Public Footpath to Welcaster; then with a suddenness in which he seemed to be drowning, Brewery Hill; to the right the High Street, Brewers Lane to the left and at last the little road up to the Mill House.

He pulled up gently outside. He was home.

The house was in darkness. Evidently she had gone out somewhere; no one expected him till tomorrow. What would Laura say when she saw him? Would the shock be too great? Should he go down to the "Wheatsheaf" and ring her from there, deceiving her for a moment into thinking he was still in Southampton? And then gently revealing to her that he was only a stone's throw away from her, twenty seconds if he ran, his feet four inches above the Aylsbourn earth? . . .

He lay forward over the wheel and closed his eyes. He was entirely content. There would be no more waiting after this. He

was home at Laura's door, the M.G. oiled and tuned and ready to
carry them away together where nobody would ever find them
and where they would make love as no two young people had ever
made love before. Soon he dozed. But through his imagination,
mescalin-bright with love, there ran an unrelated jumble of ideas
and phrases and snatches of song, a long disordered shorthand, a
broken-up code, a key to his young life: I'll be seeing you, In all
the old familiar places . . . Get those arms up in the air, Benedict,
Keep them *up* . . . Well hit, Benny, we've got time for another . . .
Adeste fideles, laeti triumphantes, adeste, adeste . . . where all the
dark and white folks meet, Basin Street, land of dreams . . . when
I consider how my light is spent, ere half my days in this dark
world and wide . . . the best this country has to give, Benny, and
then to learn to give it back again . . . hold me tighter, Benny, I
won't bite . . . oh Benny, I'm so afraid, the world's such a big place
and we're so alone . . . you lovely bastards, we're going to win
today . . . arrogance, definitely, and then appetite . . . I'm bursting
to do some Roman history with you; anyone here ever read a
book called *I Claudius*? No, well . . . Dear chums, as it is my
custom to commence with the most important item, I'll give you
a list of what I've eaten . . . when they begin the Beguine . . .
Quis multa gracilis te puer in rosa perfusus liquidis urget . . . Oh
Benny that was the very first time . . . for me too . . . I'm sure my
life will be very unhappy . . . I love beautiful things, trees, water,
flowers, scents, sounds, colours, I hate ugly things . . . alpha minus
query minus . . . he's very well *made,* all legs at the moment, but
the head is very fine . . . to you my heart cries out Perfidia . . .
when I'm married I shall expect my husband to have a horse and
car . . . Benny, why are you so sweet to me? . . . I'll be seeing you
in all the old familiar places . . . the children's carousel, the
chestnut tree, the wishing well . . . two whole volumetrics, oxalic
and H_2O_2 with $KMNO_4$ . . . Constance, please, isn't there anything we can do? . . . all dreams have to end, Benny, as you'll find
out one day . . . it's the manure, the malt, the hay, the river, the
wood, all trees breathe, they give off a sort of sweetness when
they're heavy with fruit . . . lay your sleeping head my love, human
on my faithless arm . . . promise me, when you come home . . .
that old pub at the source of the Cressbrook—remember—and we
shall make love properly as no two people ever did before . . .
sweet slob, dear old butch, darling boy, dear cadet Benedict it is

indeed a most unhappy duty . . . he used to go round secretly putting an extra polish on our shoes . . . and I shut myself in my bedroom and sobbed my heart out, for I felt as if I'd lost a little bit of you . . . shoes five and a half, stockings nine and a half, vital statistics . . . I'll be seeing you in all the old familiar places . . . Hello, Benny . . . Hello, Benny . . . Hello, Benny . . . Hello, Benny . . . Hello, Benny.

"Hello, Benny."

He opened his eyes, then shut them quickly. It was light; the early morning sun was in the sky. The face that stared so intently down at him was familiar; those mild old blue eyes, that slightly sawny weather-beaten old working-class face. . . .

"Hello, Benny. You remember me don't you? It's Mrs. Duncher."

"Hello, Mrs. Duncher. What are you doing?"

"I'm on my way to work. But what are you doing?"

"I'm waiting for Laura. She doesn't expect me till today. I must have dropped off to sleep. It doesn't matter. It passed the time."

Mrs. Duncher was staring at him as if he were a phantom.

"But didn't you know, Benny?"

"Know what?"

She turned her head away because there are moments when one human being should not look at another.

"She went away with Tony Hammond yesterday. He's been here for the last ten days, seeing her every day. They—they were married by special licence yesterday."

Mrs. Duncher, as she said this, had unknowingly shut her eyes tight, as if to help her not see anything. In a little while she slowly opened them again. Then she cried, "Benny!" And again in compassion and fear, "Benny! Benny! Benny!"

"But P.J., if I may say so with respect, you're just not with it. You're out on Cloud Nine. This is the twentieth century—remember?"

Sammy Spiral faced his managing director across the desk angrily. He was a long stringbean of a youth whose gaberdine coat had no reveres, and whose khaki-drill trousers were of the tightest possible diameter consonant with getting his feet into them. He wore a pair of dove-grey suède shoes, a thin hand-knitted wool tie, horizontally striped, and a coffee-coloured silk shirt. His thick, short hair was brushed forward over his forehead so that he resembled a moody young centurion. He had an I.Q. of 150 and dirty finger-nails. He looked like a man who played a far-out tenor sax in a cool jazz cellar, or a beatnik, or a recent product of Cambridge University. As it happened he was all three.

He had come down just three years ago and chosen to work at Diskon after going for sixty-four interviews; after resisting all the enticements that Shell, I.C.I., Unilever, Hedley's, the Metal Box Company, Granada Television, and J. Walter Thompson could offer him. Something about the Diskon set-up had intrigued him; it was not a giant outfit, but pretty swinging and on the way up quick. He had been pleased by the note Diskon had sent through the Appointments Committee: "We are looking for a young man with a first or 2.1 in economics who combines ineluctable ambition with natural arrogance. We don't give a damn what school he went to or what games he plays. He must have a real passion for modern jazz, since it is this department of our business that he will have to develop: he must dig Gillespie, Monk, Coleman, Hayes, Harriott and Dankworth. He must develop a passion for selling records to the highly intelligent and progressive people who enjoy cool jazz; that is young professional people in the 25-35 bracket. He must be prepared to work with passion all the hours God sends and in return will not be expected to clock in or call anybody sir. He will start at £800, will hit £3,000 at thirty, after which it will be up to him."

This specification sounded as if it had been drawn up in heaven by the Archangel Gabriel with Samuel H. Spiral's names inscribed on it in letters of fire. Sammy's ambition was to go places but quick. He had no doubt, not a sliver of doubt, that he and his friends would be running England well on the right side of forty. Diskon sounded exactly the kind of outfit that would fall into his unmanicured but eagerly outstretched hand one day. After all, P. J. Benedict, the gaffer, though only ten years his senior, was a doomy old nut who once or twice had talked about jagging it in; if he ever did, Sammy Spiral was waiting with itching heels in the wings. Also, in fits and starts, he rather liked P.J., as everybody called him. Not today though. He looked at the old geyser with displeasure. He saw a tall, slightly stooping man of thirty-four with very large eloquent brown eyes and a moon-like face with unfashionably long hair curling a little over his ears. He was a pretty odd nut to have built up a business like this, Sammy reflected. But then, after all, P.J. had the reputation of being the most ruthless bastard in a fairly cut-throat business. Actually, on closer acquaintance, Sammy had decided that ruthless was the wrong word; P.J. had made good *because he didn't give a damn*; he had no emotions at all and worked with a continuous, cold fury. Sammy was no sentimentalist, as God well knew, but he couldn't quite see P.J.'s angle. What was it all for? He didn't seem to have any material ambition and he certainly didn't have any restless friends with whom he felt a compulsive necessity to keep up as Sammy did; in fact the very few times he'd seen friends of P.J.'s in the office he'd been struck by their peasant-like qualities. P.J. had no family to work for, no wife, no children, not even any parents. He wasn't interested in politics even though he went without much enthusiasm through the liberal motions. It just didn't figure. However, he was enjoying his job at Diskon and only occasionally did he feel a stab of irritation. Like now.

"Even in the twenty-first century I doubt if there'll be any future for fiddling the books," Benedict replied. "There'll be room for people like you in one of those therapeutic rest-homes that will replace prisons if the Howard League get their way."

"It's not fiddling, P.J. All we have to do is stick a simple little label on the consignments saying second-hand and we save ourselves thirty-three and a third per cent tax."

"The only drawback would seem to be that the consignments

are not second-hand. When I last saw them, the discs looked kind of brand-new to my jaundiced old eye."

"But P.J., how are we going to compete? You know some of our new competitors are doing this all the time."

"We shall compete by selling better records with twice the energy and ten times the imagination."

"But nobody will ever *know*, P.J."

"I will know. And you will know."

"What possible harm will it do?"

"It will harm you and it will harm me."

"Look, P.J., I know you think I'm just an immoral young layabout. That's not so, you know. I'm as involved in morality as you are. But I'm interested in things that *really* matter. I was out in Algeria with the rebels, you know that."

"What is the good of bringing aid to the Algerian rebels— though I applaud it—if you swindle your own people with your other hand?"

"What do you mean swindle? It's only the *government*."

"Would you walk into a post office and lift a hundred pounds worth of notes from the till?"

"That's a false analogy, P.J. You have to live inside the contemporary ethical climate. You know that everyone tries to do the government for all they're worth."

"Do they? All the clergymen and schoolteachers and people on small pensions? Would your father try to do the government?"

"You know perfectly well he can't. He's just a minor civil servant. Anyway, he wouldn't have the enterprise. That's why he never got any further."

"But would he, if he had your opportunity?"

Sammy hesitated. "No. That's why I despise him."

"And that's why you despise me?"

"No, don't misunderstand me, P.J. You've done a great job with Diskon. But it seems to me you're fighting with one hand tied behind your back if you don't meet your rivals on equal terms."

"We shall still be expanding when those of our rivals who stick second-hand labels on new consignments are languishing in Pentonville," Benedict said. Then he added pleasantly, "And to bring this discussion to an amicable close, let me give you my word of honour, Sammy, that if you try it on you will be thrown out of here the very same day with one week's money. You get the idea?"

Sammy snapped his fingers in sudden inspiration. "I've got it, P.J.," he said. "You've given yourself away. It's that word honour. That's what's got you by the short and curly. You're still in the grip of an outmoded and discarded concept. Why, it's a word that's not even used seriously any more. I can't think of a single serious semantic use for it. Where did you pick the concept up?"

He had forgotten his anger; P.J.'s threat had run off him like water off a duck's back. But he was genuinely curious about his last question.

Benedict smiled at Sammy with affection.

"I think I picked it up in another century," he said, "from some despicable old nut. Maybe even my father. You'll just have to ride along with our Dickensian concepts if you want to stay here, Sammy. Now which is it to be—the new labels or a week's money?"

Sammy uncurled slowly from the armchair. "The new labels," he said resignedly, "and don't come bollocking me when you see the next quarterly returns."

"They will be fifteen per cent up on this quarter," said Benedict easily, "or you will get that swift kick in the arse for which you have been so eloquently pleading. Oh and Sammy. . . ."

Sammy turned. "Yes, P.J.?"

"Come to dinner tonight. You've got a girl friend, haven't you?"

"Sure, I have a chick. What do you think I am, made out of cement?"

"All right, bring her too. It's 223a Upper Brook Street. Seven-thirty."

"Black tie, P.J.?"

"No. Just a tie, if it's not too much bother. Send in Mr. Weston as you go out, will you?"

(b)

Felix had acquired at least one unpleasant trait from his father, Benedict reflected: a passion for black suède shoes. He glanced down at Felix's feet with disapproval. Otherwise, the picture was much as he had imagined it. Felix wore a grey

221

flannel suit and a bow tie. He was still very lean and now in maturity good-looking so that he would notice in a busy street; too good-looking, you wouldn't trust him further than you could throw him. Benedict noticed with a sharp sense of shock that there were one or two hints of grey in Felix's glossy black hair; they were the same age—with very nearly half their days run through. And those talents which are death to hide: what had they done with them? It didn't really matter, it was strangely comforting to see Felix again. He shook hands warmly.

"Now then, Felix, what'll you drink?"

"What have you got?"

"Everything: scotch, gin, vodka, sherry, tomato juice. . . ."

"I'll take a scotch please. On the rocks if you can. Thanks."

"Cheers."

"Cheers."

There was a silence. Then Benedict said:

"I've ordered a special lunch for you today, Felix. I tried to imagine what you'd like best. Finally I settled on a rough paté, some pheasant with game chips and all the usual trimmings, mille feuilles, and some Stilton. I've got out some Mouton Rothschild in your honour. I hope you've acquired a taste for château-bottled claret?"

"I can take it or leave it, Benny. But today I'll certainly take it."

"I hope you can drink seven glasses."

"Seven?"

"Yes. I make it a rule only to drink one at lunch."

"I'll drink six if you'll drink two."

"All right; it's a deal. Now then—ah here comes that paté, let's sit down—tell me all about yourself. What have you been doing since we last met?"

Felix sighed. "My dear Benny, what a question. It would take me a year to tell you. But I could just pick out the highlights for you if you really wish."

"Go on."

Felix considered. Studying his face closely, Benedict noted with compassion that there were new lines in it he had never seen before; normally, he reflected, time paints in its greasepaint so slowly, that one doesn't notice. This was quite startling; just as if the Felix he had last set eyes on had disappeared for five minutes

222

and come back in the disguise of the man he would be in fifteen years.

At length Felix decided how he would start.

"You know, Benny, there was always one writer I admired more than all the rest put together."

"Stendhal?"

"You've got a good memory. The great ambition of my adolescence was to follow in the footsteps of the young Stendhal—to be a writer of comedies and a seducer of women. It seemed in my first innocence a perfect career for me." He frowned. "Unhappily I found the second half of the project all too easy. The first half proved much more difficult."

"I thought you had decided to stay in the Army?"

"Yes, that was my idea at one point. But it grew so deadly boring, Benny. You've no idea what life in a peace-time officers' mess can be like."

"I don't even know what a wartime officers' mess is like."

"Oh no, of course you didn't get a commission, did you? Anyway, I realized I was learning nothing, not developing as a writer must. If you could have seen some of the officers' wives I was compelled to seduce to while away the tedium!" He made a grimace of disgust to remember. "Anyway, I came out, went to Cambridge, then in 1950 did all sorts of odd jobs. I was a Rolls-Royce salesman and a steward on the Queen Elizabeth, a trainee welder at Waterloo Station, a bookmaker's runner and even briefly a television announcer. But you know, it's a myth that a writer must have a multiplicity of jobs; what he must have is a clear eye and a sharp ear in the situation he happens to find himself; it might be Lloyds Bank or the Prudential, but there'll be material even in unrewarding places like that."

"Why didn't you write about us—I mean your friends?"

Felix waved the question contemptuously aside. "Have some sense, Benny. What in the name of heaven would I find to say about our peasant lives together? Why, the most interesting character in a novel like that would be me, and God knows I'm dull enough!" He was rather tickled at the thought.

"Yes, I suppose that's right. So what did you do?"

"Travelled. My trust, you see, fell in at twenty-one so I could do more or less what I liked. I went to the United States and lived in Manhattan, in Greenwich Village for a while."

"How was that?"

"Oh lots of fun—but not much material. You see, everyone seemed to behave in such closely predictable patterns. You know I've kept a notebook ever since I was a boy. Well, I meant to use it only to record those snatches of dialogue, ideas, expressions, hints, moods, subtleties, which would be significant one day, would throw a strong light into the personalities I was describing. But I got nothing to record. Oh, I had some fun among the beats. There was one I was particularly fond of. His name was Zubinsky, and he read poetry in one of those beat cafés while someone played a cool guitar. I lived in his pad a while. He was a proper comedian. Always some new joke. He used to send his girl-friend in to my room every morning with the early-morning coffee. She was Javanese, and gorgeous."

"I can't see anything particularly funny in that."

"Yes, but absolutely starkers old chap. Not a stitch on. It was a bit of a facer first thing in the morning, even to a hardened campaigner like me."

"I get the joke now."

"Anyway, in the end even Zubinsky got boring and I decided to head west: Chicago, Detroit, Minnesota, and across the Rockies to San Francisco. That was beautiful, Benny, one of the two places in the world I could happily live in."

"The other?"

"Haifa. They've a lot in common, believe it or not. Anyway I taught in California for a bit—you know I got a degree in English eventually? It was only a third, but in California that puts you in the Leavis bracket. I even played some small parts in those canned TV films they make in Los Angeles now. But I had to get out of L.A. in the end. It became quite intolerable."

"What did?"

Felix's dark face gleamed with malicious pleasure.

"You mean you don't know? My dear Benny, L.A. is run by queers. You go to a party and you have to declare your interest before a girl will take any interest in *you*. You get girls coming up and saying, 'Are you a man?' You know the first time it happened I was eating a canapé and I nearly choked."

"I bet you did."

"Mind you I made some good friends out there in California. The beauty of the place is that you can make a packet with hardly more trouble than it takes to lift a peach from a tree. Why, I met a character out in Hollywood one night who'd just got bored with the rain in New York one day in 1948 and said to himself, 'Aw hell, let's go west'."

"The slogan of the good American since the beginning of history."

"Yes. Anyway, he went. And today that fellow owns an electronics works, a laundry, a restaurant, a concession to import Mercedes cars and an art gallery. Just because it rained!"

"What about your writing?"

Felix looked almost—though it wasn't a word you could really use about him—crestfallen.

"I don't know, Benny; everything I wrote was opaque. You know writing is an odd talent. Not everybody thinks he can play a piano or paint a masterpiece. But everybody is taught to write in the literal sense, and therefore everyone feels he can be a writer. Look at the bloody generals," he added gloomily. "You know, Benny," he went on, "there are some writers who put words down on a piece of paper and they leap right off again. They write half a line and summon a character into your room. They can make you feel a woman's scent or the beer on a man's breath when there's no one there but you. But it's a bloody rare and precious gift. There's one young American writer can do it. I read a page of his and put my pen down in despair. His name is Philip Roth and he's only about twenty-nine; five years younger than us, Benny.

"Sometimes, you know, Benny, I really felt I was swinging. I'd sit down and I'd feel in a good mood and I'd say to myself: today I'm going to write the arse off all those other hacks, today's my day. And I'd write all day like crazy and go to bed not knowing if I mightn't have put down something fresh-minted like a 1960 half-crown. And then in the morning I'd wake up and read what I'd written and it would be flat, Benny, flat and lifeless as cold porridge.

"Finally I realized something. I've always resisted your all-or-nothing-at-all theory of life. But it began to dawn on me that nothing else but everything would do in this racket. I remembered reading a remark by that Russian writer, you know, *Not By Bread Alone*——"

"Dudintsev?"

"Yes. Dudintsev was quoted as saying that he'd given his whole strength to that book. Now at first that seems preposterous, a typical piece of Slav sentiment. And yet now I'm convinced that nothing less will ever do. It's a bit like taking up religion or romantic love; it's all or nothing at all. And I decided my trouble was I wasn't really prepared to pay quite such a heavy price."

"So you published nothing."

"Oh yes, under another name. Just to make quite sure it wasn't masochism, that I hadn't got a masterpiece on my hands. I hadn't. All three books sank without trace. They sold about two thousand copies each; the critics ignored them, not that that matters, though. I only wanted three friends and one girl to say yes to my book, Benny, and I'd have been happy. Three friends and a girl; all the rest is meaningless to me. But they never did."

"I'm a bit surprised that you mention a girl. Surely not one special girl?"

Felix looked a trifle shifty. "No, not really. Whatever was on the cards at the time. What a frightful bore all that bed jag is, Benny! You know I've tried all colours, white and black and coffee——"

"Some took it like the host, some like a toffee."

Felix looked genuinely surprised for a moment. "You know I was doing that sub-consciously. Good for you, Benny. I didn't know you kept up with the O.K. versifiers still."

"Felix, almost any modern poetry could be applied to you. As you were talking I kept thinking of that other one—what is it?— oh yes, something about he ran through women like a child through growing hay, looking for a lost toy whose capture might atone for his own guilt and the cosmic disarray."

"That's good," said Felix with his dark and slightly evil grin, "the cosmic disarray. But I don't believe I've ever been guilty of guilt, if you follow me."

"You just want to be left alone."

"Yes. Leave me easy, leave me alone. You see, Benny, I never expected anything out of life. Therefore I'm not disappointed. You, on the contrary, are always full of hope. Therefore you must be vulnerable always, for ever being hurt and disenchanted."

"You're wrong, Felix. I haven't had any real hope for the best part of fifteen years now, since the year I last saw you."

"Benny, I don't often say I'm sorry. But I'm sorry about what

226

I said on the rock. There was no need to make it worse than it had to be anyway. You know, there wasn't a word of truth in what I was saying. Poor Laura was perfectly innocent at Torquay, in fact I'm prepared to take money that when she ran off with that bastard Hammond she was *vierge du corps*. No, promiscuity wasn't her kick at all; it's just that"—he groped for the expression—"she was made for disaster. She was made to be snatched away. She was predestined to unhappiness. Remember, in the war, how people used to resign themselves to the possibility of death? They'd say: there's nothing I can do if it's got my number written on it. Well, that was Laura's misfortune. The good Lord wrote Tony Hammond's number on her when he slid her down the chute into the world."

"You know she writes to me each year on my birthday?"

"You don't say! Where are they?"

"She never puts an address. The letters are posted in central London."

"What on earth does she say?"

"Always the same. Just wishes me a happy birthday, says she reads about me from time to time and is glad I'm doing well, hopes I'm happy, and that's it."

"Nothing about Hammond?"

"Nothing."

There was a pause while Benedict poured out the last of the wine and they both lit cigars.

"Now tell me about our other old buddies, Benny. You know I never keep in touch. What's Milo doing?"

"He's a scientist. He's working on some diabolical new rocket in Applestreet New Town."

"Isn't that the monstrosity they've built in the Cressbrook Valley?"

"That's it. He's very respectably married by the way, to a brisk, sensible nurse he met at a dance, and they have two small girls."

"I hope the poor little bitches don't look like Milo."

"They don't look like anything very much. I haven't seen him for some time, only when he comes up to London, usually on his way through to Woomera."

"He's on the up and up, the old human slide-rule?"

"Oh yes. He'll soon have his C.B.E. and he'll get his K.

before he's forty-five. He'll be Sir Milo all right. Not that he gives a jot one way or the other."

"And Ken Heppel?"

"They run the local garage. It's a big business nowadays. They're among the most prosperous people in the town. They're supposed to have a dream-house on Cromwell Hill, but I've never seen it."

"You've never gone back?"

"No."

"Isn't that a bit melodramatic?"

"Just common sense. I tried it once, but when I was getting near I began to tremble so much—as if I'd got a shock—that I couldn't drive. I had to turn back."

Benedict paused and turned a troubling thought over in his mind.

"Do you know something, Felix?" he said at length. "Seeing you has done something quite dramatic for me. You seem—if you'll forgive the extravagance—to have broken the spell. I believe I could go back again now. No"—now he was certain—"it's not a question of could. I will go back. I'm determined to see what's happened to everybody. To hell with whether it's a mistake. I'll go late—after dinner tonight. I'll damned well stay there until I've sorted it all out. God, you know something? Felix, you've broken the spell."

"Poor old Benny. So you're what a psychosomatic syndrome looks like."

"That reminds me: Constance is still in Aylsbourn. She married Aelfric Gates—remember?—he's an assistant manager at the Brewery now. Something went wrong with him at Oxford; I never quite found out what. Anyway, he has a reasonable sort of future. You know old Keith Margrave died and one of the big breweries bought his business up. Of course the sentimentalists complained; but it means more chance for Aelfric. It also means I can buy Margrave bitter anywhere in London now."

"But now what about yourself, Benny, how did you come to encumber your sensitive spirit with all this success?"

"Oh it was just that I had no other interests in life. Anyone with a little intelligence and no other interest in life can make a pile these days if he wants to, Felix. Mind you I was lucky in my partner—he's a chap called Rupert Ripley, the best salesman in

Greater London—and of course we got in at the bottom of the market, just before the rocket went up. It was quite fun in the early days. I didn't bother about a degree you know. . . ."

"Why not?"

"Oh I couldn't face it at that stage. I wanted to get stuck into something that would take up seventeen hours of each day. And this business certainly did. We started with a capital of twenty-one hundred pounds—all the money my father left me, a bit Margrave was decent enough to give me, and Rupert's gratuity. We started off in a basement in Praed Street. Gosh, it was fun."

Benedict looked excited in a way he had been careful not to do for thirteen long years. "We started as a record club, making under a hundred copies of each record. The first discs, I remember, were fifteen shillings. We made them of plastic, not shellac, because that was too expensive. We bought an American recording instrument for £140 and cut our first concert in Birmingham Town Hall. That was in 1948. We made a loss of fourteen pounds in our first year. And now we have a turnover of £460,000."

"Do you realize, Benny, that if you'd been such a fool as to marry Laura, you'd probably be a BBC engineer by this time, making seven hundred and forty a year?"

"I expect you're right. Anyway, I'm entirely indifferent to that side of it. It's just something I'm grateful to, that's all, for using up all my energy and giving me no time to think."

There was a long silence. Each was lost in his own thoughts. In the end Benedict said: "Felix, did you tell me the other night what you are in now—export, is it?"

"Yes. I have a small shipping business in the City. That's not ships you understand—we're agents."

"Isn't that rather dull?"

"Monumentally dull. But then you know, Benny, I think I'm basically rather a dull fellow."

"What nonsense you do talk still, Felix."

"It's true. I go in at nine-thirty, I make a few calls, have lunch at Pimms, ring a few people up, sign some letters, and get back to my flat in Belsize Park. In the evening we go to the local cinema."

"We?"

Felix looked shifty again.

"Yes. Joanna and I."

"Not our Joanna?"

"I'm afraid so. Well, you know, Benny, I was always fascinated by women older than myself."

"But she's only a year older than you!"

"Yes. Well, I don't know. I looked her up when I got out of the Army. It was strange, but she seemed quite refreshing after all those awful colonels' wives. I didn't have to make any sort of effort, you see. She knew what a swine I was from the word go. Mind you, I gave her an awful time. She was only just getting over that frightful man and I was the first friendly face she'd seen in London for years. She cut herself off from her family you see, just wouldn't see them. I behaved in a despicable way, Benny. I used to use her flat as a base for my operations. Sometimes I didn't come back for weeks on end. Usually she'd throw the G.P.O. directories at me, sometimes all four, but she always took me back in."

"What was the point? Why didn't you go and live in Dolphin Square or any other of those big anonymous blocks where you could have done whatever you liked without all those tiresome scenes?"

"I dunno. It was pleasant to have someone to talk to with no artifice, no mask to the face."

"It never occurred to you to offer to marry her, I suppose?"

"Benny, have a heart. Who'd marry *me*? Actually, in a moment of gin-soaked depression I did once make her a mean sort of offer, which she declined."

"What offer?"

"I said I could give her ten years' love."

"Then years *what*?" Benedict interjected sharply. The great debate was resumed after thirteen years and he was rather enjoying it.

"Ah yes. Our semantic disagreement. I used the word love, Benny, as a convenient emotional shorthand. She knew what I meant all right, even if she wouldn't admit it to herself. I meant: I desire you sufficiently and sufficiently often to overcome the tedium of your breakfast face and the boredom of your small talk and the slightly emetic distaste I get when you squirt deodorant under your arms. Isn't that all it means?"

Benedict beamed with pleasure. "I can't tell you how happy I am to see you again, Felix," he said. "You know, growing up spoils some people. But nothing will ever erode your particular and unique charm."

"Who was right about life, Benny? You or me?"

"We were both right. And both wrong. You know, Felix, I can see an even more horrifying fate looming ahead for you, Stendhal reincarnated, Henri Beyle of Belsize Park, writer of comedies and seducer of women."

"What fate?"

"I'm very much afraid that one day you will get up and steel yourself with a triple shot of gin and put on your best suit and take Joanna off in a new hat with a veil to the Register Office. And having married her in three minutes flat you'll both go and get sloshed at the Salisbury, and you will both have got what you deserve."

"What did Joanna do to deserve me?"

"I think suffering was necessary to her, as disaster was to Laura. And you were destined to be the instrument to inflict it."

"It's not quite as desperate as all that, Benny. Sometimes we get rather soppy about each other, bring each other home ridiculous little presents, and laugh like young. You know all that stuff people go through." He paused and there was a long silence. He seemed to be struggling with a new and unfamiliar concept.

"You know what, Benny, you may be right. After all, marriage is about the only kick I haven't tried. It'll be a new sensation, and there aren't so many left."

"Mightn't it be that it would be good for Joanna? Or would that be pushing logic too far?"

"Benny, after what she's put me through, she doesn't deserve to be happy." He added absently: "The long, miserable, jug-eared, ugly, half-baked bitch."

"Felix, you've given yourself away. I never thought to hear you use so many loving words about a woman in one sentence."

There was another long silence. They puffed reflectively at their cigars. At length Felix said:

"All right, Benny. I've told you all. Now it's your turn. There's one old friend of ours you haven't mentioned yet. Someone important. Hadn't you better own up?"

"Yes," said Benedict. "I'll own up."

★ 12 ★

"HELLO, BENNY."

Benedict groaned and turned over. He couldn't think where he was; he felt as if he had been hit very hard on the head. It wasn't like coming back to the world after sleep; it was as he imagined it must be to come out of a long marijuana dream or maybe a nine-hour operation. He felt as if he had been a long way away. But it was no good shutting his eyes again; you had to come round in the end; after a long dream you had to face the grey world as best you could.

Arabella was sitting beside his bed. No, that was wrong. It wasn't Arabella he had come to see, it was——

Then he began to remember, and he closed his eyes again.

In a minute, though, he opened them again in sharp curiosity. God damn, it *was* Arabella! And this room looked a little familiar, like a room lived in during a previous incarnation. Then he recognized it under the new paint; it was Felix's room. What in the name of heaven . . . ?

"Don't talk, Benny. Just rest. You've been asleep a long time—nearly twenty-four hours."

"Arabella—what am I doing here?"

"Mrs. Duncher rang me up, when you passed out, from the nearest call-box. I got round to you in our car in five minutes and we got you here between us and put you to bed. Dr. Anderson came and gave you something to make you sleep. He thinks you've got a virus infection, probably something you picked up abroad. Also, he said you showed symptoms of shock. So it was bed for you, Benny, with a sleeping pill, and a week before you get up."

"Arabella—I must have been dreaming. I had the most awful——"

Arabella gently shook her head. "I'm afraid you didn't dream it, Benny. It's true. She's gone. But don't think about it. Go back to sleep. Here, the doctor said you must take this."

He drank without resistance; he didn't care. And it was the next day—two days since he had first seen England again—before he awoke. Arabella was at his bedside again. She wore a house-

232

coat and was stirring something seriously in a toothglass. He watched her through half-closed eyelids, pretending to be still asleep; she hadn't changed much. He had forgotten her high cheekbones and slight slant of her eyes; maybe she had a little Eastern blood in her. He'd never thought of that before. At last she noticed him.

"Good morning, Benny. Do you feel as if you're coming back to us now?"

"Yes, thank you, I feel fine now."

"There are a lot of presents for you from your friends. Look at those heavenly yellow roses. Tess sent them. And the books are from Ken. Milo, need I say, sent the grapes. No doubt he'll be round to eat them soon."

Benedict tried to sit up in his panic, found he was not so strong as he thought, and fell back again. "Arabella," he pleaded desperately. "Please don't let anyone see me. Not even my friends. I've got to get out of here...."

"You'll stay exactly where you are," she said firmly. "But I promise you faithfully I won't let anyone see you if you'd prefer that."

He lay back, relieved. Somehow he had to pull himself together again, start the long, painful job of picking up the pathetic, shattered little pieces of his life.

"Here," Arabella said, "drink this."

"What is it?"

"Never mind what it is. It'll be good for you. Take it."

He was glad to be told what to do, and he obeyed her. Soon he had dozed off again. It was afternoon before he felt able to talk. Arabella brought him some soup and a glass of red wine.

"Drink this, Benny. You haven't eaten for nearly two days. We'll soon fatten you up again."

"Arabella, this is awfully good of you. I hope Gerard doesn't mind."

"He's in Czechoslovakia, attending some Iron Curtain trade fair. Mrs. Duncher's moved in to help me look after my two boys."

"Two boys?"

"Tim and you. He's seven now, you know. He keeps wanting to come and see you. I've promised to let him when you're a bit better."

"I'd like to see him. But I can't impose on you, Arabella, I must get up...."

"The doctor says you will stay in bed for another five full days. And that means right here. Even then he thinks you should take it easy for another week. The Johnstons will want to have you then, they've been most anxious about you."

"I couldn't talk to anyone at the moment, Arabella. If I really must stay in bed, please let me stay here out of everyone's way."

"That's just what I'm telling you to do. Now do you want to sit up and read a paper?"

"I'd rather just talk to you."

She sat on the bed and said: "Now, Benny, let's talk. Tell me all your adventures while you've been away from us."

For a while they avoided the subject that was first in both their minds. At length it was Arabella who mentioned it first: "Benny, I know there's not much one can say to help. But you mustn't feel bitter about Laura. She is the one who will suffer most because of this."

"I don't feel bitter. To tell you the truth I don't feel anything. I still don't believe it."

He thought for a while. Then he said: "And yet, you know, if I search my mind ruthlessly, I believe right back, deep inside, I always knew this or something like this would happen. I had always been afraid of it sub-consciously."

"I expect you're wondering how she could have said the things she did—at least the things I imagine she said—if she didn't love you. But Benny, if you will forgive a perfectly extraordinary statement, I'm sure she did love you. She would have loved you for a long time, maybe always, in a gentle way, if it hadn't been for Tony. And what she feels for Tony is not, in my dictionary, love. I don't know if this has ever been explained. Let me give you an example of what I mean. When Masha went to Trigorin, was that *love*? I don't think so. It was compulsion. Does the fish love the hook? There is just no alternative; for some women a man says come with me and she has to go; it's inevitable as death; it's beyond logic or reason or argument or ethics. It's just that Hammond and she were predestined for each other and, I believe, for each other's destruction. I'm afraid I've explained that very badly, but I do believe it with all my heart."

"I suppose," Benedict said with a touch of bitterness, "it was the same predestination that drove you and Tony together."

She flushed under the insult.

"No, Benny, you know that's not so. I turned to Tony in despair when I realized that Gerard and I were through."

"You were through as long ago as that?"

"Oh but of course, didn't you know? The first time he was unfaithful to me I thought it didn't matter; but it did, like the little worm you can hardly see that eventually eats out the whole heart of the apple. He had mistresses even when we were married; he never gave them up."

"What sort of people?"

"Any sort—barmaids, waitresses. He wasn't fussy; on the contrary." She shivered to remember. "I've never hated anyone quite the way I hate him."

"Then why——?"

"Why stay with him? Oh the usual thing, I don't have any money of my own now, and Tim's all I've got. I must stick it out, at any rate till Tim is older and we can get a proper financial settlement."

"What was Tony really like?"

She smiled and there was tenderness in her face even after the passage of five years, when she thought of him. "Oh he was so sweet, Benny. I suppose you're feeling he must be an absolute ruffian to take Laura away. It's not so. First, I don't suppose he quite understood the depth of your relationship, but even if he had, he couldn't have helped himself. He's not really bad, you see. Just—somehow put together the wrong way—like a marvellous and powerful engine with the controls all set in reverse."

There was silence in Felix's room. Then she hesitated and decided to go on.

"He was just what I was waiting for. I *was* waiting for someone you see. I'm not ashamed to admit it now. He was so—pretty. I was afraid you'd take him away from me." (Benedict never understood that remark.) "I couldn't believe it when I first saw him, that men could still look like that. I grew up in Paris, you see, where my father owned some hotels. He had quite a lot of money once, but it all went on women. He was a brilliant man—imagine an *Englishman* beating the French at the hotel business—but he made a complete mess of his personal life. In the end I grew to hate him—yet it's his type I'm still drawn to physically."

She smiled. "He was married four times. I literally had to introduce him to the son of his first marriage. I was the child of his fourth. My mother was a dancer. I don't mean a ballerina, I mean a dancer in a *boite*. She died and soon after, so did he, but fortunately there was enough money for my education. I went away to a convent and to a finishing school in Lucerne, a very smart one where all the girls were daughters of ambassadors or viscounts. That was *fun*, Benny—I had no worries or thoughts for the future; just hours of gossip and lessons in what to wear and what to say and what makes a beautiful picture."

"You learned a lot there, Arabella; I've never heard anybody talk quite like you."

"Oh, but I learned—from the other girls let me say—to talk *franchement*; life's too short for subterfuge, for us to hide behind our inhibitions. Anyway, then the finishing school ended, and I went to live in Paris. I was supposed to be studying music. But in fact I was having a whale of a time." She smiled, and Benedict saw suddenly how men could be deflected by a woman's smile. "You know, Benny, at one time the idea of being a very grand and famous courtesan seemed quite attractive to me. There were so many men in Paris before the war who had yachts and smelt delicious."

"I remember you telling us about this subject when we had tea in this room."

"Yes, I remember. It was a wicked thing for me to tell you, but you must remember, I was in a pretty desperate state."

"You looked perfectly—serene—to us."

"That only shows how little a boy sees. But though I should never have said such an outrageous thing to you, Benny, it happens to be true. You won't read this in *Woman's Own*, but it's frightfully important for a man to have a *sympathique* smell."

"What else?"

She looked at him, studied his face carefully, then made a decision. "You think you're old enough now for the advanced course? You know, I believe you are, Benny. What's more, I think this is just the time for me to give it to you. I've got to get your poor old feet back on terra firma."

She took a breath, and pursed her lips gravely while she organized her thoughts. Then she began to talk without the

236

slightest sign of inhibition or self-consciousness, straight from the heart, straight from her experience; *franchement*.

. . . "For me Benny, it's the most important thing in the world. It's metaphysics; it's the only way of breaking out of the solitariness we each inhabit. It's crucifixion, yet it's liberation. I suppose you must know that poem of John Donne's—it's very famous—how does it go?—oh yes, something about lovers' souls descending to affections and to faculties—'Which sense may reach and apprehend, Else a great Prince in prison lies'."

"It's a marvellous poem. But tell me, what else is important in a man?"

"He must be good and heavy. You have to feel there is no escape. But please don't imagine that just physical details are the only important consideration. Making love, to a woman, you see is at least three-quarters intellectual; she can start to make love one night, and finish the next. Women are very secret people, haven't you noticed? There was always something very delightful for me in meeting my father for a terrifically respectable lunch at the Ritz—for he always cosseted me, however badly he behaved to his various wives—after having made love all the night before, and knowing one would make love again that very evening. Are you shocked, Benny?"

"Not yet, I'm afraid."

"I must try harder." She reflected, and her face was suffused with the intensity of emotions recalled from another life. "The little intricacies are never recorded, Benny; the wonderful shock of discovery; the astonishment at seeing the hair on a man's stomach turn suddenly as your eye travels down his body, from black to a glorious red—I mean it's so *surprising*. But the detail I love best is the hair just behind a man's ears and on his neck. Don't ask me why, it's always been my special thing. Oh, and another point, the hair must be soft, and yet springy. It must be resistant to a woman's touch, and have a life of its own."

There was another pause. Then she said tantalizingly: "I think that will do for lesson one, Benny. Go to sleep and I'll give you lesson two tomorrow afternoon."

The next day they were quite alone: Mrs. Duncher had gone to Winchester for the day and Tim was at school. Arabella brought up lunch for them both on a tray and a bottle of wine.

When they had finished she lit a cigarette and smiled with provoking innocence at him.

"Well, Benny," she said. "Do you want to hear lesson two?"

"Yes, please."

She considered. "It's hard to know where to begin. But this is the essence of the thing, I think. To know somebody in bed is really the only real way to know them; the Bible gets it right as usual. It's not love, but it's the sealing-wax of love; the thing is not completed until it's been sealed in bed."

"You told us once that love was rare."

"Yes, I mean that. But I'll accept passion. Passion is pure and good. What I am against with all my heart is the mechanical habitual act."

"Do you think it's true that it means more to a woman?"

"Not always—generally though. A woman, you see, doesn't *have* an erotic experience. She *is* an erotic experience."

"Do you think it's better for the woman than the man?"

"How do I know, Benny? But do you remember that old myth about the Greek God who turned into a woman? He was asked how the two experiences compared and he said for the woman it was ten times better. I will say this: for me, it couldn't be better than it is."

"You told me some fascinating stuff yesterday about the details that appealed to you. Are there any more?"

She thought. "I'll tell you a nice thing about a man. That's the exact point where his shirt disappears under his belt. Now isn't that ridiculous? Also, the smell of a man's shirt—when he's got it on of course—is specially nice. Some women get a kick out of men's socks——"

"Arabella, you're joking!"

"No I'm not. It's really quite astonishing what tricks the life force will play to get us into bed. Think of a girl's legs in a swimming costume. You don't think twice about them, do you? But if you see four inches of stocking above the knee, you think you're seeing something madly exciting."

"Yes, I see that. But *socks*. . . ."

"Benny, I'm perfectly serious. Some girls get a kick out of a pair of rumpled socks, out of watching a man's ankles move on the clutch and the accelerator as he drives a car. Oh. . . ."

"Yes?"

238

"That reminds me. One of the sexiest things I ever experienced in my life. This is good, Benny. One day when I was only eighteen, I went to a marvellous ball outside Paris. I was driven out there one summer evening by a Frenchman of forty-six who had a red Alfa-Romeo. We did a hundred miles an hour all the way. I was wearing a white dress and I had been given scent, almost for the first time I think. I'd only just escaped from the convent. Anyway, it was something to do with the contrast between the fragility of my new white dress and the virility—*the power*—of all that speed. You know that Frenchman could have had me there and then if only he'd known."

"What, in the car?"

"Certainly. A car is both an awful and at the same time an exciting place for a woman. Normally she likes space and leisure to make love. She doesn't like those quick furtive smash-and-grab affairs. But there is this side to a car—it can sometimes powerfully convey the sensation of being ravished; and I needn't tell you how primitively exciting that is to a woman."

"But you can't——"

"No—of course you can't take her by force. But I think you'll find that if you take a woman by absolute gentleness, mixed up with moments of—well—brutality only just contained, you'll find you've aroused an erotic force in her you may not be able to cope with."

"And what else should you do to reach this kind of . . . ?"

She smiled. "One thing above all, Benny. One thing the Catholic church understands to perfection. Did you ever realize, Benny, that the Catholic secret is its instinctive knowledge and understanding of sex? That's what it's about really; you know all that Bride of Christ stuff? No, what I was going to say was that the church understands the importance of abstinence. The French have a saying, 'Il n'est sauce que l'appetit.' God how true that is of making love! That's why," she added thoughtfully, "that I was so glad to have been brought up in a convent. You came to it fresh; you miss all those grubby little adventures of adolescence. For the same reason naval marriages are usually happy. They're apart for months at a time and then, Christ Almighty!—when they're together again. . . ."

"I remember a man saying something rather direct to me about that once, Arabella, but it seemed true. He said that after a long abstinence it felt as if your spine was being shaken right out of your body."

Arabella laughed. "My dear Benny! You're not quite so innocent as you look. That's marvellous and it's right. Now I shall bore you with all these theoretical lectures soon. It's time you registered for one or two practical lessons. From now on, Benny, you're on your own. . . ."

Odd, Benedict thought afterwards, how sentences are said in an ordinary way, and you receive them in your brain, and you allot them an ordinary importance and it's not for minutes or days or sometimes years after that you realize their true importance. Her last sentence was like that; an ordinary flat, English sentence, which he heard, and understood, and was about to discard again; when, in an instant he seemed to be struck, as if physically, by its significance. It was just as you might take a piece of shot silk in the hand, and it would look an ordinary green, and then as you turned it in the light it would suddenly become gold. The words echoed through his head over and over again, getting louder each time, till they seemed to explode inside him:

Now you're on your own. Now you're on your own. Now you're on your own.

What did those simple five words remind him of? Oh yes: of a different world, the innocent world in which he'd grown up, into which the first hints of love, the first tangential whispered invitations had insinuated themselves in sentences of similar simplicity and apparent guilelessness; What are you waiting for, Benny?— Yes that night in Tessa's room. And again: Will you be able to live on Platonic love for ever, Benny?—And again: Benny why have you never . . . ?

She was staring at him in amusement: "Why, whatever is the matter, Benny? You've gone quite pale."

He swallowed. "It's nothing. I——"

But it isn't nothing, Benny. Say it to yourself softly again: Now you're on your own. What does that mean, Benny? You know no woman ever says yes, not just like that. Doesn't it mean—what are you waiting for, Benny?

It's three o'clock, Benny, in the afternoon, and Mrs. Duncher has gone to Winchester for the day. Tim won't be home from school till half-past four. The door's shut, Benny, you're alone in

Felix's room with Arabella. Now you're on your own. What are you waiting for, Benny?

He tried to speak, but there was no voice left in his throat to speak with. And as Arabella looked down at him a miraculous thing happened; the smile very slowly melted away from her face and the room was suddenly full, not of ordinary silence, but an oppressive absence of sound, like the interval between a sliver of lightning and the following crack of thunder. While this was happening, Benny saw that Arabella realized what she had said; perhaps what had really happened was that she had known subconsciously what she meant all the time, but had not admitted it inside herself.

Now you're on your own. What are you waiting for, Benny?

He reached out his hand and laid it gently on hers. She had a small hand. His fingers were shaking so much that it was almost comic. But she had on her face now the intensely serious expression he had seen once before, the set and grave expression that Laura had worn that first time at the secret view. For, after all, it was a serious thing for a woman to embark on. . . .

Her fingers closed, gently but quite deliberately, round his.

The first emotion he could disentangle from the great new orchestration of his senses was a most curious access of pity. For how defenceless, he always reflected afterwards, when it comes to the heart of the matter, a woman is! How little and childlike she seems, when all her defences are removed, when her clothes, guardians of her public *persona,* make only a little tumbled silken citadel on the floor! Now that he saw Arabella properly, for the first time, saw her as she would only reveal herself for the act of birth, the act of love, the act of death, he felt for her only a compassion so overwhelming that it seemed for a moment to overwhelm even his need. But very soon she saw to it that his pity was usurped by a desire that was steel-hard; her peripatetic fingers slid over him without fuss, without hurry, and without shame. They moved over his back and through his hair, her nails sinking softly into his flesh; her tongue, her teeth, her lips flirted gently with his. She smelt a little of cigarettes and wine and scent; her lipstick was slightly smeared and her hair scattered over the pillow; knees and tresses folded to slip and ripple idly. With soft playfulness she led him into the act of love, revealing in every gentle movement the sophistication of her erotic ideas and the variety of her experience. But now a new emotion seemed to be strangling him: a sharp sense of surprise that even those unexpected and asymmetric patterns in his desire found an exact and answering analogue in her own. Still he held back, a little shy and unreleased. She too seemed untroubled yet by any thrusting sense of urgency; the rigour with which they could still contain their sensual play seemed only to accentuate their delight.

She made love with allusive and tangential skill, enticing him to try new ways of pleasing her, coaxing and refining his first amateur researches with infinite and loving care. She offered herself to him with deliberate coquetry. Then, in a very little while he felt her arms tighten round his neck and he realized that she had reached, with great delicacy and elegance, a first quiet peristalsis. She sighed and lay back in his arms, lovely in the first fulfilment of her passion, but even now solicitous not to precipitate his own enormous longing. At length, however, she began to entice him again along the swift-rising curve of their shared and needle-sharp pleasure. Now her hospitality had a new urgency: she moaned and rolled her head from side to side in delicious agony at the sweet rut. The broken words of love with which they had initiated their miraculous congress blurred and dissolved into wordless sounds wrenched from them by pure desire. Soon it became clear that they must come to the end of the beautiful matter. Now they had thrown all intellectual restraint aside and were at last free to revel in the sensual riot. Her libido was ferocious; she had the wild strength of a velvet tiger maddened by an unknown hunger. This then, must be that strange moment of hate between a man and a woman when they are still separate, before they blend in the final moment of truth. This must be that last knowledge, that exquisite crystallization; this was what it meant, in the biblical sense, to know a woman; this must be it. For a moment the blindness induced by their ecstacy seemed to lift and through a mist he saw Arabella transfixed, transformed, set free. Though the boundaries between thought and speech seemed to have dissolved away long ago, so that he no longer knew one from the other, yet some huge sub-conscious force must have thrown the frenzied question up to the surface of his mind and given it utterance: Is it now, Arabella, is it this is it this is it this? Finally, through everything, as the light was fading and despite the terrible and marvellous sensation of drowning and melting and dying he heard her say: Yes, Benny.

Yes Yes.

Yes. Yes. Yes. Yes. Yes. Yes. Yes. Yes.

Oh Yes Yes. . . . Yes Yes. . . . Yes Yes

Yes.

13

"YES," said Sammy Spiral, undoing his thin knitted tie, "it was quite a swinging affair."

"Oh Sammy, I wish you'd stop using all that jazz slang. It's all right when we're at the Flamengo but it doesn't sound right coming from a young executive."

"Hoity-toity! Who's been out to dinner with the boss? Who tried to prove she wasn't a common little slut by putting on a hyper-refined accent?" He did a mincing imitation: "Yes, P.J. No, P.J. Oo, you are *clever*, P.J."

Jackie ripped off her stockings angrily. Really, sometimes she wanted to throw things at Sammy. Sometimes, as a matter of fact, she did. But the trouble was, she couldn't help adoring him. She had loved him from that first moment he'd walked into the record shop six months ago to try and buy a new Ornette Coleman; they didn't have it in stock but they'd got into conversation and found they both dug the same music, so what more natural than that Sammy should ask her to come jiving one evening at The Marquee? Since that evening they hadn't looked back; with the wild abandon of espresso-age children they had leaped into bed at once and would soon be coming up for what Sammy wittily called their seven-month itch. She had moved out of her Y.W.C.A. hostel on the pretence that she was going to share a flat with a friend; so indeed she was, but the friend was Samuel H. Spiral, who would not have met with the unqualified approval of the Y.W.

Sammy had rented a grubby flat in Camden Town; he did most of his entertaining at lunch-time and believed in going out at night. Like all his contemporaries, he had no intention of getting mixed up with an intelligent girl who'd give out with Sartre and all that gear. He had lost no time in acquiring this cute little scrubber. She was no trouble, didn't argue, loved him dearly, and thought he was the cleverest young man in England. What more could a nut want? Only, like all chicks, there was a snag somewhere. Now this chick had met P.J. she had suddenly gone all broody. A very unpleasant fear crossed his mind: surely she wasn't expecting to *marry* him? But if not, why all this jazz about the disc-biz; why had she spent so much time yacking to P.J.'s chick? Come to think of it, how *about* that? So P.J. had a chick after all. . . .

"Well," he said, doing up his pyjamas, "they say still waters run deep. Did you dig the gaffer's chick?"

"Sammy, unless you stop using that ridiculous language I'll go and sleep on the settee. Honest I will. A boy with a brain like yours and you have to talk that rubbish."

"Aw belt up, willya?" He climbed wearily into bed.

"I thought she was perfectly sweet."

"Oh did you now?" He had put on his posh voice again. "How frightfully decent of you."

"I suppose you'll grow up one day. Why don't you try and study P.J. a bit more? He has charming manners."

"Look here, dearie, will you leave me to manage my own affairs? P.J. is a doomy old goon like I told you. He's in Cloudsville. He's just not with it."

"Then how do you explain this smashing business he's built up?"

But Sammy was not listening. He had been thinking.

"You know what, Jackie?" he said. "I think I've got the answer. P.J. must have been brain-washed at some point. He told me once he was on an intelligence jag in the war. What happened, the Russkis must have got him, taken his brain out, unscrewed the parts, then put it all back the wrong way round."

"He looks quite normal to me—no." She checked herself. "There *is* something, Sammy. But it's not what you say. There's something about his eyes."

"Or maybe," Sammy said thoughtfully, "he's been psycho-analysed. They sometimes get that very simple-broken-down look when they've had a couple of years at it at twenty quid a week."

"No," said Jackie definitely. "I'll tell you what it is. Some time, he's been horribly badly hurt. That's what his eyes say."

"Aw don't talk such crap," Sammy said, yawning. "I know that old geyser. He's hard as nails. Insults, set-backs, disappointments —they all bounce off him like peas off a Centurion tank."

"Yes, but how long have you known him?"

"Three years."

"This must have happened a long time ago. Maybe around when I was born. Maybe it was some wartime romance that went wrong!"

"Maybe it's just this chick he has in tow. She must be pushing forty hard; she must have been around a while."

"She told me they've been together now for thirteen years— ever since her little boy went away to a boarding school."

"We've been tergither nah fer thirteen years," sang Sammy irreverently. "And it don't seem a die too much. There haint a lidy lerhivin in the land. As I'd swop for my dear old——"

"Belt up will you, nut?" she pleaded. "You're not a patch on Peter Sellers."

"So why doesn't he marry the chick and get it over? He doesn't have a gig with any other scrubber does he?"

"No. She obviously can't marry him; maybe because she's already married and her husband won't divorce her. Did you see —she was wearing a wedding ring? Anyway," she added, "what does it matter to a mature, sophisticated woman like that? She's got P.J. for keeps—what does she need to tie him down for?"

"Ah," said Sammy, yawning horribly, "that's the sort of language I love to hear. How right you are, dearie! Why should a pure and honest love be fouled by the bourgeois stigmata of slavery? A woman after my own heart."

"They can't get married. We can."

"Yeah. But we wont."

"We'll see about that. Tell me, Sammy, what did P.J. say to you when we went out for coffee?"

"He told a couple of really fruity stories. Ooh, real lush they were."

"Don't lie to me, Samuel Spiral. I know he wanted to tell you something. Arabella told me he has some big business deal on."

"Yeah. Well, since you seem to know all about it, there's no need for me to tell you, is there?"

"That's it," she snapped with finality. She picked up her pillow and swung her legs out of the bed. Sammy just managed to catch the back of her nightdress.

"Come back, you lousy slut. I'll tell you."

She got back into bed, triumphant. She had Sammy on toast when it came to the point!

"Well, dearie," said Sammy, "it seems that the gaffer has

246

decided to sell out the biz. Or to put it more precisely, to establish a charitable trust which will own it. He'll draw a rentier income and an old geyser called Grumman who's failed to make good at the Bar will be administrator of the trust. It makes no difference to my side of the business; we still have to *earn* the money. It gives me a bit more chance, with P.J. out of the line, that's all."

"Who'll take over?"

"Rupert—a man after my own heart."

"But, Sammy, that wasn't the theory you had last time we talked; you said something about a public company."

"Yeah, that was the buzz, especially when he called in this old nut Grumman. But come to think of it, why should he need Grumman to float an issue? All he'd have to do if that's the scheme would be to work through a stockbroker or maybe an issuing house"—Sammy was interested in what he was saying now; the idiom had evaporated for a second—"sell off maybe twenty-five per cent of his shares at around par and probably pay ten per cent on around fifty-five thousand profit."

"You know, I don't understand all that gear, Sammy. The main fact is that P.J. wants to quit."

"Yep. He says he wants time to do a spot of thinking. Maybe take his chick round the world. Funny, in a way—whenever I got sick of working seventeen hours a day and complained, he used to tell me that was all he was in business for."

"She said a funny thing to me. She said, 'I believe at long last he's coming back to earth.'"

"Like I told you, he's on Cloud Nine."

"No, Sammy, there's more to it than that. He's a strange fish. And yet I'm sure they're very happy together."

"Yep," said Sammy. "They seem to make like young."

"Sammy."

"Yes?"

"P.J. must like you to tell you all this."

"The old geyser does give me a wintry smile from year to year. I'll be quite sorry to see him go. Still all the quicker, for me."

"Sammy, I wish you could love me like that."

"Oh but I do."

"Put your arms round me and swear to it on your honour."

"On my *what*?"

"You heard me, Sammy."

He hesitated. The first part of her instruction was one that was uppermost in his mind; it was hard not to obey. As for the second, well, in his weird and ragged moral code, you didn't tell a chick a thing like that unless you meant it. Of course it didn't really matter, it was just a semantic haggle, but there was a little, almost invisible seed of goodness in Sammy which he had probably inherited from the old cube who was his father. So at length he did as he was told and added:

"Sometimes I get to feeling I want to come back home and forget everything and just curl up with a certain slut."

It was not a very high-flown declaration of love but Jackie instinctively knew it would do. "Oh Sammy," she said "I do love you so."

Samuel H. Spiral, he said to himself, you're heading for very big trouble indeed.

(a)

"THE only thing I can't forgive," Benedict said, "is the detergent foam in the Cressbrook."

He had been staying with Tess and Ken for two days now; he had spent them wandering dream-locked about the Valley.

Tess smiled indulgently at him over the breakfast table. They were alone; Ken had already gone down to the garage. "Benny, if you could have forgiven *that*, we would never have forgiven *you*. But Ken's fighting it for all he's worth. He spends such a lot of time trying to make the Cressbrook Valley a better place to live in. He always says that if some stiffnecked old Victorians hadn't fought and sweated and worried their guts out for us, we wouldn't have had the chance to grow up as human beings; we'd still be vegetables living off the land; so what are we doing for our children and for theirs?"

Benedict let his eyes wander round the room; over the piles of *Encounter* back numbers, the Art Treasures Book Club volumes, the Contemporary Fiction books, the hi-fi, the stereo, the long rack of gay record sleeves, and then, through the enormous glass window at the view, a view which would make him drunk to live with.

"You know, Tess," he said, "you are the only girl from all our gang who just met and fell in love without complications. You had none of the heartaches and betrayals that all the other girls had to go through."

Tessa seemed to look at him oddly for a second. Then she said quickly: "Here you are, Benny—your favourite—mushrooms."

"Good heavens, Tess, how on earth did you remember?"

"Oh I remember. Make the most of them. They're getting rare. The new fertilizers they put on the fields destroy them."

"I hope somebody benefits from my loss. I could easily develop into an old Blimp, bellyaching at every step forward and regretting the end of the days when you could get a servant for thirty shillings a week. The only snag with that world was that we were the servants."

"No, you couldn't be a Blimp, Benny. Not you. You don't love people and places uncritically; you love them warts and all."

"I don't know. I'm afraid I invest all my friends with qualities they don't have. I think of them all as a hundred and ten per cent of what they really are."

"For a woman, that's a very agreeable trait."

"Maybe. But as I get older, I find my feet are coming slowly back to earth again. I no longer run along four inches above the ground."

There was a silence between them. Then Tess said: "Who are you going to see today, Benny? You've so many friends to catch up with, and since that paragraph in the *Journal* yesterday you'll find people will be ringing up all the time. You must make a programme."

"First," said Benny, "I'm going to see an old lady that I never knew at all well. It's funny how, when you're young, old people are so tiresome. But now they have a restful quality. I think first, this morning, I'll go and call on Lady Margrave."

(b)

Inside the Brewer's House there was the same stillness that Benny remembered from childhood; an overpowering calm in which the tick-tock of the grandfather clock seemed to be counting away the seconds left till Doomsday.

Lady Margrave came out herself into the hall to greet him. She was nearly seventy now, and she walked with a stick. But she was still courageous in her elegance; her skirt was fashionably short and there was blue rinse in her hair; her face had new lines in it but was still kind and good to see again. She held out her hand.

"Benny, my dear boy! This is a most wonderful surprise." She led him into the drawing-room. "Come and sit next to me. I want to hear all your news. How long is it since we met?"

He was still surprised to hear the Edwardian clarity of her vowels; she was the only woman in a ten-mile radius who still pronounced girl "gel".

"It's thirteen years, I'm afraid, Lady M." The familiar abbreviation came back naturally.

"Is it really? And you've done frightfully well in those years, so I read. Congratulations, Benny. Poor Keith would have been so proud of you. He always wanted you to come into the Brewery, you know."

"I was extremely sorry to hear he'd died, Lady M."

"Thank you, Benny. But these things must come to us all in time. We must just ask God's grace to help us bear it." There was pain in her old face for a moment; but it passed and she smiled at him.

"Now what else, Benny. Are you married yet?"

"I'm afraid not, Lady M."

"You mean that scoundrel Weston persists in his cruelty?" (All Aylsbourn knew the story.) "Poor Arabella! Never mind, she must know you would never leave her. And though one should never wish harm to a fellow human-being, one must face the fact that Weston won't be with us for ever. He's sixty-seven now, you know, and crippled with arthritis. His heart is none too sound either, I hear." She tried to suppress the unchristian relish in her voice.

"I hope you're in good health, Lady M. You look wonderful."

"Oh thank you, yes Benny; thank God, I'm still sound in wind and limb. There's life in the old gel yet. I have a companion, you know, my old friend Doris Maddocks, so I always have someone to talk to when I'm lonely."

"Not——?"

"Yes, Miss Maddocks, Keith's old secretary. Why do you look so surprised?" She laid a hand rather saucily on his. Then she added: "Oh, if you mean about Doris being sweet on Keith, why I knew all about that." She sighed and glanced up at a faintly bovine portrait of Sir Keith above the fireplace. He wore his I Zingari cap. The artist had caught the mottled tones in his indulgent middle-aged face perfectly.

"Poor Keith! He was such a dear, but rather dense I'm afraid. Poor Doris loved him devotedly for twenty years and he didn't even notice. You must think it a little strange that we live here together. Well, you know, women do not have the same fierce jealousies as men. Or, if they do, they become resigned to them. You see, Benny, Doris and I have much in common." She smiled. "We both loved the same man. I happened to be lucky to be first, that's all. We often talk about him. We are good friends."

"I can't imagine, Lady M., how a man could have someone in love with him all those years and never notice."

"Can't you, Benny? But you see, Keith wasn't as clever as

some of you young fellows. He didn't know as much about women as you do nowadays."

"I suppose so. Tell me, how is the Brewery?"

"I seldom go in now, Benny. It's most efficiently run from London, and apart from attending the annual directors' luncheon —they let me stay on the board for old time's sake—and drawing my dividends, I know little about it."

"Do they still have the big cricket match against Hampshire?"

"Heavens, yes. The only difference is, now the men have to pay for their own beer. Don't think I'm criticizing, Benny. In our day it was a different relationship. It was largesse we were offering. Wages were pitiful—often three pounds a week or less. Now these chaps have their own cars and can afford to buy their own beer. But tell me, why don't you play next summer? You're a shareholder still, aren't you?"

"Yes but——"

"Then you must play, Benny. I insist. You used to be such an elegant bat. I used to keep the score for all Keith's games and I know a good bat when I see one. Promise me you'll play?"

"You tempt me, Lady M. May I think about it and let you know? I haven't even held a bat for about fifteen years."

"I shan't take no for an answer. Now tell me about all your other young friends. I do hope they are enjoying themselves now."

"What exactly do you mean, Lady M.?"

"I always felt so sorry for you young people during the war. No lights, no clothes, not much to eat, no parties, no fun. Look at the young people nowadays with their coffee bars and scooters and such elegant clothes specially designed for them and all these newspaper articles. I mean they're so much in everybody's thoughts. No one ever had time for you young things during the war; we had so much else on our minds."

"You know, I never thought of it that way, Lady M."

(c)

"Yes, Benny," said Mr. Johnston, "there've been a lot of changes."

They sat on the old stools, side by side, in the physics laboratory. Benedict studied Mr. Johnston with interest. He realized with a shock that he was nowhere near as old as he had supposed; he might be fifty-five now, and apart from a thinning out of the hair on top of his strangely turnip-shaped head, he looked no different.

"We've got six hundred and fifty here now," he went on. "A hundred in the senior school alone—we call it the sixth now; seventy-five doing science, fifteen modern subjects, and the rest arts."

"A hundred," said Benedict in disbelief, "but the whole school wasn't much bigger than that in my day."

"Yes, well, everyone stays at school now. And we have this big influx from Applestreet New Town. Have you seen the New School yet? No? well let's walk up there."

They strolled slowly out of the school and up Windmill Hill. Benny stopped as they turned the corner. For where the footpath had once led to his secret view—their secret view—there was now a massive modern building: steel, glass, concrete stretching away in smooth planes and long perspectives. It was a beautiful building. They had built it right over the place where he and Laura....

"You've got to admit," said Mr. Johnston, "that it's a decided improvement. Yes, very pretty. And you should see the new laboratories—finest in England. They don't have anything better at Winchester I can tell you that."

"Who chose this place?"

"The architect. A bright young man from London. He walked up the hill and he stopped there and he said, that's it."

"What a splendid architect he must be. So all the children can see right to Oakhanger from their windows."

"Yes. Mind you, I don't know how many of them appreciate it."

"Tell me, Mr. Johnston," Benedict burst out without considering, "why did you come to live here? Couldn't you have been a research scientist?"

Mr. Johnston considered. "I'll tell you," he said. "I was driving along here with Milly in my bull-nosed Morris in—maybe 1926. And we stopped here and had a picnic up on the side of the Downs. And I looked down on the little place and I said, Johnston, this will do for you. A research scientist? You would really have preferred to see me grinding away in some dreary laboratory every day instead of doing the most exciting job there is—opening up the minds of the young to all the astonishing possibilities there are in the world? If I'd got to the top of the tree and made my three thousand or whatever, I'd only have come back here. I'd have suffocated in the town. Here I'm my own master and in the morning when I wake up I can hear the Cressbrook from my bedroom window. No, I'm doing what I want to do."

"Wouldn't you have liked to have been headmaster?" Mr. Johnston shook his head vehemently. "Certainly not, Benny. Then I wouldn't have been able to teach, which is all I ever wanted to do. I'm second in command here now and that's good enough for me."

"Do you have any really bright boys or girls at the moment?"

"Only boys, Benny. Didn't you know they've split the school in two. The girls are going to a new school at Applestreet."

"How do you feel about that?"

"I don't know. The educationists are all for segregation. They say it's more efficient. I suppose it's true that a boy might get eight 'O' levels instead of nine if he's only with other boys." He grinned. "You'll remember, Benny, that girls can be a distraction. On the other hand, I find boys and girls together easier to teach. It was more fun. They seemed more alive. Still, that's what the educationists have done, and we have to carry out their ideas as best we can."

"What's your new head like?"

"Leftmarker? Good chap. Nice, efficient Newcastle lad who got a first in chemistry at Cambridge. That's another thing, Benny, it's getting more competitive all the time. All the old staff have been superseded by younger, brighter people. You see, it's not just the public schools who're having to struggle for places at university now. We, the old grammar schools, are having to fight like mad too—against them, against the new big secondary school, against each other. Yes, Leftmarker's all right. And Ilex's influence is still strong here, you know. We built a new wing with some money he wangled out of a Californian trust for us. But if you want my honest opinion, the finest head this school ever had is Macpherson."

"How do you mean—*is*?"

"He's still alive. Didn't you know?"

"But he can't be. He was very old when he retired."

"He was sixty-seven. Now he's eighty-five."

"But he had a weak heart."

"He still does. But the life-force is strange, you know. It will

254

burn for a very long time if you turn the lamp down low."

"But," Benny cried out in horror, "when I left here he was——"

"Blind? He's still blind."

"You mean," said Benny, but really to himself, "that all these years I have been eaten up by my own small troubles, he has been sitting alone in the dark."

(d)

"You won't stay too long will you, sir," said Macpherson's housekeeper. "He's a very old gentleman and we have to preserve his strength."

He was sitting in the corner when Benedict came in, out of the light; it was immaterial. In old age his skin had taken on a strange, luminous quality and the flesh seemed to have sunk a little on the bones. The hands were scrubbed as pure as a surgeon's, and the finger-nails had the extra cleanness that only very old people can achieve. It was impossible to know that he was blind except by the slightly uncertain way he held out his hand.

"Well, Benny, my boy," he said. "They tell me you're a very distinguished young man these days."

The voice was higher than Benedict remembered it, high and lighter; there was not much left of the beautiful bass he remembered.

"I've made a lot of money, that's all, sir. I'm not particularly proud of the way I've made it."

"Why ever not, Benny? Ye know Johnson's remark—yes of course you do, so I won't trouble with it. I take it that you are *innocently* employed?"

"Oh it's not crooked, sir. We make gramophone records."

"Do ye now? Well they are one of the great solaces of my old age. Did ye realize they're recorded many of the great English poets and novelists now?"

"It's not our line, sir, but I did know. May I hear one?"

"Of course." The old man reached out and began to wind an old clockwork gramophone beside him. Benny intervened. "Here, let me do that, sir."

"Thank you, Benny. Please play a little of the Thomas Hardy, will you?"

Benedict put it on. The recording was all right, but the repro-

255

duction seemed dreadfully thin and scratchy to his experienced ears.

"Ay it's a great blessing. And then sometimes, once or twice a year maybe, an old pupil comes and reads a little to me. That's a most refreshing change."

"Perhaps I could read something to you now, sir, if you'd like that."

"Of course, Benny. Please help yourself from my bookcase."

He took down at random the *Oxford Book of English Mystical Poetry* and read a poem by George Herbert. Macpherson chuckled with pleasure as he ended.

"That's good, Benny. 'Cabinet of pleasure' is felicitous. The poem is well made, Benny. Ye know in my part of Scotland they still use the old, archaic word for a poet—they call him a maker. It's apt. But I mustn't start boring you with a lesson. Why don't you read me something more up to date—ye used to enjoy modern poetry if I recall rightly. There's a book somewhere there"—he indicated the shelf—"sent to me by one old pupil for my birthday. I've not been able to get anyone to read it to me yet."

Benedict searched the shelves and found a new volume of Dylan Thomas.

"I think I've got it, sir."

"Ay. Then go ahead, Benny."

He opened it at random and began to read:

> *Do not go gentle into that good night,*
> *Old age should burn and rave at close of day;*
> *Rage——*

Macpherson waited with the marvellous patience of the very old. The room was very still.

"Go on, Benny. Those are good lines."

"I'm sorry, sir. I'll begin again."

When he had concluded, Macpherson considered for a moment. Then he passed judgement.

"The poem is very fine, Benny, by any critical yardstick at all. It will last. But ye know, one can tell it was written by a very young man."

"How, sir?"

"Because of his impatience and anger at death. When ye get to ripe old age like me—as I hope ye will—ye'll find it's not so bad

256

as you think. Old age has many compensations, Benny. There's no more striving, no more broken hearts. Ye have time to think. And ye'll realize what a comedy it all is. Then maybe in the evenings there'll be a new record of Bach to play before you drop off to sleep. There are many worse fates, Benny. I'm quite content...."

(e)

On his way along the High Street he stopped at the Post Office and wrote a card to Sammy Spiral:

Would you please: a. ring our technical department and say I want our best two men to report to me here on Monday. I'm sending on a list of the equipment they'll need.

               b. get me a complete and up-to-date list of all spoken prose and poetry now on record and tape.

               c. get me a complete list of the best new recordings in the entire Bach repertoire.

Thank you

P.J.

He then sauntered up to the market square to have tea at Miller's.

But Miller's wasn't there. Instead, a green neon light said Gino's. Behind its gleaming chrome Gaggia espresso machine, were waitresses briskly serving plates of apfelstrudel, spaghetti bolognese, wienerschnitzel and ravioli. And, of course, coffee.

He pushed open the door, a little unsure of himself, and took a seat by himself in a corner.

He had been sitting there for only a few minutes when a young man who had been watching him from the other side of the room got up and crossed over. He was dressed with casual elegance in a grey flannel suit, cream shirt, and college tie.

"Excuse me, sir," he said politely, "but aren't you Mr. Benedict?"

"Yes. I'm afraid——" The young face was absurdly familiar. It was a dark, humorous face, with incipient black rings under slightly slanting eyes. "Good heavens! You must be Timothy."

"Good shot, sir."

"Well come and sit down. And for heaven's sake don't call me sir, it makes me feel so old. Call me Benny."

"Certainly. Tell me, how is"—He used the Christian name with the easy familiarity of a child whose parents have been long parted—"how is Arabella?"

"Oh, she's absolutely fine. She'll be mad to have missed you. Why don't you ever come up to the flat?"

Arabella had adopted a policy of always taking Timothy to their cottage by the sea in her turns to have him during the holidays; she had deliberately kept him away from Benedict, not wanting to complicate either of their lives.

"I'd like to very much. I have to go back to Oxford in a few days; perhaps I could call in on the way."

"We'd love that, Timothy. It's quite central and you can entertain your friends. I'm supposed to have one of the biggest record collections in London, and there's plenty of jazz too if you like that sort of thing."

"Of course I do. Thanks very much. And tell me, how is my brother?" He deliberately seemed to want to avoid saying half-brother.

"Felix? He's in great form. We had lunch together just the other day."

"I'd like to see him again. We haven't met since I was at school. He turned up a few weeks before I left, gave me a tenner and some good, if rather cynical, advice, and pushed off again."

"Which school?"

"Winchester. My father got fed up with Aylsbourn after Ilex left. Also, he's not very happy at the way Felix has turned out."

"What sort of advice did Felix give you?"

"Oh it was a sort of Polonius speech brought up to date."

"Tell me."

"Let me see—oh yes—he said on no account to marry till I was fifty."

"Ah. It used to be forty. He's raised his sights as he's got older. And yet somehow I think his bachelor days are coming to an end. What else did he say?"

"He said always to live a thousand a year above my income. And to stick to English mistresses. He said it was a bit like choosing cheese; when you're young you rush for all those exciting

French and Italian things, but as you grow older you realize that the English ones are, in a subtle way, quite the best in the world."

"Unexpected patriotism—from Felix."

"He said that of course if I could find a Chinese mistress for my old age that would be ideal. Oh, and he was very interesting about friends. He said to give all Americans a wide berth, except New Yorkers, all athletes, and all politicians. Otherwise, he said, I'd die early of boredom."

"Dear Felix! He doesn't change much."

"He was particularly adamant about the politicians."

"Did he say who you *should* cultivate?"

"Yes. He said to make my friends among Jews, Catholics, and queers. Jews, because they understand music. Catholics because they understand drink. Queers because they understand women. And all three because they understand money. As he put it himself—what else is there?"

"Felix is unique. You should see more of him; cultivate him. I'm sure you'll like him. I'll give you his address."

"That's awfully kind. Yes, I'd like that. I very much enjoyed our last meeting."

"How old are you, Timothy?"

"I'm twenty—just starting my third year at Oxford."

"My God I remember you being born. That dates me, doesn't it?"

"But you're not so old, Benny."

"I'm thirty-four; but you make me feel a hundred and four."

"But how absurd of you. We talk the same language."

"The trouble is, we *nearly* do. When you speak to someone thirty years older, you don't bother to try to communicate. But with someone only half a generation away, the language is tantalizingly similar; it's just been put through a scrambler, so one doesn't *quite* understand it."

"It's the war which produces this curious gap; I can't even remember it."

"I suppose you can't. And you can't remember a world where there was no nuclear fission. That's the main difference. The thirties were dreadful. They had a bleak, mean quality: it was Hitler's decade; we had Jarrow and Jessie Matthews and the sort of interior decoration you see in the Trocadero—and we knew the war was coming, even though we were only children. But there wasn't this all-pervasive sense of doom you get now with the bomb."

"But you see, Benny, I've never known any other world. Therefore I have no sense of loss. O.K., so the bomb goes off. So we die. But we die anyway. We're all in the condemned cell."

"True. Another funny thing, though, Tim, before the war the sun seemed hotter. It's an illusion of course, you have only to look up the records. But my God it *seemed* hotter."

"It couldn't have been hotter than the summer of 1959."

"That was dreadful, Tim; it was unnatural. I had a crawling feeling down my spine every day; to tell you the honest truth, I really thought it had something to do with the Bomb."

Tim laughed: "I can't win. All right, what about books. Shall I tell you whom I like?"

"Yes, please."

He considered: "Capote, Kerouac, Vailland and Roth among the new boys. Otherwise the usual names: Hemingway, Koestler, Huxley.

"What about the angries? Don't you dig them?"

Tim made a contemptuous gesture. "They give me a pain in the belly. Their values are so parochial. What does it matter whether people eat their peas off a knife or not? The main thing is, we've all got knives; we've all got peas." He leaned forward. "We're the world's aristocrats, Benny. Yes every one of us, even Jimmy Porter and Jim Dixon. All this manufactured social indignation must strike the average Asian as a sort of neurotic internecine squabble between pampered courtiers. The rabble are howling for bread outside." He glared out of the window and gave a wave of recognition. "Take our old Mrs. Duncher who's coming in to see us now, for example. She packs away as much food in a day as the average Chinese peasant does in a week."

Mrs. Duncher came over to the table and Benny got up to shake hands with her. "Well, Benny," she said, "it must be thirteen years since I last saw you."

"I wish I could say I'd weathered as well as you, Mrs. D. Won't you join us? Tim and I are just comparing life now with before the war."

"Thanks, I will. Oh there's no doubt about it. It's much better now. Look at this wonderful New Town. My son Joe can make fifteen quid a week easily. Before the war he'd have been lucky to make three."

"You don't think the New Town may be spoiling the country-side?"

"Spoil it? Who cares? What ever good has the countryside ever done for the likes of us? No, let's fill up all the fields with New Towns I say."

Tim got up. "Please excuse me, Mrs. Duncher," he said courteously, "but as you know, I always ring my girl-friend at noon each day. Our love affair is rather intense at the moment."

"Off you go, dear, and enjoy yourself," said Mrs. Duncher expansively. She watched his slim figure disappear with pro-prietorial affection.

"Such a charming young fellow," she said. "Much more easy-going than his brother, though they're both lovely boys. I feel so sorry for this young one," she confided "What with his father getting worse and worse and no mother—if you'll pardon me saying so."

"That's all right, Mrs. D."

"It's a shame," went on Mrs. D. to no one in particular. Then leaning forward she added: "And him illegitimate too, poor little mite."

"I beg your pardon?"

"Didn't you know, sir? It's my belief that Mr. Weston and her was never married. I once chided her for not wearing a ring, said it wasn't proper. And she laughed and said: 'Mrs. D. it's much worse than you think. As a good old-fashioned communist, Mr. Weston doesn't even believe in holy wedlock. I'm a kept woman and I rather enjoy it.' Yes, I rather enjoy it, those were her very words."

"Are you sure of this, Mrs. D.?"

Her simple peasant's face took on a new look of apprehension.

"Now don't you dare tell on me, sir. I've always been too scared to mention it, only it just slipped out then."

"I promise not to mention your name, Mrs. D. But you know, you've just given me some quite marvellous news."

(f)

"*One* two three and *one* two three and *one* two three dee dah dee dee. . . ."

261

Through the open window Benedict heard the patient voice chanting above the excruciating sounds of children's violins practising a minuet. It was a familiar voice; he remembered the first day he had heard it: "Anybody here read *I Claudius*? Well, we'll start with that. . . ."

Martin Hennessy had not changed much. His boyish, curly hair was a little sparser and he wore glasses. But still he exuded that unqualified enthusiasm which had always swept every problem away in front of him like a powerful snow-plough.

As he entered the music room in the Civic College at Apple-street New Town, Hennessy began yet again: "Now then, everybody, *one* two three and *one* two three and . . ."

It was evening; the little group of violinists was bunched together in a pool of light. Hennessy played too, rocking gently back and fro in time with the music, entirely absorbed by the back-breaking pleasure of his task.

He jumped up when he saw Benedict. "My *dear* Benny," he cried, "what a surprise." Then to the children: "All right, that'll do for this evening. Be here again tomorrow, and remember it's only a week now to the concert."

They sat side by side in the music room among the discarded music scores. Hennessy's slightly fishlike face sparkled with genuine excitement. His blue eyes seemed slightly more protrusive than ever, and his thick lips glistened with saliva. I suppose, thought Benedict, that if I'd met him for the first time today I'd have written him off as a complete prune.

"Well, Martin," he said, "this is the last place I'd expected to find you."

"Really, Benny? Why ever do you say that?"

"I had a feeling that you'd be headmaster of some famous school by this time, or a university administrator like Ilex, or maybe that you'd be a Labour M.P. . . ."

He realized this must sound condescending and stopped. But Hennessy only laughed.

"Gracious me, Benny, what a boring fate you saw ahead for me. No, I came into this business, believe it or not, with a passionate urge to teach. Of course, some of that early enthusiasm got rubbed off by the attrition of many brutal small boys, but some will always remain. And here in Applestreet I do the most exciting teaching there is."

He leaned forwards in his enthusiasm. "Here, Benny, in this rather grandly titled Civic College, I deal simply with boys and girls aged between fifteen and eighteen who have come on from the execrated secondary modern schools. They are, in other words, the detritus of our educational system; the people who simply hadn't got the brains to pass the eleven plus."

He beamed. "In two years we put them through their 'O' level and the best of them get seven subjects. Among two hundred we get about five—only five—who fail to pass in anything. And every one of these children, Benny, is a failure on arriving here!

"The third year, we put them in for 'A' level—one, two or three subjects. Some of them go on to the university—people who couldn't pass their eleven plus remember—and many go into the civil service, teaching, engineering, the church. Now, Benny, don't you think that's more exciting than working up a lot of young smoothies with IQs of 140 for Oxford scholarships?"

"Yes, I can see that, Martin. But I don't see how you do it."

"Remember first that the children who come here all *want* to learn. They realize they've missed something. Many of them are simply late developers. Our job is to open up their minds to what they're missing. To do that, you really have to enter into their world a hundred per cent. For example, recently I learned to jive, just to see what it was like. Even though I'm nearly fifty, Benny, I enjoyed it. I cut out those Pfeiffer cartoons and stick them on their notice board. At first they thought they were half-witted; now they lap them up. I take them to France for their holidays; thirty of us in a bus at fourteen pounds each. I take them up to town to see 'West Side Story'. And in between, Benny, I teach them history."

"I hadn't looked at it like that. I suppose that's why you left Aylsbourn?"

Hennessy's face clouded. "Not really, Benny. I was extremely happy there. But I'm afraid Ilex and I didn't see eye to eye."

"He was too ambitious for you?"

"Benny, the school—not the actual human beings in that school —were just cannon-fodder for his campaigns. They were instruments of his ambition. He was the most unscrupulous man I've ever come across."

"Ironic, really, when you think of all that's been written of the Aylsbourn Experiment."

"Experiment my foot! It was a disgrace. You see, Benny, Ilex bent all you young people to fit his strategy. It didn't matter what you *wanted* to do, or what you would be *happiest* doing. Look at poor Aelfric Gates—one of the cleverest boys I ever taught. He should be a scientist now, not an under-manager in a brewery!"

"I never understood quite why he failed."

"He failed, Benny, because he'd lost his faith. You know I was taking him for his scholarship?"

"Yes, I remember."

"Well, just before the examination—only two nights before if I recall rightly—Ilex took me on one side and said in that chummy way of his—'My dear Martin, I want you to give Aelfric one last cram.' Of course I was keen, so I said yes, I would. Then he said —and I always remember this—'I should give him a thorough run-through on the effect of bank rate on unemployment in the 1832 to 1845 period. And then do go very carefully into the Trevelyan Report and Civil Service Reform.' "

"Well, I don't quite see what's wrong with——"

Hennessy held a hand up dramatically: "Benny, *both those questions were in the paper when Aelfric turned it over two days later.*"

"You mean——?"

"I mean that Ilex committed a deliberate and calculated fraud. With two out of four questions served on a plate, Aelfric sailed through. Well, he would have anyway. But he never forgot. He knew, you see. He was never quite the same again. It took the heart right out of him."

(g)

"Yes," said Milo, "it's a very beautiful piece of machinery. We're going to call it 'Mac the Knife'."

They were sitting at Milo's dining-room table in his trim semi-detached house in Applestreet New Town. On the table there stood a number of bottles of Margrave Extra. Milo's wife sat in her chair by the fire, knitting briskly. She did not appear to be listening. She was a pleasant-looking girl of about twenty-five who wore a twin set and a pair of slippers.

Milo looked very little changed. His spectacular bent nose still dominated his homely face, and his ears still protruded at right angles. His always sparse hair was now thinning out rapidly, and like Hennessy, he had taken to spectacles. There were a pair of large horn-rimmed glasses perched on his nose as he talked.

Mac the Knife was a horrifying rocket; an oil picture of it hung over Milo's fireplace. "Yes," Milo added, "my chaps gave me that painting as a wedding present. Rather imaginative of them, don't you think?"

"Staggering," said Benedict. He could hardly take his eyes off Milo's brain-child. Then a question occurred to him.

"What exactly is it *for*?" he asked.

"It's a ground-to-air rocket, designed to intercept aircraft. I was out in Woomera testing it earlier this year. It's fabulous. Do you realize," Milo said with pride, "that if it came to a showdown we could now guarantee to knock one hundred per cent of enemy aircraft out of the air with this? It's got a brain inside that makes it keep going till it homes on its target. It can't miss."

"But," said Benedict, "we all know that the next war will be fought rocket again rocket. Can you guarantee to knock a hundred per cent of their *rockets* out of the sky?"

"Not yet. But as soon as we detect the enemy rockets coming up over the horizon, we shall send up our own interceptor missiles and they will work out which way the enemy rockets are coming even as they're taking off. The aim will be to get them into the same piece of sky as the opposing rockets at the same time, and then create one vast nuclear explosion in the stratosphere which will blow their rockets and ours to kingdom come. Of course, some are bound to get through."

"Milo, you're not serious about this?"

"Of course I'm serious. Can you think of any better idea?"

"Throw the whole damned lot into the sea."

"Ah, yes, unilateral disarmament. Well, I'm not a politician, Benny. My job is to make rockets, not decide how to use them."

"But doesn't it worry you? I mean the thought of all that waste? Because if it *doesn't* go off you've spent your whole professional life on nothing, and if it *does* go off you won't even survive to enjoy the excitement of seeing your charming monster in action."

"On the other hand," Milo said, "the very fact that we're making our rocket may stop them using theirs."

"Tell me," Benedict said, "what your working day is like, Milo."

"Sure. Well, I get to the works at eight twenty-five."

"Not eight twenty-four or twenty-six?"

"No, eight twenty-five. That's when everyone else starts, and I have to be there too. I work through till five twenty-five with an hour for lunch in the work's canteen. Of course, if there's a flap on I may stay late. And I always have these"—he indicated a mound of scientific papers on the sideboard—"to read as homework. I've picked up German and Russian so that I can keep up with as many of their technical journals as I can."

"But what *do* you do during your day?"

"Well, we have a big programme, you see. Each of these things costs two million pounds. It takes hundreds of electronics engineers to produce each one. It has a quarter of a million parts and nineteen thousand valves. Any of these can go wrong. My job is to jolly the chaps along, and keep the programme up to schedule."

"Do you ever fall behind?"

Milo looked a little crestfallen.

"I'm afraid so. We're running about two and a half years behind now. It's not our fault. It's the bloody government. They keep changing their minds about our allocation. The fact is, Mac the Knife will be obsolete by the time it's delivered to the R.A.F." He sighed. "It's a great pity because it really is a beautiful rocket."

"What do you do when you're not working?"

"Not much. Joan and I watch the television most evenings. Do you ever see that fellow Tony Hancock? He absolutely slays me. Then on Saturdays we go shopping in Applestreet, and on Sundays I play golf. I read the *Sunday Times*, of course, and that takes me most of the week."

"What about holidays?"

"Oh we generally get in the old Ford Consul and head for the coast. Anywhere where there are some good golf courses."

"Tell me, Milo, do you ever see any of our other friends?"

"No," said Milo. "Oh, I did see Doreen Pepper once. It was in one of those Soho strip joints. She's some sort of manageress, in charge of the girls' morals and all that stuff. Her, her, her." Milo gave his dirtiest chuckle. "Can you imagine the old Pepper-pot in charge of anybody's *morals*?"

"You didn't tell me about this, dear," said his wife. She did not look up from her knitting.

Milo peered at her over his horn-rimmed glasses. "Didn't I,

dear?" he said mildly. "Well, don't distress yourself. I have to entertain these visiting American scientists, you know, and that's their idea of an evening's fun."

"Did she recognize you?" Benedict asked.

"Of course. She said: 'Hello, Milo, old fruit.' "

"And what did you say?"

"I said: 'Hello, Pepper-pot. Fancy seeing you here.' "

"And what did she say?"

"She said: "I might say the same about you.' "

"And that was all?"

"Of course it was all. What do you take me for, a playboy?"

He poured out more Margrave Extra.

(h)

"Trust you, Benny, to arrive at the worst possible moment."

Constance stood in the doorway, her face flushed from the stove, a print apron over her old tweed skirt; she wore a powder blue jumper with the sleeves pushed up to the elbows and her hair was a little untidy. To Benedict she looked, as she always did, enchanting; proud and beautiful as ever, her head held very high and her eyes looking straight into his with mocking challenge in them.

"Constance, I do apologize; it was a wild impulse, I should have rung you up first."

"Come in, Benny. I'm only teasing you. It's wonderful to see your moonstruck old mug again. I read that you were in town and we were going to invite you. I'm just making cakes for my children; they have a party after school this afternoon. If you don't mind the mess you can come and sit in the kitchen."

But of course there was no mess in the kitchen; it gleamed with the same stainless efficiency that had once distinguished her small corner of the laboratory, and Benedict felt again a sense of regret that this splendid intelligence could not have been given space and time to flower. He sat down at the kitchen table.

"Now if you'll excuse me going on working; I'd like to hear all your news from the beginning. First though, how is Arabella?"

"She's fine, thanks."

"Why didn't you bring her with you?"

"She didn't want to come this time. She will, you'll see."

"How long is it since I last saw you, Benny?"

"Believe it or not, sixteen years."

"Sixteen years—I was only a child then. Have I altered very much, Benny?"

"Not to me. I am astonished to see how little you've changed."

It was true; there were one or two very small lines round her eyes that had not been there before and her face was more mature now; sixteen years of living, suffering, loving had touched, but not harmed her; she seemed softer now, fulfilled by—or resigned to—the ordinary cares of house and family.

"You look very grand, Benny. I bet that suit cost a packet."

"Yes, too much. I waste a lot of money. But I've never cared tuppence about it."

"You're just at your best now. Men are ripening all the time until they're forty. In their twenties they should be left strictly alone."

"But women are best in their thirties, too, Constance."

"No, Benny," she sighed. "Thirty is the great turning-point. After that, you can only take consolation in watching your children's faces change each day."

"You have two children, don't you, Constance?"

"Yes. Johnny is eleven and Kate is ten. I'd better find some pictures."

She went and searched in her handbag, and produced a small leather folder. Inside were two photographs: one of a girl with already, if only incipiently, her mother's marvellous expression of disdain in her face, the other of a delicately good-looking boy; he looked as if the demands of his intelligence might one day put stresses on his physique. Benedict stared at the pictures in disbelief.

"Constance, in a few years they'll be as old as we were when we first met. Yet now they just seem like children!"

"We were only children."

"But the things we thought and felt!"

"They think and feel them too."

"And what about Aelfric: how is he?"

"Aelfric is fine. He quite enjoys his work at the Brewery, but it's just a job to him. He should really have been a research physicist. He might have done something wonderful."

"So might you, Constance."

"No. I was just a little above the average. Oh, I would have got

268

a degree, and maybe toiled away in a laboratory for a while, but in the end I'd have married some spotty chemist and started rearing children; all that's happened is that I've had them earlier; which, as they said in Ten Sixty-Six and All That, is a Good Thing. An intelligent woman is always in an impossible predicament."

"You can't sell me that one, Constance; you desperately wanted to go to a university. I never understood why you didn't go."

"That's a long story, Benny. Here"—she poured him out a cup of coffee, then one for herself. She sat down at the other end of the table and looked at him for a moment. Then she smiled. "You know it *is* good to see you, you old loon." Another, more troubling thought passed through her mind, and her smile faded. She put a hand instinctively to her hair. "I must look an awful sight. Why do you do these things to me, Benny?"

"I'll tell you the truth, Constance. I wanted to catch you unexpectedly; I wanted to see you as you really are in your ordinary everyday life. I'm sorry if I've annoyed you."

She shook her head, smiling at him. "You could never annoy me, Benny. You're incapable of hurting anybody."

"You should tell that to the people in my office."

There was a silence. Then she said: "You'd like to know why I never took up my scholarship?"

"I'd be fascinated."

"Then I'll tell you. The first thing you must realize, Benny, is that I was born, as they say, on the wrong side of the blanket. I'm illegitimate."

"You don't know who your parents were?"

"Not so fast. I was adopted when I was a baby by the Hayleys. They were good, God-fearing, simple people, and I owe them nothing but gratitude. They're both dead now, you know."

"I didn't realize."

"One of the rules of adoption is that the real parents must give up all claim to the child. They must promise never to see it. When you think it over that makes sense."

"Yes, otherwise the child never knows who it belongs to."

"Exactly. I used to get Christmas presents from my mother when I was a little girl, though I didn't know where they came from. I never really bothered very much about it till I was about eighteen. Then one day I found my birth certificate in a desk. It gave my mother's name—Pickering is her name by the way—and an address. I wrote there—a very guarded letter, not even saying who I was. I didn't want to upset her, or even enter her life again if she didn't want it."

"And she replied?"

"Yes; Can you imagine it, Benny? We met on St. Pancras Station. We recognized each other at once. It was—well it was wordless."

"What was she like?"

"I think you would have said that she was a highly intelligent woman, Benny, and I thought she was quite beautiful. She was only thirty-seven."

"About our age now."

"Yes. She was a nurse, and she'd fallen in love with a man she was looking after in a private clinic. It wasn't till after I was on the way that he told her he was already married. She tried to keep me, but it wasn't so easy in those days, Benny. She worked in a textile mill for tenpence an hour; in the end her health gave up and I had to be adopted."

"Christ, it sounds like something out of Dickens."

"But it *really happened,* Benny. It happened to your old girl-friend Constance."

"And when you found your mother?"

She shrugged, but there was distress still in her cool and lovely face. "I won't harrow you with the details. She was still desperately poor and, Benny, she was dying. How in the name of heaven could I go to Somerville knowing that? All I felt was an anger so cold and passionate that I'd have killed my father if I could."

"Why didn't he help?"

"He did what was expected of him. The Hayleys had a regular cheque each month from him for my upkeep and education. Mind you, they were always very frugal people. The reason my skirts were always so short Benny, had nothing to do with fashion. It was simply that I wore them and wore them until I'd grown right out of them.

"I don't think my mother ever let my father know what happened to her. Anyway, she had a little fun in the last few months of her life. I took her abroad, to Switzerland and Italy, and she loved that. Of course she was upset about my first marriage, but that was inevitable really. I just ran into the first friendly arms I could find."

"What about your father, Constance? Did you ever see him?"

She raised her chin a fraction higher, and stared Benedict proudly in the eyes.

"I don't have to see him, Benny," she said. "I can read about him in the papers almost any day of the week."

"You mean—he's famous?"

"Yes. If you'll forgive me, I think I ought to keep his secret."

"Do you still hate him?"

"No. It was just one of those things. My mother should have asked for help; she was too proud, so he never really knew. I shall tell my children who he is one day; and they will be proud too."

When Benedict left, a long time later, when they had discussed all their other friends and laughed a lot and sometimes fallen silent, and then talked in snatches and laughed some more, he kissed Constance on the cheek.

"Oh Benny," she said. "That's not how you used to kiss me. You see how old we're both getting."

"You know, Constance," he said. "May I confess something to you? I realize now that, mixed up with everything else, I was a little in love with you."

"But Benny," she said, "surely you realized. We were all a little bit in love with each other."

Her lovely face haunted him as he walked slowly along the High Street.

Now I know, he thought to himself, why she always held her head so high.

15

"MR. and Mrs. Tony Hammond," said the name-plate. Benedict rang the bell and waited. Life teemed in the street all round him; small rosy children played hop-scotch and a rag-and-bone man shouted his sad needs as he rolled by in his horse-drawn cart.

It was a basement flat in Pimlico; once no doubt a prosperous merchant's flat, but now divided and subdivided into apartments; and the names of all the inmates were grubbily inscribed on cards beside the many front door bells. Benedict was no longer afraid; he felt no emotion except a vague curiosity. Constance had given him the address; she had always got on well with Laura and occasionally they exchanged letters. It was a piece of information he could easily have dug out for himself if he had ever cared; but he had never cared.

Laura herself opened the door and when she saw Benedict standing there she showed no surprise. She said simply: "Hello, Benny."

"You recognized me after such a long time?"

"Of course. I always knew you would come one day."

She led him into the flat. It smelt faintly of unwashed children. There was a pram in the hall.

The living-room was spacious but rather dark. The September light streamed in from one large basement window let in at the front. Benedict could see the sky only when he had taken a seat in the only armchair; it was a perfect autumn afternoon and the air had a tint of kodachrome blue in it. The sun on the bare solitary lilac tree and the wall in the front garden was the colour of gold: not mustard or primrose or copper or egg-yolk but like gold bullion melted down and sprayed on every branch and brick.

Laura sat at first on a small stool in the shadow; then as if to show she was not frightened to be seen, she moved forward a little, and the flood of liquid golden bullion caught and drowned her face in light, making Benny—even after so long—catch his breath.

She was thin, this was his first impression; she had lost the pleasing shapeliness of her girlhood and even her cheeks were a little hollowed, throwing into dramatic relief those still-miraculous green eyes. Her skin was still pale but overlaid now with a dull crimson flush. Her nose still had its little arrogant tilt and her hair, though shorter, was still held in an Alice band. Her wrists were fragile and her hands, though still well kept, with the nails cut square, were red with housework. She wore a full red skirt, a simple white shirt and sandals. She wore no make-up; so that she looked younger than her thirty-six years; hardly more than twenty-five until you noticed the lines round mouth and eyes.

She opened a box of cigarettes and offered them.

"Thank you," he said, "I don't."

She lit one herself and drew in the first lungful of smoke with a sense of necessity that told Benedict a lot about the last thirteen years; she had never smoked before.

"Well, Benny," she said, "how did you find where we lived?"

"Constance told me. I was down there for a few days."

"Constance!" She said it softly with recalled affection. "How is she, Benny? God, it seems such a long time ago!"

"She's extremely well and as far as I can see quite unchanged. You know she has two children now?"

"Oh yes. I even have their photographs. They're very sweet."

"Tell me about yourself, Laura. What have you been doing all these years? And how is Tony?"

She looked away. "Benny," she said, "why do you want to know?"

"Do I have to tell you?"

She shook her head slowly. "No," she said. "No. I understand. But it's such a long story, Benny."

"Tell me just a little, then."

She thought for a while. "It's no good my trying to say anything now about what happened between us, Benny. Any words of mine would be so inadequate that they would sound insulting. In any case I have no reasonable explanation to give you. But I will just say that I am sorry—sorry in a way I can never convey to you."

"Don't say that, Laura. I've thought about it a lot, and I think I do understand; a bit at any rate."

She tried to remember. "Believe me, Benny, there was nothing between Tony and me in those days—nothing that is, except a curious tension. If there was anything between us, it was like an invisible piece of fine wire looped round us both. Neither of us

273

knew exactly what it was, and we never discussed it. But we both sensed that there was something."

"This was right from the word go?"

"Right from the word go—from the first day you saw us."

"Ah," said Benny, but it was more like a sigh than a word. "So I was right after all."

"If you were, you were the only one that knew it for sure. He went away in 1942 and—apart from maybe an odd, neutral card at Christmas or birthdays—I had no more contact with him. You knew, I suppose, that he failed to get a degree?"

"No, I didn't realize that."

"Heaven only knows how he managed that. He wasn't lazy, and he had an unusually perceptive intelligence—you know that, Benny. It was just that—well, he seemed set on hurting himself. Then came those awful itinerant jobs in which he thought he was opening up his personality to new shapes and sounds and colours and scents. But of course he was doing nothing of the sort. He was just drifting."

"Did he never have a clear idea what he wanted to do?"

"No—did any of us?"

"Milo, I think."

She shrugged it off. "Well Tony didn't. The long curve downward had begun before he even left the Cressbrook Valley. He began to write to me again early in 1947. Benny, I know by any accepted standard of morality I should have told you at once; but how could I? And what would it have done to you—longing as you were for me—just as I longed for you? At first his letters were short, jocular, friendly. Gradually though, they grew more frenetic and neurotic. Benny"—she was remembering and her hands knotted and unknotted her handkerchief—"they were terrible letters. They terrified me, each one—*because I knew I had to read them. And because I knew a long way down that they were summonses, just like summonses which lead a man to prison. Summonses to which there is no alternative; no payment that will amend or lighten the punishment.*"

"Truly, Laura, I can understand something of what it was like. I promise you."

"Then he turned up. I'd told him, of course, that you would be home soon and this seemed to drive him crazy. He turned up in Aylsbourn. One day"—she bit her handkerchief and her small sink-red fingers were trembling—"he was waiting for me at the bottom of the lane. Oh Benny, if I could have jumped on a plane and come to you, escaped, everything would have been all right."

"I'm afraid it would never have been all right, Laura."

"But that was what I desperately wanted to do. Of course my parents at first thought I was crazy; naturally they could hardly approve of Tony after what had happened between him and Arabella, but—well, they didn't disapprove. They were quite fond of him, and he had no parents of his own"—she paused. "You know, I suppose, that they both died—within a year of each other?"

"Yes, I heard."

"Anyway, they saw the danger within—within two or three days. Oh Benny, it was terrible in a way I can't put in words. There was no hope for me. I was in a cage, and only Tony had the key. But he wanted me in that cage, and so he threw the key away. I'm talking nonsense, I'm afraid."

"No."

"It got worse each day, the nearer to the day you were due. And, Benny—believe me—I was so longing for you to come home, even in the middle of all this—do I sound like a lying dirty little whore?—or can you believe such an improbable thing?"

"I can believe it."

"Then—then he asked me to marry him. He said that once you got back he would never ask me again; I had to decide then. Benny, I swear to you that as I said yes—while I was actually saying it, my whole body was revolting and struggling against it, and do you know, Benny, truly I was sick when I got home. I just was sick, or in plain words I vomited; I seemed to be sicking up my heart and soul and all my self-respect."

She was not actually crying as she told Benedict this, but her voice was shaking and it seemed she had difficulty in breathing. He waited till she could go on again.

"So we were married—in a Register Office—with a couple of his boozy pals as witnesses. And I got tight, Benny—it was the only thing I could do—and we passed the night of our—our 'honeymoon'"—she used the word in quotation marks—"at the Strand Palace. When I woke up in the morning I was calling out your name. He's never forgotten that."

"I heard you call."

She seemed not to take this in. She was trying to control herself so that she could go on.

"He was working as a barman at the time. He used to come in tight—oh, he lost that job, like all the other jobs—and we used to fight. But I mean fight—nails and teeth and even fists. Benny, did you ever see a play called *Look Back In Anger*?"

"Of course, Laura."

"What did you think of it?"

"I thought what a marvellous talent, but somehow pointing the wrong way."

"But Benny, it's the greatest play ever written. Every word of it was true. It was us, Benny. He even blows his trumpet like that man in the play."

"He still plays?"

"That's how we live, Benny. He could never keep a job—but he could play jazz. He formed a group called the Ravers. They're not very great, but they make a living. They play in the South London dance halls and a few river pubs. He's come up with the boom—even bad jazz pays well now—and we often make fifty pounds a week. It's not money we're short of"—her voice broke. "It's freedom from each other."

"Has he ever gone away?"

"Has he ever gone away?" she echoed bitterly. "Do you know, Benny, his manager calculates he's had between two hundred and three hundred women—usually in shop doorways or in the back of his car?"

"*What?*"

"Benny, you can't imagine what it's like. The other day I got so crazy I put my hand through a window, I was trying to commit suicide, I think. Here"—she held out one of her small hands and he saw the new scar. It would be there for life. "And do you know what he did? He said, 'Two can play at that game.' And then he smashed his hand through the broken glass as well." She put one of her little clenched fists in her mouth and bit it hard as if to try to believe it. "Sometimes I ask him why he can't think of a quick way to commit suicide; not this slow way."

"Laura, why does he do this?"

"Why, Benny, why? Do you think I haven't asked myself this thousands of times? But I think I know why now." She took a deep breath. "It's because he's so full of life. Benny, if you'll forgive a rather crude expression, sometimes the life seems to be overflowing out of him, its pressed in so hard, out of his mouth, his ears, his eyes. . . . He doesn't exactly mean to be bad, you see, he was just given too much life and it spills out of him all wrong. I knew a woman once, Benny; I met her in hospital—yes, I've been there a few times, but I won't depress you with it—who had a most horrible illness. She would conceive a baby, only it wasn't a baby; it was all the raw material growing and spawning inside her and making nothing that anyone could ever look at. And that's what it is with Tony: it's teeming inside him and he can't cope with it; he doesn't know what to do. He drinks, he has women, he takes drugs, anything to reach a kind of clarity. He never gets it. And I'm part of his life-sentence, Benny. He can't do without me. Can you imagine, after all we've done to each other we sometimes go to bed"—and now she was sobbing—"and we make love as no two people ever made love before."

Now it was Benedict's turn to look away. Eventually her sobs died away and she put her hand pathetically out towards him. Reluctantly he took it.

"Benny," she said. "I've just realized what I've said."

"It's all right."

"I can't hurt you any more, can I? I couldn't if I tried."

"Tell me, Laura, isn't there any good side to all this? Aren't you ever happy?"

"Oh sometimes, for a little while. Sometimes he even brings me home something. And of course we have the children."

"You have *children*?"

"Yes. Four. And, Benny, do you know what this terrible surplus life in him has done? As if to make it up, it's given us the four most beautiful children you ever saw in your life. I know I'm their mother, but it's not just maternal pride. People stop and stare at them in the streets."

"How old are they?"

"Mike is eleven, Louise is seven, Angela is five, and Pete is one. I'd like more, but the doctors said I'd die for sure if I had another. They're beautiful children, Benny, you should wait and see them come home from school."

"Laura, not now. I don't think I'd like to today."

He got up slowly. Over the fireplace, though hidden in the

shadow, was a painting in oil. As he came closer, he saw that it was of Tony Hammond.

"That was painted last year. It's by Carlo Rewson, his best friend. He's mad, everyone knows that, but God he's a marvellous painter."

Benedict studied the picture with interest. It had a ferocity about it that was a little unnerving; the colours seemed to have been hurled on to the canvas and the face that now stared out at him conveyed an impression of super-reality. The painting spoke about its subject in a way that no photograph could ever begin to do. Hammond looked—well it was an odd word to use, but to Benedict he looked—possessed. There was still beauty in the curious wedge-shaped face, but the eyes behind the thick glasses were frightening: they seemed to stare out of the picture with the hopelessness of a soul in Bedlam. Rewson had painted Hammond with his battered yellow trumpet raised to his lips, and so powerful was the painter's talent that you could almost hear him hitting one of his high notes.

"Tell me, Laura," he asked with interest, "does he really play so badly? I always thought he was wonderful."

She went to a long cabinet that lay along the wall, and turned a switch. "He made this tape the other day," she said. "Judge for yourself."

Benedict felt his skin crawl at the first note of the trumpet. It was exactly the sound that had first thrilled him over twenty years ago. But as he listened, he realized with astonishment that the sound Hammond was making was appalling; he had not moved on one iota from that day in 1930. His timing was ragged, his tone poor and his ideas naïve.

"He was sloshed that night," she said. "Some people think jazzmen play better when they're a bit high." She shook her head. "They have to think it out and orchestrate; and the farther out they are the more thought they need to put into it."

"Still, the kids love it, I expect."

"Oh yes—but all they want is a good old thump, thump, thump to jive to. Now listen"—she manipulated the knobs and the tape raced forward—"here's the one you always used to love, Benny."

She turned up the volume and Benny started—so taut had his nerves become—at the flood of sound. It was the Original Dixieland Onestep, the tune Tony Hammond had played on the night

278

of the second great football game, and as Benedict heard it he felt the old delight leap up in him again. And this time Hammond seemed to be inspired; his tone was urgent and driving and full of joy. Laura and Benedict stood looking at each other as the magnificent sounded pounded and pulsed through the shivering basement room. When it was over she snapped the switch off.

"That's all, Benny," she said. "That's all he'll ever do now. And he could already do that when we were all children, growing up together."

16

ARABELLA was sitting at her desk, writing a letter. He was touched, as he always was, to see that she was wearing her glasses. She was, like all women, resentful at having to wear them at all, and tried never to do so when Benedict was there. She took them off as he came up behind and kissed her.

"Hello, Benny darling. Did you have a wonderful time?"

"Wonderful. But I wish you'd come. I met Tim."

"Oh, then I am sorry. How was he?"

"Diabolically good-looking—all that buccaneering Felix stuff crossed with your slightly mysterious Oriental look."

"Benny, you're quite ridiculous. Who else did you see?"

"Oh, everybody. Constance, and Milo's father, and Tess and Ken send their love of course; and I went over to Applestreet to see Milo and Martin Hennessy. . . . But who else do you think I've seen?"

"There are so many people you might have met, Benny. Tell me."

"Laura."

Arabella turned round quickly.

"And?"

"It was just as I expected."

"They're unhappy?"

"Dreadfully. They live in a squalid basement in Pimlico."

"I suppose you felt you'd got to help them?" There was a bitter note in her voice. "You feel you have to help every lame dog over the stile, even the ones that have bitten you."

"No. I can't help them. They don't need money. All they really need is someone with a pair of pliers to cut an invisible wire."

"You're talking nonsense as usual, Benny."

"I'm sorry. Oh and I saw Lady M. She said I should play for the Brewery team next summer. And you know what, Arabella? I went to see the estate agent. I suddenly thought how marvellous if we could get a house in the Cressbrook Valley. Maybe we could even find one where it ran through the bottom of the garden so that. . . ."

Arabella's face had grown serious. "Benny," she said, "I want you to sit down and listen carefully. For thirteen years—thirteen wonderful years—I've lived with you and tried to help you do whatever you wanted."

"Of course, Arabella. You know how I feel about . . ."

"But you are not going to live in the Cressbrook Valley."

"Why not?"

"Because for you, it would be a disaster. You'd never do another thing. You'd sit on all the local fatstock committees and judge baby competitions, and become a J.P. Benny, you'd be quite appalling as a squire."

"I assure you, the picture you paint sounds grisly to me too."

"Yes, but you'd get talked into it. I can see you, Governor of your old school, Lord Lieutenant of the County, Master of the Hunt, Conservative M.P. for the Cressbrook Division . . ."

"Not on your life!"

"All right. Let's leave that for a moment. The next point is that you are not going to turn the business into a charitable trust so that you can sit and dream all day and salve your conscience by remote control. That's too easy, Benny. You will keep the business. If you really have this masochistic desire to give something back—I'm pulling your leg now, Benny, so don't look so crestfallen; you know how I feel about that—but frankly you've got to do it some much harder way. You've got to stay in the rat-race. Also, you will keep the business because I am an extravagant slut and I want you to marry me."

"Yes, I was coming to that. Why in hell's name didn't you tell me . . ."

"Because, Benny, in the first place I wasn't sure about you. No, don't look so hurt. You're such an idealist, and you fell in love so deeply when you were very young, that I wondered if you'd ever get over it. I know we've been very happy and that in a quiet way I've helped."

"Arabella, don't be ridiculous. If it hadn't been for you . . ."

"There'd have been somebody else to bring you slowly back to earth. You know something, Benny; you used to say that you felt as if you were running along with your feet four inches above the ground. Well, now you're coming very gently back to earth. The spell is breaking. Only promise me you'll always stay a quarter of an inch above sea level. You've acquired some arrogance. You have the greatest appetite for life of any man I've ever met. And you have a very pleasing smell. I have, therefore, decided to marry you. I always wanted to have a chance to ask a man that and now I have."

"You know perfectly well, Arabella, I'd have married you years ago if I'd known. . . ."

"Benny, I didn't want your chivalry or your charity. I didn't want you till you were looking at me straight and cold and clear and saying to yourself: she's a raddled old bag of forty, six years older than me, and she's been around a bit but I'll have the old slut all the same."

"That's not quite how I see it."

"Well that's how I see it."

"I can't understand why no one ever told me you weren't married to Weston."

"You'd have found out if you'd ever gone back to Aylsbourn. And as soon as you did, Mrs. D. told you. Similarly, if Felix had ever come home, we'd have told him. Before, he was too young. We arrived from our honeymoon when the poor little fellow was only twelve and trying so hard to adjust to a new mother. We didn't—I didn't—want to give him an added problem to struggle with. Anyway, enough of these squalid recriminations. Is it yes or no?"

"It's yes."

"Good. One other point. I want to have your child, Benny. I always have. More than one, if there's time."

"I'll see what I can do. And now I'm going to give you one or two orders."

"Yes, my lord." She got out a pad to write them down. It was a harmless game they played.

"Lay in twelve dozen bottles of the dryest champagne you can find—Bollinger or Krug I should think."

"Yes, my lord."

"Get the grub from Fortnums and see they include vol-au-vents made with Cressbrook mushrooms."

"Yes, my lord."

"Go to Victor Siebel tomorrow about your dress."

"Yes, my lord."

"Send invitations first to our personal friends. Mr. and Mrs. Kenneth Heppel. Mr. and Mrs. Aelfric Gates. Tell her I shan't take no for an answer. Mr. and Mrs. Milo Johnston. Mr. and Mrs. Henry Johnston. Mr. Felix Weston and Miss Joanna Johnston. I'll tell you all about that later. Squadron-Leader Rupert Ripley and friend. Tell him she'd better be presentable this time—we're getting respectable in our old age. Mr. Samuel H. Spiral and Miss Jackie Mason. Tell him if he doesn't bring her he's fired. Mr. Timothy Weston and friend. Mr. and Mrs. Martin Hennessy. Lady M. and Miss M. Oh and Mrs. D. of course. . . . I'll think of some more later."

"Yes, my lord."

"Book us in at that hotel at Portofino. You know, where we had that other honeymoon."

"Yes, my lord."

"And come here."

"Yes, my lord."

17

KEN HEPPEL and Tessa sat in front of the fire. He was reading Alan Sillitoe's latest novel; she was sewing. It was Tessa who broke the silence first.

"Darling?"

"Yes."

"I can't help thinking about Benny."

"What about him?"

"Well it's so long since he was last in the Cressbrook Valley. Thirteen years at least. Why do you think he came back?"

"Because seeing Felix again seemed to liberate all his old inhibitions. He was bound to come back one day, but there had to be some moment which would tip the scales. Felix provided it."

"What does Benny really believe in?"

"That's simple. Benny is a man haunted by the incorruptible. He is out of phase with his time. He happens to believe in a heresy and a blasphemy. His heresy is that to live is sweet. His blasphemy is to claim that life is good."

"What's strange about that?"

"How can a man like that be in gear with the world nowadays? Of course he's doing better than most people; in fact he's made a great material fortune, and that, I suppose, is the index of success in 1960. He's made it from his own disillusion. He's made a quarter of a million, Tess, in a fit of absent-mindedness."

"How has he done it, though? I mean he used to be so gentle and unaggressive."

"He's done it because—leaving aside his natural intelligence, which thousands of other men have—he never gave a damn whether he made a packet or lost it. Consequently, the world being what it is and the genuine competition pretty thin, he made it."

"He didn't care?"

"No, he didn't care. He was trying to forget what he had lost. Remember, he had no orthodox religious faith, only the ordinary humanist's belief in men and women."

"But, even I know, darling, that that's a pretty reckless belief to stake your life on."

"I know. But he did. He never understood why those who lost their trust in God should also lose their trust in people. In fact Benny works on the reverse theory: that if there is nothing else then we are of infinite importance to each other. And that all of us, therefore, should live as if this were so."

"But he was disappointed in his belief?"

"Yes, and it hurt him more than anyone has ever understood. Yet, you know, I believe he accepted all the time, a long way inside, that he would have to be disenchanted."

"Had to be?"

"Yes, you see he really is no Pangloss. He doesn't see life in perfect perspectives and glossy colours. On the contrary, he loves it unaffectedly, warts and all, as a man may still love a woman after seeing her face each day for fifty years. If you put Benny to the stake and called on him to recant, he would still cry out that life was good as they cut the hot entrails out of him."

"But is Benny's view so unusual?"

"No! the longer I live the more I see that the world is entirely a subjective illusion. And our view of it is entirely independent of our circumstances; we find it heaven or hell because of the way we are made, the disposition of our hormones, our genes, our glands. Some of us were born rich and despise life; others as poor as church-mice love it all the way. Felix's father has a hundred thousand, yet Felix despises life, I was always in favour of life, even when my father had only three pounds a week."

"This is where he always disagreed with Felix."

"Yes; I've listened to the debate between Benny and Felix for nearly fifteen years now; neither is right, neither is wrong. But both views should be heard and understood. Benny's view is out of favour."

"But what exactly *is* Benny's view? I mean in a nutshell, so that I can understand it?"

"Benny divides people into two simple categories: the life-enhancers and the life-diminishers; he is a believer in the first, a leader of the pro-life party."

"Yes, I've heard Laura use that phrase."

"That doesn't mean he accepts things as unmovable. He's a radical; he's grasped that the only way to preserve a country's true essence—or a man's—is to carry that essence onwards in changing material forms from one generation to the next. Radicals seek to preserve the best by continuously altering the outward forms; conservatives destroy the best by a rigid adherence to the external shape of a civilization at the expense of its true inner meaning."

"You make it sound rather complicated, darling."

"O.K. Let me put it more simply: see what happens to a ship when the wheel is held straight. To keep it on course you have to keep swinging the wheel."

"You may be right. But that doesn't sound like the Benny I know."

But Kenneth wasn't listening to her now. He was on his favourite theme. "Benny argues," he went on, "that we are living on a spiritual island; all our most talented young men are firing their beautiful, white-hot bullets out to sea at the traditional enemies, while the real enemies are creeping up behind us; or are already inside the barricades. He argues that far more fortresses have fallen through treachery inside than ever did from exterior assault."

"You're serious about him being a radical?"

"Yes. Today's young angries are the true conservatives; they are not against the Establishment, only against not being in it themselves. Otherwise, when they want to launch an assault, why do they choose the most boring Aunt Sallies in the world: God, the Government, the Middle classes, parents—traditional chopping blocks of the young since the beginning of human history?"

"Benny has different causes?"

"Yes, Benny on the other hand, has chosen something really unpopular to champion; something that genuinely puts him in the world's pillory. You know we've cleaned up some of our four-letter words recently, washed their faces and restored them to respectable use again. But can you imagine anyone taking Benny's four-letter word seriously?"

Tessa, the girl who, as Benny thought, was the only one of all his friends who had never been tormented by love unreturned; who, as he believed, had only loved once, said: "Even I know which word that is, darling."

"Remember the story of his examination fiasco? He wrote down his entire faith in his own four-letter word that morning."

"Does he have any other key words which he lives by?"

"Yes, an even more ridiculous one: honour. Turn it over in

286

your mind; can you think of a single serious use to which it could now be put? We've not only scrubbed it clean, which was necessary; we've scrubbed it away. No one can get up and use that word now, except as a joke, without being howled down; it has *no serious meaning*."

"But there must have been something wrong with the word or we wouldn't have had to treat it so drastically."

"Yes. Of course it had to be cleaned and overhauled. Maybe it should be put back into the machinery of our civilization in a different gearing or fitting or angle. But it must go in somewhere; I mean people have got to live in a certain moral framework, however sophisticated, or we really are finished."

"You're beginning to talk in riddles, darling. But I think I understand. Benny came to see us because he's trying to get his bearings back, to decide what he can do next; what he can give back."

"Yes. That's exactly it. Take a humdrum thing like the question of his business. He thought of giving it up. But he's going to carry on with it; it would have been too easy to opt out. He's going to marry Arabella—and about time. He'll probably have children, and later they'll come into the business."

"But there's only one business in which he's really interested, darling, and that's the business of loving."

Kenneth Heppel looked at his wife with new interest. "You know, my dear," he said with genuine affection, "you're not half so silly as some people think."

"Tell me, Ken," she said without seeming to notice, "what was it that Benny found so strange about the air here? It's good, I know, but there's nothing unique about it, is there?"

"Good heavens no. Benny, you see, is a romantic. He has a way of bending the world to fit his view of it. The paradox is that this makes it no more or less valid than anyone else's view. There is no objective world: only our own conception of it. I can see the world quite easily through Benny's eyes if I try; on other days I see it the way Felix does."

"What was it, though, about the air?"

"The beech-trees. I'm convinced that's all it was. They have a special fragrance. It's been noted in the local histories for four hundred years now. You'll find references to our 'delicate sweet air' in one of the Elizabethan poets."

"So that's all it was."

"That's all. Everything is amenable to reason; there's a rational explanation for everything. We live in the age of the picaresque hero and the positivist philosopher; we must do without our illusions. There's no magic in the world, except what we put into it.

"And that," he concluded, "is all there is to it."

Tessa went and looked out of the window.